ONCE UPON A TIME...

A beautiful waitress and her father met up with a dog who wasn't a dog but a prince who'd been turned into a dog...

And then the most evil woman in the world escaped from prison and sent three bad Trolls and a very dangerous wolf to find the prince....

And then the wolf fell in love with the waitress and didn't know whether he wanted to marry her or eat her...

Don't worry. It's not confusing. It's just the 10th Kingdom....

Hallmark Entertainment Books

JOURNEY TO THE CENTER OF THE EARTH
Jules Verne

LEPRECHAUNS
Craig Shaw Gardner

THE 10th KINGDOM
Kathryn Wesley

And coming in Spring 2000

ARABIAN NIGHTS

JASON AND THE ARGONAUTS

THE 10TH KINGDOM

Kathryn Wesley

based on a screenplay by
Simon Moore

HALLMARK ENTERTAINMENT BOOKS

Hallmark Entertainment Books is dedicated to providing readers with compelling companion books to our television mini-series. Our corporate mission is to delight, entertain and engage our viewers and readers of all ages.

HALLMARK ENTERTAINMENT BOOKS are published by

Kensington Publishing Corp.
850 Third Avenue
New York, NY 10022

Copyright © 2000 by Hallmark Entertainment Books, a division of Hallmark Entertainment, Inc.

Cover photos and insert photos copyright © 2000 by Hallmark Entertainment Books, a division of Hallmark Entertainment, Inc.

All rights reserved. No part of this book may be reproduced in any form or by any means without the prior written consent of the Publisher, excepting brief quotes used in reviews.

If you purchased this book without a cover you should be aware that this book is stolen property. It was reported as "unsold and destroyed" to the Publisher and neither the Author nor the Publisher has received any payment for this "stripped book."

Hallmark and the Hallmark logo Reg. U.S. Pat. & TM Off.
Kensington and the K logo Reg. U.S. Pat. & TM Off.

First Hallmark Entertainment Books Hardcover Printing: January, 2000
First Hallmark Entertainment Books Paperback Printing: January, 2000
10 9 8 7 6 5 4 3 2 1

Printed in the United States of America

For Paul

An Introduction to *The 10ᵗʰ Kingdom*

Dear Reader,

Fairy tales have enchanted audiences for centuries. They began as oral tales and were made legends by folklorists like the Brothers Grimm. While most believe that fairy tales are little more than stories for children, these often grisly and wickedly funny morality plays were originally intended for an adult audience. Over the years, adult tastes in literature changed and the stories were softened for younger eyes and ears. So murderous parents became wicked stepparents and gruesome punishments for evil deeds were toned down or discarded altogether.

The 10ᵗʰ Kingdom follows a traditional adult fairy tale plot. The original fairy tales weren't concerned with "Happy Ever Afters." Instead they took us on a journey of transformation in which the trip is just as important as the ending. In *The 10ᵗʰ Kingdom*, we encounter dangers that threaten, but we will also find glorious things from magic mirrors to talking dogs. Most importantly we learn that our greatest strength comes from ourselves.

This story, set in the Nine Kingdoms two hundred years after the reigns of the great queens (Snow White, Cinderella and Little Red Riding Hood), brings us to a land where "Happy Ever After doesn't last forever." In addition to finding parts of our favorite fairy tales here, we also find old wives' tales, Greek myths, and references to mid-twentieth century British Literature.

The 10ᵗʰ Kingdom is more than just a fairy tale. It is a

modern fantasy that whisks us into a land of enchantment and danger. At the core of the tale is the enduring bond and the magical journey of a simple, young waitress and her ne'er-do-well father. Their wondrous, mystical and often dangerous adventures in the fantastic world of the Nine Kingdoms allows them to flee the mundane existence of their everyday lives, deepens their love for one another and opens their eyes to the magic that has always been around them, the magic that is known as the 10th Kingdom.

Beneath all *The 10th Kingdom*'s texts and subtexts is a wonderful story. It is funny and scary and tragic, just as good stories should be. It has an engaging heroine and a flawed but good-hearted hero. It has kings and queens and princes, not to mention magic beans, magic rings, and magic fish. It has evil trolls and a wicked witch. It even has an unusual role for the Tooth Fairy.

If you want to read something else like *The 10th Kingdom*, well, there isn't anything else exactly like it. But there are books that inspired it. You might want to return to the Grimm Fairy Tales you read (or that were read to you) as a child.

Enjoy the 10th Kingdom. We hope it's a place you'll want to come back to again and again.

Robert Halmi, Sr.
Chairman, Hallmark Entertainment, Inc.
Executive Producer, *The 10th Kingdom*

Part One

THE DOG FORMERLY KNOWN AS PRINCE

Chapter One

Virginia rested her elbows on the windowsill and leaned into the breeze. If she closed her eyes halfway, the trees in front of her looked like a vast forest: cool and green, filled with possibilities and adventure. Sometimes she sat there for hours, imagining herself a princess trapped in a tower, waiting for some handsome prince to emerge from the woods, find the key, and set her free.

She touched her brown hair, wrapped in its neat bun at the back of her head. It wasn't even long enough for her to pull a Rapunzel on the guy—no way could she let down her hair and have him climb up it. The strain of that would be too much. She didn't even like having other people brush her hair. They pulled too hard. Imagine how it would feel to have someone *climb* it.

As if it had heard her thoughts, the breeze tickled a loose strand of her hair. She leaned even farther forward, hoping to catch a bird's call or perhaps the roar of a wild beast.

Instead a siren wailed in the distance.

Virginia blinked and opened her eyes the whole way. The trees before her weren't part of any forest. They were a small grove on this side of Central Park in the middle of the most urban environment in the world—New York City, land of the concrete jungle, a place where sunshine was rare and exhaust fumes ruled.

She could smell them now, toxic and foul. A bus belched on the street below, and some passerby, caught in the cloud of black smoke, yelled an insult. Her tower was really her apartment, the one she shared with her father. They were on the edge of the Park not because they were rich—they weren't even close—but because he was the janitor in this building and the apartment was part of his pay.

Her bedroom was tiny, like the rest of the place, but at least it was hers. She glanced at the alarm clock beside her bed and sighed. She'd daydreamed the afternoon away. Her shift would start soon, and she wasn't ready for it. Her feet still ached from the last one.

She worked at the Grill on the Green, a restaurant at the edge of the park. She liked waitressing; it allowed her to meet people. Sometimes it was a trial—like last night, when the place had been full of tourists looking for the New York experience—but mostly it got her out, seeing things, and forgetting where she was at.

So many women in the city were just like her: dead-end jobs, no hope for advancement, no way to make new friends, and no way to meet anyone. Last night, one of the tourists had said to her, "It must be great to live in New York."

She'd had enough of that kind of talk. She'd been late to work because some joker had grabbed her bike in the park and she'd had to kick him away with her foot. The cook had spilled a jar of jelly on her in the kitchen, and the shirt she'd swiped from the boss's closet in the back had been several sizes too big. She'd had to go through the entire night holding a tray in one hand and her shirt front in the other.

Great to live in New York? The comment was like putting a flag in front of a bull. Still, she restrained herself.

"Great?" she'd said. "Close your eyes."

The woman, a middle-aged bottle-blond from some Midwestern town, did.

"Now," Virginia said, "imagine the most boring day of your life."

The woman nodded. She had a little smile on her face.

"Right," Virginia said. "Now you have my life in perfect focus."

The woman's little smile faded. She opened her eyes and looked confused. And Virginia had walked off, tossing her cocktail tray up and down like a baseball.

But she hadn't been lying. Lately she'd been saying to herself that after a woman reached a certain age—and was still living with her father!—nothing exciting would ever happen in her life. The best she could hope for was finding a partner and opening a restaurant of her own.

As if that was ever going to happen. It'd be as likely as opening the front door and finding a satchel of cash.

Virginia grabbed the window frame by its peeling paint and tugged the window closed. Then she left her room to make sure her chores were done before she left. Her father spent his evenings in his fake leather recliner, drinking beer and punching the remote. If she didn't leave him dinner, he wouldn't eat at all.

She hurried to the kitchen, then stopped. There were potato chip packets and empty beer cans in front of the armchair. The mess would be worse if she left it for the morning.

With one hand she grabbed the foil wrappers, and with the other she picked up the cans. She carried them into the kitchen and dumped them in the trash. Then she pulled open the ancient white refrigerator—the thing was so old that it groaned—and stared at the frost-covered freezer door, which was at her eye level.

Maybe she'd add a new frost-free refrigerator with side-by-side doors and ice and water dispensers. Or, if she got extravagant, a stand-alone freezer instead of this puny one that barely fit ice and two days' worth of leftovers.

She took a frozen dinner out of the freezer, shoved the door closed with her hip, and placed the food beside the microwave. Then she went back into her bedroom and got her bike.

It was a used model her dad had found in a pawnshop, although he'd lied and said he'd bought it from one of the bicycle places in the Upper West Side. She let him have his fiction. It made him feel better. She'd been in some of the bike shops. They wanted to see the rider so that they'd sell a bike that fit her frame. She was petite, and the bike he'd bought was a little too big. She was used to it now, but another of her small dreams was to ride a bike that fit.

As she wheeled the bike out of the bedroom, she steered to avoid the tools and paint cans stacked against the hallway's walls. A couple of times, her dad had spilled nails here and hadn't bothered to pick them up. After blowing one tire, she'd learned to be careful around her father's workspace.

Before she went out the door, she checked to make sure she had her keys. Then, with one hand on the hard seat, and another on the handlebars, she wheeled the bike into the hallway.

Her dad was standing by the elevator. His bright blue uniform stood out in sharp contrast to the brown-and-tan flocked wallpaper. He had the call box open and wires dangled from it. The elevator doors were jammed open with his toolbox.

And her way to the street was effectively blocked.

He didn't notice, of course. "Look at this," he said. "Feast your eyes on this."

He held out a wire for her to study. She peered in as if she were interested. "This," he proclaimed, "has been gnawed."

Oh, great. Rats eating the wiring. She wondered why she hadn't seen any furry electrocuted bodies lying around if that was what they were really doing, but she wasn't going to ask. Her dad would have a theory.

He always had a theory. The guys down at his favorite watering hole seemed to love his theories and sometimes she did too. *Tony*, they'd say, *what do you think of . . .* , then give him a topic and sit back. When he expounded, his brown eyes lit up and his familiar rumpled face lost some of its perpetual disappointment.

But she didn't have to prompt him to tell her this theory. He already had a speech prepared. He'd just been waiting for an audience. "This isn't my job, you know. This is an electrician's job. But who has to fix it?"

That was her cue. She was supposed to say, *You, Dad*. But she missed her entrance.

He shoved the wire back into the box and frowned at her. "Where are you going?"

"To work, Dad," she said, sighing. "Like I do every day."

Tony snorted, stuck an "Out of Order" sign on the wall above the open wiring box, then motioned for her to get in the open elevator. She wheeled her bike in and turned it around, giving him room to follow her in and get to the control panel. It too had the cover off and old wires were exposed. His toolbox was open on the floor under the panel.

Tony studied the mess of old wiring for a moment, then stuck his screwdriver inside, and with a clank the doors slid closed and the elevator started down.

"Take the stairs on the way back," he said, staring at the exposed mass of wiring in front of him. "Just in case."

She nodded. She'd been planning to do that anyway.

With one hand still holding the screwdriver, Tony reached into his toolbox and grabbed his emergency can of beer. He wasn't supposed to drink on the job—it was a firing offense—but Virginia had long since stopped warning him about that. All he had done was learn to sip the beer in a new way, hiding the can, and trying not to slurp. That, at least, was an improvement.

His hand slipped on the screwdriver and the elevator jerked. Virginia braced herself. He reestablished the connection, then shook his head as if the blip were the elevator's fault.

"You know, I'm starting to think the only people they want in this country are people like me, guys who'll work for scraps, who'll do anything, six jobs, who will basically bend down and take it."

Virginia nodded, just as she was supposed to do. She had her responses to this speech memorized. She heard it almost every day.

"Ten, fifteen years tops, and this country is finished as a democracy, as a caring society, as a place where people do things for others." Tony took another swig of his beer. "We're finished. We're gone. We're out of here."

She didn't believe in a caring society. She'd learned early on that other people were trouble. Her philosophy—often thought and never stated (unlike her father's)—was *Stick with yourself and you won't get hurt.* That had proven true for her more often than not.

Her dad had stopped talking. She wondered how long he'd been silent. Rather than letting him start with another speech, she said, "Your barbecue ribs are on top of the microwave."

Tony frowned—perhaps she hadn't given the appropriate response—and then the elevator jerked to a halt. As the doors started to open, she realized that the frown hadn't been for her. It had been for their stop.

The third floor.

Tony crouched and hid his beer in the toolbox. He was still rummaging through it as Mr. Murray and his eight-year-old son got on.

Mr. Murray owned the building and somehow believed that gave him the right to be a petty tyrant. Virginia braced herself for some unpleasantness. She didn't even smile at the boy as she used to do. The kid was beyond hope. And who wouldn't be? He was wearing a tiny suit that matched his father's, and their faces had the identical expression, as if they had both swallowed something bad.

Her dad stood at attention. Mr. Murray both frightened and angered him. Frightened because Tony knew that Mr. Murray could fire him on a moment's notice, and angered because Mr. Murray was usually unreasonable.

Virginia had heard her father lecture on this topic ever since they moved in here. And on this topic, she agreed with him.

Mr. Murray was frowning at the open box with its dangling wiring and the screwdriver stuck into the mess. "Tony, I've been calling the elevator for half an hour. I thought you'd fixed it.''

"I had," Tony said, "but it's broken again."

"Well, don't spend all night on it," Murray said. "You've got to look at that boiler. It's driving everyone crazy. There's air in the pipes."

"I know," Tony said, but he spoke softly. Virginia wondered if Mr. Murray even heard him.

"The system's got to be drained and bled."

"I've just got to do the drip in number nine, then I'll be on the case." Her dad had a tone in his voice when he spoke to Mr. Murray that Virginia never heard at any other time. It had a hint of eager puppy dog mixed with an edge of annoyance.

Murray Junior pointed a stubby finger at Tony. "That man's breath smells, Daddy."

Virginia closed her eyes for just a second. The beer. She had warned him. But apparently, Mr. Murray wasn't concerned with Tony's breath.

"I'm only going to say this once," Mr. Murray said. Once a day was more like it. Virginia resisted the urge to mouth the next part with him: "There's an awful lot of people who'd like your job. An awful lot of people."

Virginia clenched her fists, but Tony only smiled and nodded.

The elevator reached the ground floor, and the doors slid open. Mr. Murray and Murray Junior got off. Even their walks matched.

Tony waited until Mr. Murray's back was turned and then gave them the finger.

"Drain the system. Drain the system," he said in a singsong voice. "I'd like to drain his system."

Wouldn't everyone? But Virginia knew better than to agree with her father. That might launch another theory, which would mean she'd be late for work.

"I'll see you later, Dad." Virginia rose on her toes to kiss his cheek, and then wheeled her bike out of the elevator.

She thought she had made good her escape when her father said, "Don't go across the park." Every day he said that. Every day she ignored him. "You hear me? You promise?"

And as she did every day, she said, "Sure, Dad."

She was almost to the door.

"Have you got a jacket?" Tony called.

He should have looked earlier. Of course he hadn't. Too wrapped up in his own problems. She didn't bother to answer.

"What have you left me for dinner?"

The same thing she always left him. But she didn't answer that either.

The doorman at the front desk gave her a look of sympathy. She wheeled past him and out the front entrance. The moment she stepped out the door, she took a deep breath.

Exhaust fumes. Uck. The concrete jungle.

She got on her bike and rode across the busy street, dodging cars on her way into the park. The trees made her day worthwhile. The trees and their valiant struggle against the bad air, the graffiti artists trying to carve their love lives into the trunks, the dogs fouling the exposed roots. If those trees could survive in this place, so could she.

Virginia veered off the path and took a shortcut, rising over a small crest until she reached another path. She couldn't see her building from here. She couldn't see any part of the city.

She loved it here. It was her reward for the sameness of her everyday life.

His feet hurt in the magic shoes, but the rest of him felt pretty good. Pretty darn good. Relish, the Troll King, resisted the urge to chuckle as he made his way down the hall in the Snow White Memorial Prison.

Getting inside hadn't been hard. A little pink Troll dust, the magic shoes, and he was through the main door. Only the vulture outside—the real one, the one sitting on the sign—had seen him cross the manicured grounds to the drawbridge. And that bird wasn't going to confess nothing to nobody.

The corridor was wide and dimly lit. The shadows were dark. Every few yards, however, there were squares of light, with bars, as a bit of moonlight came through the grated windows. The torches on the walls burned brightly, but they couldn't dispel the gloom.

He liked it gloomy. And darkness suited his purposes. He would do well here.

He held his hand out in front of himself. Nothing. The shoes were doing their trick. No one could see him. And if he was careful, he'd accomplish his mission without anyone being the wiser.

He turned into another corridor. The stone walls seemed even wider here, but the ceiling was lower, giving the place a tunnel effect. A warder carrying an iron lantern was going about his rounds. He was tall for a human, with a face so mean it could almost be a Troll's. His skull was shaved. It looked like a pale, shiny globe of light flashing through the shadows. He wore the dark green uniform of all the officials in the Fourth Kingdom, and it looked as ridiculous on him as it looked on the rest of them.

The warder stopped. Obviously he had heard Relish's footsteps. Then the warder shook his head and continued on. Relish walked behind. The magic shoes he wore over his boots made soft footfalls.

The warder stopped and turned. Relish grinned, knowing the human couldn't see him.

''Who's there?''

Relish waited as the warder did. Then the human shook himself as if berating himself for imagining things, and started down the corridor again. Relish followed, picking up his pace. He was close to the cell now. He wanted to get there before the magic shoes took away all of his self-control.

The warder stopped again, obviously spooked. ''Who's there?''

This time, Relish continued forward, hand in the pouch of pink Troll dust. The warder shrank back from the sound of the footsteps, but Relish was moving too quickly. He rushed up to the warder and threw a handful of pink dust in his face.

The warder's eyes widened and he looked as if he were going to sneeze. Then he fell backwards, body tangled in a heap. Relish peered at him. Pink dust covered the human's face. He'd be uncomfortable when he woke up. Especially from the way that arm was bending. Pins and needles and maybe a pulled muscle or two.

Relish grinned. He bent down and grabbed the warder's keys. Then Relish carried them to the cell where his idiot children had gotten themselves imprisoned again.

The cell door was sturdy, made of wood with metal strips reinforcing it. A thick wooden bar covered the front and was held in place by the lock. Relish stuck the key in the lock, turned it, and raised the bar, pulling the door open.

His idiot children got off their cots, whirling and turning until they lined up in front of the door. It wasn't even a good defensive position. He couldn't believe how little they had learned of the things he taught them.

They had lined up in age order. Burly and Blabberwort were seven feet tall—the perfect height for Trolls. But Bluebell was only five feet tall. He crouched beside his sister Blabberwort and looked even more pathetic than the other two.

Relish frowned at his children. What a motley crew. Burly had pulled his black hair away from his face, revealing his excessively pale skin—like his father's—and his gray eyes. His two lower canines rose like fangs, nearly touching the steel bone he'd pierced through his nose. He wasn't as ugly as a Troll could be, but he was close.

Blabberwort would have been Relish's pride and joy if only she had the brains to go with her fabulously bad looks. Her hair was orange and she wore a tuft of it in a straight-up ponytail shaped like a poodle's tail. Her hooked nose was pierced, and she wore a gold ring in the side. She had her mother's dark looks, and they seemed to suit her more than her younger brother Bluebell.

On Bluebell the dark looks made him seem unfinished. His frizzy black hair was out of control, and his hooked nose hid his imperfectly gnarled teeth. He bent his head when he grinned, making him seem shyer than any Troll should be.

"You are pathetic," Relish said as he stepped inside the cell. "You call yourself Trolls? You make me ashamed."

They looked surprised at the sound of his voice.

"Sorry, Dad," Burly said.

"Sorry, Dad," Blabberwort said.

"It won't happen again," Bluebell said.

As if Relish believed that. "This is the last time I come and rescue you. Especially for minor offenses."

"Come on, Dad," Burly said. "Take off the magic shoes."

Apparently his son didn't like his father to be invisible. Apparently that made Burly nervous. Which was good. "I'll take them off anytime I want to," Relish said.

"Mustn't wear them longer than you need to," Blabberwort said.

"Shut up!" Relish ordered. "I can handle them."

But maybe he couldn't. He was a bit woozy, and he was enjoying baiting his idiot children a little too much. He felt drunk—a feeling he liked—but it was probably a dangerous feeling when he was inside a cell inside the Snow White Memorial Prison. Getting caught like this by making judgment errors made him almost as much of an idiot as his idiot children.

Which was not a good comparison at all.

He put one invisible hand against the cold stone wall and pulled off a magic shoe. Then he removed the other shoe and staggered a little as he became visible.

He watched his children as they saw him appear. All three of them leaned away from him.

Good. They were still scared of him. As they should be.

"Take this," he said after he got his balance. He thrust the bag of Troll dust into Burly's hand. "I think I got all the guards, but I might have missed some."

Burly took the dust and looked at it as if he'd never seen

it before. Relish glowered at him. Burly cupped his hand around it. Relish raised his eyebrows.

"Do you want to stay in here forever?"

"No, Dad," Burly said.

"No, Dad," Blabberwort said.

"I never want to be in here again," Bluebell said.

"Then let's go."

Relish led them out of the cell. He was still clutching the keys, and he still had his shoes, although that wasn't enough anymore. He felt naked now that he wasn't invisible, and he had the beginnings of a headache—but whether that was from the magic shoes or the presence of his children, he couldn't tell.

They crept through two different corridors, retracing his steps. He had done a pretty good job of dusting the guards. Not a single one was awake.

Wait.

A woman's voice spoke in his head. It was faint, but strong and alluring. Relish stopped and so did his kids. They all looked at each other. Apparently his children had heard the voice too.

Come to me.

Well, he didn't have to be asked twice. The guards were out, and he wanted to see what kind of female owned a voice like that. He had his imaginings—and so, apparently, did his sons, who looked more focused than he had ever seen them. Even Blabberwort looked interested, although probably not in the same way the men were.

They turned off the main prison corridor toward a sign that read: MAXIMUM SECURITY WING. He'd never been in this part of the prison, not even on his own. And of course, his idiot children weren't talented enough to even contemplate the sort of despicable deeds that got someone assigned here.

At the end of the corridor was a stout oak door. It looked even more solid than the one his children had been stashed behind. Relish pawed through his keys until he found the right one. He unlocked the door. It opened, revealing another corridor.

Somehow that disappointed him. He wanted to see the owner of the voice.

He led his children farther, and within a few moments they reached another locked door.

Burly's fangs bit into his upper lip. "This is where they keep the Queen," he whispered, the fear filling his every word. "No one is ever allowed in here."

Somehow Relish had known that, but he had ignored it. Now he was too curious to stop.

He opened this door and found himself in yet another corridor. At the very end of it was only one cell. Its door was even thicker—he could tell that from this distance.

As he led his grown children down the corridor, he passed a sign: ALL FOOD TO BE LEFT IN COLLECTION BOX. It made a shiver run down his back. Whenever he'd been in this prison, the guards had handed him his food.

A little farther along was another sign: NO PHYSICAL CONTACT! His headache was growing worse. Still his curiosity moved him forward.

As he passed a third sign—ALWAYS TWO WARDERS WITH PRISONER AT ANY TIME—Blubberwort looked at him as if she questioned the wisdom of his decision to continue. If he weren't questioning the same thing, he would have cuffed her for the expression alone. And then he saw the fourth sign: NEVER ENGAGE PRISONER IN CONVERSATION.

Did a voice in the head count as conversation?

Open the door.

Relish looked at his children. They were looking at him.

Open the door to everything you desire.

Okay. That did it. That was enough to convince him. He took a step forward and peered through the little barred window that was just above his eye level.

A human woman sat on the edge of a cot. She wore a gray hood over her hair, but the hood was pulled back enough to reveal her stunningly beautiful face. She had delicate features and wise eyes. He wouldn't have found that attractive in a Troll, but in a human—he nearly whistled in appreciation.

Beside her sat a golden retriever. She was stroking it with one gloved hand. Relish watched the hand movement, mesmerized.

The woman noticed him. Her gaze met his, and she smiled.

There was something reassuring in that smile, but another shiver ran down his back nonetheless. In that smile lay his future. He didn't know how he knew it, but he did.

The fate of the whole world turned on that smile.

And on what he decided to do next.

Chapter Two

The sun was shining, the birds were singing, and Prince Wendell wished they would stop. All that cheerfulness was annoying him, especially when he couldn't be outside, enjoying the day. He put an elbow on the window of the carriage and leaned out. The forest beside him looked thick and lush, the light filtering through the trees. There'd be lots of game in that forest. And he would so much rather be chasing it—even without a bow and arrow or any other weapon for that matter—than he would like to be inside this carriage, heading to the hinterlands.

He couldn't stand it anymore. He leaned his head back against the velvet seat. At least he didn't have to feel wood beneath him. This carriage was cushioned. In fact, the cushions were so thick, a person could sleep on them as if they were a bed. The old royal carriage, the historic one, the one in the basement of the palace, had wooden seats and no padding at all. He wondered how his royal ancestors and their equally royal posteriors managed to survive rides like this one.

"Where exactly are we going?" He managed to sound as disinterested as he felt. At least he resisted the urge to study his fingernails. His man, Giles, who had known Wendell since he was a baby, would have seen through that.

"To Beantown, sire, in the southwest corner of your kingdom. You are accepting the throne that the craftsmen there have made for your coronation." Giles was frowning at him anyway. A seventy-year-old man's frown had more power than a younger man's. Wendell would swear to it. And Giles always frowned when Wendell asked questions to which he should have known the answer.

Fortunately, Wendell had Giles around to listen to all the chatter from the ministers. Yes, Wendell had been briefed about this trip and no, Wendell hadn't paid attention. That was what Giles was for.

"Is it much farther?" And then, because Giles had seen through his restlessness anyway, Wendell added, "Can't we stop and go hunting?"

"Very shortly, sire." Giles's mouth tightened around the edges, a small movement, one probably no one but Wendell noticed. The only reason Wendell had learned to see it was because it made Giles sound even more disapproving than usual. "We must make a brief stop at the Snow White Memorial Prison first."

Wendell sighed. A prison. What a spectacular place to go on such a lovely day. Doom and gloom instead of sunshine and a quiet romp through the woods. He looked out the window again, only this time he leaned forward. The two spirited horses pulling the carriage had red plumes on the tops of their heads, and it looked as if the entire carriage was part of a parade. Which it would be, of course, if there were anyone around to look at it.

"I hate these outer provinces," he said. "The people are so common."

Giles made that small face again. Wendell resisted the urge to roll his eyes. Giles hated it when Wendell dismissed his subjects like that. If Giles had had his way, Wendell would have spent a year among them, getting his hands dirty in some sort of forced labor and bathing not at all.

"Your stepmother has applied for parole again," Giles was saying, "which we will, of course, turn down. This is simply a routine courtesy visit."

The carriage rounded a corner. Some time ago, the forest had given way to manicured grounds. Wendell wasn't sure when. He wasn't even certain if they had gone through a small town. He had been staring at the horses, not at his surroundings.

But now he focused on them. Snow White Memorial Prison was shaped like an ancient palace, from the days when palaces doubled as fortresses. It had towering stone walls and a foreboding gray exterior. The grounds were rather lovely, but even that beauty was marred by the vulture that never seemed to leave the brown-and-white sign at the base of the property.

The carriage followed the narrow road. Here the bumps were so great that even Wendell's royal posterior, swaddled in cloth, cushioned on the finest velvet in the Nine Kingdoms, felt every single jolt.

As they wound their way to the top, Wendell glanced at Giles. Giles's frown was even deeper. Wendell was frowning too. The last time he had been here—and he had no idea how long ago that was (although Giles would probably know)—there had been all sorts of people outside, waving and shouting and laughing. Then there had been the warden and the guards. They had stood in a grim semicircle farther inside the grounds, waiting to greet the Prince and his entourage, such as it was.

Today there were no screaming people, no grim welcoming committee. Had Giles finally gotten a date wrong?

"Well, this is marvelous, isn't it?" the Prince asked. "Not exactly the red-carpet treatment."

"I'm sure they can't have forgotten about our visit, Your Majesty," Giles said, although his tone belied his words.

The carriage pulled to a stop in front of the drawbridge— which was down—and before Wendell could move, Giles had opened the carriage door. Oh, the old man was angry. He would storm to the door, pound on it, and demand that Wendell get treated like the Prince he was. Wendell did so like having Giles around.

Giles was halfway to the door by the time Wendell got out of the carriage. He followed, a smile playing across his face. He could hardly wait for the confrontation. No one riled Giles without paying for it dearly.

When Giles reached the large, arched wooden doors, he grabbed the knocker and pounded so hard, people probably heard the sound three kingdoms away. Wendell stopped beside Giles and worked very hard at keeping a serious expression on his face.

Instead, he found himself looking across the grounds and yawning. Giles glared at him—Wendell couldn't see the look, but he could feel it—then knocked again.

The door opened. Wendell heard it more than he saw it. Then he turned toward Giles in time to see the old man stagger backwards. He was bleeding at the neck. His throat had been cut.

Suddenly, Wendell was awake. He reached for Giles, but as he did so, someone grabbed his arm and yanked him inside. Wendell tried to pull himself free, but he couldn't. The grip on his arm was extremely tight. The door closed behind him, and he had to blink to see what was happening in the gloom.

He wasn't sure exactly what was going on, but he knew it involved Trolls. He recognized the stink of them—the smell of old leather, sweat, and something rancid, like spoiled meat.

The hand let go of his arm and he stepped forward, trying to get away. Then someone kicked him in the rear. He nearly fell, but he righted himself. He started to run, but someone punched him in the face. He fell backwards, was caught by heavy hands, and got kicked again. Wendell flailed with his elbows, but it did no good. He had at least two assailants and they had to be Trolls. One of them was as big as a house.

They half dragged, half kicked him down the corridor, punching him every time he put up a fight—which was all the time. Finally they made it to the reception hall. The door was open. Wendell was about to shout for help when he was shoved inside.

He sprawled on his belly and cringed as a boot headed for his face. He deflected the blow but felt half a dozen others. As he moved this way and that, staggering up only to fall again, he caught a glimpse of the two beating him. One of them was fairly short for a Troll. He didn't punch that hard either. The other one, the one who had some power behind her kicks, was female, with orange hair. Wendell focused on the gold ring hanging off her nose. If he could grab it, maybe he could get somewhere.

"Enough," said a female voice. A very familiar female voice.

"Since when do you give the orders?" That was a male voice, and it wasn't familiar.

The kicking stopped. Wendell got to his feet and resisted the urge to dust himself off. He stood at his full height, even though it didn't match the Trolls'. And as he looked toward the door, he got a sense of how much trouble he was in.

The two Trolls who had beaten him had gone to the door. They were now standing with two other Trolls—male, tall, and hideous—who flanked Wendell's stepmother, the Queen.

He was in trouble now. The entire Nine Kingdoms were in trouble now. Unless he could do something. But he didn't know what that something would be. Giles had warned him about traveling without an entourage, but had Wendell listened? Of course not. That was what Giles was for. Had been for.

Oh, dear. Wendell had to listen on his own now.

"You're a long way from your castle, Wendell. Perhaps you should have stayed there." The Queen was smiling her secret little smile. He swallowed hard. He'd never forgotten that smile.

"You'll pay for this," he said, more to stall than anything else. If he had a moment, he was certain he would figure a way out of this.

The Queen laughed. She had a soft laugh, but that only made it more menacing. "On the contrary. I think you will beg at my feet for food."

Only then did he notice the dog beside her. It was large and golden and had strange eyes. They seemed to be brighter than a dog's eyes should be.

"Do you know what this is?" she asked, stroking the dog.

"It's a very special kind of dog. Magical. I hope you like dogs, Wendell. You're going to spend the rest of your life as one."

She bent down as she said that last, and let go of the dog. It bounded toward Wendell. He tried to back away, but the dog reached him and put its paws on his chest. Wendell raised his arms in a gesture of surrender—damn her, she'd known how much he hated dogs—when he suddenly felt quite loose inside his body. It was as if he wasn't attached to his own skin anymore.

He was shrinking and the room had grown dimmer. It had also gotten louder. His perspective had shifted. He had been staring at his stepmother, and now he was looking at—his own sash. How did that happen?

He glanced up and saw his own face. Only his tongue was out, the way a dog's would be, and his front arms were cocked and bent like those of a dog standing on its hind legs.

Oh, no. He didn't like this at all. He glanced down and saw that his own hands were feet. Hairy feet. Golden hairy feet.

"Come, come, Wendell," the Queen said in a tone that had a motherly chiding behind it. "You don't greet people on all fours, do you?"

"You'll never get away with this," Wendell said. Or tried to say. Instead, he barked.

"You know, I do think he's trying to tell us something," the Queen said.

The Trolls applauded. Wendell shook his head, felt his ears flap against his skull, and something move around his royal posterior. He glanced over his golden, hairy shoulder.

He had a tail. He really was the dog.

The Trolls were laughing and applauding. The real dog—who looked for all intents and purposes like the Prince (did he really have such curly blond hair? And such a goofy expression on his long face? Or was that the function of the magic, the dog, and the Queen's maliciousness?)—was exploring his face with his hands. He swayed on his feet as if he weren't used to balancing on two legs.

The Queen's smile had faded. "Grab him!" she ordered.

One of the taller Trolls hurried toward Wendell. Those creatures could move fast. The Troll reached for Wendell, and Wendell did the only thing he could do.

He bit those stubby, pale, filthy fingers. They tasted like they smelled.

"Ow!" the Troll cried and pulled away.

Wendell resisted the urge to spit. He wheeled around, nearly getting tangled in all four limbs, and ran from the room. It was easier to run on all fours as a dog than it was as a human. It only took him a moment to get into the loping stride. The tail was throwing off his balance, but he bet he could get used to that too.

He veered into a corridor and was scampering down it when he heard the Queen shout: "Stop him!"

Wendell cursed and the sound came out as a growl. There was an awful lot to get used to in this dog body, not to mention trying to outthink the nastiest woman in the kingdoms while he tried to make his escape. And, to make matters worse, he had a hunch he was going deeper into the prison instead of getting out of it. And he didn't even want to think about trying to open doors.

If he could apologize to Giles, he would. This was not the kind of hunting Wendell had had in mind.

Who would have thought wimpy Wendell would be this much trouble? The Queen narrowed her eyes as Wendell's tail disappeared into a darkened corridor. And to make matters worse, the smelly Trolls she was stuck with weren't as swift as she wanted them to be.

"We'll get him," Burly shouted. "He's not going anywhere."

"He can't escape," Blabberwort said. "It's a prison."

Oh, wonderful. Pronouncements. And obvious ones at that. The Queen was about to push them from the room when all four Trolls took off, limbs flailing.

If Wendell had any sense at all, he would be able to keep them busy for hours. And Wendell had just proven to have a lot more sense than she had ever given him credit for.

She turned toward the Dog Prince, who was still looking at himself with wonder. Apparently Wendell had been smarter than any animal. The look on the Dog Prince's face was definitely a lot dimmer in the intelligence department. How come she hadn't noticed Wendell's brains before?

Probably because he had always played spoiled heir to the throne to perfection.

"Well?" she asked the Dog Prince. "Do you have anything to say for yourself, Your Highness?"

The Prince glanced over his shoulder slowly, then growled, "Where's my tail gone?"

An involuntary sound of disgust escaped her. She had had a very small hope of sending the Dog Prince after Wendell, but that obviously wouldn't work. Instead, she would need other help.

She clutched the keys she had lifted from the Troll King—delicately, not because she thought he would notice, but because she really didn't want to touch his leather-and-suede coat—and walked back into the prison proper. She avoided her old corridor, the one that led to maximum security, and instead went toward the cells.

As the inmates saw her, they shouted at her to let them out. Some hung near the bars, others reached for her as she passed. They were a motley bunch, scarred and hideous-looking, but without any real strength. Bulky, burly men didn't run well. She needed someone with speed, agility, and cunning.

Not that she would find anyone like that here. Anyone with speed, agility, and cunning should have been able to outrun all the king's horses and all the king's men.

Then she smiled. The only king the Nine Kingdoms would have would be a dog.

She was about to give up when she saw a flash of dark hair, of intelligent eyes, of a narrow, handsome face that somehow made her think of wolf-like cunning.

Speed, agility—and cunning. Hmmm. How perfect.

"You," she said.

The man came closer. He was slender and moved with the kind of quickness she was looking for. He grinned at her, and there was a bit of the rake in that smile.

"Hello," he said.

A melodious voice, deep and rich. The kind of voice a man should have. She raised her chin slightly. He was charming, too, and knew how to use it. This was more than a human male. This was something else.

"What are you?" she asked.

"Me?" He raised his eyebrows as if he couldn't believe the question. "A very fine chap, falsely imprisoned on a trumped-up—"

"Do not make me ask again." She knew he was more than that. His gaze caught hers. Apparently he realized that she was not someone to be trifled with.

His eyes changed, flared green for a moment, and then returned to normal. "I am a half wolf."

She unlocked the cell door, but hung on to it to show him her control. "If I let you out, you must serve me without question."

He grinned. "Breakfast, lunch, dinner, I'll serve you anything. I'm your wolf. Loyalty is my middle name."

She let go of the door and took a step toward him. His grin faded and he stopped babbling. She looked at him, stared at him, and his eyes went flat, the way an animal's did while it tried to figure out the best way to deal with its fear.

"Give your will to me." She used her Power voice.

Still that flat look. He wouldn't be an easy one to convince.

"Be mine to summon and control whenever I call on you."

For a moment, she thought he was going to say no. Then

he blinked, looked away, and nodded. Now she was the one who smiled. He was hers, and she knew that no matter how smart Wendell was, he lacked cunning.

He could never outrun a human wolf.

Chapter Three

Wendell scampered through the corridors of the prison. His brand-new tail kept flopping behind him. If it weren't for all his doggy feet, he would have fallen long ago. He finally figured out how to tuck the thing between his legs. Miraculously, it curled when he did that so that he wouldn't trip on it as he ran.

He had no idea where he was going. The corridor seemed bigger than it had before. The ceiling was far away and the walls were wider apart. He doubted that was because this part of the building was actually bigger. He suspected it was because he was smaller. He knew he was missing a lot of opportunities here, opportunities a real dog would see, because he thought of himself as larger than he now was. He had to focus on his dog size—where would a Golden Retriever fit?—because he certainly wasn't man-sized anymore.

If only he'd been paying attention. He'd been warned long ago to be on his toes when he was within ten miles of his stepmother. Of course, he hadn't paid attention to that. Giles had—but on that one, apparently, Giles hadn't listened hard enough.

Wendell's heart twisted a little at the thought of Giles. The old man had been a good companion all these years. But if Wendell didn't take care, he would end up like Giles. Or worse. He'd be on one end of a leash and his evil stepmother would be on the other.

Wendell rounded a corner, his claws scraping against the

cobblestone floor. If only they'd keep the flooring the same around here, but he'd had to adjust to regular stone, then brick, and then cobblestone. He wasn't used to four feet, and he wasn't used to running barefoot and the effect of his toenails scraping on everything was driving him insane.

At least he'd solved the tail thing.

His heart was pounding and he was lost. He had no idea where he was going. He kept stopping at door after door after door, but they were all locked. Or as good as locked. He'd never missed his thumbs so much in his entire life.

Guards were everywhere. Unconscious guards lying on their sides, their faces covered with pink dust. There had been a coup in the Snow White Memorial Prison and he was the only one who knew about it.

What would his advisors think when the Dog Prince returned to them? Would they know it was Wendell? Would they be startled when it barked at them?

"There! There he is!" one of the Trolls shouted.

That voice was very far behind him, yet he heard it. Hmmm. He'd been told that dogs heard better than humans. Now he knew it. It didn't make up for the lost thumbs, the diminished eyesight, or those scraping claws, but it did help a little.

He glanced over his shoulder and saw movement behind him. He didn't have that much of a lead.

He saw some stairs ahead. Down. Down would be good. Maybe there'd be a back exit.

A dog-sized back exit.

"Out of my way, amateurs," a new voice said. It was clearly not the voice of a Troll. "This is a job for a wolf."

A wolf? A talking wolf? Weren't wolves superior to dogs? So much for hiding in a small, dog-sized space. The wolf would smell him out in no time.

"We are best at tracking." Those Trolls were real whiners.

"In your dreams, Troll boy," the wolf said.

The stairs led to a narrow corridor filled with high arches. He followed them and ran toward a dank, forgotten room, filled with cobwebs and dust and more junk than he'd ever seen. There were crates and chests and even half a rotted carriage—blue with a white emblem on it. On top were rotted clothes and curtains. The entire place smelled forgotten.

He resisted the urge to sneeze. He was still going at top speed. He wasn't quite sure how to stop. He rounded the corner into the far side of the room, lost his doggy balance—his feet sweated when he was nervous!—and slid into a towering pile of junk.

It clattered around him, sending dishes and goblets and things he couldn't identify toppling to the stone floor. He was sliding horribly—and the slide didn't stop until he crashed into a large mirror at the far end of the room.

It was a full-length mirror with some kind of elaborate design on the frame. As he looked at it, the silvering shifted.

"He's over there!" one Troll shouted.

An amazing world opened before him. First an ocean—or perhaps a sky—and then a statue of a large green woman holding a torch. He stared at it.

The image kept shifting. Now it showed a bridge and a city like none he'd ever seen. Buildings that reached for the sky crowded together like peasants waiting for his coach. The sun shone on this place, and it glittered in the light.

He heard footsteps behind him, clattering and slapping and coming toward him.

The image was moving in, toward the buildings. They had smooth glass windows and walls that appeared to be made of a better, smaller stone than he'd ever seen.

At the base of the mirror, he saw his own reflection, and it confirmed what he already knew. The golden dog's body was his now. The only difference between the one the Queen had held and the one he had now were the eyes. These eyes were his. He recognized them, even though he didn't know how he could.

The footsteps had gotten very loud. Wendell's heart was pounding. Someone had gotten close. There was no other way out of this room. He had to go through the mirror.

''What's going on here?'' the wolf said.

The image now showed a grassy place. It looked manicured, but it was full of trees, full of places to hide.

Wendell leaped into the mirror, silently praying that he wouldn't just bump his head on the glass and give himself seven years of bad luck (not, of course, that his luck could get any worse).

He didn't hit anything, except a thick liquid that had to be the mirror. Suddenly, he was in complete darkness. But worse than that was the silence. He couldn't even hear his own breathing.

Then he was in the trees, branches slapping against his face as he hit the ground. There was real dirt beneath his paws, but there was a stink to the air he'd never smelled anywhere else—a heavy, oily scent as if someone were burning too many lamps in one place.

He bounded forward, determined to get away from the entrance site. The wolf would come after him, and if Wendell wasn't careful, the wolf would find him. Wendell had to find water to hide his scent. That would throw the wolf off. Then, in this strange place, he might be able to find help.

There was a path before him. It seemed to be made of dirt and gravel, but he couldn't really tell. A woman riding a strange metal contraption was coming down the hill toward him. Wendell tried to jump out of her way, but the contraption slammed into him.

He flew through the air. A dog was whimpering, and then he realized that was him. As he soared, he saw the woman fall and hit her head. Then he landed near a rock. He wanted to get up, but he couldn't.

Instead, fighting it as hard as he could, he slipped into darkness.

A faint clatter echoed through the prison, and then three voices rose in disgust. The Queen closed the door to the reception hall. She didn't want to hear the sounds of failure.

Wendell had escaped her, for the moment anyway. He couldn't go forever. He would be too challenged as a dog. He wouldn't know how to survive. But the Queen didn't want to use her newfound freedom to search for the little inconvenience, not when she had so many deliciously evil plans.

She folded her gloved hands together and turned toward the Troll King. What a disgusting example of Trolldom. He was tall and square, with the same hooked nose two of his children had. His skin was as pale as his older son's, only unlike his son's, the Troll King's eyes glinted with something like intelligence.

She could use him. She could use him very well.

"Within a month," she said, catching his attention, "I will have crushed the House of White. I will have Wendell's castle and his kingdom."

She took a step toward the Troll King, making certain her voice was at its most seductive. "And for helping me to escape, you will have half his kingdom to rule."

The Troll King's eyes widened, and he licked his lips. She half expected to see him rub his hands together with glee, but apparently he restrained himself.

"Half the Fourth Kingdom?" the Troll King asked. "But it's huge . . ."

That word must have triggered something in his small brain, because he suddenly frowned.

"What's your plan?" he asked. "What do I have to do?"

She raised her chin slightly, modulating her voice just a little. "Allow me the use of your children until they have caught the Prince for me."

"That's all?" The Troll King sounded relieved.

"And tell no one what you have seen, of course."

To her surprise, the Troll King didn't answer for a moment. Instead his eyes narrowed. She could almost see his troll-sized brain attempting to work. He was actually contemplating this— or trying to. He obviously thought there was a catch to it.

Of course, there was, but she wasn't going to tell him that for a long time.

Finally, he asked, "Do I get to choose which half of the kingdom I have?"

The Queen closed her eyes. Never underestimate the power of greed. Then she opened her eyes, smiled at him, and told him what she thought he needed to hear.

A magic mirror. Wolf didn't like the look of that. Nor did he like the look of that dog—the dog that would give him his freedom if he but captured it. That dog looked much too smart. It was studying the images changing in the mirror as if it were waiting for the right one.

Wolf hadn't tried to be quiet. He had announced his presence just a moment before. But now, as he approached, the dog looked over its shoulder and saw him.

Those eyes were too intelligent to be a dog's eyes.

Then the dog looked forward again. The image in the mirror had changed to trees and greenery. At the base of the mirror, he saw the dog, then he saw his own image behind it. He was a good-looking man, if he did say so himself. Just tall enough, just handsome enough—

He lunged for the dog just as the dog leapt forward. The dog disappeared into the mirror, and for a moment the image winked out.

Wolf uttered a perfectly wolflike curse, thought for maybe a half a second about his own foolishness at following a dog through a magic mirror, then leaped just as the image of trees and bushes returned.

The stuff inside the mirror coated his skin and he was enveloped in utter darkness. He couldn't smell anything, see anything, or hear anything.

Then he found himself tumbling in a group of bushes. The branches tugged at his clothing and he was getting grass in his hair.

He was outside! He hadn't been outside in a long, long

time. He wanted to let fly with a wolfish howl, but that would reveal his position. Instead, he stood, dusted himself off, and glanced behind him.

There was a mirror-sized shimmer by the bushes. Faintly, he could still see the storage room. The Trolls were thumping their way through the arch—late, just as he'd predicted. They had no idea how to track anything.

Tracking. That was his job. He had to move away from the image so they didn't see him and wouldn't know where he had gone. He moved, then sniffed. The air wasn't quite fresh, but it didn't stink as much as the air in many of the villages. Here there was only a slight scent of urine overlaying the greenery. No. The dominant scent was something unidentifiable and metallic. Then, above that he caught the faint odor of sudden fear, and beneath it—dog!

Wolf grinned and loped in the direction of the smell, thinking this assignment was getting more pleasant by the minute.

Virginia sat up slowly. Her entire body ached, but her forehead ached the most. She'd fallen off her bike before, but never had she crashed and burned like this. She hadn't seen that dog until it was too late.

Her hands were trembling. She willed them to stop shaking, and one did. That was the one she used to touch her forehead. It was bleeding. She stared at the blood on her fingertips for a moment, then decided it wasn't enough to worry about. She probably had a cut. She'd had them before.

Then she looked at her bike and moaned.

The front wheel was completely buckled. There was no way she could ride it and no way she could fix it. Not here.

She would be late to work, but at least this time she had an excuse.

The condition of that wheel meant she'd hit that dog pretty hard. She looked for it, and saw a bundle of golden fur lying beside the path.

Unmoving.

"Oh, my God," she said. "I've killed it!"

She'd never killed anything before, not even accidentally. She moved toward it, and as she did, the dog twitched. It wasn't dead after all. She let out a small sigh and put her hand on its soft fur.

The dog looked up at her with surprisingly intelligent eyes.

"Are you all right?" she asked as she felt through its fur, searching for broken bones, blood, anything that would require immediate care. She found nothing.

"Where's your master?" She looked over her shoulder. A dog this well cared-for usually had someone trailing it. Or had it gotten out? That wouldn't do her any good. There had to be millions of dogs in the city of New York. That meant there were millions of dog owners, and all of them brought their dogs to this park. How would she find the right owner?

How would she deal with this dog at work?

She felt around its neck, but of course, the dog didn't have a collar. Some people were so irresponsible.

"Why haven't you got a collar, hmm?" she asked.

The dog seemed reassured by her voice. It moved too, and as it did, she realized it was a he.

Behind her, she heard a low, wolf-like howl. The hair on the back of her neck actually stood up. Even the dog seemed alarmed. Then she realized how precarious her position was. A woman alone in the park after dark, in a secluded wooded area. There were no real wolves in Manhattan, but the human wolves were very dangerous indeed.

She looked at the dog and he looked at her. Apparently they belonged to each other now, at least for the night. She got up, picked up her bike, and straightened its mangled wheel enough so that she could wheel it along.

The dog stood with her, and as she hurried out of the park, he followed faithfully along.

Chapter Four

Blabberwort stepped out of the mirror and onto a grassland. There were trees around her, but they'd been tamed. It was dark here, but it smelled delicious. There was a lovely tang to the air she'd never noticed before. It was almost rotten, at that perfect stage when bad things became delectable.

Bluebell pushed her aside as he climbed out of the mirror, and she was about to turn around and shove him when Burly glared at her. Apparently Burly was still sore that the wolfman had followed the dog through the mirror first.

"Suck an Elf!" Bluebell shouted from behind her. "Where are we?"

She hadn't even thought about that. She'd never been here before. She ran her tongue over her broken teeth and stared. Rising above the trees were buildings, and they were filled with light. Even the path ahead of them had a large lamp above it, illuminating the darkness.

What a strange place.

"Get a look at that," Burly said, pointing at one of the tall buildings. It towered over the others and had lights on its side that were multicolored. It seemed very far away. This appeared to be the only greenery in a sea of buildings.

Blabberwort knew a lot about the Nine Kingdoms. It was her one and only specialty.

"This is not part of the Nine Kingdoms," she said. "It is a magic place. Look at all those lights."

"They must have a ton of candles," Bluebell said.

If this wasn't part of the Nine Kingdoms, then it was some-place else. Blabberwort smiled at her own logic. And if it was someplace else, then it didn't have any rulers. She could fix that.

"Maybe we should claim this kingdom," Blabberwort said.

"That's a sensational idea!" Burly shouted. "Let's grab it before anyone else does."

Blabberwort spread her arms and said in her loudest voice: "I claim this land and all its inhabitants for the Troll Nation. Henceforth it shall be known as . . ." She stopped. She wasn't good at making up names. If she had been, she would have thought of a new one for herself a long time ago. She looked at the others. "What shall we call it?"

"The Tenth Kingdom," Bluebell said.

Blabberwort grinned. How absolutely perfect. She clapped her tiny brother on his puny back and made him stagger forward a little. Then she looked around for something to help with the celebration of their newfound power.

Farther down the path, a pair of humans sat on a bench. They were scrawny things, fairly young, and they were kissing in that disgusting, mouthy way humans had.

They seemed quite involved.

Blabberwort pointed at them. Burly nodded his approval. He moved Bluebell's head so that Bluebell could see, and all three of them crept toward the bench. A little mayhem, a little theft, would be the perfect celebration.

Blabberwort reached the couple at the same time her broth-ers did, and as if they'd planned the whole thing, they shoved the couple around. The woman—hideously blonde—screamed, and the man—with those awful, delicate human features—did nothing to save her. Instead he protected his own face.

Humans. How disgusting they were. Blabberwort decided to punish these two for being part of that ugly race. She got lost in a frenzy of slapping, hitting, and kicking until she realized that her victims were leaning on the bench and moaning.

The woman's hideous blond hair was covering her ugly

face. The man had his head tilted back as if he couldn't stand it anymore.

"What have we got, then?" Burly asked, as ready, apparently, as Blubberwort was to get to the thieving part of this celebration.

They all grabbed the couple's feet and stared at the puny white shoes. Blabberwort squeezed one. It was soft and mushy, not at all like a good pair of boots.

"Rubbish!" Bluebell said, disgusted. "Look at these. These aren't even leather."

They dropped the couple's feet, and the man moaned. Burly cuffed him. Bluebell looked at the woman's jacket. It wasn't appropriately Troll-like, but it had a certain charm to it. It had the emblem of some ruler across it. Bluebell pulled it off.

Blabberwort didn't like the fact that her brother had gotten one of the choice items. She grabbed the bag that had been between the couple.

"Any more shoes in here?" she asked the semi-conscious couple. When they didn't answer, she dumped the bag's contents on the ground. Boxes of powder and tiny metal tubes and papers fell to the dirt. So did a big black box.

"What's this?" Blabberwort picked up the box. It felt smooth. It was made of a material she'd never touched before. Nice. Solid. Strong.

The man sat up slightly and she swung the box at him, hitting him in the head. He fell back, but the box seemed to come alive. It vibrated, and then high-pitched voices and music came out, singing a very catchy tune about nights and fevers.

She felt herself move involuntarily to the music. As she looked, her brothers were doing the same thing.

"More magic!" Burly shouted.

They continued to bounce to the music. How wonderful it was. But of course, Bluebell had to ruin it. He looked at Blabberwort and Burly.

"Come on, bring it with us," Bluebell said. "We must find the Prince before he gets away."

Blabberwort sighed. She wanted to stay here. But she knew their father would be very angry if they did.

Burly stared down at the humans on the bench. "You are now our slaves. Remain here until we return."

The couple put their arms around each other, slowly, as if it hurt. Blabberwort followed her brothers away from the bench, but she couldn't resist one look back.

There, on the back of the bench, illuminated in the strange light, was her brother Bluebell's handwriting. In some kind of chalk he'd scrawled: TROLLS ROOL.

Blabberwort grinned. Trolls rule. Yes, indeed they did.

Virginia was feeling a little stiff and sore as she walked. In addition to the cut on her head, which ached, there were other bruises that were beginning to make themselves known. Her bike was making a scraping sound, and the poor dog was still following her.

She had no idea how long she had been unconscious. Probably long enough for someone to mug her and she wouldn't even have noticed. At that thought, she felt inside her coat pocket and groaned.

"My wallet . . ."

The dog looked at her as if she had said something important. She stopped, sighed, and turned around. She doubted she had been mugged. She was still wearing her necklace, after all, and any garden-variety mugger would have taken wallet and jewelry. Which meant that the wallet had to be lying on the ground next to the accident site.

She started walking in that direction. The dog glanced at her again, as if he were questioning her judgment. But a dog couldn't do that, could he? She decided not to worry about it.

As she reached a small grouping of trees, she saw something. Green and flashing. It almost looked like a pair of eyes. The wind had built up and it was cold. The night seemed even darker than it had before.

The dog was still looking at her as if she were crazy.

"Leave it," she said to herself. "You'll never find it now."

She turned around again, and this time she ran to the edge of the park. The dog trotted to keep up with her.

Fortunately, the Grill on the Green was as close to Central Park as a restaurant legally could be. She went around the back and leaned her bike in the alley. The familiar scents of grease and beer wafted out of the kitchen, and the lights were reassuring.

Virginia went inside, leaving the door to the alley open as it usually was. The cook ignored her, as usual, but as she walked by the grill, Candy came into the kitchen. When she saw Virginia, she let fly, just as Virginia knew she would.

"Where have you been?" Candy asked. "I've been covering for you—"

Then Candy stopped. She had almost reached Virginia. "Your head! You're bleeding."

She air-touched Virginia's forehead. Virginia ducked so that Candy wouldn't irritate the wound.

"I smashed my bike," Virginia said. "And I lost my wallet. And I've picked up a new boyfriend."

The dog was standing in the doorway, his tail between his legs. He looked groggy and a bit overwhelmed.

"Oh, aren't you the cutest cooch'ms?" Candy said, hurrying to the dog. She crouched by him and started petting him. "What a lovely doggy."

"I hit him with my bike, but I think he's okay," Virginia said. "He's not bleeding or anything."

Candy seemed to have a serious dog fetish. She was ruffling the fur around the dog's face, and the dog was looking both baffled and tortured.

"Don't let the boss see him in here," Candy said. "What's his name?"

"I don't know," Virginia said. "He hasn't got a collar."

Candy stared at the dog for a moment, then said, "He looks like a Prince to me." She patted the dog. "Hello, Prince."

Virginia grabbed a tissue off a nearby counter. "Hello,

Prince,'' she said, thinking Candy was right. The name did sound appropriate.

The dog preened just a little.

Virginia dabbed at her cut with the tissue, and was relieved to see it hadn't bled any more. Candy got up and grabbed a piece of hamburger off one of the plates stacked haphazardly by the busboy. She went to Prince and waved the hamburger in front of his nose.

He looked at it with complete disgust.

Candy glanced over her shoulder at Virginia, surprised. Virginia shrugged. She didn't pretend to understand that dog. She wasn't really sure she wanted to.

Blabberwort smelled blood. Fresh blood. And, it seemed, Burly did so at the same time.

''Here!'' Burly hurried to a spot on the path where there was the blood, yes, the smell of dog, yes, and some scraps of metal lying about. ''There's been an . . . incident.''

Blabberwort hurried to his side. She didn't want him to get all the goodies. Of course, Bluebell was lagging slightly behind.

Burly was looking at all the shiny things. But Blabberwort saw a dark shape in the grass. ''Lookee look!''

She scooped it up before her brothers could get it. Leather. It was very good leather. She held it to her nose and sniffed, enjoying the marvelous fragrance.

''Calfskin,'' Blabberwort said. ''Nice. Squeaky clean.''

Burly watched with obvious disappointment that he hadn't found the leather. Bluebell was standing as close as he could get without touching the prize.

Blabberwort decided to torture them with it. She held it out slightly and examined it. It wasn't a shoe, that was for sure. It was something else. And it had strange things inside.

Bluebell grabbed the square and opened it. He pulled papers and things out of it, throwing them to the ground. Blabberwort looked at them, but they all seemed useless to her.

Finally, when the square was empty, Bluebell brought it

close to his face. He squinted his beady eyes at it. "If found please return to Virginia Lewis," Bluebell read, "Apartment 17a, No. 2, East 81st Street."

Ah. Blabberwort grinned. Finally. A destination.

Bright lights, strange roaring sounds, a metal object three times the size of a house hurtling at him on a strangely covered street. Wolf stood at the edge of the grass and watched everything. He had never seen so many lights in his life. Or so many magical things. Carriages of all shapes and sizes that moved under their own power. Buildings with all sorts of exotic names. Smells such as he had never encountered before.

"Well, huff-puff," he said in admiration. "What a place!"

He wanted to follow all of the smells—he even wanted to roll in some—but he banished that thought quickly. He liked to think of himself as an enhanced human, but sometimes his animal natures got the better of him.

They couldn't here, though. He wouldn't allow it. He had a job to do, and he would do it, just as he was supposed to.

He sniffed, separating out all the scents, labeling and identifying the ones he could. Then he caught one that made his stomach growl. "Meat!"

How long had it been since he'd had real meat? Not gruel, not that prison slop, but real, tasty succulent meat?

He honestly didn't know.

He scanned the area around him until he saw the place where the smell was coming from. It was well lit, and even the sign above it had lights hidden behind it. GRILL ON THE GREEN.

He hurried over to it and stopped outside. The window glass was smooth and clear, and provided a lovely view of the tables inside. Two rather plump humans had plates before them heaped with food. The woman right beside him was eating a steak. Rare.

Saliva formed in his mouth and he started to drool. Oh, those animal natures. He hated drooling, but he couldn't stop himself. He licked his lips and could almost taste the steak that woman was eating.

How wonderful. How spectacular.

"Don't forget what you're here for," he said to himself. He had to control those animal natures. Had to control those desires. Had to stop thinking about steak. "Find the Prince."

The woman took another bite. She looked at him, her expression both annoyed and disgusted. No human should look at him that way. He pressed his face closer to the glass.

"But huff-puff," he muttered, "a wolf's got to eat, hasn't he? Can't work on an empty stomach."

He made his way from the window to the door, pushed it open, and stepped inside. It was as if he had entered a smorgasbord of smells. Chicken, fish, even a bit of fresh lamb. Mmmm. His stomach growled again in anticipation.

Then another smell wafted over the top.

"I smell dog!" Wolf said out loud. "Would you believe it? Work and pleasure combined."

The woman stared at him as if he were a crazy man. Slowly she removed the piece of steak from her mouth. He resisted the urge to steal her meat. If she was going to waste it, he should have it, shouldn't he? Shouldn't he?

Maybe he should go for the dog first. Maybe he could grab a snack as he did so. Maybe.

Work and pleasure. He had been right. This job *was* getting better and better all the time.

Chapter Five

Virginia's forehead still tingled where she had put some antiseptic on her cut. Now she had to take care of Prince before the boss found him. She didn't want to leave the dog in the alley, so she led him to the storeroom. The boss never went in there.

It was dark and rather dingy, with large restaurant-quantity cans of everything from chicken broth to garbanzo beans cluttering the shelves. There was a dry-food smell in here and, like every other building this close to the Park, an ever-so-faint odor of mice.

At least, she liked to think it was mice. Although she knew it was probably rats.

Prince stopped at the door. She had to force him to come inside. He did, his tail still lowered. Was he in pain? He hadn't really wagged his tail since she careened into him on her bike.

"Now don't make a sound," Virginia said, crouching so that she could face the dog. He really did have the most intelligent eyes. She almost believed he could understand her. "I'll come back when I can and check on you. Don't make a noise or you'll get me the sack."

Prince barked. Virginia grabbed him.

"Shhh! Or I'll put you outside."

He seemed to like that even less. He sat down and looked at her with the saddest, most mature expression she had ever seen on a dog's face. She almost—almost—apologized, but she always thought less of people who apologized to their pets.

Not, she hastened to remind herself, that he was her pet. But he was her responsibility.

She left the storage room without looking back, so that the guilt wouldn't get her. Then she took the staff keys off the wall, and locked the door. That way, the boss wouldn't inadvertently find Prince, and Prince—with that sharp brain of his—wouldn't figure out a way to get out.

Virginia wiped her hands, grabbed an order pad, and stuck it in her apron along with a pen. Then she went out into the crowd.

Candy had all the tables because Virginia had been so late. And, since Virginia had to clean up, Candy was taking the newcomers as well. The guilt got Virginia again. She would have to help with side orders, salads, and drinks until the workload evened out.

There were two new tables, a large group of rowdy people who were banging their menus for attention, and a good-looking guy toward the back of the room. Of course Candy went to him first. Virginia frowned. Good-looking but strange. Something about his eyes didn't seem quite human.

She shook off the thought. Maybe her head was injured worse than she thought. She seemed to be reading a lot into eyes tonight.

She went to the rowdy table and pulled out her order pad and pen. Just as she was about to take the order, she heard a crash from in the back.

From the storage room.

She cursed under her breath and left the man, in the middle of ordering his drinks, to shout after her. She ran for the kitchen. The cook looked up from the grill, his face shiny with sweat.

"Was that you?" she asked.

He shook his head and flipped a hamburger. This place could get robbed and he would stay behind the grill, calmly cooking any order that had been placed in front of him.

Virginia grabbed the staff keys as she hurried to the storage room door. With shaking fingers, she unlocked it, and pushed the door open.

A broken jar had sent glass everywhere, and beside it, a container of flour had fallen and spilled open. Prince stood beside the flour, his tail wagging hesitantly.

"That's it," Virginia said. "I'm putting you outside and—"

And then she froze. Crudely scraped into the spilled flour was a single word. *Danger*. She stared at it uneasily for a moment—this night had been too strange for words—and then she realized what was going on.

"Okay, Candy, come out," she said, looking around. "Funny joke."

Wait. Candy was in the main room, taking the order of some good-looking guy who reminded Virginia vaguely of a wolf. She looked at the keys in her hand. She had locked the door and she had unlocked it. And there was no one else in the room.

Feeling a little silly, she said to the dog, "I don't suppose you wrote that, did you?"

Prince barked and she moved backwards just a little. The night was getting stranger and stranger. He couldn't have done it. The flour had to have been spilled before. She just hadn't noticed.

Like she hadn't noticed that Prince, even though he was covered in flour, had most of it concentrated on his right front paw. Just the way it would if he had written something with that paw.

Dogs couldn't spell, could they? What was he, a trick dog escaped from the circus?

She looked at him for a very long time. Those intelligent eyes of his met hers.

Finally she gave in to the absolute weirdness of it all. "Bark once."

Prince barked once.

"Bark twice."

Prince barked twice. Virginia was so startled, she jumped backwards.

"Stop it!" she shouted at the dog. Then she took a deep breath. "Okay, Virginia, you've fallen off your bike and cracked your head and you're in hospital. You're in hospital and they've given you morphine or something and that's why—"

Prince barked twice again. Virginia glanced at the word *Danger* and then back at Prince. He was covered in flour. He had too much of it on his right front paw for any explainable reason. He could bark on command.

He had the most intelligent eyes she'd ever seen in a dog. Hell, there were some men who didn't have eyes as intelligent as that.

He was staring at her with such intensity that she couldn't ignore him.

"Can . . . can you understand everything I'm saying?"

Prince barked once.

Virginia resisted the urge to cover his mouth. The boss would hear. Everyone would hear.

"Stop it!" she said. She found herself backed against the wall, and she had no idea how she had gotten there. Her heart was beating so hard, she thought it would carve a hole in her chest.

Okay, she thought to herself, using a tone she'd only heard from her grandmother. *Okay. Get a grip. The dog says there's danger. Let's find out what this is about. No matter how ridiculous it seems.*

"Who's in danger?" she asked. "Both of us?"

Prince barked once more, then grabbed her sleeve gently between his teeth. He dragged her arm toward the door. There was no mistaking this message. He wanted her to leave. With him.

That meant both of them were in danger. What kind she wasn't sure, but she remembered that feeling she had in the park, the eyes staring at her, the growing darkness.

Danger. Both of them. And now she was taking advice from a dog. Prince tugged harder on her sleeve.

Could this night possibly get any worse?

Wolf had given in to his animal nature. He simply had to have something to eat. And there were so many choices here! The menu was quite extensive.

He figured he had time. The dog was hiding nearby and probably wouldn't come out, thinking he'd found the perfect bolt-hole. Wolf could smell him, tantalizingly close.

But not as tantalizing as the steak. The chicken. The fish . . .

The waitress was standing near him, chewing gum, and looking completely vapid. Her nearness was making him nervous. Humans were meat. Good meat, although hers would probably be a bit tough. And he really didn't want to go for a human tonight, although she was standing awfully close.

So many choices, so little time.

"No, I just can't decide," Wolf said.

The waitress chomped harder on her gum. Her eyes didn't quite meet his as she said, "The specials are lamb and—"

"Lamb?" That was right! He had smelled lamb when he first came in here. Good, succulent fresh lamb. He had been thinking of how wonderful it smelled when he caught a whiff of dog.

"Ohhh," he said, thinking of the delicacy of all of it. "New season's lamb, I hope. Young and juicy and frolicking provocatively in the fields, bouncing up and down with soft fluffy wool—"

He shook his head. "Stop it, pull yourself together."

The waitress had tilted her head slightly as if she heard something far away.

And he thought of lamb and couldn't stop his mouth from running on. That animal nature again. "Some little shepherdess not really paying attention to the flock," he said, his thoughts of delicious lamb turning again to delicious girl. "Probably asleep if I know little girls . . . I mean I'm not going to eat her, not if there's a nice leg of lamb going . . . no, no . . . I mean I *could* eat her of course, especially if she's dozing in the meadow, breathing soft, warm breaths . . . ohhhh . . . but if there's lamb fillet, or a nice fat rack of chops . . . I'm not greedy. Well, I am greedy, I don't know why I said that. I have a substantial appetite. Born to gorge, that's me.''

The waitress hadn't really heard him. Or if she had, she hadn't cared. "So," she said, "is that a yes on the lamb?"

"Of course it's a yes. If, of course, the lamb is fresh. If it isn't, I want steak."

"It's fresh," the waitress said. Her gum snapped. That was a disgusting sound. He couldn't believe he was thinking of eating her. He was human after all. Humans didn't eat their own kind. Not even enhanced humans. Not even enhanced humans with wolf-like tastes.

"So, it's the lamb, right?" she said, as if she weren't exactly sure.

"Yes," he said. "And make certain it's undercooked."

"We don't undercook nothing," she said.

"I want it undercooked."

She frowned. This girl was not one of the most brilliant specimens of humanity he'd ever encountered.

He was losing patience. "What's your name?"

"Candy," she said.

Named for food. The wrong kind, but food nonetheless. "Candy, my dear," he said, "I want my lamb undercooked."

"You mean rare?"

"No, no, no," Wolf said. "Listen, rare implies dangerously cooked. When I say rare, I mean just let it look at the oven in terror and then bring it out here."

She squinted at him. "You want fries, baked potato, mashed, coleslaw, or rice with that?"

Wolf winced. "No fries. No vegetables, no blue cheese, no sour cream—just meat, red as a young girl's first blush. And six glasses of warm milk."

"That's the lamb special and six glasses of warm milk," Candy said. "Got it."

Wolf sighed. That sounded fantastic. He could imagine himself sitting here all night, eating to his heart's content.

And then he thought he heard a dog bark, faintly, through a wall behind him. Wolf reached out and grabbed the waitress's arm before she managed to leave.

"I almost forgot," Wolf said. "I'm looking for this lovely lady who found my doggie."

To his surprise, Candy smiled. She looked younger when she smiled. Fresher.

"Oh, is it yours?" she asked. "Virginia's out back. I'll tell her."

She hurried away as if she were on some kind of mission. He left his seat and followed her, through the kitchen (cooking beef, sizzling on the grill, ah, the smells, the delightful succulent smells!) and toward a storeroom.

At that point, Candy noticed him. "You can't come in here."

The smell of dog was strong here. There was another scent underneath it. A delectable feminine scent. Tantalizing. Beautiful.

Wolf reached around Candy and whipped the door open. The room was empty. But it hadn't been for long. The smell of dog was strong here, and so was that delightful female scent. They had been together here. The dog had a helper.

Then he saw *Danger* written in the spilled flour, and he cursed. The dog had found a way to talk.

He rubbed out the message with his foot before Candy noticed it.

Candy was frowning. "Maybe she went home. She hurt herself when she fell."

She. That's right. Candy had mentioned a she. A Virginia, she of the lovely scent.

"Oh, poor little sausage," Wolf said. "Where does she live then, this lovely lady? I can't wait to thank her."

The storage room door swung shut behind them. He stifled a small smile. Candy looked nervous.

"Well, I can't really tell you where she lives, you know, I don't know who you are . . ."

Wolf backed Candy against the wall and trapped her between his arms. He tried to look at her the way a prospective lover would, but all he could think of was how wonderful her flesh might taste. Still, he had to find out about that dog . . .

He made his eyes flash hypnotically.

"Oh," he said ever so gently, "you can tell *me*."

Virginia got off the bus at the end of her block. It was amazing how empty New York streets could be at night. She was used to seeing more people around—or maybe she just didn't notice when she was on her bike.

Her poor wounded bike was still at the restaurant, but Prince was with her. He'd followed her obediently onto the bus, even though he'd looked around as if it were something strange, and he was following her now. It seemed that he looked a little less worried than he had before.

Now she was judging the mood of a dog. She shook her head. "I'm going to go straight home," she said to the dog, "and phone the police, or the dog pound."

She glanced at Prince. He didn't seem unduly upset about that last phrase. Maybe he didn't know English as well as she thought he did.

She frowned at him. "I don't know if you've escaped from a circus or what, but I am obviously not well and I need to go to bed."

The street was in shadow. There seemed to be people sleeping against the small iron gate two buildings down from hers. That was unusual. Homeless people usually slept in the park. It was close enough, and they'd be much more comfortable than they were on the sidewalk.

Or the stairs. She frowned. A man was sprawled on the stairs leading into her building, his hand on a paper bag, his face turned away from her. She couldn't smell the booze on him, but she wagered it was there.

"This used to be a nice street," she said, more to herself than Prince. The dog gave the man a wide berth and followed Virginia inside.

No one sat at the desk, which was unusual, and the lobby was dark. Was she getting home later than usual? She thought she was early. She had spent hardly any time at work.

The old TV was still on, broadcasting to no one. Maybe her father had desk duty tonight. He was sometimes known to disappear for hours, raiding beer from the fridge and then smuggling the cans to the lobby.

"Dad?"

He didn't answer.

She tried louder. "Dad?"

He wasn't around. Prince looked at her expectantly. Virginia shrugged and went to the elevator. She pushed the call button several times. It flashed on, then off. She sighed heavily and kept pushing until the light stayed on and she heard the clink and rattle of ancient elevator cables.

Prince raised his head and looked at the closed doors as if they were doing something strange.

"Look," she said to the dog, "you can stay tonight and then you're on your own. Understand?"

Prince barked once. His instant response startled her, just as it had before.

She put a hand to her cut forehead. "How can I be talking to a dog? I've gone crazy."

Prince barked twice.

"Yes, I have." She sounded irritable and she didn't care. "Don't try and reassure me."

This time, the dog was silent. The elevator arrived and the doors whooshed open. She got in and pressed the button for her floor, then wondered at the wisdom of that. Her father had told her to take the stairs on the way home just in case.

Oh, great. She might get stuck in an elevator with a talking dog. Even Prince seemed a little alarmed. He was whining softly in the back of his throat. Apparently, where he grew up there weren't such things as elevators.

Lucky dog.

The elevator arrived on the seventh floor with a clunk. The doors hesitated for a moment—and Virginia's heart did too—then they opened.

The hallway was darker than usual, and there were people lying in the hallway. One of them was snoring. Virginia stepped carefully out of the elevator. Prince followed. His whining had stopped.

One of the people was holding a leash that led to a sleeping dog. A Dachshund. Prince went and investigated. As he got close, he started snarling.

Virginia's heart started beating hard. "That's Mrs. Graves from next door," she whispered. "And her husband and their son, Eric. What's happened to them?"

She almost expected Prince to bark some sort of coherent response. Behind her, the elevator doors whooshed shut, then opened, then closed. Virginia turned. The elevator was continuing its little door dance, and she noticed her father's toolbox sitting below the still-open call box. But her father was nowhere to be seen.

"You wait here," she said to Prince. "I'm going to see if Dad's all right."

The entire floor was quieter than she'd ever heard it. No far-off tinny voice of a television set, no fighting in the apartment down the hall, no barking Dachshund just inside the Graveses' apartment door.

Light came through the skylight, but it was marred by a strange shape. Virginia looked up. A bird lay spread-eagled on the glass. It appeared to be asleep.

She touched her forehead again. Maybe this was all an elaborate dream. Maybe she was the one spread-eagled in the park, her bicycle beside her, the back wheel slowly turning with the momentum she'd had before the accident.

But this seemed too real to be a dream.

She reached her apartment door and stopped. Her heart hit jack-hammer rhythm. The door was splintered open, as if someone had hit it with an axe. It barely hung on its hinges.

Inside, the cold light of the television illuminated her sleeping father's face. It was covered with pink dust.

"Dad?" Virginia whispered. "Wake up. . . ."

She didn't want to be too loud, afraid that whoever had attacked the door was still around. She peered at her dad. He made a slight, gargly, sleeping sound and then exhaled. At least he was alive.

She tiptoed across the room and down the hallway. Her bedroom door was open just wide enough for her to see through. The light was on and inside the room were three of the strangest people she'd ever seen.

Two were as tall as basketball stars—one with orange hair Dennis Rodman would have been ashamed of, the other with frizzy dark hair. The third was short, but seemed to have more energy. They were pawing through her belongings as if they were looking for something.

"Look!" the tall dark-haired one shouted. "Here they are!"

He grabbed a shoe from her closet and sniffed it, closing his eyes as if he were smelling a delicacy. Virginia raised an eyebrow. This was getting stranger and stranger.

"Soft cow," he said. "Nicee nice."

Virginia glanced down. Prince was beside her, staring into her room. He barely moved. He didn't seem surprised by the people at all. And surprisingly, he didn't bark.

The tall, dark-haired one was trying to stick his huge gnarly foot into her shoe. The short one watched for a moment, then said, "No! Try the red ones."

Virginia was about to back away when all three faces turned in her direction.

"Hello there, girlee," the orange-haired one said.

Virginia started. Orange-Hair was female, and she was cradling an armful of Virginia's shoes.

"These have been very badly cared for," Orange-Hair said in a tone that suggested Virginia had committed mass murder. "Scuffed and cracked and neglected."

She dropped the pile. They clattered against the floor. The other two creatures staggered toward Virginia unsteadily. They had managed to shove their huge feet into her high heels.

"You have nice shoes," the taller male said. "And so tiny."

"We have hundreds of pairs at home," Orange-Hair said.

"—so we know what we're talking about," said the shorter male.

Now Virginia finally understood how Alice felt when she tumbled into Wonderland. She wondered if Alice had this same sinking feeling in the pit of her stomach, the feeling that things had just gone from bad to worse.

The creatures were still tottering toward her. Virginia backed away, making it to the living room before they trapped her against a wall.

What had all those self-defense classes taught? Attitude was everything. Show them that she wasn't afraid.

"Who are you?" Virginia demanded. "And what have you done to my dad?"

"Hit him with a bit of Troll dust, that's all," the tall one said.

Prince slinked behind the sofa. He was watching, undoglike, no barking, no attacking. It almost seemed as if he had a plan. She hoped so. If her dad could be felled by Troll dust, then she could be saved by a dog.

"Troll dust?" Virginia asked.

The tall one slammed his hand against his chest. "I am Burly the Troll, feared throughout the Nine Kingdoms."

Then he bowed, followed by Orange-Hair, who said, "I am Blabberwort the Troll, dreaded throughout the Nine Kingdoms."

"And I am Bluebell the Troll," the short one said as he bowed, "terrified throughout the Nine Kingdoms."

Nine Kingdoms. Trolls. Dogs that could write. Magic sleeping dust. Virginia was trying to take it all in when Burly twirled, produced an axe, and slammed it into the TV. The set exploded in a poof of smoke and a shower of sparks.

"*So where is he?*" Burly shouted.

Okay. Virginia got it. Trolls were psychopaths. "I-I-I don't know what you're talking about."

"Prince Wendell," Blabberwort said. "We're going to count to three, then we're going to make you into shoes."

Burly grabbed Virginia's leg and squeezed so hard, she almost yelped. In the hand that had held the axe, he now held a pair of scissors. Where did he keep all that equipment? Under his smelly jacket?

"One," Burly said. "I'll cut the shoes."

Blabberwort ran a small curved knife gently along Virginia's arm. The blade felt smooth and sharp. Virginia held her breath and wished the dog would do something.

"Two," Blabberwort said. "I'll shape the shoes."

Bluebell grabbed Virginia, pulled her forward and held a huge needle to her eye. Or maybe it only seemed huge because it was so close. These three were serious and they were seriously crazy and they had a seriously crazy shoe fetish and they just might do something . . . well, something serious and crazy.

"Three," Bluebell said. "I'll stitch the sh—"

"All right! All right!" Virginia shouted. "I'll tell you where he is."

Prince slunk even farther behind the sofa. No help from that quarter. She had to come up with some kind of lie. A good lie.

"He—he's here," she said. "He's just outside."

"Show us," Burly said. "Take us to him."

She didn't have much of a choice. The three of them grabbed her and dragged her out of the apartment, the metal on their clothing clanging as they moved. The sound didn't wake her father, and Prince still wasn't doing anything.

The hallway didn't look any different. The people were still sleeping. At least two of them were snoring. Virginia struggled, but she wasn't going to get away. She had to think her way through this one.

As they dragged her toward the end of the hallway, she saw Prince come out the apartment door. He remained in the shadows so that they couldn't see him. Smart dog, considering the shape of that Dachshund.

Bluebell shook her, and Virginia, out of ideas, pointed at the closed elevator.

"He's hiding—behind those doors," she said.

As they approached the elevator, the doors opened. The Trolls gasped.

"Ah-ha," Burly said. "That room was not there a moment ago. You are crafty."

The Trolls shoved Virginia into the elevator and got in beside her. They started to look around. They touched its flocked wallpaper and the sides, making little noises of delight. Somehow it didn't surprise her that they had never seen an elevator before.

Then Blabberwort peered at Virginia suspiciously. "There's no one in here."

"Oh, yes, he's here," Virginia lied. "I'll, uh—operate the secret door to show you where he's hiding."

She punched the "close" button. The doors actually obeyed her command. As they started to close, she stepped out of the elevator. Then she grabbed the loose wires dangling from the control panel outside the elevator and wrenched them out. A small electric shock ran through her hand, but she didn't care. She just prayed the Trolls wouldn't figure out how to stop the door.

"No!" Burly shouted. "It's a trick."

The doors were nearly closed when stubby fingers shoved between them.

"Open these doors!" Blabberwort demanded.

The fingers tried to pry the doors open. They were going to succeed too. The last thing she wanted was those creatures loose in this hallway again. She grabbed the nearby fire extinguisher and slammed it down on the fingers as hard as she could.

"Ow! Ow! Ow!"

The fingers disappeared and the doors slammed shut. Then Virginia grabbed the remaining wires, yanked them out of the control panel, and gave it a good whack with the fire extinguisher just in case.

The elevator doors stayed shut this time, and she thanked the mechanical gods for small favors. Inside, she could hear the Trolls banging.

"Let us out!" Bluebell shouted. "Let us out!"

Prince ran up to her, barking for the first time, his tail wagging, something she'd never seen before. It was almost as if he were congratulating her.

"All right, all right," Virginia said, feeling a little grin build. She had done pretty well. But she had to keep moving. "Let's get out of here."

Prince didn't need to be told twice. He ran with her to the stairs and down the fire escape. As she stepped outside the building, she heard Troll voices growing fainter.

She didn't like leaving her father with them, but it didn't look as if they were bent on destruction. Only on defending shoes. Of course, if they looked in his closet, they might get really upset.

Chapter Six

Tony slowly woke up. There was a terrible smell in his nose, something like rancid meat, and he wondered if the ribs Virginia had left for him weren't good. He'd eaten them quickly, and then he'd fallen asleep.

His eyes felt gummed shut, and there was an awful taste in his mouth. And he'd been drooling. He hated it when he drooled in his sleep. He wiped at his face and felt himself drift off again, but something was preventing it. Something loud.

The doorbell was ringing.

And ringing.

And ringing.

"Whatever it is," Tony said, "go away . . ."

There was a man outside his door. A man he didn't recognize. How come Tony could see him through the door? Tony rubbed at his eyes. He had to wake up.

"Good evening." The man smiled warmly as he stepped through the door. That was why Tony could see him. Someone had splintered the wood. Didn't he dream that? It was just as he was dropping off. Not that it mattered right now. There was a stranger in his apartment.

Tony stood, swaying just a little, wishing he could wake up all the way.

The man surveyed the apartment and he seemed to be sniffing something. "Trolls have visited you first, I see."

Trolls? Tony frowned. What was this guy doing here?

"No matter," the man was saying. "My name is Wolf, and

I have come to you with a proposition. Tonight and tonight only I am authorized to make a unique offer, namely the end to all your personal and financial problems.''

A scam artist. Tony crossed his arms. ''One more step and I'm calling the cops.''

Wolf grinned. His name suited him. He made Tony very nervous.

''I'm . . . I'm in charge here,'' Tony said. ''This is private property.''

Wolf spun around the room, tested the sofa, ran his fingers across the back of Tony's chair. Then he reached into his pocket and pulled out a small but elaborate golden case. He whipped it open and some glimmering light flowed out. The light had a faintly disgusting odor, like dried cow dung.

Tony tilted his head and blew out slightly to get the smell out of his nose.

Inside the case was a black bean the size of his thumb.

Wolf said, ''Under the terms of this policy, I am—in exchange for the information as to the whereabouts of your daughter—able to offer you a magic bean that, once eaten, will give you six glorious wishes.''

Six wishes. What was this? Wasn't the norm three?

It was as if Tony was in a fairy tale, which he definitely was not. He was in his apartment.

Wolf didn't seem to notice his hesitation. He'd found a framed photograph of Virginia and had picked it up, studying it. ''This her?''

How did this guy know of Tony's daughter? What was going on here?

''This can't be her,'' Wolf said.

''Why not?'' Tony asked.

''She's succulent,'' Wolf said. ''Wow, what a dreamy, creamy girl.''

He ran a hand over the picture, looking mesmerized. Tony peered at him. This guy was really strange, and Tony wasn't sure he liked the way that Wolf was looking at his daughter—

or at least at the photograph of his daughter. First he was looking at it like a lovesick puppy and now he was leering at it as if he wanted to—

"Tasty or what?" Wolf said. "Where is she?"

As if Tony would tell him. Not after that last look. "She's . . . she's not back from work yet."

Wolf tilted his head and then shook it reprovingly, as if he had caught Tony in a lie. "Oh, she's been back, all right. I can smell her."

He flicked the bean across the room and Tony caught it. It was hot, and it started to jump inside his hand.

"Hey," Tony said, "what's it doing?"

Wolf slid nearer to Tony and his eyes flashed green. They seemed to fill his sockets, turning everything, including the whites, the color of emeralds.

"Six big wishes," Wolf said. "Imagine having anything you desire."

The bean bounced insistently against his hand. Everything he desired. Hmmm.

"And from the look of your modest surroundings," Wolf said, "I'm sure there are many things you'd love to change."

Of course there were. First he'd buy a new chair, real leather this time, and then he'd start on the walls. The flocked wallpaper made him feel as if he were in a decrepit bordello. He nodded slightly and said, "Well, I—No!"

What had he been thinking? He'd actually considered it. He thought of letting this . . . this . . . wolf get near his daughter. "Get out of my apartment!"

Tony's shout didn't seem to faze Wolf at all. His eyes had gone so green that they reminded Tony of a forest. A magic forest. "Six lovely wishes . . ."

"I . . ." There was a reason he was protesting. He just couldn't remember it.

"Yes?" Wolf asked.

Six wishes. Anything he wanted. He could get more than a chair. He could get a thousand chairs. He could get enough money to have a new chair every day. He smiled just a little. It was a goofy smile, he knew, but the idea of having everything he wanted was more than he had allowed himself to contemplate before.

"Just supposing this . . . this thing works," Tony said, "what's to stop me asking for a million dollars?"

The bean was still jumping insistently against his hand. He really wanted to try this.

Wolf grabbed a spare rib from the plate on the floor beside Tony's chair. He brought the rib to his mouth and ran his teeth along it, cleaning the meat off the bone as if it were merely sauce. But his gaze remained on Tony.

"You can ask for anything you want." Wolf tossed the bone over the back of Tony's chair.

Tony's brain wasn't working as well as he wanted it to. That long sleep had affected him. Or had those eyes? "But there must be a catch."

"Oh, no." Wolf whipped a contract out of his pocket and spoke very fast. "It's a standard multiple wishes deal: six wishes, no going back on wishes once made, no having five wishes and then wishing for another thousand . . . Well, come on, is that fair or what? Now where's your lovely daughter?"

Wolf thrust a pen in front of Tony. Wolf's eyes seemed even greener. Tony reached for the pen. Six wishes. Six lovely wishes. He almost touched the pen and then stopped.

What had Wolf said about his daughter?

"Wait just a minute," Tony said. "What do you want her for?"

"Oh, nothing bad," Wolf said. "Simply to reclaim my little dog that she found earlier."

"Your dog?" Tony asked.

"There's even a reward," Wolf said, "which I intend to give her *personally*."

Wolf smiled. He had beautiful teeth. And nice green eyes. The bean was still bouncing in Tony's hand. He looked at it; then he watched his own hand reach for the pen and scribble a signature. He didn't remember giving his hand that instruction, but somehow it didn't matter. This man seemed quite nice, after all, and he was missing his dog. . . .

"If she's not at work she'll be at my mother-in-law's." The thought of his mother-in-law made Tony's stomach turn. "She's always trying to turn Virginia against me."

"Does this mother-in-law like flowers?" Wolf asked.

"She likes money," Tony said. "That's the only thing that impresses her."

"Address please," Wolf said.

Tony's hand moved of its own volition again, writing down the address. Out of the corner of his eye, he saw Wolf caress Virginia's photograph and then pocket it. Tony wanted to protest, but found that he couldn't.

"It's been a pleasure," Wolf said.

That bouncing bean was still slamming against his palm. Tony looked at it. It didn't really look like a bean. It looked like an oversized beetle. Maybe he didn't want to do this after all.

"How long before this takes effect?" he asked.

"Don't worry," Wolf said. "The first three hours are the worst."

"Right," Tony said. That made sense after all. Or rather, it didn't. He frowned. "What does that mean?"

But Wolf was gone. Tony didn't even see him leave. Well, they'd made a deal, and Wolf had made certain promises.

"Anything I want . . ." Tony whispered.

He took a deep breath, then swallowed the bean. He waited. He didn't feel any different. He wasn't even more awake. If a man ate a magic bean, shouldn't he feel something? Even a minor tingle of magic power?

Apparently not. He shrugged. "All right," he said, beginning to like this idea. "For my first wish—"

His stomach cramped in horrible agony. Pain shot through his abdomen and down his back, up into his throat, and he barely held the contents of his belly down.

The first three hours are the worst, Wolf said.

And this was what he meant.

Tony closed his eyes. "Oh, my God!" he moaned as the pain got worse.

Virginia unlocked the door to her grandmother's Gramercy Park apartment. She put her finger to her lips so that Prince wouldn't bark—not that he seemed to do it like any other dog would anyway—and then eased her way inside the door. Prince slipped in with her.

She started to push the door closed when her grandmother shouted, "Who is it?"

"Only me, Grandma." Virginia turned. Her grandmother was standing at the other end of the hallway. She wore her velour bathrobe and had her peach-colored hair pushed back in a style sixty years out of date. She wore too much makeup, as usual, but it fit the style of the apartment: sumptuous and gorgeous, at least in terms of the 1930s.

"What are you doing here at this time of night?" Her grandmother had her hand over her heart. "I nearly died of shock." Then she looked down at Prince. "And what in God's name is that?"

She yanked the dog forward and peered into his face. He struggled to get free. Virginia found she didn't like the way her grandmother was handling him.

"I found him," Virginia said. "He's a stray."

Prince gave her a withering look.

"A stray," Grandma said, disgusted. "Well take him somewhere and get him destroyed. He's probably riddled with fleas."

Prince probably had fewer fleas than any dog on the planet. Not that her grandmother would know that. Grandma let go of Prince and then swayed slightly to one side.

Virginia sighed. Her grandmother was drunk again.

"I don't want him going near Roland."

Roland, her grandmother's pampered poodle, lay on his satin pillow. He looked at Prince suspiciously, little dog eyes narrowing. Now Roland had poodle eyes with poodle intelligence. Prince had human eyes. Virginia was becoming more and more convinced. She'd never believed until tonight that a person could read intelligence in an animal's eyes.

"When I saw you," Grandma said, "just for a moment I thought you were your mother."

Here they went again. "Sorry to disappoint you," Virginia said.

"She'll come back one day, you know," Grandma said. "She'll just swan in without a word. You don't think she could be in Aspen? She loved the snow."

"I think she would have come back by now," Virginia said. "Fourteen years is a lot of *après ski*."

"Don't be cheap, dear," Grandma said. "Would you like a glass of champagne?"

She poured a glass from an almost empty bottle. Virginia glanced down the hall at her grandmother's bedroom, where the satin-covered bed was slightly mussed and the shopping channel was on.

Staying here would drive her crazy, but it was better than going home to the smashed door and those psychopathic Trolls stuck in the elevator.

"Would it be all right if I stayed the night?" Virginia asked.

Her grandmother smiled. It was a gloating smile. "He's thrown you out. I knew it would happen." Her voice rose as she sank in her own imaginings. "Your forehead's cut. He's hit you—"

"Don't be stupid," Virginia said, disgusted. She hated dealing with her grandmother when she was drunk. Which was getting to be most of the time. "I fell off my bike."

Roland advanced on Prince and yapped. Prince moved away as if the little dog were nothing more than a fly.

"Why don't you come and live with me?" Grandma asked. "You could have much more space here. You could be something in society, Virginia. You've got your mother's looks."

"I don't want to be something in society," Virginia said.

"My debut at the Ritz Carlton was like a coronation," Grandma said, clearly lost in the memory. "I was on the cover of every society magazine. And your mother . . . at seventeen she was so beautiful, it hurt to look at her. She could have had any bachelor in New York. And who did she end up with?"

Virginia knew this script as if it had been written in stone. "Dad."

"I rest my case," Grandma said.

Grandma leaned forward and poured more from the bottle. Then she picked up her glass and swung it as she spoke.

"I gave her everything. If only she could have been like you. You never get angry or shout, do you? You're such a good girl."

A good, quiet girl who clenched her fists a lot. Virginia bit her tongue. Literally.

Grandma didn't seem to notice. She picked up a cigarette holder, put a new cigarette in the tip, and lit it, then put it to her red-painted mouth like the star of a Depression-era movie.

"I can see it happening all over again. You're a waitress, for God's sake. Who are you going to meet? An eligible short-order cook? Don't throw your life away like she did."

Roland yapped at Prince. Virginia watched this out of the corner of her eye, wondering what Prince would do. Prince looked over both shoulders, and then punched Roland in the face.

The little dog yelped and Grandma scooped him up. "I'm taking him away from your bad old dog," she said and stalked to her bedroom, trailing smoke like a Disney villainess.

Punched him? Virginia frowned. It must have only looked that way. She sighed and walked down the hallway to the guest room. Prince followed, looking very satisfied with himself. She waited until he got into the room, and then she closed the door.

Was she a failure like her grandmother said? She didn't feel like one. But she didn't feel like a success either. She was just a waitress who had gotten a bump on the head, inherited a dog that seemed more human than canine, and who locked evil Trolls in elevators.

She didn't know how any of this would look in the morning, but she had a feeling it couldn't get any worse.

Chapter Seven

Blabberwort could not see the source of the light that was flickering on and off. She had never seen a light that had such a cold glare. It hissed and popped and fizzed, but there were no flames in it, nothing that allowed her to put it out.

This entire room was strange. The doors did not function. The walls had velvety material on them that appeared to be glued on. She had run her fingers over every inch of this place, and still she could not figure out how to leave.

There was a great magic here, one they should have protected themselves against before they stumbled into this building.

Her brothers were rubbing their feet. They had taken off the shoes, but occasionally they would pick them up and hold them as if they were a talisman.

"I'm thinking back over the years," Blabberwort said, "and I feel this is quite the worst spell we have ever been put under."

"We've had some stinkers," Burly said, nodding, "but nothing like this."

Bluebell had his arms crossed. He was watching them as if it were their fault they were all trapped.

"She's a powerful little witch, that one," Burly said.

"I would have had her if she hadn't ... had me first," Blabberwort said.

"Absolutely," Burly said.

They looked at each other; then they felt the walls of the

cell again. This was worse than the Snow White Memorial Prison. At least there they'd had some natural light.

Some food.

A bed.

"I can't stand it anymore!" Burly shouted. "I've got to break this spell!"

He brought out his axe and Blabberwort had to scramble out of the way to avoid his backswing. Burly hacked at the door once, twice, three times, and then looked at his work. It seemed to make no difference, which made him even angrier. He turned into a hacking machine, chopping, chopping, chopping until he had moved from the door to the wall to the floor.

Suddenly his right leg fell through. He screamed. Blabberwort and Bluebell grabbed him and pulled him up.

There was a hole in the floor. Blabberwort peered down it. There was a cable attached to this room, and it went down into impenetrable darkness.

"Ahh," Blabberwort said, staring down into the blackness below them. "She is far more powerful than we imagined."

"Suck an Elf," Burly said. "It goes on forever. It leads to the deep, dark place below that has no bottom."

"I hate those kind of places," Bluebell said.

Didn't they all.

The bathroom smelled of fresh vomit and other disgusting things. Tony moaned and clutched his stomach. He had never been this ill before, not even the time he ate his mother-in-law's special—and week-old—meatballs. He had no idea what possessed him to eat that bean or whatever it was, given to him by a stranger. What had he been thinking?

He had the horrible suspicion he hadn't been thinking at all.

He hauled himself off the bathroom floor and turned on the tap, splashing water on his fevered face. He hiccuped violently, prayed that he wouldn't dry-heave yet again—he'd probably lost everything, including half his internal organs—and then the doorbell rang.

Wonderful. Charming. Wasn't this just the best day of his life.

He used the wall to brace himself as he staggered into the other room. Through the remains of the door, he saw Murray, looking quite mad.

Tony debated opening the door, not that it really mattered. If the door had a peephole like it was supposed to instead of being shredded, he might have had a choice. But he didn't.

As he leaned out the door, he cringed. Murray started into him, just as he expected.

"So of course you never fix the pipes like you promise. That I've come to expect. But this—" He pointed to the hallway. "What the hell is this?"

Tony leaned even farther out of his apartment. What a mess. In addition to the ruined door, the hallway was covered in pink dust. Someone had ripped all the wires out of the elevator's control box and flung them across the floor.

He felt a flush building in his cheeks. "Oh, sorry, Mr. Murray, sir. I can explain everything." Even though he couldn't. He tried to cover by saying, "I'll get right to it."

"No. No," Mr. Murray said. " 'Right to it' isn't good enough. I want you and your daughter out of this apartment today. You're fired."

Oh, no. Tony couldn't be fired from yet another job. He wouldn't be able to find work anywhere. Especially not work that had a free apartment with it.

He'd never tried to suck butt so hard in his life. "No, please, Mr. Murray—"

"What, you little creep?" Mr. Murray asked.

Tony froze. He'd had his door demolished, been attacked by pink dust, seen a man who called himself Wolf, and ate a bean that tasted like bat dung. Then he'd vomited half the night—not to mention other things—and, through no fault of his own, got fired. Mr. Murray wouldn't change his mind, no matter how hard Tony sucked up. Mr. Murray was an idiot and he deserved to know it.

Tony leaned forward as though he was going to impart the secret of the universe.

"I wish you and your entire family would kiss my ass," he snapped, "and be my slaves forever."

Mr. Murray's eyes narrowed. "What did you say . . . Master?"

That last word he just breathed out. His eyes were glassy, and his entire posture was one Tony had never seen before.

Then Murray crouched and grabbed Tony by the hips, kissing his behind. Tony yelped, pushed Murray away, and then paused.

I wish you and your entire family—

Tony giggled.

"What, O Master?"

"Clean this hallway," Tony said. "And get someone to repair my door."

"Yes, Master."

Murray scampered away. Tony walked inside his apartment. He suddenly felt better. He had just made a successful wish— and he had five more.

He went into the bedroom, put on his robe and slippers, and got himself a cigar from his secret stash, the one Virginia never found. He walked into his living room to find Murray there, bobbing up and down like a kid who had to go to the bathroom.

"I have someone cleaning the hallway, Master. And my mother shall fix your door. What else do you desire?"

Tony grinned. Murray had made him feel like a toad for years. He could only return the favor.

"I want you to clean my boots," Tony said.

"Yes, Master," Murray said.

"With your tongue."

"*Yes,* Master." Murray seemed just a little too eager. It took a bit of the fun out of it. But not all.

"They're in my closet. Bring them into the living room so that your entire family can watch."

"Yes, Master."

Murray scrambled off to the bedroom. Tony wandered into the kitchen. Well, he had his own personal servant. What else could a man want?

He pulled open the refrigerator. Only one beer left. That wasn't enough for a man who had just become king of his own castle. He closed the door.

"Okay, Wishmaster," he said, "give me a never-ending supply of beer."

He chuckled. No one else would have thought of that. He opened the door and saw another bottle standing next to the first. He slammed the door angrily.

"Two?" Tony said. "Is that what you call a wild night where you come from?"

He opened the door again and now there were four bottles. That was better. He closed the door, then opened it like a kid who'd just learned that doors opened and closed. This time there were eight bottles.

Every time he opened the door, the number of beers in the fridge doubled. How cool. He opened and closed the door a couple of times, and then counted.

Thirty two bottles of beer.

Kinda like the song. Only the beers weren't on the wall. And they appeared faster than a man could sing about them.

"All right!" Tony said. "Oh, you've got to see this, Murray."

He grabbed a handful of beers and kicked the door closed with his foot. He carried the beers into the living room.

Murray was clutching a boot between his hands. "I'm worried they're not clean enough, Master. Shall I lick your boots again?"

Oh, Tony was enjoying this too much. He smiled. "Show me your tongue."

Murray's tongue was black. But not black enough. "Well

maybe another five minutes. How's your mother getting on with the door?''

"Almost done now, Master," Mrs. Murray said.

Tony peered into the hallway. Seventy-five-year-old Mrs. Murray Senior was groaning as she tried to fit the door back into place. He probably should go help her, but then he remembered all the times she'd called him names when she'd seen him in the elevator.

Nope. She could heft that door all by herself.

Something brushed against his buttocks. Tony turned to see Murray reaching for his behind again. That was the only bad part of this wish.

"Hey, thanks," Tony said. "Once was enough."

Murray nodded and backed away.

Tony got his behind out of Murray's line of sight just in case. He sank into his chair and crossed his feet. Then he put the cigar in his mouth. He was feeling better all the time. And he still had four wishes. "I wish . . . uh . . . what do I wish?''

He glanced at the pink dust all over the floor. He was beginning to hate the color pink.

"I wish I had something that cleans the place up on its own without me having to lift a finger. Yeah."

The closet door opened and the vacuum cleaner, the one that hadn't worked in three years, came out with a roar of power that it hadn't had in its youth. It sucked up the dust like it craved the stuff. Tony laughed and clapped his hands together.

Life was perfect, and he still had three more wishes to go.

The apartment building was tall and beautiful and old, and made of a kind of brick Wolf had never seen before. He took the last bite from his BLT—he had thrown out the L and the T, but the B was delicious. More than delicious. It was life-giving. It was sumptuous. It was as close to perfection as a man—a wolf—a man got in this lifetime. He licked off his fingers and contemplated the address.

"Well, huff-puff," he said, "this must be the place."

He bounded up the stairs like a puppy, and went to the door marked with the number he'd been given. Then he paused for a moment, slicked back his dark hair, and practiced his charm. He put the flowers he'd stolen in the crook of his left arm and the chocolates he'd stolen in his left hand, the box prominently displayed. Then he knocked.

The door opened ever so slightly. A chain held it in place. A woman peered through the door. She looked much older than he had expected, and smelled of sweat and perfume. Clearly not the woman he was seeking.

Still, he'd expected this. This had to be the owner of the place. The aforementioned grandmother.

He smiled his most winning smile. "There must be some mistake," he said. "I do apologize. I was looking for Virginia's grandmother."

The woman frowned slightly. "I am she."

Oh, wonderful. She put on airs. At least he could use her vanity to his advantage.

His smile grew. "It cannot be. Virginia's sister, perhaps, her young mother perhaps, but her grandmother? You are a dazzling beauty."

She touched her skin. It looked as if she had slept in her makeup. "Oh, well, I don't have my face on or anything yet."

Obviously. "May I come in?" he asked. He took a step forward, but she closed the door just enough to let him know he wasn't welcome.

"Who are you?"

"I am Virginia's suitor," Wolf said. "Her betrothed."

He held up the picture of Virginia he had stolen from her father and kissed it. Then he had to kiss it again. And then one more time for good luck.

"Betrothed?" Grandma said slowly. She was obviously coming around. "But she said nothing about a fiancé."

"How like her," Wolf said. "How modest. Most girls would brag and boast about dating the heir to an enormous fortune, but not Virginia. Please follow her example and judge me on my personality, not my society connections."

That did it. Grandma undid the chain and pulled open the door. "Do come in. I'll get dressed."

He slipped inside the door and set the flowers and chocolates on a nearby table. "You don't need to change. You look perfect as you are."

She smiled at him. She wasn't much to look at, not like Virginia. But she would be a delectable meal. The meat might be slightly tough, but she was clearly well fed. She would be plump and delicious and—

Oh, he was being so bad.

She primped her hair again. "Do I look all right?"

He nodded. "I can see where Virginia got her looks."

Grandma smiled, but the smile had an edge now. Apparently Grandma thought she was prettier than Virginia. Bad Grandma. Bad.

"In my day," Grandma said, "I was considered one of the most beautiful women in New York." She waved a hand toward a wall covered with strange paintings that looked almost lifelike. Wolf followed her.

"You still are one of the most beautiful," he said.

She smiled.

It was the smile that caught him. He couldn't help himself. He wrapped his arms around her and sniffed. Yes, delectable. She struggled, but didn't scream. She seemed to welcome his advance.

He was liking Grandma less and less, but wanting to eat her more and more. He grabbed the cord off her robe and bound her hands, then found a scarf on one of the tables and gagged her. Then he used the bottom half of the cord to tie her feet.

He carried her into the kitchen. She was squirming now and trying to scream. Meals were better in silence. He searched until he found a large roasting pan, then set it on the table. He put Grandma in it, and she squealed even louder. He grabbed the chef's apron off the wall, and put on a chef's hat. The best meal of the day should be prepared in the very best way.

As he looked, he found rope and he used that to bind her better. He also found salt and pepper and poured them over her unnaturally colored hair.

Then he paused and studied her. She really was quite frightened. Did one human being do this to another? No, of course not.

"I'm so bad," Wolf said. "I can't believe I'm doing this. Still, I suppose you'll look better surrounded by potatoes."

She had to have potatoes. She had a large roasting pan after all. He didn't see potatoes, but he did see the spice rack. He peered at it, then bopped her on the head with one hand.

"Call this a kitchen?" he asked. "Where's the garlic? The rosemary? What have I got to work with—some three-year-old dried herbs?"

He put his hands on his hips and surveyed her. "Oh, huff, you're not going to fit in the oven, are you? Not in one piece anyway."

She was squealing and shaking her head. Why didn't they build ovens big enough for elderly women in this place? He studied the oven door.

He grabbed some dried garlic—Yeech. Who thought of this stuff?—and sprinkled it on her head. The old lady was whimpering. He stopped and peered at her. She was crying softly.

"What am I doing?" Wolf said. "I should untie you, a poor old lady, frightened out of her wits. I should untie you . . ."

He tapped a finger against his lips, considering.

". . . but first, I'll put a dollop of fat in the oven tray."

"Grandma?" Virginia's voice called out through the apartment. "Are you awake yet?"

"Oh, no," Wolf said. "The guests are up and breakfast's not ready."

He examined the rack of knives before settling on an old

cleaver. He shook it in Grandma's face. "Do you ever sharpen these knives?"

She whimpered and cringed as if she expected him to chop off her head.

He slapped the heel of his hand against his forehead. "What a sick thing to say. How can I say such a thing?"

He heard a rustling sound from the far bedroom. The fair Virginia. He ran out of the kitchen and slipped through the open door to what had to be Grandma's room. Disguises. Disguises were always good.

He pulled on her hairnet and robe, then slipped under the covers.

"Grandma?" Virginia called out.

"In here, darling," Wolf said, trying to make his voice weak and grandmotherly sounding.

He peeked through the covers and saw a movement in the hallway. Virginia's voice was lovely. As lovely as her photograph.

"You want some coffee? Toast?" She was getting closer. She was in the room now, and he could hear the squeak of her shoes as she walked on the hard wood floor.

"Mmmmmm . . ." Wolf said, keeping his voice as high as he could.

"Have you got a cold or something?" Virginia asked.

She was right near the bed. He could smell her. Ah, that wonderful fragrance. It was so much better up close. Then the covers flew back.

"Surprise!" Wolf shouted.

She screamed. He whipped out the cleaver and—froze, struck by the vision before him. She was tinier than he'd thought she'd be. Delicate. Her beauty was profound.

"Boy, oh, boy," Wolf said, staring at Virginia. "You're fantastic. Your picture doesn't do you justice. Wow!"

He noticed the cleaver in his hand. He had forgotten that he held it. In fact, he didn't know why he held it. What had he been thinking?

"Oh, no," Wolf said, desperately trying to cover. "How did this get here?"

Virginia was backing toward the door. He sprang out of bed, trying to stop her.

"By the way," he said, "where's the dog? Sleeping in, if I know my royalty."

Virginia dove for the door, but he got there first, bounding across the room and trapping her. Sometimes his little wolfly talents came in handy.

"You smell great," Wolf said. "I've had little teasers of your scent before, Virginia, but in the flesh ... perfumes are not for me. No, I respond favorably to the audacity of a woman who flaunts her own aroma. And you ... ohh, Virginia, you smell like Sunday lunch."

"K-keep away from me," Virginia managed to say.

"Beautiful eyes, beautiful teeth, all the right stuff in all the right places ... no doubt about it, I am in love."

She grabbed a vase from the nearest table and broke it over his head. He felt the impact, the shards of glass falling around him, but it really didn't faze him at all. In fact, it might have knocked some sense into him. He'd have to wait a while to make certain, of course, but it felt that way.

She yanked the door open while he stood there, slightly stunned, and ran down the hall. He removed Grannie's things—obviously a man shouldn't woo a woman while wearing her grandmother's clothing—and followed. He didn't quite understand why the women in this family were so afraid of him.

"Let me put your mind to rest," Wolf said. "Now that I've seen you, eating you is completely out of the question. Not even on the menu."

He put the cleaver down on a side table to show his good intentions. Virginia was pressed against the hallway wall, near an open window. Her ratty blue robe didn't do her justice at all. He would have to make certain she was properly garbed one of these days. When they were closer.

"Now, this is going to come out of the blue," Wolf said, "but how about a date?"

She grabbed a walking stick that had been leaning against a door. She held the stick like a sword, brandishing it as if she actually knew what she was doing. He doubted she did. He held out his hands, and moved closer.

"All right," he said, "we've started badly." He reached for her, but Virginia whacked him on the side of the head. The stick cracked against his skull. Now that hurt.

He frowned, trying to remember what he was saying. Oh, yes. "I take all the blame for that."

That should soften her up. He took another step closer, and this time she jabbed the stick in his balls. He screamed in pain. That was not necessary. Not necessary at all.

"Oh, come on, give us a chance at least," Wolf said. "You are one dynamic lady, no question there."

She took the stick in both hands and swung it like a club. It hit him under the chin and sent him flying backwards. At the last moment, he realized that she had opened the window when she was standing by it, and he tried to reach for the sides to prevent himself from falling through.

But it didn't work. He fell backwards for a long way. As he fell, he saw Virginia peek out the window, grimace, and close it. Then, as he turned to see the pile of garbage below him, he thought he heard her squeal.

"Oh, my God! Grandmother!"

He grinned as he landed, rapped his head on something hard, and passed out.

Chapter Eight

Blabberwort sat in her corner of the magic room, legs drawn up to her ample chest. Even with the hole in the room's floor, the hole open to eternity—or perhaps because of it—the room had gotten extremely hot. And it smelled of her brothers in a way that the prison cell never had.

It was their fault that they were all trapped. If she hadn't come with them. If she hadn't let them lead her into this awful place, then she would be fine. She would be somewhere else, where she could tell if it was day or night, night or day, or even day. Maybe night. She would be able to tell. And here, she couldn't.

They were glaring at her too, as if she were the one who was crazy. And they were wrong.

She couldn't take this anymore. She had to do something. She sprang to her feet and looked at the magically lighted buttons beside her.

"What are you doing?" Burly asked.

"I was just going to press all the buttons again," Blabberwort said.

"You've done it thirty thousand times already," Burly said, disgusted. "How many more times do you have to do it before you realize they don't do anything, dwarf brain."

Above her, the strange light spat and frizzed. She sank back down, knowing that Burly was right and hating to admit it.

"How long do you think this spell will last?" Burly asked.

"It can't be that long," Blabberwort said.

"A hundred years?" Burly asked.

"At most," Blabberwort said. "Maybe only fifty."

She was trying to minimize their situation, but it wasn't working. Her words seemed to depress them more than anything.

They depressed her.

Fifty years. That was longer than they had been condemned to the Snow White Memorial Prison.

"Well, we'll just make the most of our confinement," Burly said, "and agree not to fall out."

"Absolutely," Blabberwort said, "we'll do the hundred years, and maybe if we get lucky we'll only have to do two thirds of the spell and get out early."

Bluebell had been silent through all of this. But at that last, he turned toward his brother.

"No!" Bluebell shouted at Burly. "I cannot spend a hundred years with *your socks.*"

He leaped on Burly, and they started to fight, rolling and punching, biting and kicking, screaming and shouting, narrowly avoiding the hole in the floor.

"Stop it!" Blabberwort shouted. "This is just what she wants. She wants us to panic. We will find a way out of this spell, trust me."

She grabbed them and pulled them apart. They stared at her like tiny babies.

"I trust you," Burly said.

"I trust you more," Bluebell said.

She sighed and flung them away. It was all well and fine that they trusted her. But what did it matter when she didn't trust them?

She didn't trust them at all.

Murray had a gorgeous wife. She was tall—although not as tall as Tony—blonde and blue-eyed, with the most beautiful skin he'd ever seen on a woman. Murray used to be jealous of any other man even looking at his wife, but now he was more concerned with the growing beer problem in the kitchen.

The other member of Murray's family didn't seem to notice his looks either, and there were at least eight of them in the room. Strange for a bunch of little tattlers.

Tony was enjoying this. All except for the butt-kissing part. Every time he turned around, another member of Murray's family was reaching for his ass. He had to shoo them away like flies.

Murray's wife stood in front of him, and Tony had his hands on her slender shoulders. He wondered how much he could do to this woman without incurring Murray's wrath.

He wondered how much he could do to this woman and not lose his own self-respect.

Only one way to find out. Tony said, "Murray, I'm taking your wife out to buy her some underwear, is that okay with you?"

"Okay, Master," Murray said. "Help yourself."

Tony could hear the rattle and groan of the refrigerator. At last count, there were 108 bottles of beer in it. Probably more now. Certainly more than the thing could hold.

As if on cue, he heard bottles smash against the floor. He grinned. "Where's my beer?"

The newly repaired door to the apartment opened, and Mrs. Murray Senior entered. She looked a bit winded from her repair work earlier. Her eyes were glazed just like the rest of her clan's.

"Master," she said, "I think there might be someone trapped in the elevator. I can hear voices and banging."

"Well, in case you haven't noticed," Tony said, "I'm no longer Mr. Do-It-All. Get off your rich ass and fix it yourself, you miserable old crone."

"At once, Master," Murray's mother said.

She toddled off. Tony stroked Murray's wife's hair. He'd have to learn her name sometime. Maybe after a sun-soaked week in the Bahamas. She could call him Master all the time and never wear any clothes. And he wouldn't try to stop her if she reached for his butt.

The Bahamas. Did he wish for that? Or should he be more pragmatic? After all, he only had a few wishes left.

"Okay, Wishmaster," Tony said. "Mrs. Murray and I require some spending money. How about a million dollars?"

The doorbell rang. Tony left Mrs. Murray's side and hurried to the door. He pulled it open, and saw no one. Then he looked down. A satchel sat in front of the door. The satchel was slightly open—and it was filled with money.

He crouched, running his fingers through the money as if it were Mrs. Murray's hair.

"Rich!" Tony shouted. "I'm rich!"

He grabbed it and hauled it inside, dropping money as he went. The vacuum cleaner sucked it up behind him, just as it had sucked up the rugs. Its bag was bulging badly. He'd have to figure out how to solve that at some point, but not now.

Not when he was rich for the first time in his life. He showed the money to Mrs. Murray.

"Rich!" he said.

She didn't seem any more impressed than she had been earlier. But he didn't care. The Bahamas, sunshine, no more work *ever*. How much more perfect could life get?

He'd had dreams of bacon, a beautiful woman, and . . . garbage. Wolf opened his eyes. His head ached. It took a moment for him to realize where he was. The building he had fallen out of loomed in front of him like a nightmare. He couldn't even tell which window was Virginia's.

Slowly he got to his feet and brushed himself off. He'd had a plan, but the blow to his head had knocked it out of his brain. He frowned. He had to do something. He walked to the nearest door and stood, trying to get his bearings.

A woman approached him. She wore large glasses and had her red hair pulled away from her pale skin. She looked too smart to eat.

"Can I help you?" she asked.

"Oh, I hope so," Wolf said. "I'm very confused."

"You must be Paul's referral. I'm Dr. Horovitz." She tried to shake his hand, then seemed to realize she was holding a cup of dark liquid and a pastry. She shrugged. "Paul said you'd drop by to make an appointment."

"Can you tell me what I'm doing here?" Wolf asked.

She smiled at him. "Let's get to know each other a bit before we tackle the big question. Okay?"

That was okay with him, he thought, although he wasn't sure why. What had he been planning? A roast? It seemed hazy to him.

Dr. Horovitz unlocked the door to her office. He glanced at the sign as he followed her through: DR. MARIAN HOROVITZ, PSYCHOANALYST. He had no idea what that meant, but a man didn't fall out the window and land at a doctor's feet without needing help. Maybe he was injured. Maybe she could fix it.

She flicked on a light switch, revealing a dark-paneled room full of books. A leather couch smelled of a meal too old to be edible. She set her liquid and pastry on a wooden desk and pointed to the couch. After a moment, he realized she meant for him to sit on it.

He did, gingerly.

"It is better if you lie down," she said.

He tilted his head at her. She didn't seem like she was about to seduce him. He knew what women were like when they did that, and they weren't like this. Still, he lay down partly because he wanted to see what she would do, and partly because he was still a bit woozy.

She sat in a leather chair and folded her hands in her lap. "Now, then," she said. She had an accent he didn't recognize. "I'm going to say a word, and I want you to give me the first word that comes to mind."

He grabbed a pencil from a nearby table. The wood felt good in his hands. Then he stuck it in his mouth. Dr. Horovitz was looking at him expectantly. What had she said? Words. She'd say one, he'd say one.

He could do that. He nodded.

"Home—" Dr. Horovitz said.

"Cooking," Wolf replied.

"Coward—"

"Chicken."

"Wedding—"

"Cake."

"Dead—"

"Meat."

"Sexual—"

"Appetite."

"Love—"

"To eat anything fluffy." Wolf snapped the pencil in half. He was more nervous than he thought. Dr. Horovitz was staring at him. He shrugged. "Sorry, more than one word. Start again."

She leaned forward as if she were the predator and he the prey. And he found he kind of liked the feeling. . . .

The vacuum cleaner problem was getting out of hand. The bag was five times its normal size, and the vacuum was belching black smoke. It was trying to pull the curtains down from the rods.

"Give it a rest, won't you?" Tony shouted at the vacuum cleaner.

He whacked at it with an old baseball bat, but that only seemed to make the vacuum cleaner more determined. It growled and tore at the curtains like a mad dog.

Tony whacked at it again and again until it wheezed, burped some more black smoke, and stopped. Silence. Merciful silence. But somehow the vacuum had leaked fluid. His feet were wet. He looked down.

The fluid didn't come from the vacuum. It came from the kitchen. And it smelled suspiciously like beer.

Tony hurried to the kitchen. Murray was hugging the refrigerator like it was a live thing trying to attack the apartment. He had tied it with bungee cords, and the cords were straining. Beer bottles were falling through the small crack in the door.

"I can't stop it, Master," Murray said.

What a mess. Tony leaned his weight against the door. With his strength and Murray's determination, they managed to force the door closed. He whipped off his belt and wrapped it around the door handle, then added a few more bungee cords.

The refrigerator rocked like a caged animal.

"It's not going to hold," Murray said.

Everything was coming apart. But Tony wouldn't let his final dream be destroyed. He had to leave the apartment before the refrigerator blew.

He grabbed the satchel of money and then took Mrs. Murray by the arm.

"That's it, enough," Tony said. "We're going out. 'Bye, everyone."

He opened the front door—and jumped back as a group of police officers—SWAT team members, it looked like—scurried in, all holding large guns pointed at him.

"Hands behind your back. Now!" A policeman shouted as they pushed Tony toward the wall. They trapped him there and turned him around. Somehow he'd dropped the money and lost Mrs. Murray at the same time.

He had to fight for himself here. It was his last chance. Besides, this looked bad.

"What's going on?" Tony demanded. "What have I done?"

"Here's the money," one cop said.

"No. No. No," Tony said. "There's been a mistake. This money just appeared outside my door."

An officer grabbed his hands and yanked them behind his back. He wanted to protest that that hurt, but thought better of it. They held his hands there and then slapped handcuffs on him. The metal was cold and bit into his wrists.

Then the cops turned him around. The Murray family was

lined up, watching the whole proceeding. Two cops were poring through his things. Another had headed toward the kitchen.

"I haven't left the apartment all morning," Tony shouted. "These people will all vouch for me. They're independent witnesses, aren't you?"

"Yes, O Master," everyone said as one. Then they bowed.

"Look, you've got the wrong man," Tony said. "I was just having a quiet beer with my friends."

The cops looked at each other as if they didn't believe a word of it. Tony knew he was screwed. He was about to say something else—anything else—when the refrigerator exploded.

Virginia got off the bus. She was tired. Prince was following her, and she wished he wouldn't. Everything had been strange from the moment she met him.

She turned down the block to her neighborhood. There were more cop cars parked outside than usual. Maybe they finally caught those strange Troll people she had locked in the elevator. She would wait until they finished whatever they were doing, and then she'd try to contact her dad.

She'd been meaning to talk to Prince anyway. She stopped near the entrance to the park. Prince stopped too, his tail wagging expectantly.

"This is it," she said. "This is where we say good-bye."

Prince barked twice, his sign for no.

"Yes," Virginia said. "Since you've entered my life, I've been attacked by Trolls and a wolf, and my grandmother never wants to see me again. Not until she gets the seasoning out of her hair, anyway. And I can't go home either."

Prince stood at the edge of the park. Virginia waved a hand at him.

"That's it," Virginia said to the dog. "Hasta la vista. Shoo."

Prince didn't move, and neither did Virginia. She couldn't just leave him here. But she had to. Things were just too weird.

Virginia sighed. "Okay, this is the deal. I'm going to take you back to exactly where I found you, and then we're going to go our separate ways. Okay?"

Prince barked twice. She ignored that and walked into the park. She followed the trail that she usually took. It wouldn't take long to find the scene of the accident.

"Look," Virginia said, "I'm not the adventurous type. I'm just a waitress. This is way too scary for me, thank you very much. Whoever these people are who want you, they can have you."

As they got closer, Prince ran in front of her, tail wagging. For a dog that had been reluctant to leave her moments before, he was certainly happy to be here.

There were scrape marks in the grass where her tires had skidded, and a tuft of hair near one of the branches. Dog hair.

"Okay, we're here," Virginia said. "This is where we really do have to say good-bye."

She backed away from him. Prince turned those lovely doggy eyes on her—human eyes, actually—and stared at her plaintively. Then he barked twice. It was as if she were abandoning him to horrors not even she could imagine.

But she had to.

It was for the best.

Or so she tried to believe.

Chapter Nine

"I think you're still holding back," Dr. Horovitz said. "What's really troubling you?"

This woman was amazing. Wolf bit his lower lip, tasted blood, thought of food, and then remembered his dilemma. He sat up on the couch, ran a hand through his hair, and peered at the books. They all had scientific titles and seemed to be of no help.

"All right, all right." Wolf leaned forward and grabbed Dr. Horovitz's arm. "Doc, I've met this terrific girl, and I really, really, really like her. But the thing is . . ."

He couldn't tell her. He shouldn't tell her. The difference between his animal nature and his human nature was so . . . so . . . *personal.*

"Say it," Dr. Horovitz encouraged gently. "Say it."

Wolf grabbed the arm of the chair, trying to restrain himself, but unable to. "I'm not sure whether I . . . I . . . I want to love her or eat her."

"Oh," Dr. Horovitz said.

Wolf leapt to his feet. Dr. Horovitz didn't move, which made her the first human ever to not cringe from him when he was in this kind of mood. He paced in front of her, hands clasped behind his back.

"I blame my parents," Wolf said. "They were both enormous. They couldn't stop eating. Every day I came home from school and it was eat this, eat that, eat her . . ."

"You shouldn't punish yourself," Dr. Horovitz said.

"I should, I should," Wolf said. "I'm bad. I've done so many bad things. But that wasn't me, you see. That was when I was a wolf."

He threw himself onto the couch. It groaned beneath his weight, which wasn't considerable—was it?

"Doc, I want to change. I want to be a good person. Can't the lion cuddle up with the lamb? Can't the leopard rub out all its spots?"

Dr. Horovitz glanced at her watch. She pushed her glasses up on her nose and said, "I really have to see my next patient now."

Wolf couldn't believe what he was hearing. He stood, and Dr. Horovitz stood, putting one hand on his back and propelling him to the door.

He had just confessed his deepest darkest secret, and *she hadn't even cared.*

"But I'm desperate, Doc," Wolf said.

"Such deep problems can't possibly be solved in just one session."

"But I'm in love and I'm hungry," Wolf said. "And I need help now. Throw me a lifeline."

She had somehow gotten him to the door. This woman controlled him, and he didn't even want to eat her. She leaned over and grabbed a piece of paper off her desk.

"Here's a reading list I'd strongly recommend." Her tone hadn't changed during the entire session. She didn't seem to feel the urgency that he did. "Now why don't you come and see me next week?"

"Don't you understand?" Wolf asked. "I won't be here next week."

She tilted her head reprovingly. "You're not going to intimidate me with suicide threats."

Then she shoved him out the door and closed it behind him. He had never been so skillfully maneuvered in all his life. He turned, thought about banging on the door, and then decided he'd left enough of his dignity in that room. He didn't need to discard the rest by banging like a half-grown pup against the door.

Thrown out of the nest was thrown out of the nest. It had happened to him once before. At least she'd given him a list of instructions, which was more than his parents had done.

He was on his own, and truth be told, he did better that way.

Tony's arms hurt. They felt like they were going to be pulled from their sockets. He was surrounded by police, and even the hallway smelled like beer. Up ahead, he saw Mrs. Murray Senior working on the wiring for the elevator. Where had that elderly woman gotten her skills?

One of the cops shoved him forward. Tony stumbled, wondering how it could have gone from free beer, beautiful, willing women, and a satchel of money to this within fifteen minutes.

"If you cooperate and give us your dealer's name," the cop was saying, "maybe we can put in a word for you."

Tony shook his head. "What dealer?" he asked. "I'm not taking drugs."

They had nearly reached the elevator. Mrs. Murray glanced at them, but didn't seem to notice anything out of the ordinary. Weren't the Murray family supposed to be his servants? Shouldn't they try to save him? Or did he have to ask?

And if he had to ask, then the cops would shoot her, and much as he disliked the old crone, he didn't want to be the cause of her death.

"I've almost fixed the elevator now, Master," Mrs. Murray said.

Bully for her. The cops continued to shove him toward the stairwell.

"You said you don't remember stealing the money," the cop said, "because you were under the influence of these magic mushrooms."

"Beans, not mushrooms," Tony said. "Yes, I'd eaten the bean, but . . . oh, God."

They shoved him into the stairwell. He had to concentrate to keep his balance. There was no way out of this. Everything had gone weird since those creatures had smashed his door. And that bean, that magic bean. What a curse it had been!

He almost wished he had never eaten it, but it had taught him the power of unthought-through wishes. So he kept his lips pressed tightly together and concentrated on surviving the next few minutes.

The strange flickering light came back on. Blabberwort glared at her brothers. They looked as though they had been melted and then sewn together. Their eyes were big and dull and sad.

Then the light went out. The darkness was absolute. She wrapped her arms around her knees. Eternity in this place would just be too damn long.

When the light came on, Bluebell had his large forehead scrunched up. It was as if he'd actually had a thought.

"I think we might be in her pocket," Bluebell said.

The light went out. Which was good. That way he wouldn't be able to see Blabberwort's reaction.

"What?" Burly asked.

"I think she might have shrunk us and put us in a matchbox in her pocket."

"That is ridiculous," Burly said. "You're falling to pieces. Get a grip on yourself. How can we be in a matchbox, you idiot? Where are the matches?"

"Exactly." Blabberwort couldn't have agreed more. Where had Bluebell come up with this thing? It was too dumb to call an idea.

The light came back on.

"I'm sorry," Bluebell said. "That was a stupid thing to say. I'm just getting very hungry, that's all."

They were all hungry. Blabberwort narrowed her eyes. That presented a completely different problem. They would have to eat sometime. Trolls had fearsome appetites. And none of them were carrying food.

"Say what you mean." Apparently Burly had the same thought she had. "Out with it, come on."

"I didn't mean anything," Bluebell said. "I just meant I was hungry. Don't read things into everything I say."

But it was too late. The idea had come to the surface. Blabberwort stared at her brothers. Neither of them looked all that appetizing, but eventually, she knew, that would probably change.

"I'm really hungry, too," Blabberwort said.

"*I want to get out of this box before we start eating each other!*" Bluebell shouted at the ceiling. "*I can't stand it any—*"

Suddenly the box shifted. All three of them grabbed the wall. Something whirred. The lights came back on—all of them, not just the annoying fizzing one, and the box started downward.

Blabberwort leaped to her feet and so did her brothers. They stared at the walls of the box as if it would give them answers.

"We're moving!" Burly shouted.

Blabberwort corrected him. "We're going down."

Bluebell covered his head. "We are about to arrive in the underworld! Prepare yourselves!"

The box stopped moving, and slowly the doors opened. Blabberwort recognized this place. She'd seen it before, only then it had been dark.

"This isn't the underworld," Burley said. "This is where we came in."

"Magic indeed," Blabberwort said. "How did she do that?"

At the mention of *her,* they glanced at each other. An attack could come from anywhere at any time. They plastered themselves against the walls and eased out of the room, looking from side to side to make certain no one was around.

No one was.

They stepped into the main area, where black-and-white images were showing themselves in another, smaller box. So that was how she kept track of her prisoners. Blabberwort thought of showing that to the others, but changed her mind when she realized they weren't going to be attacked.

Burly and Bluebell seemed to realize the same thing at the same time. They let out a whoop of joy and ran out the front door.

Blabberwort followed. They were heading back to the trees and the grass and the familiar stuff. And she couldn't wait to get there.

He'd never sat in the back of a police car before, especially not with his hands cuffed. As they drove out of his neighborhood, Tony looked around for some help. A lot of people were walking down the street, but they kept their eyes averted as if he were the one who had done something bad.

All he had done was eat a magic bean that tasted like— well, he wasn't going to go there again—but it wasn't a felony for heaven's sake. Couldn't these cops understand that?

Maybe he could make them understand.

He leaned toward the mesh that separated him from them.

"Listen," Tony said to the two cops in the front seat, "can't we do a deal? I can give you whatever you want, I promise. A house in the Hamptons, cars, boats, women. I've still got two wishes left."

"You're not making it any better trying to bribe us," one cop said.

"What have I got to lose?" Tony said. He thought for a moment, swallowed hard, and sighed. Two wishes left. Well, he wouldn't get to use any of them if he didn't get out of here. "Okay, *I wish I could escape from this police car now.*"

The cops laughed. Then the driver went very pale.

"Paul," the driver shouted. "The brakes have failed."

Oh, great. This wasn't what Tony had meant. The car shot through a red light, scattering pedestrians. The driver fiddled with the wheel—didn't they teach cops how to stop moving brakeless vehicles in cop school?—and the car hit the curb, going over it, narrowly missing a knish vendor and slamming into a store.

Glass tinkled all around them. Tony blinked twice. He wasn't hurt. But the cops were. They were out cold. He stared at them for a moment before realizing what he had to do.

A glorious place. Wolf had no idea who had come up with the idea of having all the books in the world in one place, but it was fabulous. Someday when he wasn't looking for Virginia and chasing Prince Wendell, he would come back here and read everything there was on food—an entire section!—and cooking and spices and . . .

But he already had more books than he could carry. He had them balanced under his chin, and he was still trying to catch one or two as they slipped.

The woman beside him, the "clerk," as she'd said she was called, still looked a bit overwhelmed. Apparently she'd never had anyone want to read *everything* in the self-help section before, at least not all at once.

"You've been very helpful indeed, miss," Wolf said to the bookstore clerk. "Thank you very much. If my plan is successful, I will certainly invite you to the wedding."

She smiled at him uncertainly and slipped into one of the aisles. Wolf put his free arm around his books so that none of the other customers would grab one. Then he walked toward the main door.

The window—which had been fine when he came in—was broken and one of the mechanical horseless carriages was stuck in it. That was the problem of attempting to steer without benefit of horse.

People were crowded around it, and men in blue were trying to get out of it.

"Stop that man!" one of the men yelled.

Wolf focused. The man was pointing at a familiar figure who was sprinting toward the street. Virginia's father, Tony!

Better and better. Wolf clutched his books and ran toward the door. A different clerk reached for him.

"Sir, have you paid for those?" she asked, but he ignored her. He ran through the small barricade before the door and sirens went off. But he couldn't stop now.

Tony was headed for the park, and Wolf ran after him, still clutching his stack of research to his chest.

Chapter Ten

It was hard to run with his hands cuffed behind him, but Tony was doing a fine job. He occasionally lost his balance on the trail, but he never fell. Track, all those years ago, too many to even think about, paid off now.

Except for the extra pounds and the age and the fact that he was barely keeping ahead of those cops.

His breath was coming in harsh gasps as he went off the regular path to use Virginia's old shortcut. The trees were a little thicker here, and he felt a little safer. Not much, but enough.

As he rounded a corner, he saw someone who looked suspiciously like Virginia, crouching in front of a dog.

"Dad?" The girl called out.

"Virginia?"

"Dad!"

That clinched it. It was Virginia. Tony ran to her, not wanting her to shout any more. The police would hear.

It only took him a second to reach her, but it took a minute for him to catch his breath. When he did, he said, "You won't believe what's happened to me."

"Don't bet on it," Virginia said.

She was standing by that dog, which was watching him with eerie golden eyes. Weird people, weird beans, weird dogs. Somehow it all made sense.

"Is this the dog they want?" Tony asked. "Just give him back. Please?"

"I don't think he is a dog," Virginia said. "He's trying to talk to me, but I can't understand what he's saying."

Well, he could solve that, and probably find out why this damn dog was so important.

"Watch this." He moved Virginia out of the way and crouched in front of the dog. He stared into the dog's eyes and said, "I wish to understand everything this dog is trying to say."

Virginia looked at him like he was nuts.

Tony ignored her.

"You're in terrible danger, both of you," the dog said. He had a surprisingly aristocratic voice.

"It worked!"

"What?" Virginia asked.

"If you value your life, you have to do exactly as I say," the dog said. "We have to find a way back."

"He's talking," Tony said, pointing to the dog. "He's talking. Can't you hear him?"

Now Virginia was really looking at him like he was crazy. Like he was rip-roaring crazy, the kind they put people away for. "No," she said slowly, like she was talking to an elderly person who refused to wear a hearing aid. "I can't hear him."

There was crunching behind them.

"Ssh," Tony said.

More crunching. Thick, heavy footsteps. Police? Tony wondered. Then what was that smell?

He grabbed Virginia and pulled her into the trees. The dog was already there, looking at them with those eerie eyes.

An instant later, one of the people who had attacked him—the ones the wolf guy had called Trolls—strolled past. She—he—it was very tall and wore too much orange. Some of it even poofed into a straight ponytail on top of her—his—its head.

"It's over here somewhere," the Troll was saying. The voice was, frighteningly, female. "I marked the tree."

The Troll that followed her was shorter, and its sex was

just as indeterminate. "Look out for the witch," it said. Or rather, he said, because the voice was deep and masculine. These were the ugliest creatures that Tony had ever seen. Even uglier than he had remembered them from the time they'd axed their way into the apartment.

A third Troll followed them, but remained silent, its gender, therefore, a mystery.

Tony glanced at Virginia. She didn't seem surprised by them. Instead, she was watching them intently. Only the dog looked nervous. All three of them waited until the Trolls were gone before slipping out of their hiding place.

"Okay," Tony said. "What's next?"

"Next," the dog said, leading them off the path, "is to get us out of here. I need to find the magic mirror. It'll send me back to my home. I can't do anything here, like this."

"A magic mirror?" Tony repeated. He didn't know why he was having trouble with this concept. Trolls in the daylight didn't seem to bother him this much.

"It's a mirror," the dog said inside Tony's head. "But it may not look like a mirror from this side. You have to look very carefully."

Tony glanced over his shoulder. He thought he saw a lot of men in blue combing the woods. Overhead, a police helicopter zoomed by and he ducked.

"Why are so many police officers after you?" Virginia asked. "And why are you wearing handcuffs?"

"They think I did a major bank job," Tony said. "I'll explain later."

"Stop rabbiting and help me find the mirror," the dog said.

"We're looking for a magic mirror," Tony said to his daughter.

"Of course we are," Virginia said.

And they'd better find it pretty soon, Tony thought, or he'd be in jail. He was all out of wishes.

"Look for a piece of the forest that doesn't fit," the dog

said. "I'm sure this is where I came through—there! There it is. Look."

Tony looked at the copse of trees the dog was staring at but saw nothing except undergrowth and trees.

"Over there," the dog said. He sounded exasperated.

"Yeah, there's something weird . . ." Tony frowned. It was almost as if there was a blank spot in the trees. A pulsating blank spot the size of a full-length mirror. As he got closer, he realized it wasn't blank. It was black.

Virginia stopped beside him and looked too. She bit her lower lip.

Tony squinted. It looked as if there was a room beyond, a room full of tumbledown junk. "What is it?" he asked.

"Lookee look," said the female Troll from a short distance behind them. "There they are."

Tony glanced over his shoulder. All three Trolls were running in their direction, followed by some police. The chopper had circled back and was heading this way too.

"Follow me if you value your lives," the dog said as he jumped into the mirror. The image winked out and then reappeared.

"Do as he says," Tony said, shoving Virginia toward the mirror with his shoulder. "Quick."

Virginia jumped into the mirror just as Tony did. It felt as if he had jumped into wet rubber. All the sounds of Central Park vanished, even the heavy beat of the chopper overhead, and then suddenly he stepped into the room he had seen through the opening.

It smelled of dust and mold. There were metal dishes scattered everywhere and ruined curtains, and several broken chairs. It was worse than the storage room in the apartment building.

"Where the hell are we?" Tony whispered.

"I don't know," Virginia said. "But I'm pretty sure it's not Central Park."

"We're in the southernmost part of my kingdom, where I was attacked and turned into a dog."

The dog led them into the corridor and down a narrow hallway. "This is the Snow White Memorial Prison, housing the most dangerous criminals in all the Nine Kingdoms."

"Back up a second," Tony said. "The nine what?"

"Kingdoms." The dog rose on his hind legs. The movement was oddly formal. "I am Prince Wendell, grandson of the late Snow White and soon to be crowned King of the Fourth Kingdom. And who might you be?"

Tony glanced at Virginia who, since she couldn't hear the dog, had no idea what he was saying. Tony stood up a little straighter too as he replied, "I'm Tony Lewis, janitor." He tried to give that last word as much dignity as possible. "I think you know my daughter Virginia."

"Is that dog talking again?" Virginia asked.

The dog—Prince Wendell—Tony couldn't believe that he believed him, but he did—went down on all fours and cocked his head. "Shhh," he said. "I can smell the Trolls."

"Shhh," Tony said to Virginia. "He can smell Trolls."

Virginia rolled her eyes, but then she sniffed too, and her eyes widened. Tony caught the familiar stench as well.

All three of them hid behind some barrels just in time. The Trolls had apparently come through the mirror. They were walking through the same hallway, the huge ugly female in the lead.

"What shall we do when we have our own kingdom?" she asked.

"Servants," the short male said. "We must have hundreds of servants to polish our shoes."

"And we'll have footwear parties where you have to change shoes six times an hour," the third Troll said. Apparently he was male too.

"And anyone found with dirty shoes will have their faces sewn up!" the female said as if she liked that idea.

They continued talking as they passed. They went up a flight of stairs, still mumbling about shoes. When their voices faded, Tony, Virginia, and Prince Wendell emerged from their hiding place.

"We must find my stepmother's cell," Prince Wendell said. "Perhaps there's a clue as to where she's gone. Follow me."

"He says to follow him," Tony said to Virginia.

Virginia glanced over her shoulder as if she preferred going back through the mirror to going deeper into this place. But she followed along. Prince Wendell led them up the stairs, and suddenly Tony realized they really were in a prison. There were cell doors everywhere and high dark corridors. The guards, though, were asleep on the ground, pink dust on their faces.

"What's happened to everybody?" Tony asked.

"The same thing that happened to you," Prince Wendell said. "Troll dust."

No wonder his place had been so filthy. The very memory of the stuff made Tony want to sneeze. One warder rolled over and snorted in his sleep.

"And it's starting to wear off."

"Dad, let's go home," Virginia said.

"I can't go back yet, can I?" Tony snapped. Sometimes Virginia was so inconsiderate. "The police are swarming all over Central Park looking for me."

"Well, we can't stay here." Virginia tugged her blue sweatshirt jacket tighter around her neck. She clearly wasn't comfortable. Neither was he. He had run into a prison to escape going to prison and somehow he didn't like the irony in that.

Prince Wendell led them around a few more columns into the main prison dining room. It was empty, but it still smelled of grease and unwashed bodies. On one wall was a giant map. Prince Wendell leapt onto a nearby table as Tony and Virginia walked closer to the map.

It was hand drawn and prettier than the maps he was used to. A big red arrow pointed to an area marked Snow White Memorial Prison, and beneath the arrow, it said, YOU ARE IMPRISONED HERE. At least they were polite in this place. Prince Wendell said he was the soon-to-be-crowned king of the Fourth

Kingdom, which was marked in green. It was a long, thin strip in the center of the map, bordered by all the other lands.

Virginia peered at it, reading aloud, "The Troll Kingdom. Red Riding Hood Forest . . ."

"What is this place?" Tony asked Prince Wendell. "Is this like Sleeping Beauty and Cinderella and fairy stories and stuff?"

"Well, the Golden Age was almost two hundred years ago, when the ladies you refer to had their great moments in history," Prince said. "Things have gone downhill a bit since then. Happy Ever After didn't last as long as we'd hoped."

Tony didn't like the sound of that. If you couldn't believe in fairy tales and Happily Ever After, what could you believe in?

"And who's this stepmother who's turned you into a dog?" Tony asked.

"She is the most dangerous and evil woman alive."

Now that, Tony understood. He nodded. "I have several relatives like that."

But that didn't ease his mind either. He was beginning to think jumping through the mirror hadn't been a very smart move after all.

The prison looked no better from above. The Queen crossed her arms and stared at it. She still wasn't certain how she had allowed herself to be held in that place all this time.

At least she was out. The air felt good, the sunlight better. Even the Dog Prince seemed to be enjoying it. He was on all fours, scuffing the knees of his trousers and getting his gloves dirty, as he sniffed the ground.

Maybe he was enjoying it too much.

The Queen stared at him for a moment. He had been a great dog, but he was making a terrible prince. Relish, the Troll King, came out of the woods and looked at the Dog Prince in disgust. The Queen said nothing. Instead, she looked at the royal carriage. She would have to leave this place. She couldn't wait any longer. To do so would be to jeopardize her chances of taking over the Nine Kingdoms.

"Where are they?" the Queen demanded. "I should never have trusted Trolls to do everything."

"Be careful what you say," the Troll King said. "I'm the only reason you got out of prison in the first place."

She let out a bit of air, not quite a sigh and not quite loud enough for him to hear. She still needed him for a short time anyway. She would have to keep him mollified.

"Of course, Your Majesty," the Queen said, "and for that I am eternally grateful. But I can't wait here any longer. No one can see the Prince like this."

They both turned toward the Dog Prince. Now he was on his back, rolling in some disgusting smell he'd found and trying to scratch his neck with his hind foot. His booted hind foot.

This time the Queen did sigh. "Have your children bring the dog to me when they return."

The Troll King narrowed his eyes. "I am not your lackey. I am Relish, the Troll King, and you would do well to remember it."

Oh, some day he would pay for this. But not yet. Not while she still had plans for him. She made herself speak softly. "Of course, Your Majesty, and I will reward you handsomely for your help, as I promised, with half of Wendell's kingdom."

He walked up to her, so close that she could smell the oil on his leather jacket. "When, exactly, will I get it?"

He was a little shrewder than she wanted him to be. She would do well to remember that.

"Soon," she said. "Now I must go. I have stayed too long already."

She bent down and cuffed the Dog Prince on his right ear, the way she used to do when he was a dog. He rolled over and looked at her, his expression sad and puppyish.

"In the coach," she snapped. She had no time for whimpering dog games.

"Where are you going?" the Troll King asked. "There's

nowhere you can hide. When they find out you've escaped, there will be roadblocks everywhere. They'll search every house and carriage in the Kingdom.''

The Dog Prince got into the coach and she followed him. Then she leaned out, touching the royal emblem as she did so.

''They won't search every carriage,'' she said, and smiled. Then she tapped the side of the carriage, and the team started forward. The Troll King stepped out of their way. The Queen pulled the window curtain enough so that she could still see out, but no one could see her.

The Troll King stood on the hillside for a moment, then slipped on his magic shoes and vanished.

The Dog Prince stuck his head out the window beside her, tongue lolling, and barked in excitement. She cuffed him on the side of his head and he whimpered.

''Humans don't do that,'' she said.

He nodded, but she knew he didn't understand. She leaned back inside the carriage and closed the curtain all the way. This would be a very long trip. A very long trip indeed.

Prince Wendell led them past rows and rows of cells. The deeper they got into the prison, the more uneasy Tony became. Virginia had her hands wrapped around her torso as if her arms could shield her.

Tony'd never been in a prison before, but he didn't think they looked like this. All the cells had barred windows and barred doors, and they seemed larger than the average cell. But they did stink of urine and body odor so old that he wondered if the place had ever been cleaned. Below each cell door was a sign with the prisoners' numbers, their names, and details of their crimes. Fortunately, Tony walked past them too quickly to read anything.

As they passed one cell, though, a hand jutted out.

''Give us something to eat.'' The man who spoke was bald and looked meaner than Jesse Ventura in his fighting days. ''I haven't had anything to eat since yesterday.''

Prince Wendell didn't even look up. Virginia gave the cell a wide berth, and so did Tony.

The next cell was smaller. Tony peered inside. A dwarf—not a short person, but a dwarf straight out of the Brothers Grimm—looked at him. And then Tony realized the dwarf had a hideous scar running along one side of his face.

"Let us out," the dwarf said. "Come on, just get his key and let us out."

"Terrible people," Prince Wendell said. "They deserve all they get."

Virginia stopped as she reached the next cell. It was barely a foot off the ground. That seemed strange, even to Tony.

Virginia crouched and read, "Deadly mice?"

Tony knelt beside her to read the inscription. Sure enough. It said DEADLY MICE.

"They're only serving eighteen months," Tony said.

"It's a life sentence." Prince Wendell sounded unmoved. "Come on."

They passed another cell with just a skeleton hanging from manacles. Tony almost asked—and then decided against it.

They turned into a corridor with a sign at the end that said, MAXIMUM SECURITY. Tony hadn't liked what had been, apparently, minimum security. He had a hunch he'd hate this.

But Prince Wendell soldiered on, and Tony felt he had no other choice but to follow. They went past a few cells, then a door with another sign on it, something about no talking to the prisoner and two warders at all times. He wasn't able to catch everything, but what he did see made him wonder if he should go on.

Prince Wendell was already halfway down the corridor, so Tony kept going too. Virginia was looking more and more disgruntled the deeper they went.

Finally, they reached an open cell, the only one in this wing. Prince Wendell went inside. Tony did too, but the air grew darker, and he could almost feel a presence, one that was gone but not forgotten.

It was not a pleasant feeling.

"Look," Prince Wendell said, "there's a dog bowl down here. That's the dog that's got my body. It's outrageous."

Tony looked at Virginia. She was still clutching her arms, her knuckles white.

"What did she do, this woman?" Virginia asked.

"She poisoned my mother and father and tried to kill me as well," Prince Wendell said.

Virginia didn't respond to that. Apparently she still couldn't hear the Prince when he spoke.

"Basically," Tony said, "she poisoned his mother, his father, and tried to kill him as well."

Prince Wendell sniffed the floor, his tail down. "I think the Trolls were in here. Very strange . . ."

Virginia swayed to one side. Tony reached for her, but she caught herself by putting one hand against the wall.

"Are you all right?" Tony asked.

"I feel weird being in here." She looked queasy. He knew that look well from her childhood. There was a roller coaster on Coney Island that always brought that look to her face.

"Virginia, honey," Tony asked, worried, "are you okay?"

"No, no." She stood up straight and attempted a smile. "I'll be all right. I just need to get out for a minute."

Then she walked out of the cell. Something had really freaked her out. She was usually tougher than that. Tony looked after her, torn between remaining with Wendell and taking care of his daughter.

Then he heard a *whack!* followed by a thud. A loud thud, like someone falling.

"Virginia?" Tony called out into the corridor. "Are you all right?"

She didn't answer. He hurried to the cell door, but as he did, the door slammed shut. He heard a low chuckle. He rattled the door and looked through the bars, but saw nothing except the feet of a sleeping warder.

"Virginia? Virginia?"

She wasn't answering, and she was the only one outside the cell. Tony shook the door harder.

"I don't believe this," he said. "Prince?"

He looked around. Prince Wendell had vanished. He was alone here, in maximum security, without any way of getting out!

Just as panic started to set in, Prince Wendell slipped out from under the bunk. "I wasn't scared. It's just ... people mustn't see me as a dog, Anthony. It's deeply, deeply embarrassing."

Oh, great. Embarrassment before sense. "I couldn't care less about you being a dog," Tony said. He turned back to the door and rattled it so hard that the sound hurt his own ears. "Virginia? Virginia?"

Then the feet he saw moved. The warders were waking up. They would find him in here, with the dog, just like the Queen. He was beginning to wish he was still in that cop car. Prison here was worse than prison in New York. Here they had magic and all sorts of things he couldn't imagine. There they had only—He winced, and backed away from the door.

He had no idea what he would do.

Wolf stepped through the mirror, carrying his books in a bag he had slung over his shoulder. He'd stolen the bag from a man sleeping on a bench. The man obviously hadn't needed it; it was filled with dirty clothes and some inedible food called protein bars which Wolf tried and immediately spat out. He'd followed the scent of Virginia and the dog, overlaid with the smell of Trolls, back here.

Now she was in his world. Life had gotten better.

He turned to the mirror and saw the greenery he had just left. The men in blue were getting closer and closer. Soon they would find this thing and come through, and everything would get very messy.

There had to be a shut-off mechanism. All magic items had them in one way or another. Wolf used his free hand to search the side of the mirror's frame. And then he saw it, a protruding piece of frame that had to be the secret catch. The dog must have activated the thing when he jumped through it, or something like that.

Wolf reached forward and pushed the catch back into the frame. There was a loud whoosh as everything vanished, and the mirror shut off.

Wolf jumped backwards at the sound, but then he noticed he was staring at himself. And what a good-looking fellow he was too. He couldn't understand why Virginia had screamed at him. True, he needed a shave, but still. He rubbed his chin and then grinned.

He was the only one who knew the secret of the mirror— and he would keep it that way.

Chapter Eleven

It felt good to be home, if one wanted to call the Snow White Memorial Prison home, which Blabberwort surely did not. But back in the Nine Kingdoms, the real world, whatever someone wanted to call it.

She was walking behind Burly, who was carrying the witch over his shoulder, her head and arms bobbing up and down like a rag doll's. She looked very uncomfortable, but she couldn't look uncomfortable enough for Blabberwort.

They were walking outside the prison toward the main gate. They'd already searched the inside. Behind them alarm bells were ringing, and once Blabberwort had turned around to see the warders from the main gatehouse falling all over each other, as humans waking from Troll dust were wont to do.

Burly took one look at them and frowned in disgust. "Where's Dad? And the Queen?"

"I suppose we are a little late," Blabberwort said.

"Stop!" a warder shouted. "You. Stop where you are."

He was running from the gatehouse, or actually trying to run was a better way of describing it. He was carrying a large stick and looked a bit frightening.

But Blabberwort knew better than to be frightened of one dusted human. So did her brothers.

Burly reached up with one meaty fist and, when the warder got close, kaboshed him on the head. "Shouldn't we go back for the dog? The Queen will be very angry."

"The Queen can suck an Elf as far as I'm concerned,"

Bluebell said. "We've captured the witch from the Tenth Kingdom. Let's go home and tell Dad."

Blabberwort grinned. It was time that they had redeemed themselves. Dad would be so very proud. And Dad was rarely proud.

The all-powerful witch of the Tenth Kingdom was theirs forever.

Wolf had smelled the Trolls before he saw them in the corridors of the prison, carrying the beautiful Virginia as though she was a sack of meat. That angered him more than anything, them treating his Virginia like food. Never mind that he had once planned to do the same to her grandmother. Never mind that he had greeted her with a cleaver in his hand. He had changed. He was reformed. He was carrying a bag of books over his shoulder to prove it.

He followed the Trolls out of the prison and was now watching from the woods as they made their way to the river. Several boats floated on it, but none of them seemed to notice the Trolls or beautiful Virginia's plight.

The dog wasn't with her, but the dog could hang for all he cared. Wolf had a chance with Virginia now. He could save her, be her knight in shining white armor—or actually a slightly dusty blue overcoat—and then he would have her love forever.

It was such a lovely image that he held onto it for a moment before he scampered down the hillside toward the path.

The Trolls had reached the river. They had found a boat and were in the process of throwing the boat's owners overboard as Wolf made his way toward them. He stayed in the shadows so that they wouldn't see him.

They dumped his beloved Virginia onto the bottom of the boat and pushed off. Wolf got closer. He stared at the water for a moment, then at the sign near it which read, YOU ARE NOW LEAVING THE FOURTH KINGDOM.

Quite a sacrifice his Virginia was asking of him. But he was more than willing to make it.

For her.

Sloshing water and a splitting headache . . . and something damp against her back. Virginia's eyelids fluttered as someone picked her up and slung her over their shoulder so hard that all the air left her stomach. She tried to cough, but couldn't. There was a terrible stink that seemed to be coming from the leather jacket she was facing. She didn't want to think about that.

She craned her head slightly, and the movement made her dizzy. There was an alarm ringing far away, and as she bounced, she saw that her captor was walking on a dirt path. An upside down sign—she squinted to read it until she realized that she was upside down, and then she could decipher it—read, YOU ARE NOW ENTERING THE THIRD KINGDOM.

She got a vision of this place from that beautifully drawn map that she had seen earlier in her dream (this *was* a dream, wasn't it? *Please?*). In the Third Kingdom, it said something about Trolls.

The grass was overgrown here, and something had died in it, making the stench of the leather jacket seem almost palatable. Everything, from the wood to the buoys to the boats, looked rotted and unkempt.

Toward her left were several unused carts, and a road that wound its way up a dark and forbidding mountain. Toward the top she saw an ugly castle and somehow she knew, with the certainty of dreams, that that was their destination.

She turned her head again, and ahead she saw a series of wooden huts. Men sat before them wearing yellow uniforms, smoking and drinking as if they didn't care about their work. There were three arches that stood over the path.

The first read: TROLL CITIZENS. The second read: FOREIGN CITIZENS. The third read: SLAVES. That last was a very bad sign. Virginia winced. She hadn't meant to pun, but her head ached as it never had before, and she could feel a lump forming on the right side. She had been in a prison and then someone had whacked her.

Her captor strode through the first arch, making him a Troll. She winced again, and felt the dizziness grow. This had to be one of the Trolls she had locked in the elevator. Things were getting very, very bad.

The men in uniform scrambled to their feet and then bowed.

"Welcome back, Your Majesties," they said in unison.

Very, very bad indeed.

Tony no longer had feeling in his hands. Maybe, if he did, he would attempt to bash the warders who held him over their heads and then tell Prince Wendell to run for it.

Then again, maybe not. These warders were the toughest looking men Tony had ever seen—and he'd grown up in a very bad neighborhood. But the prison governor looked even tougher. They'd brought Tony in front of this governor. He looked mean, he looked bad, and he looked pissed about the Troll dust.

But then, who wouldn't be?

The warders had led Tony into the governor's office. Wendell followed. The office was as dark and foreboding as the rest of this horrible place.

"It is some kind of spell," one of the warders was saying to the governor. "Me and the lads have been laid out for over a day. We've searched every inch of the prison but the Queen is gone, sir."

The governor's beady eyes stared at the warder for a very long time, as if this Queen's disappearance were his fault. Then the governor turned those beady eyes on Tony.

"I have been the governor of this prison for twelve years. No prisoner has ever escaped before."

Tony started to shake. But he managed to sound calm as he sucked up. "That's a very impressive record."

"Whatever you do, don't tell him I'm a dog." Prince Wendell sounded very close.

"Why not?" Tony asked.

"Speak when spoken to," the governor snapped.

"Because the Queen has got some terrible plan," Prince Wendell said. "My whole kingdom may be in jeopardy. No one must know I'm helpless."

The governor cracked his knuckles. Tony jumped.

"Where is the Queen?" the governor asked. His tone was menacing, his shoulders were broad, and those cracked knuckles looked like they could do some serious damage.

"I wish to be home, now, this instant!" Tony shouted. *"I wish I was back home safely tucked up in bed."*

Tony clicked his fingers and snapped his heels together like Dorothy in Oz. The governor stared at him. The warders stared at him. He was willing to bet that Prince Wendell was staring at him too.

And that was all that happened.

"Well," the governor said, "it seems you're not."

Tony's stomach turned, and then it flattened, and then it ached. He retched. Something was coming up, and it was coming up now. He coughed and gagged, and bent over. All that work and then—a shriveled-up black husk flew out of his mouth and landed on the governor's desk.

"Oh, no, Anthony," Prince said. "You didn't swallow a dragon-dung bean? You moron."

Tony closed his eyes. "Guess that means I've had all my wishes."

The governor flicked the fizzing husk into his garbage bin. Then he turned on Tony. "How did the Queen escape?"

"I have absolutely no idea," Tony said.

"Then why were you found locked in her empty cell?"

"I am an innocent victim," Tony said. "I have never been in trouble with the law in my whole life."

The governor raised a very faint eyebrow. "Then why are you wearing handcuffs?"

"Because I'm wanted for armed robbery," Tony said. "But I didn't have anything to do with that, either."

"Carry on, Anthony," Prince Wendell said. "You're doing spectacularly well so far."

Tony's shaking had grown worse. "I've come here from a different dimension, led by this dog, who is actually Prince Wendell."

"I told you not to say that," Prince Wendell said.

"Prince Wendell?" the governor asked.

The governor trained his beady eyes on Prince Wendell, who met his gaze, and then turned them back on Tony. "I can make you break rocks with your teeth for a hundred years."

He probably could too. "It's the truth," Tony said. "I swear."

"This is the Queen's dog," the governor said. "She has been permitted to keep him in her cell for three years. Don't insult my intelligence."

"It's Prince Wendell," Tony said. "Look, I'll show you." He bent down and looked at the Prince. "Bark once if I'm telling the truth."

Prince Wendell didn't even look at him. "I have no intention of barking, Anthony."

Oh, great. Oh, great. The damn dog was going to get them both killed. Him and his stupid pride.

"He's just being awkward," Tony said. He looked toward the door. He had to get out of here. He needed some kind of plan. Maybe honesty would work.

He licked his lips. "I must be released immediately," he said. "I think my daughter has been abducted by Trolls—"

The governor pounded on his desk so hard that everything in the room bounced. "Enough!" he roared. "I'll have the truth out of you soon enough. Warder, remove his handcuffs, issue him a prison uniform, and put him in, uh . . ."

He ran his finger down a chart that listed all the prisoners. His dirty nail stopped at one number, and a slow smile spread across his ugly face.

"Oh, yes," the governor said. "Put him in 103 with Acorn the Dwarf and Clay Face the Goblin."

"Clay Face?" Tony said. "I don't want to be put in a cell with anyone called Clay Face."

"What about the Queen's dog, sir?" one of the warders asked.

The governor looked at Prince Wendell. The dog looked more regal than ever. How'd he do that, when all Tony wanted to do was run?

"Get the furnace going," the governor said. "I'll slip some rat poison in his dinner tonight and we'll chuck him in the incinerator tomorrow."

Now Prince Wendell's regalness faded. "Did you hear that? Did you hear that, Anthony? You have to get me out. It's your duty."

Oh, yeah, as if Tony could do that with his hands cuffed and two warders dragging him toward cellmates Acorn and Clay Face. Still, Tony put up a valiant struggle. He shifted and shifted and shifted again, but the warders held him tightly. He couldn't even elbow them. He couldn't escape. He wouldn't know where to escape to.

Except that mirror. Wherever it was. Even though it was in this building, it seemed very far away.

His only hope was Virginia and he had no idea where she was—or if she was even still alive.

Chapter Twelve

Virginia's dizziness was fading, but she kept her eyes closed. She felt as if she was inside a large shoe, a large *old* shoe, a large old *tennis* shoe that should have been discarded before it could stink up an entire room. She wanted to bring her hand to her nose, but she couldn't. It was stuck.

Her lashes fluttered, but she still didn't want to open her eyes. Her arm hurt, stung actually, and she was immobile. Since the last thing she remembered was being carried, she knew that this wasn't good.

Someone chuckled nearby. Finally her eyes flew open, and she saw the three Trolls she'd locked in the elevator smiling at her. One of them held a very large needle and a bottle of blue ink. She looked down. They had tattooed her! And it wasn't a nice tattoo either, not the rose she'd been thinking of, or a delicate little butterfly.

Instead, it was a huge Troll death's head with snakes and rats and things she couldn't identify, and below it were the words, TROLL TOY.

"She's awake," said the Troll who'd been carrying her. She recognized him from his leather jacket. "Strip her."

She cringed, but to her surprise, they grabbed her feet. They pulled off her shoes and socks and held her ankles.

"You are a captive of the merciless Trolls now," said her captor.

"Merciless," said the female.

"Without mercy," said the short one.

They sniffed her shoes and examined them carefully, bending the toes back and forth. She looked around. She was in a large room that had stone walls covered with leopard-skin prints and other materials that looked slightly rotted. A fire in a nearby fireplace covered some of the smell with the scent of smoke. A chandelier hung above her, but the lights flickered as if there were candles in it instead of light bulbs. Everything was dirty and falling apart, but even if it weren't, the room would be horrible. The mixture of oranges and browns and yellows made her think of sixties decor gone wrong.

"Look, look, Blabberwort," said Virginia's captor, thrusting a shoe at the female.

She took it, and smiled. "Thanks, Burly."

"What about Bluebell?" the short one asked, and it took a moment for Virginia to realize he was referring to himself.

But the other two didn't pay him any mind at all. Instead, the female—Blabberwort—grabbed Virginia's feet and hovered over them.

"Pretty little feet," she said. "Nicee nice."

The short Troll, Bluebell, leaned over Virginia's feet and sniffed them. Virginia turned her head away as if she were the one being forced to sniff her own feet. He seemed to be enjoying it a lot more than she would.

He put the palm of his hand against her toes and pressed them backwards very slowly. It was beginning to hurt when he asked, "Who runs your kingdom?"

The pain was sudden and sharp. He'd bent her toes back as far as they could go. "My kingdom?"

"Who's in charge?" Blabberwort asked.

Virginia blinked, uncertain how to answer. It really was hard to think when she was in pain. "The President," she said finally.

Blabberwort leaned in even closer. She had a bulging forehead that was the main cause of her unattractive looks. "Wendell was trying to rally an army from your kingdom, wasn't he?"

''No. No.''

Bluebell shoved even harder on her toes. Virginia wondered if they would break.

''Ow!'' she said.

Her captor, Burly, picked up a jug next to her and swallowed its contents. Then he approached her, and spat it in her face. It was stinky and sticky and smelled of apples.

''This could be a long torture session,'' he said.

She liked being spat on even less than having her toes bent. ''I'll tell you anything you want to know.''

''I torture first,'' Burly said. ''Then you talk. It's better that way. Rush a torture, ruin a torture.''

Suddenly, the wooden door behind them flew open. Virginia heard footsteps but couldn't see anyone. Then the door slammed shut.

''Dad's back,'' Burly said. He didn't sound happy about it.

The footsteps crossed the room and stopped in front of Virginia. Her heart was pounding, but she knew the heavy breathing she heard wasn't her own.

''How about taking off the shoes, Dad?'' Bluebell asked. ''You don't need them indoors.''

There was a click from a nearby wall, and a door Virginia hadn't noticed slid back. Behind it was a wall filled with hundreds of shoes, every type she'd ever seen plus some.

''I can rule the world in these shoes,'' said a voice Virginia had never heard before. ''I am all-powerful.''

''Come on, Dad, you've done the hard part,'' Burly said. ''Just slip them off.''

There was a rustle of material and a slight thud. Then a Troll more hideous than the others appeared. He was taller, had dark hair, and his ears stuck out so far that Virginia thought at first that they were part of a hat.

''I can handle them,'' the Troll said. ''I can take them off anytime I want to.''

''But you never used to put them on first thing in the

morning," Blabberwort said. "Imagine the Troll King under the influence—"

"Enough!" said the newcomer. He was the Troll King, then, more powerful than the others. Virginia scooted back as far as she could in the chair, but they had tied her so tightly that she could barely move.

He shoved the shoes into the closet and turned toward his children.

"Where've you been? You're a day late." Then he jabbed a finger in Virginia's stomach. "And who's this? You were supposed to bring back the dog."

"Forget the dog, Dad," Burly said. "We have discovered another kingdom."

"It's the mythical Tenth Kingdom," said Blabberwort.

"Talked of only in myth," Bluebell added.

"Don't talk rubbish." There was menace in the King's low voice, and an intelligence in his features that was missing in those of his children. Virginia liked him even less than she liked them. "There is no Tenth Kingdom."

"There is," Bluebell said. "And this witch put us in a box of matches."

A box of matches? Did he mean the elevator? Virginia didn't have time to think about that. The Troll King peered at her as if he were trying to see inside her.

"You were captured?" he asked slowly. "By this girl?"

"She's a witch," Bluebell said.

The Troll King clearly didn't believe him. "How many of their soldiers did you kill before you were captured?"

"None," Bluebell said.

"None"—Blabberwort glanced at her father sideways—"survived."

But he didn't fall for her lie. "Who wants to be whipped first?"

It was all Virginia could do not to cringe.

"Dad, it's true," Burly said. "I can prove it. Look at this." He pulled a sack from behind her chair. Virginia recognized it. She had seen the shorter one carrying it when she shoved them into the elevator. She had simply thought it part of his outfit.

Burly reached inside the sack and, to Virginia's surprise, pulled out a small boombox. He carried it to the area rug—which looked like a cheap thing made from fur—and dropped it upside down.

The other Trolls stared at it as if they expected something to happen. Burly pushed on it, and Virginia recognized the pre-tape hiss. The Troll King frowned as if that were what they wanted him to hear.

Then, suddenly, "Saturday Night Fever" blared out of the player. The younger Trolls bobbed up and down to the music as if they couldn't resist its charm, but their father stared at the cassette player as if it were going to bite him.

"They are called the brothers Gibb," Bluebell said excitedly.

"The song concerns a deadly fever that only strikes on Saturdays." Blabberwort's fingers did a small dance to the chorus.

The Troll King's frown grew. "There is more to all this than the Queen is telling me."

The Queen. Virginia froze. They were working with that awful Queen Prince was telling them about? The one who had been imprisoned? The one who had tried to murder his family? The one who had changed him into a dog?

The Troll King must have seen the recognition in Virginia's eyes, for he crossed the room and stopped in front of her. "You will dance for me," he said. "And when you finish dancing, you will tell me how to invade your kingdom."

Virginia swallowed. Hard. "I'm not much of a dancer, really."

The Troll King walked to the wall of shoes. He studied it for a moment, passing up large platforms, tiny heels, and an oversized pair of boots. Then he grabbed the ugliest shoes on the wall, an iron pair that looked as if they weighed a ton.

"You'll dance when you wear these," he said.

Then he walked to the fireplace and carefully placed the shoes in the middle of the blazing flame.

"Wake me," he said, watching her reaction, "when they turn red."

She blanched. She had to have. It felt as if all the blood had left her face at once. He smiled just a little, and left the room. His children went to the fireplace and watched the shoes heat up.

The warders opened the door to a cell and tossed Tony inside. He rubbed his wrists. They had marks on them from the handcuffs. The door clanged behind him and he stood for a moment, letting his eyes adjust to the semidarkness.

The warder said, "Middle bunk," and it took Tony a second to realize that was a command. There was a triple-bunk bed pushed against one wall. His cellmates were already in their bunks, their backs to him. He couldn't see their faces.

In fact, the only face he could see was that of Prince Wendell—his human face, which had been a mystery to Tony before now. The prince looked nothing like the dog, except that they both had brown hair and intelligent eyes. In human form, the prince was good-looking in a bland sort of way and had enough of a receding jawline to make him look vaguely goofy.

Beneath the prince's picture were the words: WORK HARD AND HONESTLY. Apparently that was supposed to be inspiring, but Tony found it laughable. Put anything like that in New York and it would be covered in graffiti in an instant.

He climbed the ladder to his bunk as quietly as possible and hesitated for a moment before getting on the mattress. It smelled faintly of sweat and urine and straw. He had a hunch it was crawling with bugs. But he was very tired and uncertain what to do, and there really was nowhere else for him to go. So he hoisted himself onto it and tried to ignore the cloud of dust that surrounded him as he flopped down.

"So," said the guy on the lower bunk, "what are you in for?"

Tony's heart was pounding. "Quite a serious bank job actually. A few people got hurt but, you know, that's the way it is. What about you?"

"Aggravated assault," said Lower Bunk. "I'm very easily aggravated."

The entire bed rocked, and then a man's face peered up at Tony. It was a small but very hard face with squinty eyes and thin lips.

"I'm Acorn," he said. "Got any metal on you? Knives, forks, coat hangers?"

"Sorry," Tony lied.

"They won't let me have metal," Acorn said. "If you get stabbed, you'll save me the knife, won't you?"

"Of course," Tony said.

Acorn grinned and then settled on his lower bunk. Tony leaned back cautiously, wondering if his mattress felt just the tiniest bit damp and if it did, whether or not he should worry about that.

Suddenly, a massive hairy arm lolled down from the top bunk and Tony had to bite his hand to suppress a scream.

"Do you like carving?" said the guy in the upper bunk who had to be, by process of elimination, Clay Face.

Tony had to swallow three times before he could reply. "Uh, well, not flesh or anything like that, no."

"Look what I'm doing." The massive hand opened to reveal a piece of soap which had been carved into a sculpture. On closer examination, sculpture proved to be too erudite a word for the thing which, if Tony put it in a museum, would have to be called Four Blobs on A Pedestal.

"You have real talent," Tony said.

The whole bunk rocked violently, and Clay Face leaned over the edge. Upside down, he seemed massive, and Tony realized he probably wouldn't be much better viewed right-side up.

"My name is Clay Face the Goblin."

Tony didn't want to say that he'd already figured that out. "Tony Lewis. What are you in for?"

Clay Face smiled. Somehow it made his entire face even more hideous. "Carving."

He said the word the way most men would say their lover's name. Then he leaned in closer.

"Will you be my friend?"

"What exactly does that involve?" Tony asked and then wished he hadn't.

As they got closer to the palace, the Queen felt herself relax just a little. She no longer wanted to cuff the Dog Prince, who still had his face outside the window, tongue lolling. At least he had stopped that hideous barking.

The palace looked worse than she remembered. Neglected, abandoned. She'd have to have her servants fix that.

The coach pulled up behind the massive stone wall, and she descended, followed by the Dog Prince, who looked tempted, for a very short moment, to walk on all fours.

The windows were gone and the wind rustled the curtains. The Queen picked up her skirts and walked up the dusty steps to the main door. As she let herself in, a servant she vaguely recognized hurried toward her and bowed.

"Conceal the coach," the Queen ordered. "Then prepare a room for the Prince."

"Welcome home," the servant said. "We have missed you, Your Majesty."

She ignored the niceties. He should have known better. But she had been gone for years. He could have forgotten. Still, she'd keep an eye on him. No sense having servants who didn't understand her wishes.

The Dog Prince was already inside, his thin body shuddering, his hands still curved like dog's paws in front of him. He was standing at the base of the curved staircase. It had been so grand once, and now it looked even worse than it had when she left, the mighty wood rotting and bits of the banister falling away.

"Who's that then?" the Dog Prince asked.

She followed his gaze. The portrait was still there. It was a full-length portrait of a beautiful woman, her face improved by her cruel cunning.

The Queen smiled. "She was the stepmother who poisoned Snow White with the apple all those years ago. She was once the most powerful woman in the whole of the Nine Kingdoms, and this was but one of her five castles."

"W-W-What happened to her?" the Dog Prince asked.

"When she was finally caught," the Queen said, "they heated a pair of iron slippers over red hot coals and made her dance at Snow White's wedding."

The Dog Prince winced. For once, she had caught his sympathy. She resisted the urge to pet him on the top of his head as she used to do when he was in his dog form.

"Exactly," she said. "Isn't it amazing how cruel good people can be when they put their minds to it? She crawled out into the snow, dragging her raw, blistered, useless feet into a swamp nearby, this crippled woman who was once the fairest of them all. But she kept her magic mirrors and searched for her successor. And that, of course, was me."

The Dog Prince looked at the Queen. She resisted the urge to wipe at her eyes. She was showing a bit more emotion than she should have.

So she clenched her fist and took strength from her plan. "I will finish her work and destroy the House of White forever." Her voice was low and menacing. "And pity the fool who tries to stand up to me."

Chapter Thirteen

The iron shoes were now bright red. Virginia tried not to look at them and failed. She didn't really want to draw attention to them, but she couldn't help it. Her mind was focused on the shoes and how they would feel on her cold, bare feet.

She'd been struggling with her bonds, but she hadn't even been able to loosen them. She wasn't sure what she was going to do. She had a hunch she'd end up dancing for the Troll King and that wouldn't be a pretty sight.

It would also be extremely painful.

The three Trolls who had captured her were studying the shoes too. Virginia wished she knew a way to make them stop, but she didn't. Nothing she had tried had worked.

Blabberwort grabbed a large pair of tongs and walked to the blazing fireplace. Virginia bit her lower lip. They were actually going to go through with this.

She didn't remember fairy tales being so nasty. Then she frowned. Yes, she did. In the original Cinderella, the evil stepsisters carved up their own feet so that they could wear the glass slippers. And didn't that end with birds stealing the stepsisters' eyes? And what about all that blood in the original *Little Mermaid?* Children's movies hadn't done anyone a favor by cleaning up the gore in fairy tales. If they hadn't done that, she would have been better prepared.

Blabberwort stuck the tongs into the shoes and pulled them out of the fire. "Frying tonight," she said. "Frying tonight."

"Keep away from me," Virginia said, as if that would do

any good. Still, she curled her toes under and tried to steel herself against the chair.

Suddenly there was a bang on the other side of her. She turned. A beautifully wrapped gift box had landed on the balcony. Blabberwort set down the red-hot shoes. They burned the dust on the floor, sending little wisps of smoke into the air. She walked toward the package, followed by her brothers.

They circled the box as if it might be a bomb.

"It's a present," Burly said.

Bluebell peered at it. "Does it say, 'To Bluebell'?"

The Trolls weren't looking at Virginia for the first time since she had arrived. She struggled as hard as she could, trying to break the ropes that held her. They burned against her skin, but that was better than those still-red shoes.

Burly bent down and grabbed the gift tag on the side of the box. "It's for me," he said. "Listen to this. 'A present for the strongest, bravest Troll.' "

Blabberwort snatched the note. "You the strongest?" She laughed. "Butter boy. It must be for me."

Virginia struggled even harder. There had to be some way out of these ropes.

"I saw it first," Bluebell said.

"Finders keepers," Burly said.

They both reached for the box, but Blabberwort pulled them back.

"Wait," she said. "It could be a trap. Who knows we're here?"

All three of them backed away from the box. Virginia cursed silently. She wanted them to focus on it so that she could escape.

"Suck an elf," Burly said. "You're right."

"I wonder what it is, though," Bluebell said.

They looked at the box. Virginia could see the temptation on their faces.

"You know what it smells like?" Burly asked.

They crouched and sniffed, getting dreamy smiles on their faces.

"Leather!" they said in unison.

Virginia was struggling so hard that the chair was wobbling. If the Trolls had been paying attention, they would have heard the thuds. She tried to tell herself to keep quiet, but she knew this might be her last chance.

She glanced at the iron shoes. Still red. They were making scorch marks on the floor.

"Shoes," Bluebell said, waving his hands over the still-closed box.

"It could be boots," Blabberwort said. "Look at the height of the box."

"Boots," Burly said. "And my size by the looks of things."

He bent to open the box. Virginia looked away, concentrating on those pesky ropes. Then she heard a whack, followed by a thud. When she turned back, she saw Burly unconscious on the floor, Blabberwort holding a poker over him, and Bluebell looking at her as if she were trouble.

"Had to do it," Blabberwort said.

"Of course you did, of course you did," Bluebell said. "I would have done the same."

"They're clearly not his, are they?" Blabberwort said. "They're not addressed to him."

"You did the right thing," Bluebell said. "It's mob rule otherwise, isn't it?"

"Exactly," Blabberwort said. "A box like that can contain only one thing. Ladies' boots."

The two remaining Trolls looked at each other. Virginia held her breath. Who'd have thought that she might get free because of infighting?

"They're mine," Bluebell said. "You know they are. They're a present for me."

"They're mine!" Blabberwort shouted back.

"Mine!" Bluebell shouted.

They started to punch each other, then stopped and smiled

at each other. The smiles were obviously fake. Even Virginia could see through them.

"Look," Blabberwort said, "obviously we can't both have them. Let's just spin a coin to decide who gets them."

"Fair enough," Bluebell said. "See if you've got a coin in your pocket."

"You have to look as well," Blabberwort said.

They both pretended to reach into their pockets and then both swung fists at the same time. Virginia saw it coming, but apparently they didn't. They knocked each other out, and fell to either side of her.

She let out a small breath. One problem solved, at least for the short term. But she still hadn't figured a way out of these bonds. And the Troll King would be back at any moment. He was a lot more dangerous than his children. He would probably blame her for their unconscious state.

She shuddered, and then she heard a rustling behind her. As she turned, she saw the man who had attacked her at her grandmother's house swinging in the balcony window by a rope.

"Well, hello," he said as he swung back and forth. "Rescue is at hand."

"Don't come any nearer!" Virginia ordered.

He dropped off the rope and walked toward her, smiling. "Don't worry," he said, "I'm not who I used to be. I've had extensive therapy. I realize I have been using food as a substitute for love, and I have the books to prove it."

He opened a grungy pack he'd been carrying on his back and showed her the books inside. She looked down, fascinated in spite of herself.

"*How to Survive in Spite of Your Parents, The Courage to Heal, When Am I Going to be Happy?*, and *Help for the Bedwetting Child*, which I picked up by mistake. I've got the lot."

She struggled against those damn ropes. "You come an inch nearer and I'll shout my head off."

"That is what is known as an empty threat." He got quite

close to her, his breath against her neck. She flinched. He licked his lips, sniffed her, and then sighed with pleasure.

She remembered her grandmother, trussed up like a Christmas goose, still angry because of all the spices in her hair, and shuddered. He reached for her ropes and started to untie her. Apparently, he hadn't missed the shudder either.

"I hope you don't mind me saying this," he said, "but I get the feeling you still don't completely trust me."

"I don't trust you at all," Virginia said. "You tried to eat my grandmother."

"Oh, no," Wolf said. "I was just being playful. Wolfies just pretend to do naughty things. I would never have really eaten her. She was a tough old bird."

His eyes were gleaming. He had a wicked smile. But it was charming, just the same. Virginia steeled herself so that she wouldn't be drawn into his spell.

"I wouldn't hurt a sausage," he said. "Butter would not melt in my mouth. Well, it would melt, of course it would, but very slowly."

The moment her hands were free, Virginia leapt to her feet and backed away from him, nearly tripping on a Troll. He moved toward her, hands out. It seemed as if he were trying to calm her. But if that was what he was trying to do, he was failing miserably. She looked around for a weapon, but didn't see anything close at hand.

"Huff-puff," he said, "I give you my solemn Wolf word that you are safe with me. You are safe as a brick-built pig house. Now, wait here a moment while I plan our escape. We are in romantically reckless danger."

He nodded once to make sure she would stay put, and then he walked to the balcony and looked over. Wolf word? She frowned. Was that really his name? Wolf?

Stranger things did happen. She backed a little farther away from him and continued to look for something, anything, to get her out of this mess.

"How are you at climbing?" Wolf asked. "I nearly fell off three times coming up."

She stared at the shoe closet. The magic shoes glittered. They called to her. They were beautiful. And if she put them on, she could escape him. She could escape all of them.

She walked toward the shoes. "Those incredible shoes," she muttered. "They made him invisible."

"Yes, I know," Wolf said.

"But they made him *invisible*," Virginia said, wondering why she was speaking out loud.

"Don't touch them," he said, as he surveyed the room. "They'll make you want to wear them all the time." He frowned. "Balcony or corridor, that is the question."

He walked across the room to the door and opened it an inch. She walked up to the shoes. She'd never seen a more beautiful pair.

"I'm not going to touch them," Virginia said. "I just wondered how they worked."

"They're working on you even now," Wolf said. He sounded annoyed. "Leave them well alone."

She snatched the shoes and was about to put them on, when Wolf murmured, "Corridor, I think."

His words brought her to herself. She glanced at him. He got a panicked look on his face. "No! Quick! Balcony!" he said. "There's someone coming."

And that would be the Troll King. She didn't have time to put the shoes on. She ran to the balcony. Wolf waited for her, holding what she had thought was a rope but which was actually a bit of ivy. She hoped the vine was strong enough to hold both of them.

She shinnied down it, amazed at what fear could make her do, and the moment she hit the ground, she ran. She could hear Wolf behind her, breathing hard. The first chance she got, she'd put on those shoes and give him the slip.

Two guards were running toward them, but she dodged them as she crossed the unkempt lawn. She ran as far as she could down the rutted road, but she wasn't up to a marathon. Her head still hurt. She slowed down to a fast walk.

Still, Wolf had to struggle to keep up with her. She glanced over her shoulder. What had she done to this guy? He seemed determined to be near her. And she didn't want to end up like Grandma, no matter how he thought he had reformed. No matter how cute he was.

It was still daylight out here, but the sky was growing dark. And it wasn't the darkness of night, but the darkness of an impending storm. She'd been unconscious for most of the trip to the Troll palace. She hadn't seen the countryside, and she really wasn't sure where she was. One glance at that map in the prison had been helpful, but she hadn't memorized it.

"Excuse me, miss?" Wolf said. "Where do you think you're going, exactly?"

"Back to the prison," Virginia said.

"*Back* to the prison?" Wolf asked. "That would not be my first—"

"I've got to find my father," Virginia said. "And then I want to go straight back home."

"All right, all right," Wolf said, "but not this way. Virginia, listen, please, you won't survive five minutes unless you follow me. We must avoid the road and go this way."

He was behind her. She turned and looked in the direction he was pointing. They were facing a forest, but it wasn't like any forest she'd ever seen before. Among the normal trees were huge beanstalks. Giant beanstalks. She couldn't count all of them. They rose up to the sky, dwarfing the regular trees. And they looked hideous. She hadn't realized that beanstalks were so ugly up close.

"Oh, my God," she said. "I'm not going in there."

But she had a hunch she'd have no choice.

Tony was on his hands and knees in the corridor. He was scrubbing the flagstone floor. His hands stung—the soap wasn't Ivory and it had a peculiar smell—and the water was ice-cold.

His skin was already red and raw. He couldn't imagine what it would be like after hours of this stuff.

If he had a wish left, he'd wish for his old life back. Sure, he'd hated the janitorial job and Mr. Murray, but it hadn't been anything like this.

"Pssst, Anthony?" The voice belonged to Prince Wendell.

Tony looked around and realized he was outside the governor's office. Wendell still had to be inside.

"How did you know it was me?" Tony whispered.

"You have a distinctive, unwashed smell," Prince Wendell said. Tony flushed. "What are you doing?"

"Cleaning the floor," Tony said. "What do you think I'm doing?"

"Have you got a soap bar?"

"Why, do you want me to wash you?"

"Stay there!" Prince Wendell said. "Don't go away."

As if there were somewhere he could go. Still, Tony crawled over to the door and peered through the keyhole. He could see the Governor in an adjoining room talking to a couple of the warders. Prince Wendell had jumped on a table and was walking toward a key ring. He took a key off the ring, jumped off the table, and came toward the door.

Tony backed away as Prince Wendell shoved the key under the gap between the door and the stone floor.

"This is the Governor's master key," Prince Wendell said. "Make an impression in the soap. Hurry, he'll be back any moment."

Tony took the key in his hands. He was shaking. What would they do to him if they found him with this key? He didn't want to think about it.

He grabbed the soap bar and shoved the key into it, pressing hard. At that moment, a warder walked by. Tony nearly swallowed his own tongue.

"Very stubborn stain, sir," Tony said.

The warder didn't seem to care. Tony waited until he was gone before taking the key from the soap. He looked both ways down the corridor before shoving the key under the door. Then he watched as Prince Wendell reattached the key to the ring.

Tony went back to his soap bar and studied it for a moment. Funny how something as small as a mold for a key could give a guy hope.

Relish the Troll King was throwing all his shoes from his closet, but he already knew that his favorites weren't there. The girl had taken his magic shoes. His invisible magic shoes. And he hadn't even seen her dance for him.

He'd come in, found his iron shoes cooling, his children out cold, and a box in the middle of the floor. He'd slapped his children awake, but that hadn't given him any satisfaction. And now that he knew the shoes were missing—well, he threw the remaining ones at Burly, Blabberwort, and Bluebell.

"Idiots!" the Troll King shouted. "Fools! I can't leave you alone for a minute."

"It wasn't our fault," Burly said. "She made this magic shoe box appear."

They were convinced that tiny girl was a witch. He glared at his son, then walked to the box that they had somehow failed to open. He flicked off the top. Inside was a pink child's purse and a note.

Relish grabbed the note and read it aloud. " 'Best wishes from Wolf.' "

His children bowed their heads.

"Imbeciles!" Relish shouted again. "We must go after them immediately. Get the dogs."

The dogs would find her and her friend Wolf. And his favorite shoes. And once he had them, they'd never escape again.

Chapter Fourteen

The beanstalks had a strong green smell mixed with a hay-like odor and the dry stench of overcooked beans. The smell was powerful and unlike anything Virginia had ever sniffed before. She walked beneath the stalks, the vines and branches winding over her head. The tallness of them made her think of a trip she had taken to California as a young girl. The redwoods had seemed magnificent to her, but they were tiny in comparison to the beanstalks.

She wasn't trying to get away from Wolf now. There really wasn't any point. He was the one who knew how to get from this beanstalk forest to the prison. She could only hope that he really would lead her there.

The shoes, though, tempted her like an itch that she knew she shouldn't scratch.

Up ahead, she noticed a large stone statue of a young boy. As she got closer, she realized that the statue had been neglected. It was covered in vines, and part of its head had been hacked off. Troll graffiti marred the base, but she could still read the inscription:

BRAVE JACK
FIRST MAYOR OF BEANTOWN

She frowned. Everything was so strange here, and yet oddly familiar. The tales she had learned as a child mingled with what she could see and made the world she had believed in turn into something that wasn't quite real.

She turned to Wolf. "Is that Jack of—"

"Jack and the Beanstalk, yes," Wolf said.

She nodded. The shoes tingled against her. She reached for them, felt them beneath her fingers. They glittered.

"This used to be a very prosperous area," Wolf was saying. He wasn't looking at her. "Before the beanstalks sprouted everywhere and polluted the land."

She slipped the shoes over her feet, and felt the tingle run through her body.

"The Trolls were given the land here as their kingdom," Wolf was saying.

She held her hand up to her face and almost giggled when she saw nothing.

"And that's why they hate Prince Wendell so much, because he has a juicy, fertile kingdom, and—" Wolf stopped talking and turned around. Then around again. Virginia suppressed another giggle. He couldn't see her.

"Virginia?" Wolf called out.

He continued to spin like a wind-up toy on low, and then he stopped, putting his hands on his hips.

"Please tell me you didn't take the Troll King's magic shoes," Wolf said, clearly disgusted.

All right, she thought. *I won't tell you anything at all.* She put a hand to her head. Slightly dizzy. Almost drunk. The urge to giggle rose within her again. She wondered how long she could suppress it. Long enough to escape pretty boy here?

She didn't know, but she was going to try to find out.

Tony stood at a table in the center of the dining room, on the far side so that he could see the guard pacing above. The room seemed smaller and narrower when filled with most of the prison population.

So far as Tony could tell, they were all men, although some had wings. Others had scrunched up faces like those Trolls that he and Virginia had been running from. Others—like the guy across the table—had scars dividing their faces as if they were baseballs.

The Governor stood in the front of the room with a few other warders. The map was behind them. And on the table in front of the convicts were bowls of something that smelled like four-day-old pea soup combined with overcooked baked beans and rotting hay. Tony had a hunch mealtime was not going to be his most favorite time here at the Snow White Memorial Prison.

Everyone was standing with hands clasped in front, although no one would tell him why. At a short movement from the Governor's whip, the convicts around Tony started to recite. In unison, they said:

"We promise to serve Prince Wendell, kind and brave Monarch of the Fourth Kingdom, and pledge to mend our naughty ways so that we may all live happily ever after."

Then they sat down. Tony suppressed the urge to look at all of them as if they were crazy. Crazy they might be, but they were also dangerous.

"I have some very bad news," the Governor said. "A new era of punishment is upon you. From now on, all privileges will be withdrawn."

The prisoners at all of the tables started banging metal cups and fists against the wood. The entire room seemed alive.

"Unfortunately, a new inmate, who must remain anonymous for his own safety, has refused to tell me how he helped the Queen escape."

Oh, great. Tony tried to duck his head but it didn't help. The Governor walked toward him, making sure everyone knew who he was talking about.

"If you should find out who this man is, please treat him with compassion, as you would any other new inmate." The Governor stopped right behind Tony. "Don't think 'well, I can't have any visitors or get any exercise because of this scum' and use it as an excuse to kick him unconscious."

The pounding had stopped. Everyone was looking at Tony, even the guys with one eye or, worse yet, one eye in the middle of their foreheads. The Governor moved away, then signaled the warders, who stopped at their posts by the door.

The convicts continued to stare at Tony. He gave them his best Mr. Murray-suck-up grin and said, "Boy can I understand why no one likes that guy."

And unsurprisingly, no one laughed. Tony licked his upper lip, then looked down at the green slop in his bowl. That was where the stench was coming from. The slop was still steaming slightly, which made it seem even more unappealing.

"What is this?" he asked.

His words were like a cue to the others to eat. Most of them turned their attention to the food, such as it was. Clay Face was slurping from his bowl as if he hadn't eaten in a week.

"It's baked beanstalk," Clay Face said between slurps.

"Baked beans?" Tony said hopefully. He took a spoonful and swallowed.

"Beanstalk," Clay Face said.

Tony spat out the food into his hand. "I can't eat this. It tastes like an old mattress."

"No, it doesn't," an old convict said. "Old mattress has a sweaty, meaty taste."

Tony didn't want to know how the old guy knew that. "How often is this on the menu?"

"Three times a day," Clay Face said.

Tony lifted his glass. It was full of pale green juice. It looked like something Virginia would buy at the vegetarian juice bars that dotted the trendy parts of Manhattan. He took a deep breath and a sip.

It tasted like cold pea soup mixed with baked beans and hay, with some rancid meat thrown in for flavor.

He spat the juice out all over the table.

"That's beanstalk juice," Acorn said. "Takes a bit of getting used to."

Tony put the glass down. He was thirsty but not that thirsty.

He could see, just beyond the doors, the stairs to the cellar. Down there was the mirror that would get him back to his world, where green juice tasted like lemon-lime Gatorade and where green slop would at least have some salt in it.

"Supposing I wanted to, uh, speak to someone about getting a, for sake of argument, small piece of metal made," Tony asked. "How would I go about that? Who's the Mr. Big around here?"

Baseball Face looked both ways to make sure no one was listening, then leaned forward and whispered, "You want anything bought, sold, borrowed, or made in here, you have to go see the Tooth Fairy."

Tony wasn't sure he heard that right. "The who?"

"The prison dentist," Acorn said.

"And how would I get to see him?"

"Easy," Baseball Face said. He brought his right hand back and punched Tony in the mouth. Tony recoiled backwards. Pain shot through his upper jaw. Then he stared at Baseball Face as if he were crazy, which he probably was.

"Tell the Governor what happened, and you won't see tomorrow," Baseball Face said with a green-goo grin.

"Teef . . ." Tony said, hand over his bleeding mouth. "He's knocked my teef out."

"Shh," Acorn said. "We'll take care of it."

Tony felt the blood ooze through his fingers. The other prisoners watched as if the show weren't quite good enough. Acorn finished eating his green slime and then stood. He went to one of the warders and beckoned Tony to follow.

Tony did.

"This man hurt his front teeth on dinner," Acorn was saying as Tony approached. "I think he needs to see the Tooth Fairy."

"Prisoners aren't supposed to fraternize outside of the dining hall," the warder said.

"Then you tell Prince Wendell, the next time he comes here, that a man can't get good and necessary dental treatment."

The warder frowned. Apparently Wendell—in human form—had some pull around here. "Make it fast," he said.

Acorn nodded. He crooked a finger, and Tony leaned down. The pain in the front of his mouth grew worse. Acorn gave him instructions on how to get to the Tooth Fairy's cell and then pushed him in the right direction. Tony looked over his shoulder. The other prisoners were grinning. Maybe he would finish his meal, blood or no blood.

"Go," Acorn whispered.

Tony sighed and hurried down the corridor. The bleeding had stopped, leaving an iron taste in his mouth. His tongue played with his front teeth. They wiggled and there were some strands of skin around them that hadn't been there before.

It didn't take him long to reach the Tooth Fairy's. A filthy sign above the door let him know it was the right place. The cell door, surprisingly, was open. Tony went inside.

The Tooth Fairy turned and grinned. The Tooth Fairy was not the pretty woman of childhood myth, but a dumpy guy with long blue wings. He had the worst teeth Tony had ever seen.

"It's no good," the Tooth Fairy said. "They'll all have to come out."

"You haffn't looked in my mowf yet," Tony said.

"Do you want some candy?"

"Candy?" Tony asked. "You're a dentiff, you're not supposed to be giving people candy."

"Why not?" the Tooth Fairy asked.

"Because it rots people's teef."

"Rubbish."

"Of corf it does," Tony said.

"Well excuse me," the Tooth Fairy said, "but who's the tooth extractor here? You or me?"

Tony sat down nervously. If he wasn't in so much pain, he wouldn't have done it. But something had to change. He was getting a headache that ran up the bridge of his nose and into his forehead.

"I'll just put the straps on you," the Tooth Fairy said.

"The what?" Tony asked.

"The Straps of Comfort," the Tooth Fairy said.

"I'm not being strapped in," Tony said.

The Tooth Fairy strapped him into what looked to Tony like an electric chair. Since all of the lights were candles, though, he could only hope that the one torture these creatures hadn't heard of was an electric chair. And he wasn't about to tell them.

"Tooth decay is caused by three things," the Tooth Fairy said. "Number one, poor diet; number two, not brushing properly; and number three, Bad Fairies."

He pulled down a roller chart with pictures of the mouth and pointed to a diagram of malevolent-looking fairies.

That was it. This wasn't Oz and Toto, nor was it even as good as the worst dentist in New York. "I'm going," Tony said.

The Tooth Fairy leaned forward and reached into Tony's mouth with stubby, dirty fingers. Tony tried to move his head away. The Tooth Fairy waggled Tony's front teeth and the pain was enormous.

"Does that hurt?" the Tooth Fairy asked.

"Yes!"

He waggled them some more. The pain grew.

"Does *that* hurt?"

"Yes!"

"What about *this*?"

The Tooth Fairy yanked with all his strength and pulled out Tony's front teeth. Tony's mouth felt like fire. He screamed as blood dripped onto his tongue.

The Tooth Fairy proudly held up two front teeth that Tony had never before seen in their entirety. They had been good front teeth. Tony missed them already.

"Loose teeth," the Tooth Fairy said. "I thought so. Don't worry, I've got a whole bag of magic teeth here."

The Tooth Fairy grabbed a filthy bag and opened it. Inside were hundreds of teeth.

Tony's tongue played with the empty spot in the front of his mouth. He knew enough about medicine to know that someone else's teeth—someone else's dirty teeth—would make him sick forever. He had to turn the Tooth Fairy's attention to something else, and quickly.

He went back to his real reason for coming here.

"Look, please help me," Tony said. "I have to get a key made from this."

He reached into his pocket and removed the bar of soap. The Tooth Fairy's eyes narrowed. He looked over both shoulders to make certain no one else was watching.

"What's it worth?" the Tooth Fairy asked.

Tony took off his watch and waved it. He was certain these creatures had never seen anything like it before.

"This is a hand-worn clock," Tony said. "See, it's got miniature hands, and it tells the time perfectly."

The Tooth Fairy walked across the room and swung open a cupboard door. Inside were fifty gold and silver pocket watches.

"I know," the Tooth Fairy said. "We call them watches."

Tony closed his eyes. His mouth ached and was still bleeding. The soap bar made his fingers itch. And now, all of this had been for nothing.

The hope he'd felt after Wendell's good idea was fading fast.

Wolf could just barely smell Virginia ahead of him in the forest. The stench of beanstalk knocked out all but the keenest scents. If he wasn't so attuned to her, he probably wouldn't have been able to follow her.

She was making her way to a giant thousand-year-old beanstalk, surrounded by barbed wire and spikes. At its base was a sign that read, NO CLIMBERS!

It was accompanied by the image of a giant, and another warning: TRESPASSERS WILL BE BREAKFAST!

Not that anyone would want to trespass. Above, Wolf could hear the sound of booming drunken voices and what might have been breaking glass.

For a moment, he lost her scent. His eyes narrowed.

"Virginia?" he called.

He was more than a little panicked. If he lost her now, he lost her for good. "I know you think you're safe in those shoes, but nothing could be further from the truth. Anything you get from a Troll is bound to be bad and dangerous."

He sniffed, but he couldn't catch her lovely scent.

"Oh, Virginia, where are you?"

He thought he caught her scent, but he wasn't sure. And she wasn't saying anything. Then the air near the base of the stalk rippled, and slowly Virginia appeared.

"Oh, no," she said.

He gave her his most rakish grin. He really was pleased to see her. "Hello, again," he said.

Virginia jumped. Apparently she hadn't realized he was right beside her.

Wolf leaned against the nearest tree, relaxing now that he had found her. He said, "They're not fully recharged, you see. They don't stay invisible very long without a proper break. That's a design fault in the shoes, one of many, in fact."

Virginia tried to run from him but he leapt out and grabbed her arm. She punched him with her free hand before he pinned her with the other arm.

"You're not having them," Virginia said.

She was talking nonsense. "Having what?" he asked.

"The shoes," Virginia said. "They're mine."

He wrestled her for a moment, then yanked the shoes off her pretty little feet. She put out a hand to catch her balance. Her eyes were glassy, as if she were drunk.

"If you don't get rid of them now," Wolf said, "you won't be able to later."

She shook her head, and her eyes cleared. Maybe the spell

had broken. "You're right. I don't want them. They made me feel very strange."

He held on to the shoes so tightly that the strange material bit into his hands. Virginia stared at them. They were sparkling.

"It felt so powerful being invisible." Virginia gave a weak little laugh as if she knew how ridiculous she sounded. "How did you know where I was?"

"I could smell you," Wolf said. "Follow me."

He led her through the forest, passing another giant beanstalk. He couldn't help himself: he had to look up. Virginia did too. The stalk seemed to disappear into the clouds.

Then a loud, booming voice echoed down from above. The sound of it shook the ground.

"There's someone up there," Virginia said.

"He's started fee-fi-fo-ing." Wolf shuddered. He'd been through this before and it was not one of his most pleasant memories. "Let's get a move on in case he's sick."

They ran through the beanstalk forest. They stopped for breath beneath another stalk. This one had the number 19 painted on it in red. Words were written into its trunk: CONDEMNED. MOULD. DO NOT CLIMB.

Virginia peered at it as if she couldn't believe what she was reading.

"There are about seventy beanstalks left, but not many are occupied these days," Wolf explained. "Giants drink so much they rarely have time to reproduce."

"Can I ask you a question?" Virginia asked.

"Of course," Wolf said.

"Do you think I'm sexy?"

He turned to face her, astonished. She was leaning against one of the stalks, her body jutted out provocatively at him. She was beautiful, from the tips of her little toes to her perfect mouth to her—he sighed. Her glassy eyes.

"You're the kind of man I suppose I should be scared of," she said softly in a way that made him know she was going to make an exception for him.

An exception he very much wanted.

"Oh, Virginia," Wolf said, "much as I would love to believe what you're saying to me, I'm afraid it is the shoes talking. You will say anything to put them back on again."

She blinked, then shook her head. "Oh, my God," she said. "Yes, I'm really sorry. I don't know what came over me. You're quite right to take them off me."

"They bring out very strange things, the shoes," Wolf said. "Whatever you're suppressing."

"I'm not suppressing anything," Virginia said.

She could believe that if she wanted, but he didn't. And he found the whole incident quite curious, and quite hopeful. Then a stench wafted across the air. He sniffed, and the hair on the back of his neck rose.

"Trolls," Wolf said. "They have found us. Oh, cripes. Are we in big, big trouble now."

Through the trees, he could see distant lanterns swinging, and far away, the sound of barking dogs.

"They have dogs," Wolf said. "They'll sniff us out. Run! Run!"

Virginia lit out like she'd been made to run. Wolf had to hurry to keep up with her. He only hoped it would be fast enough. If the Trolls caught them now, things would go bad for them.

Very bad indeed.

Chapter Fifteen

🔳 Prince Wendell was tied to the table. Three meals sat in front of him, and with his new doggy nose, he could smell the poison in them. His stomach rumbled, but his self-control never wavered. How dumb did the prison governor think he was anyway? Even a dog—a real dog—would have discovered this trick.

A familiar smell caught his nose. Wendell turned. Tony was outside the Governor's office. Wendell made his way to the door, stood on his hind legs, and peered through the keyhole. Tony was staggering down the hallway. His shirt was spotted with blood and he appeared to have new front teeth.

How could that be possible?

Wendell sat down in front of the door and waited, hoping Tony was coming to him.

A moment later, he heard Tony whisper, "I've got it, Prince."

"Brilliant," Wendell said. "The Governor's in the kitchen making me another poisoned dinner. Use the key now. Open the door. There's spare uniforms in here. You can put one on and just march me out of the prison."

Wendell could hear Tony fumbling with the lock. He shoved the key in the keyhole and attempted to turn it. It didn't turn. Wendell started panting, then made himself stop. Panting was so undignified.

"Hurry up," he whispered. Then he peered under the door.

Two warders grabbed Tony from behind. The Governor stood beside him, with a steaming plate of meat.

Wendell's stomach growled again.

"You must really love pain," the Governor said.

"No, oh no, please," Tony begged. "I was just walking along the corridor and I slipped over and hit your door and ended up kneeling in front of it."

The Governor removed the key from the lock and examined it. He didn't look happy.

"Take him downstairs," the Governor said. "Tie him to the dining table and give him fifty beanstalk lashes in front of the entire prison. Right now."

Beanstalks were the toughest thing known to man. Wendell had seen backs after they'd been lashed. It wasn't a pretty sight. Wendell buried his head in his paws. "Sorry about that, Anthony."

Then the door opened. The Governor came inside. Tony was nowhere in sight, but Wendell could hear him, screaming, down the hallway.

The Governor set the plate of meat in front of Wendell, and the acrid scent of poison nearly made him gag. Next time, he wanted to say, get a poison a dog couldn't smell.

But the Governor didn't seem too concerned with him. Instead, the Governor indicated that three other warders follow him into the main room.

"I've got keys going missing," the Governor said. "I've got Trolls and wolves and Queens missing. What in the fairying forest has happened to basic security in this prison?"

Faintly, Wendell heard the snap of a lash and another scream. Poor Tony.

"Sir," one warder said, "while we were searching the prison we found that the door to the cellar was unlocked at the time of the Queen's breakout. It is possible she escaped that way."

Another snap of the lash. Another scream. Wendell winced.

"What's down there?" the Governor asked.

"Just a load of old junk," the warder said. "It's been there for hundreds of years, before this was a prison."

Snap. Scream. Wendell wished he could cover his ears.

"Take tomorrow's work detail off the laundry room," the Governor said, "and have them clear out the whole thing, top to bottom."

The warders nodded; then they left. The Governor went with them, probably to supervise Tony's torture. Wendell stretched his rope to the limit to peer at the Governor's desk. On it was the work detail. Wendell could just barely reach it.

He grabbed a pencil in his teeth and slowly scrawled Tony's name on the bottom of the sheet.

Downstairs, the lash snapped again, and Tony screamed.

It had been a long time since Wolf climbed a beanstalk. His hands were scratched. This one wasn't well cared for. He crouched on a vine twenty feet above the ground, Virginia beside him. He kept the magic shoes as far from her as possible, but she didn't seem to want them anymore.

For all he knew, that was a ploy to make him careless. He wouldn't be careless, not with those things.

She was peering down intently, breathing very softly. He was having trouble breathing that quietly. Her proximity was quite arousing, even if there were Trolls and dogs lurking nearby.

As if in answer to his thought, the Troll King appeared below them, leading two giant Dobermans. The dogs were snarling and drooling and sniffing the ground. Wolf felt his hackles rise. He wanted to leap on their backs and tear their guts out. He wanted to bite their necks until they died. He wanted to—but he wouldn't. He would hide up here like a good human until they went away.

"Keep moving," the Troll King said. "They are very near. The dogs can smell them. Don't let them escape again."

"No, Dad," the three children said in unison.

After a moment, the Troll King and the dogs passed by.

Wolf could see only the tops of the children's heads and that didn't help him distinguish between the males. Only Blabberwort's orange hair made her stand out. Fortunately, he recognized the voices.

"Got any magic mushrooms, Blabberwort?" Burly asked.

"I've got some dwarf moss," Blabberwort said. "It'll blow your head off, though. I saw fairies for three days last time I took it."

"Roll us a giant," Bluebell said. "This could be a long night."

The Trolls moved away, following their father deeper into the forest.

Virginia was clinging to the vine so hard that her knuckles had turned white. Apparently she had thought they were going to find her.

Wolf turned to Virginia and whispered, "Beanstalk has a very potent smell. It puts off the dogs."

Virginia rubbed her nose with the back of one hand. "You don't have to tell me."

"We'll stay here until it's safe," Wolf said.

The lanterns were small blobs in the distance.

"How did you get involved in all this in the first place?" Virginia asked.

Wolf, fortunately, was looking down. The last thing he wanted to do was tell her the truth. "Well, I happened to find myself at a loose end . . ."

"You were in that prison, weren't you?" Virginia asked. "What were you in for?"

Sharp girl. He glanced at her. "Oh, nothing much. Just a bit of sheep worrying, you know. And putting a wolf in a prison cell with nowhere to bound, only able to stare at the sky through the bars, it's inhuman."

Virginia nodded. "So you think I should put them on again?"

"What?" He frowned at her.

"I'm sure the shoes are fully charged up again now."

Virginia tried to grab the shoes from him, but Wolf held them away from her.

"No!" Wolf said.

"They're mine," she said. "They—what's that?"

"Oh, it's just my tail," Wolf said. He was embarrassed that it got out. He stuffed it into a little hole in the back of his trousers. The wolf parts of him always seemed to appear at the most inopportune moments.

"Your tail?" Her eyes were wide.

"It's not very big at this time of the month," he said. "Just a little brush."

"You've got a tail?" Virginia said.

"So?" Wolf snapped. "You've got succulent breasts, but I don't go on about them all the time, do I?"

Virginia was peering at his back end which, if truth be told, wasn't such a bad thing. Finally, he smiled.

"Go on," Wolf said softly. "Touch it. It's perfectly normal."

She reached out, then closed her hand into a fist. "If it's normal, why do you keep it hidden all the time?"

"Because, in case you haven't noticed," Wolf said, "people don't like wolves."

Her gaze met his. He nodded encouragingly. "Give it a stroke," Wolf said. "Go on, it's not going to bite."

Virginia stretched out her hand and touched it. Her fingers were very gentle.

He moaned and then shifted slightly.

"What?" Virginia asked, pulling her hand back.

"With the fur," Wolf said. "Not against it."

She touched it again. Her fingers felt better the second time.

"It's very soft," Virginia said.

"Thank you," Wolf said.

The Queen lifted the cellar door. Billows of dust flowed around her but she barely noticed. The two servants behind her coughed. She grabbed a lamp and held it out as she walked down the cellar steps.

Cobwebs and dust and darkness. The place smelled of damp and rot. It had been a long time since anyone had been down here. She shivered slightly. It was cold as well.

She could feel the servants' fear behind her. But she knew better than to fear. She knew what she was looking for.

When she reached the dirt floor, she slowly drew a large circle with her feet. Then, carefully, she marked five Xs in it. When she was done, she stood aside.

The servants glanced at her as if they didn't believe what she wanted. But she had briefed them before they came. They lifted their shovels and dug on the first X, carefully, just as she had explained.

It only took a few moments to unearth the mirror from its shallow grave. One of the men went to pull it out, but she held out a hand, stopping him. It was better to remove them all at once.

The servants dug the second hole, then the third, fourth, and fifth, unearthing the remaining mirrors. Then she nodded and let them bring the mirrors forth.

Each mirror was ancient, and each was different, a product of its time. Some had metal frames, some wooden. One was smaller than the others and yet she could feel its magic.

She stared at them all, still covered with dirt, and longed to have them in the privacy of her own room. She smiled at her own reflection presented in all five mirrors, and said, "It's so good to have the power back."

Chapter Sixteen

Tony's feet were chained together and he was manacled to fourteen other prisoners. They shuffled, shuffled, shuffled their way to the prison cellar. He looked at it in anguish. He had wanted to return here since he'd arrived—well, not quite since he'd arrived, but since he'd found out what a horrible place this was—and now he couldn't escape.

Heaven knew he wanted to more than anything. The whipping last night was a new low in his life. He could still feel the sting of the beanstalk lash on his back and shoulders. If only he had one wish left, he'd wish for good health for the rest of his life—or maybe he'd make it a combined wish. Good health and freedom. Certainly no one would deny him that.

No one except the Prison Governor.

The line of convicts extended from the pile of junk to a back wall that was made of wood. As Tony watched, the wall went up to reveal a dock and a boat moored alongside it. He was at the very edge of the opening. The fresh air smelled better than he expected, better than it did in Central Park even, and the sky was so blue and beautiful, it made him want to cry.

From where he stood, he couldn't even see the pile of junk clearly. He had no chance of searching for that mirror.

"Pay attention," the Governor said. "Everything in here has to be cleared out. Form a human chain and chuck everything into that boat."

The warders spread the convicts out to the limits of their

chains—about four feet apart from each other. There was no one on the other side of Tony. He looked at the boat. There was at least twelve feet between him and the boat itself.

"Uh, excuse me?" Tony said.

"What?" the Governor asked.

"Well, it's quite a long way," Tony said, pointing to the boat. "Won't we break some of the more delicate objects?"

"What do you think this is, Lewis?" the Governor demanded. "An elves' underwear party? This is scrap. Now do as you're told and shut up."

The convicts picked objects up and threw them along the human chain. It took a moment for the first item—a box made of wood and full of splinters—to reach Tony at the end. He tossed it to the boat. The box smashed on impact. So did the china that followed, and then the carriage wheel.

Tony tried not to look at the mess by the boat. Instead, he kept watching for the mirror. He'd go through it, dragging the convicts with him, if he had to.

A bowl fell to the ground halfway up the chain. He winced at the sound.

He'd go through the mirror with everyone attached, only if the mirror made it all the way to him. In one piece.

Blabberwort stood near a huge, menacing dog. She yanked on its collar just to hear it whimper. It did, and she grinned. Her father didn't even notice.

He seemed distressed to be in front of the prison again. She didn't like it either and neither, it seemed, did her brothers. Nor did the contingent of Trolls who accompanied them, most of whom had spent time in this prison at one point or another.

Her father was pacing up and down and down and up, which was always a bad sign.

"I'm not questioning your judgment, Dad, but what are we doing hanging around the prison?" Bluebell might not have been questioning their father's judgment, but Bluebell's was clearly lacking. No one spoke to their father when he was in this kind of mood. "We've only just got out."

Blabberwort cringed, expecting an outburst, but all her father said was, "Shut up."

She frowned. He wasn't paying attention to anything except his own pacing and the little bits of flour he was dropping as he moved. The flour was turning the grass white, like the first snowfall of the season.

He moved to the front of the prison gate, sprinkling flour as he walked.

"Why did the witch steal the shoes?" her father said suddenly. "Obvious. To get back into the prison."

To rescue someone! Blabberwort was beginning to understand what her father was thinking. There were only a few ways to catch someone in magic shoes.

"Flour," Blabberwort said. "Brilliant idea, Dad."

Her father ignored her praise, but he did stop pacing. "Burly, patrol clockwise around the prison. Bluebell, go the other way to clockwise around the prison. Blabberwort, wait with me in the bushes over here and check the flour every fifteen minutes for invisible footsteps."

She nodded. And even though her father hadn't given the last instruction, she knew what it would be. If she saw footprints, she would go get him.

She never wanted to face the witch alone again.

The morning sunlight was cooler than Virginia expected. She had a vague headache, as if she had been drinking. And she really wanted to put on those shoes. Hair of the dog, as some of her customers would say.

Or hair of the wolf.

She frowned, not liking that thought.

She was beside Wolf in a grove of trees, not far from the river. Ahead she could see the giant dogs that accompanied the Trolls and the Trolls themselves pacing. Wolf assured her that they couldn't see, hear, or smell them from this angle, and since he seemed to have a relatively strong animal component himself, she believed him.

She was believing him more and more these days.

"Do you think Dad will be okay?" Virginia asked. "I'm worried sick about him. But he can look after himself, can't he? He can stay out of trouble for one day?"

"From what I know of your father," Wolf said, "I very much doubt it."

Then he focused on the Trolls. He held a hand against her shoulder, keeping her back. The prison loomed above them, dark and menacing. She couldn't believe she was actually considering entering it again.

"All right," Wolf said. "You wait here. I'll put the magic shoes on and go back inside and pre—"

"No way," Virginia said. "You'll never come back. You just want them for your own."

"I don't," Wolf said.

"You do," Virginia said.

Wolf frowned. "All right, I do. But I'm fighting it, unlike you."

She reached for the shoes and managed to grab them. But Wolf hung on to them too.

He licked his lips. "I'll wear the shoes, and you hold on to me. As long as you're touching me, we'll both be invisible."

"No," Virginia said. "I'll wear them, and you can hold on to me."

"You are hopelessly addicted to those shoes," Wolf said. "And I'm not far off."

She yanked the shoes away from him and put them on. He grabbed her, and as he did, she watched them both disappear.

Tony felt as if he'd lifted all the junk in every junk shop east of the Mississippi. He looked toward the pile. It was mostly gone.

No mirror. He took a shallow breath. It had to be there somewhere.

Just as he had that thought, the man at the far end picked up the mirror. Tony watched as it made its way from person to person, nearly falling a few times, but somehow making it to him unscathed.

He clutched it to his chest like a long-lost child, then held it up, and whispered, "Mirror on! Mirror on!"

A warder looked at him as if he were mad.

"Mirror on! Mirror on!"

Tony looked at the mirror. The frame was right. The silvering was right. Only he couldn't see any vision of Central Park in it. All he could see was his own bruised face and his brand-new front teeth.

"Lewis!" the Governor shouted. "What in the fairying forest do you think you're doing?"

Tony held onto the mirror, touching the frame, the glass, every part of it he could, to find a way to turn it on.

"It's not working . . ." he mumbled.

"Lewis, you little prison princess, throw that mirror on the boat. Now!"

"I can't, sir," Tony said. "I'm frightened it'll get broken."

The Governor walked slowly toward Tony. "As you have refused to obey me," the Governor said, his voice cold and intense, "I am going to push you into the river. And as you are connected by leg irons to all your comrades, they will also, sadly, drown."

The other convicts looked at him murderously. They'd drown with him, but they'd beat the crap out of him as they did so. What an awful way to go.

The Governor got nearer and nearer to Tony. If he threw the mirror, it would definitely break.

"All right," Tony said. "I'll do it."

He looked at the pile of smashed junk in the boat. His entire future would be gone in one swing. Gone. Still, he tried to throw the mirror, but his hands wouldn't release it. He bit his lower lip and tried again.

The Governor watched him, eyes cold.

Tony was breathing shallowly. He measured the gap between the boat and his arms, wondered how hard he could throw the mirror without breaking it, and then decided he had no choice. He had to go for it.

He gave it an almighty heave and closed his eyes, waiting for the sound of broken glass. He held his breath and then, just as he expected, something shattered in the boat.

He turned toward it and opened his eyes, expecting to see the mirror shattered forever. Would that give him seven years of bad luck in this place? What kind of luck could be worse than the kind he was having, anyway?

But the mirror was fine. The pot it had landed on was hopelessly broken, however. Tony felt like jumping up and down and applauding.

Then the Governor spoke. "Thank you, Lewis. As for punishment for your disobedience, you are confined to your cell for the next seven—yes, you heard me—*seven* years."

Tony closed his eyes again. Had the man read his mind? Or was that the going rate for throwing mirrors these days?

The warders grabbed him, unhooked him from the chain gang, and led him back to his cell. He couldn't leave the mirror. It was his only chance. He struggled, but the warders held him tightly. One of them pressed on the wounds on his back and Tony had to bite back a scream. His throat was already raw from all the screaming he had done last night.

Finally, they got to his cell. They tossed him in it and slammed the door shut behind him. Seven years. The mirror would be long gone by then.

He walked to his bunk, feeling more dejected than he had ever felt in his life. It took him a moment to realize that Acorn and Clay Face were covered in dust and staring at him.

"What?" Tony asked Acorn. "What have I done now?"

"Curses," Acorn said.

"Now we'll have to kill him," Clay Face said.

Tony stared at them and gasped. The picture of Prince

Wendell was on hinges, and now it was folded back to reveal a gaping hole in the wall.

"A tunnel?" Tony asked.

They grabbed him and Acorn covered his mouth with a dirty hand. "Shhhhhh."

"We've been burrowing for thirty-one years," Clay Face said.

Tony wriggled his mouth free. "Take me with you. You can trust me. I've got *Escape from Alcatraz* on video and I feel I have a genuine expertise in this area."

Acorn stared at him for a moment, then said, "Best to suffocate him, I think."

"No," Clay Face said. "I trust him."

Clay Face reached into his pocket and removed something. He studied it, then handed it to Tony. It was the little soap statue he'd carved earlier. Tony clutched it without really looking at it.

"Thanks," Tony said. "I'd give you my watch but that's gone already."

Clay Face shrugged, then clapped a meaty hand on Tony's back and shoved him forward.

The tunnel was dark and menacing. But it was the only way to the boat, the mirror, and freedom.

Tony crawled inside, praying there was an opening at the other end.

Getting into the prison was too easy. All they did was knock on the door, a warder opened it, and then they walked inside. Virginia loved being invisible. She even loved holding on to Wolf as they walked together through the prison corridor.

"Follow those two warders," Wolf said. "The key holder's room is straight ahead and down the corridor."

They followed the warders, who were unlocking doors as they walked. It took Virginia's magic-fuzzed mind a moment to realize what they were doing. They were going deeper and deeper into the security parts of the prison.

Finally, the warders reached the key holder's room. A warder was inside, leaning back on his chair, reading a book. The cell keys were on a hook on the wall behind him and beside him was a blackboard with the list of prisoners in their cells. Virginia noticed, rather absently, that there was no mention of the dangerous mice.

Wolf had his arm around her and had pulled her close. She didn't really mind. She thought maybe she should mind, but she didn't. Really. She had her arm around him too. She'd been thinking about his tail and how soft it was and—no way would that help her dad.

She shook her head a little and led Wolf to the blackboard. Together they found her father's name and his cell number and Wolf lifted the appropriate key.

Just as they started to leave, Virginia glanced into the office next to the key holder's room. Prince was in there, tied to a desk leg. There were a dozen plates of food in front of him.

A bald-headed man who looked quite fierce sat at the desk. He was eating and seemed very intent on his food.

"It's Prince," Virginia whispered to Wolf. "Let's get him."

"We can't," Wolf said. "These shoes won't take an extra person. We'll drain all the power and become visible."

Virginia shook her head, and then realized that Wolf couldn't see her. "No," she whispered. "I'm not leaving without him."

At that, Prince's ears went up. He barked. Once. Their signal.

"You can shut up," the man said to Prince. "There must be something you like down there."

Virginia untied the rope from the desk leg. The man above her didn't even seem to notice. She put her hand on Prince's head, and in her ear, Wolf moaned his disgust.

"If you can understand me, Prince," Virginia said. "Take us to where Dad is."

Prince slowly vanished, and then started down the corridor, Virginia's hand clinging to the scruff of his neck. Wolf was hanging onto Virginia's waist, and she felt like the fluffy white stuff in the middle of an Oreo cookie. The image made her want to giggle, which would ruin the effect of all of this.

Why did the shoes make her want to laugh? She had to think clearly. They were on the way to rescuing her father.

Chapter Seventeen

Wolf clung to Virginia and every moment was sweet agony. Her scent up close, her body so soft, her—he couldn't think that way, not here. Not in the prison. But the shoes were affecting his judgment as well, even though he wasn't wearing them.

They had stopped in front of Virginia's father's cell. Wolf read the little inscription up top while Virginia struggled with the lock. Apparently, he was rooming with two charmers: Acorn the Dwarf and Clay Face the Goblin. Both of them had been in the prison longer than Wolf had been alive.

He could hear the Prince's breathing, heavy and doggy. That creature smelled terrible, and he wished Virginia would leave it behind. But she seemed to have a soft spot for him, however much trouble that would cause Wolf. He kept his hand on the small of her back as she finally got the key to work.

She pulled the door open and stepped inside. Then she stopped so abruptly that Wolf walked into her.

The cell was empty.

"Where's he gone?" Virginia asked.

Virginia's dark hair was tantalizing. Then Wolf blinked. He could *see* her, and the dog, standing with its tail between its legs. The shoes had stopped working.

"Oh, no," Wolf said. "They're exhausted. I told you this would happen."

He felt woozy. He put a hand to his head. Virginia was

doing the same thing. Even the dog staggered a little as the effects of the shoes wore off.

Prince looked up at the wall and barked. The sound reverberated in Wolf's head and made him want to howl. Oh, he would have a headache when this was over.

"Look," Virginia said and pointed in the direction that Prince was looking.

A picture of Prince Wendell in his human form—which was not, in Wolf's opinion, an improvement—was hanging at an odd angle, revealing a hole beyond. Wolf walked over to it, deliberately put his hand on the Prince's face, and shoved the picture aside.

"Boy," he said, "your father is a fast worker. I'll give him that."

Then an alarm bell went off, adding to the aggravation in Wolf's mind. He put a hand over his ears as, in the corridor, shouting started.

"Prison break! Break out! Prisoners escaped!"

"Any ideas?" Wolf asked Virginia.

"Into the tunnel," Virginia said.

There were footsteps running in their direction. Virginia pulled the cell door shut. Wolf went for the shoes, but Virginia reached them first. Wolf growled softly and leapt into the tunnel. Virginia and Prince followed him, but stopped long enough to try to put the picture of Prince Wendell back in its place.

"Come on," Wolf whispered.

They did. He hurried through the tunnel. The ground was already packed down as if a couple of people had been through it. The tunnel seemed to go on forever, and the deeper they went, the darker it got.

Prince could hear his own breathing, and that of the others, and it made him wonder about the air. He'd heard that tunnels sometimes lacked oxygen. He didn't know where he'd learned that, but somewhere, and it made his heart beat a little faster.

Then it got slightly lighter, as if sunlight were coming

through a crack in a door. It took him a moment to realize what he was seeing.

"There's something fat blocking the tunnel," Wolf said. He sniffed. There was something over the scent of dirt. A faintly unwashed odor that was somehow familiar. "Tony, is that you?"

"Who the hell is that?" Tony asked.

"It's me. Wolf. I gave you the magic dragon dung bean, remember?"

"Stay away from me," Tony said.

"How can I do that?" Wolf asked. "We're in a tunnel together."

The alarm bell seemed to be louder than ever. Behind him, Wolf could feel Virginia and the dog.

"I'm almost out, but I'm stuck," Tony said. "Give me a push."

Wolf considered for a moment before putting his hands on Tony's buttocks and pushing as hard as he could. It didn't work. So Wolf leaned into Tony's back end and, bracing with his feet, used his entire body to shove.

Tony slid through the opening like a fish through a novice fisherman's hands. Wolf didn't catch himself in time, and followed Tony out the hole. Dust and bricks fell around him, and he landed beside Tony on the hard ground.

Virginia and the dog followed a moment later. Tony grinned when he saw his daughter, then sat up and hugged her.

It was a tender moment. Wolf watched with something like pride.

"You're alive!" Tony said, laughing. "You're alive."

"Dad!" Virginia seemed as happy to see her father as he was to see her. They hugged for what Wolf considered to be a moment too long. He glanced at Prince, who was staring at the river. The dog didn't ever seem to pay attention to the right things.

"Where's the mirror?" Virginia asked her father.

"It's on this boat," Tony said. "We can go straight home—"

He looked toward the river as he spoke. Then his forehead creased. Wolf had a bad feeling even before Tony started to shout, "They've taken it! They've stolen the boat. Look, there it is!"

A single dwarf sat on the back of a heavily loaded boat. He was far down the river. When he saw Tony jumping up and down on the bank, he waved.

Tony moaned. Virginia closed her eyes. Wolf suppressed a smile. She'd be with him a bit longer then. This wasn't so great a tragedy after all.

For one brief moment, Relish the Troll King thought everything was going his way. Two dainty footprints in flour, two larger footprints beside, had meant that the witch had gone inside the prison, just as he had expected. But from there everything had gone horribly wrong.

Alarms were ringing, warders were shouting about a prison break, and Relish had a hunch who had caused that break. Maybe his children weren't as incompetent as he thought. Maybe this witch did have more powers than he expected.

He had run to the side of the prison, his son Burly ahead of him. Burly shouted, "There they are!" and Relish saw them as he hurried down the hill.

The witch, the Wolf, a man he'd never seen before, and Prince Wendell were casting off in a large boat, almost a ship. They were much too far away for comfort.

"Don't let them get away," Relish ordered.

His children sped past him down the towpath. Relish had to hurry to keep up. Blabberwort and Bluebell reached the water first, but they couldn't stop properly and they fell in. Burly narrowly missed landing on the boat. He swam behind it and grabbed the rudder.

"You are dog food!" he shouted, his voice echoing to the

shore. Relish stood at the water's edge, ignoring his flailing children, hoping Burly would stop the boat.

Burly hauled himself onto the stern. Relish felt a bit of hope.

"Hit him!" Wolf shouted. "Get him!"

The man Relish didn't recognize backed away from Burly as if he were afraid of him. But the witch grabbed a piece of wood and smashed Burly on the head.

He screamed and let go, disappearing underwater as the boat pulled away. By the time Burly surfaced again, the boat was too far away to reach.

Relish crossed his arms and shook his head. "What a pathetic display."

Light filtered into the Queen's bedroom, revealing years of dust and cobwebs near the ceiling. She'd had her servants clean this room and it wasn't as bad as it had been, but it still needed work. The work would have to wait, however, until she was ready. Her bed was cleaned, the mattress aired, and the blankets newly washed. The furniture was dusted, and the floor gleamed. But it didn't gleam as much as the five newly cleaned mirrors that surrounded her.

She stood in front of her favorite mirror. It was dark green, ornate, the edging a mass of squiggles like a thousand snakes. And unlike the others, it reflected nothing. All it showed her was a deep blackness.

"Mirror?" she said. "Wake from your sleep."

For a long time, nothing happened. Then there was a noise like the scraping of sandpaper. The mirror bubbled ever so slightly, and behind the darkness something started to glow. Then the surface moved, becoming liquid.

The Queen smiled. The power was strong, even now. When it seemed ready, she said, "Summon Relish the Troll King."

One by one, Relish's children climbed out of the river. They were soaking wet, and they all shook themselves off like dogs.

"How dare you call yourself my children!" Relish shouted. "You are the most—argghh!"

A blinding pain flashed through his head. Something was in there with him. A command. More than a command. A compulsion. A voice, deep and haunting. He closed his eyes, trying to fight it, but that only made the pain worse.

"Are you all right, Dad?" Blabberwort asked.

"What's wrong?" Bluebell asked.

"Mirror," Relish said. "Find a mirror."

Getting the words out made the pain recede a little. But his children were watching him as if he were crazy. He kept his hands clasped to his head, and he wandered away from the prison, down the towpath toward Beantown.

The pain made his eyes water and he stumbled forward for what seemed like a very long time. After a while, he realized he was mumbling, "Mirror. Find a mirror."

His children were following him, asking idiot questions. What else could he expect? Support?

"Are you all right, Dad?" Burly asked.

He tried to answer, but all that came out was, "Mirror. Mirror."

They were in Beantown now. He recognized it through the haze of pain. People were moving out of his way as if they'd never seen a Troll before. Probably not a Troll under a spell.

He staggered until he saw a tailor's shop. They would have a mirror. He shoved the door open and shouted, "Everybody out. Now."

A dwarf and a tailor ran outside. Relish didn't see anyone else in the small space. But there was a mirror. He pulled the door closed so that his children didn't come in, and then he went to the mirror.

Its surface rippled and finally revealed the Queen. She was standing in her palace bedroom, her hands clasped before her.

"Thank you so much for joining me," the Queen said.

His headache and the compulsion were gone, leaving only a faint tinge of embarrassment.

"Don't you ever do that to me again," Relish said. "Or I'll kill you."

A new pain shot through his face, and his nose exploded as if he'd been punched. He put a finger up to it. It was bleeding.

"Well?" the Queen asked.

He wiped his nose with the back of his hand. She'd pay for this. Only he knew better than to say that aloud this time. "Well, what?"

"Have your children got the dog for me?"

His embarrassment grew, but so did his fury. She had no right to order him around like this. "Not exactly," he said.

"You do surprise me, Your Majesty," the Queen said. "How did he possibly escape your tiny little grasp?"

"Don't you talk to me like that!" Relish shouted.

"He must be caught," the Queen said. "Send your children after him. And what are you doing still in Wendell's kingdom? Return to your palace and await my further orders."

"I do not take orders from y—"

But she had already vanished. All the mirror showed him was his own furious, blood-spattered face.

Chapter Eighteen

Wolf sat on the bow of the ship, his legs stretched out before him. The setting sun reflected off the water, and the river had a strong algae smell. He had to squint to read, but he continued. The books were helping him. He knew it.

Virginia sat beside him, clutching the magic shoes. She hadn't let them out of her grasp since she took them off. The addiction was getting worse.

"Virginia," Wolf asked, "would you say you were 'desperately hungry for love and approval, but destined for rejection?'"

"I'm quite happy as I am, thank you."

He smiled at her. She smiled back trustingly. Then he attacked. He grabbed the shoes and, in a single movement, threw them overboard.

"No!" Virginia shouted. "No, no—"

She got to her feet and was about to dive in after them, when he grabbed her around the waist. She was stronger than she should have been and she whipped him back and forth for a moment before he managed to hold her down.

"What did you do that for?" She sounded like a child who'd had her favorite toy broken.

"I had to," Wolf said. "For your own good."

She struggled against his hands. 'You threw away my shoes!"

"You were already dreaming of wearing them tonight, weren't you?" Wolf asked.

"Yes," Virginia said. "How did you know that?"

She stopped struggling and for the first time that day looked at him with clear eyes. She was coming back. He liked that.

"Magic is very nice," Wolf said, "but it's very easy to get addicted."

She glanced at the water. She was obviously still addicted, but it was wearing off. It would only be a matter of time.

"But why didn't you want them?" Virginia asked. "Why were you able to resist the shoes and I wasn't?"

Good question, and one he wasn't sure he should answer. But he did, as honestly as he could.

"Because," he said gently, "you have such a strong desire to be invisible."

Tony stood a few feet away, Prince Wendell at his side. Prince Wendell had been watching Wolf and Virginia. Tony had been taking deep breaths. He'd never enjoyed freedom so much before. It really was true. A person did take things for granted until those things were taken from him. Never again would he complain about his job or his life or Mr. Murray. Well, maybe Mr. Murray if the old fart had reverted back to normal. But nothing else.

"Anthony," Prince Wendell said, "if you value the safety of your daughter, then we must get rid of this Wolf immediately. He'll have her for breakfast."

Tony frowned. At that moment, Wolf looked at him. Tony himself wasn't sure whether or not to trust this guy. After all, he had given him the magic bean—which turned out to be dragon dung. Tony shivered. *That* experience hadn't been what the fairy tales said it would. Except it did allow him to talk to Prince Wendell, for whatever that was worth.

Wolf raised his eyebrows as if questioning Tony's intensity.

"Prince says he doesn't trust you," Tony said to Wolf.

"I don't trust him either," Wolf said. "A dog is a wolf crossed with an old pillow. They are tail wagging slipper collectors. And wolves can be shot on sight in his miserable kingdom.''

''Chicken rustlers,'' Prince Wendell said. ''Granny eaters, shepherdess worriers. Name me one story where the wolf is a good guy.''

''What's he done so far, apart from get you in trouble?'' Wolf asked. ''Nothing. Whereas I have saved your life so many times I've stopped counting. Dogs zero, Wolf thirty-seven thousand, as far as I can see.''

Tony sighed. This wouldn't help. And Virginia, for all her struggles, seemed to like both Wolf and Prince Wendell. Right now, Tony believed, they needed both man-animal hybrids. He shook his head at the thought, one he'd never have had in New York, and shoved his cold hands into the pocket of his very soiled jacket.

There was something in the left pocket. He pulled it out. It was the carving Clay Face had given him. Tony looked at it properly for the first time.

It was a tiny heroic statue that reminded him faintly of the one of the guys raising the flag at Iwo Jima. Only this one had no flag. Just two men, a woman, and a dog. Beneath it were the words: THE FOUR WHO SAVED THE NINE KINGDOMS.

Tony stared at it. He shook his head, just a little. He didn't want to think about it. In fact, the little statue gave him the creeps. With a sharp movement of his hand, he flung it overboard.

It floated away, leaving a slightly soapy residue on the surface of the water.

''What was that?'' Prince Wendell asked.

''Nothing,'' Tony said as he watched the carving float away in the growing darkness. ''Nothing at all.''

Relish the Troll King carried a torch and led one of his huge dogs on a lead. Who'd have thought Beantown rolled up the sidewalks at dark? He glanced over his shoulder. His henchmen were kicking at shop doors, overturning barrels, egging on the dogs. That was all well and good—a mild evening's entertainment—but it wouldn't last them for an entire week.

He should have thought of that before making Beantown his home base.

The little Mayor of Beantown, with a self-important strut, hurried up to Relish.

"I insist you leave," the Mayor said. "Trolls are not allowed in the Fourth Kingdom without proper permits. This is a gross violation of the Nine Kingdoms Treaty."

"Shut your mouth," Relish growled.

That should have flipped out the Mayor, but he was too dense to notice a warning when he heard it. He said in his wobbly little voice, "Unless you leave this instant, I shall notify Prince Wendell. And soldiers will be sent."

Relish looked at the self-important creature before him. They could argue the night away, but that wouldn't be entertaining at all. Better to let the idiot know who was boss.

With a quick right cross, he punched the Mayor. The Mayor's flesh felt soft against Relish's knuckles, and the self-important idiot fell backwards, unconscious from the first blow. If that was the kind of resistance they'd find in Beantown, then this place would be even less entertaining than Relish thought. And he hadn't had high hopes.

He turned and saw the preparations for Wendell's coronation. The flags, the banners, the pretty throne that someone had done up all because the Prince had come of age.

Beantown residents were staring at Relish as if he'd done something horrible. He grinned. They hadn't seen horrible yet.

He walked to the podium and hesitated for a brief, dramatic second, knowing the effect this would have on his audience. Then, with a flourish, he sat on the throne.

There were gasps from all sides.

He leaned forward and said in his most official voice, "I am declaring war on the Fourth Kingdom, and I challenge

Prince Wendell to come and face me within seven days, or I will claim his kingdom as my own.''

That should put the Queen's twist in a bundle. Not to mention Wendell's, if news of this reached his poor little doggie ears. Relish grinned. Then he tilted his head back and indulged in his most evil laugh.

Virginia put a hand to her eyes as she climbed onto the deck in the early morning light. She had a slight hangover, which she would not mention to Wolf. He was steering the boat, but he noticed her arrival on deck. He was watching her with a wariness that showed her he anticipated this reaction.

So she gave him a different one.

"Everything's soaking wet down there," she said. "I didn't sleep a wink."

"You should have joined me on deck, sleeping under the stars," Wolf said. "It was quite magnificent."

He closed another self-help book, its spine horribly creased—did he always have to break the spines of the books?—and then tossed it overboard. Virginia watched it go. She guessed it didn't matter now that he'd broken the spines. The water would do even more damage.

"Are we in Wendell's kingdom now?" Virginia asked. "Or the Troll Kingdom?"

"Neither," Wolf said. "This river divides the two. The left bank is the Trolls', the right bank Wendell's."

Virginia looked at Wendell's side of the river. A group of anglers stood there. They didn't look like expert fishermen. Instead, they looked like thugs. They had anxious, angry expressions that seemed incongruous with everything she knew about fishing.

Virginia's father had come up from below decks. He was standing beside her, looking at the fishermen just as she was.

"Must be a lot of fish around here with all these anglers," he said.

"No, just the one," Wolf said.

"The one?" Tony asked.

"There is only one fish in the whole of this river," Wolf said.

"Let me guess," Virginia said. "Is it magic?"

"Oh, Virginia," Wolf said, "is it magic? Every year, around this time, some lucky fisherman catches the fish, and if he agrees to throw it back, then the next thing he touches with his little finger will turn to gold."

Virginia sighed. She now knew where this was going.

"Gold?" Tony asked. "A man could touch anything?"

"Exactly," Wolf said.

"You could turn a mountain into gold," Tony said, starting to get really excited.

"Indeed you could," Wolf said.

"Dad, no," Virginia said.

"Wait a minute," Tony said. "I just thought of something. What if you catch the fish, and now you're Goldfinger, but you forget and touch your forehead, or swat a mosquito on your leg or something?"

"Then you become one of the many aquatic statues called 'The Gold Anglers Who Line the Bottom of the River,' " Wolf said. "Look down and you may be able to see one."

"Boy," Tony said, "you want to be careful with this fish."

"That's right," Wolf said. "In fact, you'd do better to steer well clear of it."

"There isn't a fish in the world Tony Lewis can't catch."

Virginia hoped that was one of her father's exaggerations. Because she was beginning to believe Wolf was right. Magic was dangerous. Especially in the wrong hands.

Like her father's.

Blabberwort was rowing. Her brothers were rowing. And it felt good. The magical music from the magical box made everything seem easier. She was singing at the top of her lungs. So were Burly and Bluebell. Bluebell was getting so into it that he removed his jacket and was starting on his shirt when the music began to sound odd.

It slowed down. It made wo-ow sounds. It was going bad.

She picked up the box and shook it, but that only seemed to make the sounds worse. Bluebell's eyes widened in panic. They all knew what happened when magic went bad.

She tossed the black box overboard. "Their magic is useless. The Brothers Gibb. Hah!"

Suddenly rowing wasn't nearly as much fun.

"Row faster," Burly said. "Faster."

"But we've rowed all night long," Bluebell said.

"Bluebell," Blabberwort said, "stop eating your head lice."

"I wasn't chewing," Bluebell said. "I was just putting them under my tongue."

"Row faster," Burly said. "Faster."

"Lookee look," Blabberwort said, pointing at something in the water. "Over there."

She reached into the water and fished out a book. But it was unlike any book she had ever seen—except in the Tenth Kingdom. She frowned at it. *Women Who Love Too Much*. Hmm, she thought. That sounded interesting. It might take some study. . . .

The Queen stood in front of her mirror. On it, she saw Relish the Troll King sitting on the coronation throne. Behind him, his henchmen were looting and sacking Beantown.

This was not part of the rules. She should have trusted her instincts. He thought he was more intelligent than he really was.

Well, he would find out exactly who he was messing with.

"Exactly what do you think you are playing at?" the Queen demanded. "We had a bargain. I would give you half of Wendell's kingdom in return for your cooperation."

"You've done elf-all since I broke you out of prison."

And now he was swearing at her. She had to swallow a

vicious retort. She wanted to bend this man to her will, not scream at him.

"It is essential to my plans that the coronation proceeds as planned," the Queen said. "If you remain in Wendell's kingdom, then a crisis will inevitably ensue."

"What's ensue mean?" the Troll King asked.

"Leave Beantown!" the Queen ordered. "Return to your kingdom or you'll ruin everything."

"I might." The Troll King shrugged. "I might not. How are my kids doing, anyway?"

"Their intellect and bravery quite take my breath away."

"Yeah?" the Troll King asked. "Well you look after them. I want them back in one piece."

"If you will only be patient, Your Majesty," the Queen said, "I will give you Wendell's kingdom on a plate."

"Yeah?" the Troll King said. "Well, I'm hungry now."

She waved a hand, and his image vanished.

"Moron," the Queen said to herself. She turned to the other mirror. "Why haven't you found Wendell yet?"

Shapes appeared in its liquid surface. Shapes and colors and nothing else.

"He is with others," the mirror answered in its dry voice. "But I cannot see them."

"Who?" the Queen asked.

"Three travel with Wendell," the mirror said. "One who can talk with him and one who can hurt you. They are traveling down the river, toward us, unknowingly."

"Show me." The Queen grabbed the mirror and pulled it close. "Show me."

"I cannot."

She pushed it away from herself and thought for a moment. Then she smiled. She had a solution.

"The wolf is with them. Work on him. Make him talk to me."

Once she spoke to the wolf, everything would be as she wanted it to be. They would have a real wolf in their midst, and they wouldn't even know it.

Chapter Nineteen

Wolf didn't like the quarters below decks. They made him feel claustrophobic, almost as if he were back in prison. But there were times when a man needed to be alone, and shaving was one of them. He'd found a small, rusty mirror and he was shaving as delicately as a man could with a knife and cold water.

He could never explain to Virginia why he had to be alone for this. A sharp movement, a loud voice, and suddenly he'd be bleeding.

He was looking a bit worse for the wear. Even though he'd slept, he had shadows under his eyes. His hair needed a trim too. And he normally wouldn't have shaved on a boat. But he was in love now, and he was trying to convince Virginia that he was the man for her. And a man in love took risks.

Suddenly the image in his mirror changed. Fortunately, he'd been dipping his knife in the cold water or he would have sliced his own neck for sure.

The Queen's face was where his reflection should have been.

"Hello, Wolf," the Queen said.

He dropped his knife and picked up the mirror with shaking hands.

"Go away," Wolf said. "Leave me alone."

"You agreed to obey me," the Queen said. "Yes. I control you."

"No!" Wolf shouted into the mirror.

"Why can't I see your companions?" the Queen asked. "What magic is going on?"

He threw the mirror facedown on a nearby bunk and ran up the stairs to the top deck. He was looking for Virginia, but he didn't see her. Instead, he saw Tony, fishing. Wolf grabbed the book he'd been reading and waved it in Tony's face.

"Tony," Wolf said. "I must bond with you."

"What?" Tony didn't look away from the river.

Wolf had to get Tony's attention. He had to get his mind off the Queen. If he thought about her, she would have an entry, and if she had an entry, then she'd get to Virginia, and if she got to Virginia, then he'd never forgive himself.

"It says in this book here, *Ironing John,* that we've lost our masculinity and need to do more man to man bonding," Wolf said. "And perhaps that bond is fishing?"

Tony didn't answer. Wolf stared at Tony's fishing line, wondering if he should get his own. He really didn't want to catch the fish. Maybe he could divert Tony's attention from that fish, too. Wolf smiled. "Boy, I love fishing with my future father-in-law."

"I want you to stay away from Virginia," Tony said. "You hear me? You've got a criminal record."

"We're on a small boat," Wolf said. "How can I stay away from her?"

"Will you both stop talking about me as though I'm not here," Virginia said.

Wolf turned. He hadn't seen her. The love of his life, and he had missed her as he had come up on deck. She was steering the boat and she looked beautiful.

"What's the biggest catch you've ever had, Wolf?" Tony asked.

"A young mountain girl called Hilda," Wolf said.

"I caught a mullet once. It was this big if it was an inch." Tony held his hands a yard apart. No fish ever got that big. "Biggest mullet caught in New York State in 1994."

"That's nothing," Wolf said. "I caught a fish last year. It was this big."

He held his hands twice as far apart as Tony had.

"Really?" Tony asked.

"No, no," Wolf said. "I just made it up. Are we bonding yet?"

Sunlight glinted toward them. Wolf shaded his eyes. The light was reflecting off a solid gold cottage on the bank.

"Wow, look at that," Tony said. "He was probably a simple guy like me. Now I bet he's got a hundred servants."

Wolf doubted that, but he said nothing. He'd seen too many people mess with this fish even though, rumor had it, only princes, nobles, and foundlings caught magic fish. So if the rumor was true, Tony was safe.

"You see, bait is crucial," Tony was saying. "If this fish has been caught and thrown back lots of times, he's going to be smart. If it's a tench, I'd go for the heavy-feed, big-bait approach, whereas if it's a carp, I'd prefer sweetcorn or maple peas, or sour-bran specials if he's a chub or a roach."

"I hope we'll be bonding soon, Tony," Wolf said. "I can't take many more of your fishing stories."

Tony's line suddenly jerked.

"Hey, hey," Tony said. "I got a bite."

Wolf looked at it in surprise. He hadn't expected this.

"It's a big-un, that's for sure," Tony said, working the line.

"Oh, my goodness," Wolf said. "I think you *have* caught the elusive magic fish."

Tony got leverage on the boat and tried to pull again. The silly dog woke up and sat beside them. Tony gave him an angry look, as if the dog had said something Tony didn't like.

"Be careful of your back, Dad," Virginia said.

Tony played the fish out, the pulled it in hard. As he started reeling in the line, a beautiful choir started to sing. Wolf winced. He had a feeling this would be bad.

"Who tries to catch the magic fish?" The voice was female and beautiful and magical.

Wolf's wince got worse.

"I've got her," Tony shouted. "I've got her. Baby, you're mine now."

He fell backwards on the boat, and the fish flew out of the water. It landed on his chest before slithering off and flapping on the deck in front of all of them.

Wolf watched it, feeling a kind of foreboding and pity. Curiously, he wasn't hungry for the fish at all.

"Throw me back immediately," the fish said. "I demand you throw me back."

Virginia left the wheel and crouched beside the fish. Wolf crouched beside her. The fish was giving off tiny gold stars.

"Give up the gold and we'll throw you back, Flipper," Tony said.

"Very well," the fish said. "The very first thing you touch with the little finger of your left hand will turn to gold."

"Guaranteed no side effects?" Tony asked. "One touch and then my finger goes back to normal?"

"What is this? A fish quiz?" the fish asked. "I'm dying. Throw me back."

"All right, it's a deal," Tony said. "I'll throw you back."

"Not you!" the fish screamed. "Don't you touch me. Someone else do it."

Virginia grabbed the fish so fast that Wolf didn't have a chance. Not that he wanted to do it. But he did want to prove to her that he could see food and not be tempted.

She tossed the fish overboard and it disappeared with a splash. Tony held up his little finger in wonder.

"I've got a magic finger," Tony said. "I've got a magic finger."

"Keep that digit away from us," Wolf said. "Your finger is now a deadly weapon, Tony."

Tony moved his hand as far away from his body as he could.

"What do we even want gold for anyway?" Virginia asked.

"What a stupid question," Tony said. "Because it's gold. When we get home, I can retire. We've won the lottery."

Wolf didn't know why that was a good thing. He was hoping that Virginia would never go home. But he didn't say anything. Instead, he went to the wheel.

They were near Rivertown. Soon they'd see more boats. Ahead, he saw a ruined castle on the hill. Apparently Tony did too.

"Maybe I'll turn a whole castle into gold," Tony said. "Like that place."

"And how are you going to carry a golden castle?" Virginia asked.

"You're right, you're right," Tony said. "I need to choose something as big as I can possibly carry."

That castle made Wolf nervous. There was something up there, something he really, really, really didn't like.

"Wolf?" Virginia asked. "What's wrong?"

"Nothing," Wolf said. "Just a feeling."

"That looks like Acorn's boat," Tony said. "Moored over there. He's here."

Tony was pointing at the docks in front of Rivertown. And it did look like one of the moored boats belonged to Acorn. Wolf glanced at Virginia. She seemed excited. He felt even odder. He didn't want her to find that mirror and leave.

"Everything's coming up roses," Tony said. "We're going home with Olympic Gold."

The silly dog started running up and down the boat. Wolf turned to Prince, but didn't say anything. It looked as if the dog was feeling the same way he was.

"What's with Prince Wendell?" Virginia asked.

Tony shook his head. "He says he feels like two people at the same time."

Wolf gave the castle a sharp look. Was Wendell's human body up there?

"He says he has to go to the castle." Tony peered at Prince. "Why?" he asked the dog. "It's just a ruin."

Prince Wendell shook his head, and then took a flying leap at the rail. Before any of them could stop him, he had landed in the water and started swimming toward shore.

"Prince!" Tony shouted. "Come back."

"We can't go after him," Virginia said. "Let's find Acorn and get the mirror."

That was Wolf's girl. She knew what was important. But Tony stared after the dog as if he were puzzled, and just a little bit worried. Which made Wolf a little bit worried. Tony was a nice guy underneath it all, but he was, after all, the biggest screwup that Wolf had ever seen.

"He'll be all right," Wolf said, not sure if that was true or not. "He's got his own mission now."

Blabberwort's hands ached, and she missed the magic of the Brothers Gibb, even though she had complained about it. The music of it still ran through her head. She wondered if it poisoned her thoughts, if it would ever leave her mind.

She didn't think on it too hard, however, because she used the rhythm of the music to continue rowing. They were just getting to a bend in the river. The area was looking familiar, but she really didn't have time to examine it. Instead, she had to concentrate on what she was doing.

"Faster, faster," Burly said.

"I can't go any faster," Bluebell said. "My hands are bleeding."

"Look," Burly said. "The ruined castle. Should we report to the Queen?"

They all looked up at the ruined castle. A report would save their arms for a few hours. What could it hurt?

"Excellent idea," Blabberwort said. "Pull over to the bank."

The boat was empty. No Acorn, no mirror. Virginia hadn't felt this dejected in her life.

Her father seemed to feel the same way. He was staring at

the boat as if it had stolen his life savings. Wolf had a slight smile on his face, though, and Virginia didn't want to ask why. He wasn't saying anything. In fact, it had been Virginia who'd been asking all the questions of the boatman who was standing on the dock.

"Acorn's been here all morning," the boatman said. "He left—oh, not half an hour ago."

"When's he coming back?" Virginia asked.

"He's not," the boatman said. "He swapped me this lovely boat for my pony and cart. Reckon I got a good deal."

"Oh, no," Virginia said. "Which way did he go?"

"He said he was taking the forest road," the boatman said. "You might still be able to catch him if you hurry."

"Good idea," Wolf said. "Let's go."

"What about Prince?" Tony asked.

Wolf looked at the ruined castle anxiously. What was bothering him about that place? He wasn't telling Virginia. She wondered if he even knew himself.

"He's off. He wants to be on his own," Wolf said. "My heart is breaking, but let's follow the mirror. Anyway, Tony, you said yourself he's been nothing but a nuisance."

"Yeah, I know, but it doesn't feel right to just run off and leave him. He must have bounded off for a reason."

"You'll lose that mirror," Wolf said.

"Dad," Virginia said, knowing what her father was thinking. She felt concern for Prince Wendell, but she also knew they only had one real chance at that mirror.

"Stay here," Tony said. "I'll be back in fifteen minutes."

Virginia sighed, but she didn't try to stop him. She was feeling guilty too for leaving Prince Wendell alone. Maybe her father could do something. Or at least find out what was going on.

She'd give him his fifteen minutes, and then he'd have to catch up to her. If they had to split up, they had to. She'd bring the mirror to him if she found it.

She looked at Wolf. Wolf was still staring at that castle, a faraway look in his eyes. He seemed almost frightened.

Her heart started pounding. She tried to shout to her father, but he was already too far away to hear.

She had changed her mind. She'd wait here for fifteen minutes, and then she'd go after him, no matter what Wolf said.

Or what waited for them back there at that ruined castle.

The morning had been a dismal failure. The Queen tried to keep her impatience in check. First that aborted attempt at influencing Wolf, and now this—trying to teach the Dog Prince how to act human.

She had dishes and cutlery laid out before him on a simple table. She'd been afraid to use the good table, thinking that perhaps he would scratch it somehow. Dishes could be replaced, but her good table couldn't.

The Dog Prince was studying the dishes before him as if he wanted to bury his face in the plate. He longed for the meat. She knew it. Meat—of any kind—was his favorite food. She had deliberately given him a piece too big to bite easily.

"When waiting to eat," the Queen said, "try to keep your tongue inside your mouth. It is somewhat vulgar to have it hanging out all the time."

"I'm starving," the Dog Prince whined. "Where's my bowl?"

"You're going to have a lovely meal," the Queen said. "But only when you've learnt to eat with a knife and fork. Until then you will starve."

She placed a knife in his right hand and a fork in his left. He looked at them as if they hurt his fingers.

"Would you like a drink, Your Majesty?" she asked, just to confuse him.

"Bowl of water."

"*A glass* of water," the Queen said. "A Prince does not drink out of a bowl."

He rolled his eyes. He'd drink from the water closet if she let him, and they both knew it. "A glass of water," he said. *"Please."*

In spite of the fact that she didn't like his tone, he did ask properly, so she poured him a glass of water. He stared at it as if he were trying to figure out how to put his snout in the opening.

"Now," she said, "is there anything else you want?"

"My woolly ball," the Dog Prince said.

She let out a horrible sigh and was about to lecture the Dog Prince yet again on the fact that he was now human and not a dog when the door opened. A servant entered. She didn't recognize this one either. A few years in prison, and the staff turnover was uncontrollable.

"Majesty," the servant said. "The three Trolls have returned."

Ah, they must have found Prince Wendell. Good news then. She turned to the Dog Prince.

"Practice using your knife and fork," she said to the Dog Prince. "I will return to test you in ten minutes."

And then she left him alone. She hoped his wooly ball wasn't anywhere in sight.

She hurried down the corridor to the main entry. The Trolls stood there, adding a stink that was unwelcome, and looking quite proud.

She didn't see Prince Wendell anywhere. Had they—perhaps—killed him?

"Well?" the Queen asked.

"We are here, Your Majesty," Burly said.

"And?"

"Just that, Your Majesty," Bluebell said.

"Where is Prince Wendell?"

"Oh, yes," Burly said. "Prince Wendell."

"I sent you to get him."

"A noble mission for any Troll," Blabberwort said.

"So where is he?"

"A question we have been torturing ourselves with, Your Majesty," Bluebell said.

"But we are here," Blabberwort said.

"And we are ever vigilant," Bluebell said.

"You idiots!" She walked in front of them and slashed their faces with her fingernail. The pain from that would keep Wendell in their memory for a long, long time. They screamed, but not as hard as she would have liked.

Someday she would roast those Trolls over an open pit. Someday, after they had found Wendell.

"I have just spoken with my mirror," the Queen said. "Prince Wendell is very near. He may be in Rivertown by now."

"Wow," Burly said. "What a stroke of luck."

"Go and find him," the Queen ordered. "If you return again without the dog, I will make you eat your own hearts."

They looked at her in disgust as they hurried out of the castle. She wiped her fingernail on a curtain, then waved her hand at one of the servants.

"Wash the Troll stink out of here," she said and left before she heard his answer.

Wet fur was a definite inconvenience. Wendell had never realized how heavy it was. It slowed his progress. And he had to hold back the occasional sneeze. He hated the smell of wet dog, even if the wet dog was him.

He was drier than he'd been since he'd gotten out of the river. He was almost to the castle. As he scurried up the path, he saw the bars of the dungeon and, looking down on him, was his own face. Or rather his human face. Or rather, the face that the real dog was using.

The Dog Prince started to bark before catching himself and realizing that he had to speak real language.

"Yes, please," the Dog Prince said. "Swap, please. Four legs, please."

The Dog Prince thrust his hands through the bars. He knew

instinctively what Wendell knew. If they only touched, they would revert to their real forms.

"Yes, good dog," Wendell said, uncertain whether or not the Dog Prince could understand him. "If we can just touch, then we'll turn back. Reach down."

The Dog Prince leaned out as far as he could. Wendell jumped as high as he could, but they couldn't quite reach each other. He kept jumping and jumping, but to no avail. He needed help. Maybe he could get someone to lift him. Maybe Anthony and Virginia had landed. Maybe they would help.

He ran down the path toward Rivertown. And who should be coming up it but Anthony!

"Anthony," Wendell shouted. "I've found myself."

Anthony hadn't seen him yet. So he looked surprised when Wendell shouted.

"Prince!" Anthony sounded relieved. Then he got a panicked look on his face. "Look out!"

Trolls shoved their way through the bushes and grabbed him. Wendell cursed himself. He had been so excited, he hadn't even bothered to sniff the air.

He recognized these Trolls, too. They were the three who'd been plaguing him.

"Hold him still while I kick him," the tall male said to the female.

"Leave him alone, you cowards," Anthony shouted. "He's a dog. Pick on someone your own size."

Then Anthony came to Prince's rescue.

He wasn't at any of the docks. He wasn't anywhere near the water's edge. Virginia shaded her eyes with her hands and gazed up at the ruined castle.

Wolf was right. It gave her a feeling of foreboding.

Wolf followed her gaze. He didn't see her father either and worse, he said, he didn't smell him.

Virginia glanced over her shoulder at the woods beyond.

They had lost the mirror. She knew it. They had already wasted too much time.

And now her father was missing.

Just as she had that thought, her father suddenly appeared on the path down from the castle. He was walking slowly, as if he had just received news that someone had died.

Virginia ran up to him. Wolf followed.

"Dad!" Virginia shouted. Her father looked up. He hurried toward her.

When he reached her, she hugged him close. "Thank God you're all right," she said. "Did you find Prince?"

He didn't answer.

Her breath caught in her throat. She moved back, out of the hug, so that she could see his face. "Are you okay?"

"I've defeated the Trolls," Tony said. "That's good news."

He didn't sound as if that was very good news. Virginia shot Wolf a worried glance. He was looking at her father.

"Any bad news?" Wolf asked.

Her father swallowed hard. Virginia recognized the look. The bad news was really bad, and it was her dad's fault.

"I can go back to that boatman guy and borrow a chisel," Tony said. "He'll come away from the others quite easily."

He was talking nonsense, maybe on purpose.

"Dad," Virginia said, "exactly what is the bad news?"

His eyes were dark and sad. He took her hand and pulled her with him toward a pile of bushes beside the path. Wolf hurried along after them.

Gold glinted in the sunlight. Virginia stopped, mesmerized. In front of her was a golden tableaux. Three gold Trolls, frozen in attack, were attached to one gold dog, frozen as he tried to escape them.

"Oh, Prince Wendell," Virginia murmured.

Part Two

WELL OF FORTUNE

Chapter Twenty

All around her, incompetence. And she—she needed to be more competent than the rest. Somehow she felt as if she weren't doing enough.

Even her mirrors were failing her.

The Queen sat at the edge of her good table, hands on the polished surface. She half thought she could see her reflection in it. *Mirror, mirror.* She smiled at the thought of the old rhyme. It wasn't the moment for that yet.

Although it might be. Soon.

A presence had joined her in the room. She looked up. The Huntsman stood before her. She felt her shoulders relax. Finally, someone competent.

She knew she could count on him.

"You summoned me, my lady?"

His voice was as deep as she remembered it. His pale eyes held an intelligence almost equal to her own. He looked good. His blond hair was still thick, his shoulders still massive. He wore a coat made of pelts, just as he had the last time she saw him.

She didn't let her relief show. "Neither Wolf nor the Trolls have captured the dog yet. Someone is testing me."

"They are nothing compared to you." He came up behind her and touched her neck. She closed her eyes at the tenderness of his touch. Perhaps she could share her fears with him. Just a little.

"I cannot see them in my mirrors," the Queen said. "Something is clouding my sight. But they are near. They have left the river and are about to enter your forest."

"I will find them." His smile was as cold as the moon on a winter night. "Nothing escapes the Huntsman."

Wolf stood in front of the giant forest. The trail winding through it was dark and foreboding. He hated this place, but knew it was what would lead them to the mirror.

His Virginia wanted the mirror, and he would take her to it, even though he knew it meant her loss to him. Perhaps he could learn to survive in her world.

The books from that place were marvelous.

He glanced at the book on the forest floor, open to the page he had marked. Then he sniffed. The subtle aroma of bacon made his mouth water.

No. He had to focus. They were getting to a dangerous place. Virginia needed him to be strong.

He closed his eyes, took a deep breath, and slowly exhaled.

"I am free of pain, anger, and fear," Wolf said. "In every aspect of my life, I am guided to my highest happiness and fulfillment. All problems and struggles . . ."

Damn. He forgot the next part. He opened one eye and glanced at the book again. He had to crouch to read it. Then he stood and closed his eyes again.

". . . now fade away. I am serene. I . . . I . . ."

The bacon was getting too crisp. There was the faint smell of charred meat in the air. It broke his concentration.

"Tony!" Wolf shouted. "You're ruining the bacon. I can smell it burning."

No one answered. Wolf picked up his book and hurried to the camp. An unattended pan sat on the open flame. Tony wasn't even looking at the meat, which was shriveled and dark brown. Wolf grabbed the pan and pulled it off the flame, then winced as the heat of the pan's handle bit into his palm. He carefully set the pan down, then shook his hand to cool it off.

"I feel terrible," Tony said. "Look at him."

Wolf couldn't resist the look. The poor dog was still gold, frozen with a look of sheer determination on his little doggie face. Tony had made a cart for him, and had tied a lead around Prince's neck so that they could drag him along.

"It was a simple magic-fish-spell, gold-finger mistake, Tony," Wolf said. "It was almost predictable."

"But I've killed him," Tony said.

"Things have a way of bouncing back here," Wolf said. "I wouldn't worry about him too much."

"You're not just saying that?" For the first time, Tony looked hopeful.

Wolf sighed. There was nothing worse than false hope. "Yes, I'm afraid I am just saying that. Watch this simple Prince alertness test."

He threw a stick. "Fetch," Wolf said to the golden dog. "Fetch."

"It's not funny," Tony said.

"It might get funnier if we keep doing it," Wolf said.

Virginia picked that moment to come back to camp. She was carrying a bucket of water. Wolf was glad that she hadn't seen him make fun of her father.

"What are you both still sitting around for?" Virginia asked. "I told you to get packed up."

"We were just having a sandwich," Tony said.

"The mirror is getting farther away all the time," Virginia said. "If we lose the trail, we'll never get home."

Wolf bent over the bacon, intently putting it into sandwiches so that Virginia would think he had been industrious. Besides, he was afraid she'd make them leave without eating. No wonder the woman was dangerously slim. She let food be a second priority.

"But Virginia," Wolf said, "breakfast is bacon. Nothing sets my nostrils twitching like the smell of bacon in the morning. Little pigs, parading up and down with their curly corkscrew tails. Bacon sizzling away in an iron frying pan."

She smiled at him in bemusement. He handed her a small

sandwich, keeping the larger one for himself. Tony took one too. Apparently guilt hadn't robbed him of his entire appetite.

Wolf bit into the bacon sandwich and drooled. It was absolutely the best thing he'd eaten all day. Maybe the best thing he would eat all day. He just loved bacon. He had to share the feeling. He licked his lips and said, "Baste it, roast it, toast it, nibble it, chew it, bite right through it. Wobble it, gobble it, wrap it round a couple of chickens and *am I ravenous.*"

Virginia looked nauseated and Tony had actually turned green.

"Let's finish these off on the move," Virginia said.

Wolf wondered what he had said. He was just trying to share.

She had gotten to her feet and was finishing packing. They would leave soon, and he didn't like this tension between them.

"Virginia," Wolf said. "Stop a minute. What do you see?"

She looked around, not really taking any time to *see.* "A lot of trees. Let's go."

"No, you see nothing," Wolf said. "Look at everything that happened last night while you slept."

She turned to him. "Like what?"

He put his arm around her, pulling her close as he pointed. "See that clearing? About midnight a badger trotted across there."

She frowned as if she were trying to imagine it.

"Then," he said, "two hours later a mother fox took the path, but our presence spooked her, and she went back into the trees. About half an hour later another fox appeared, male this time, young and out courting. I reckon he got his porridge."

He pulled her even closer. She didn't seem to mind. "See, over there, where the undergrowth is disturbed?"

She nodded.

"There was a noisy little wild boar snuffling about. I can't believe he didn't wake you up. And right in front of you, see the passage of the mole."

She squinted, intent.

"Or over there, a stag and a doe watched the sun come up with me. And that's not mentioning the all-night rabbit party, or the weasel, or the pheasants. And you saw nothing."

She was silent for a moment. He held his breath, wondering if she understood. Then she smiled.

"I stand corrected," she said.

"You most certainly do," Wolf said fondly.

"Great," Virginia said. "Now can we go?"

When they turned around, Wolf was startled to see that Tony had packed up their cart. Amazing what guilt would do. Wolf glanced at Virginia, who gave him a silent sign to say nothing.

They made their way along the path. The forest was dark and quiet, almost too quiet. As much beauty as there was here, Wolf was not comfortable in this place. The Huntsman was too strong a presence.

They'd been walking a while when Tony suddenly stopped and pointed. "Here," Tony said. "Look. Someone's definitely brought a cart up here. You can see the tracks of the wheels."

Virginia stiffened. Wolf could feel her interest.

"Dwarf," Wolf said. "Definitely."

"You can actually smell a dwarf?" Virginia asked.

"No." Wolf scooped up a handful of fragrant dirt. On top were small cut brown leaves the size of ants. "But this is a dwarf shag. Very strong rolling tobacco. No one else in the Nine Kingdoms touches it. He has taken the main forest road, and so must we."

Wolf went deeper into the giant forest, knowing that Virginia and Tony would follow him. He could hear the squealing of the wheels on the little cart. It must have been a lot of work for Tony to drag Prince along, but Tony wasn't complaining. That was a surprise in and of itself.

If Tony could change, perhaps Wolf could also. There was always hope.

Around a corner, Wolf stopped. He smelled something—some*one*—coming toward them. Virginia stopped too and looked quizzically at him. Wolf only had to wait a moment for Virginia's question to be answered.

An elderly woman carrying a bundle of twigs was walking toward them. When she saw them, she held out a thin, bony hand. "Ah, I am but a poor old lady. Spare me some food."

Food. If she'd asked for anything else, Wolf might have obliged. "Sorry," he said, "but we're down to our last six bacon sandwiches."

The woman turned to Tony. "Good sir—"

Tony held out his hands. "I only give to registered charities."

"Young lady," the old woman said, turning to Virginia, "would you spare me some food, please?"

Virginia smiled. "I'll give you what I have."

She reached into her bag and gave the old woman her last two sandwiches.

"Virginia," Tony said, "you are a soft touch."

A soft touch? Wolf would have called her a saint. People did not give up food so easily. Or at least, wolves didn't.

"Since you have been kind, I have a lesson for all of you. Take this stick." She handed Virginia one of the twigs she had gathered.

Virginia took it and looked a bit confused.

"Break it," the old woman said.

Virginia did.

The old woman handed her another twig. "And this one."

The snap echoed through the trees. Virginia looked even more confused. Wolf was fascinated.

"Put these three sticks together," the old woman said, handing three more twigs to Virginia.

Virginia bundled them together neatly, as if she were going to be graded on her work. Wolf was frowning. What was the old woman getting at?

"Now try to break them."

Virginia bent them as she had the first two. But she couldn't even get the twigs to move. She looked up at the old woman. "I can't," Virginia said.

"That is the lesson," the old woman said.

Wolf tilted his head slightly. He didn't get it. Apparently neither did Tony. He frowned.

"At least give one of the sandwiches back," Tony said.

"When the students are ready," the old woman said, "the teacher appears."

"Not in our school they didn't," Tony said.

But Virginia didn't seem upset by this lesson. She said to the old woman, "Have you passed a dwarf driving a cart?"

"Very early this morning," the old woman said. "He has taken the main forest road, but you must not. You must leave the path."

Wolf drew in a sharp breath. A warning. He had felt it all morning. But he gave the old woman the argument he'd been giving himself. "The road's the only safe thing in this whole forest."

The old woman stared at him for a moment. Her eyes were rheumy, her face a little too calm. "Not for you," she said. "Someone is following you. They intend to kill you."

Then she walked away, bent double under the weight of the twigs. Wolf watched her go, the disquiet he'd felt since they got off the river growing.

"What's this 'intend to kill'?" Tony asked, staring after the old woman.

Wolf was afraid he knew. "There is a man who controls this forest. The Huntsman. I have heard that he serves the Queen. But he certainly won't expect us to leave the only road and go through the forest itself."

"Why not?" Virginia asked.

"Because only a fool would go through the disenchanted forest." Wolf stepped off the path. His hackles rose, but he kept going. He would have to be vigilant.

"Oh, great," Tony said. "Talk it up some more."

Wolf resisted the urge to take Virginia's hand. It was better if they went single file.

"From now on," Wolf said, "I will lead. Step only where I step."

He hoped Tony and Virginia would listen and do as he said. Any mistake here could cost them all their lives.

Chapter Twenty-One

The Queen stood in front of one of her mirrors, disgusted with the scene before her. Beantown was a war zone. Barns were burning in the background, buildings were obviously pillaged, and some were covered in graffiti. She could hear the faint sound of screams coming through the magic glass.

The Troll King stood before her, his hands on his hips. He had soot on one side of his face, and he did not seem happy to be summoned by her.

"What do you want?" the Troll King asked.

"You are inviting trouble," the Queen said.

"I'll tell you something," the Troll King said. "War is great fun when there's no enemy."

Behind him, a crowd of locals were being herded toward the river by Trolls. The locals looked beaten and bloodied, the Trolls victorious.

"You are very stupid, even for a Troll," the Queen said. "Wendell's kingdom borders all the others. They're not going to let it fall without a fight. The other kingdoms will send in troops and crush you."

"I'll kill them, too," the Troll King said. "I'm not scared of anybody."

She leaned toward the mirror. Something had to interest this creature. "Listen to me. I will give you everything you desire, but you must leave Beantown. Now."

A battalion of Trolls marched behind him. They had banners and were singing marching songs.

"Beantown's old news," the Troll King said. "We've got control of every village within twenty miles of here. And it's not stopping there. I'm taking my half of the kingdom right now. Want to make something of it?"

He walked away from the mirror, laughing. She tried to summon him back, but he did not come. With a wave of her hand, she got rid of his image and replaced it with another.

The Huntsman stood in the woods, gazing at her in a hand mirror. He did not seem upset that she had contacted him.

She said, "Wendell's council don't believe the letter I sent, telling them Wendell was recovering in his hunting lodge. I watched their stupid meeting and they have sent a man to the lodge. He must not return."

"It is done," the Huntsman said.

The Queen smiled at him. He, at least, was a worthy ally.

Virginia followed Wolf deeper into the forest. Her father walked behind her, the wheels of poor Prince Wendell's cart squeaking in a regular rhythm. She found that almost comforting. Everything else was not.

It was dark, even though it was the middle of the day. The trees were so close together that she had to search for pockets of light. In the distance, she could hear screeches and howls. They were unlike any noises she'd heard before, yet they made the hair rise on the back of her neck.

But those noises weren't what unnerved her the most. It was the whistle of the wind, the groaning of the trees, and a sound she couldn't identify, a sound almost like breathing, as if the entire forest were alive.

"Hey, is it just me," her father said, "or can you hear moaning?"

"You'll hear lots of things," Wolf said. "The forest is magical."

He sounded so calm about that. Virginia had now spent two

days in the presence of magic, and she still wasn't used to it. Nor was she used to the threats that seemed to come from everywhere.

If it wasn't an old woman warning that they'd all be killed, it was Trolls chasing them, or horrible magic fish granting her father's wishes. Wolf led them to a clearing and Virginia groaned. This was a prime example of what she had just been thinking about.

Dead animals were strung up all around them: rabbit, deer, even a bear. Hanging from the bottom of another signpost were these words:

IF YOU ARE READING THIS,
YOU ARE TRESPASSING.
ALL TRESPASSERS WILL BE CONSIDERED POACHERS.
ALL POACHERS WILL BE SHOT.

—BY ORDER OF THE HUNTSMAN

And beneath that was a large circle of dried blood, fur, and feathers, apparently to make the point to all species. Virginia didn't like the forest, the clearing, or the sign. Especially the sign. It showed a knowledge of Aristotelian logic that made her shudder.

The Huntsman was smart.

"Do you actually know where we're going?" Virginia asked Wolf, trying to keep the worry out of her voice.

"I am following my nose," the Wolf said.

The screech of the wheels on Prince Wendell's cart stopped. Virginia and Wolf turned at the same time. Virginia's father was using all of his strength to pull Wendell's cart from a rut in the narrow path.

"Tony!" Wolf shouted. "Don't move!"

Her father looked startled. "What? Why?"

Wolf picked up a stick and threw it just in front of Tony. There was a loud slam as a concealed bear trap snapped shut.

Virginia felt all the blood leave her face. If it had caught her father, it would have taken his leg off.

"That's it," Tony said. "Let's get back on the road."

"No, come on," Wolf said. "Keep moving. Let's get as far as we can in daylight."

"Daylight?" Virginia asked. This time she let her nervousness in and she didn't care if he heard it. "What do you mean in daylight? We're not going to spend the night in here. Exactly how big is this forest?"

"The Thousand Mile Forest is approximately one thousand miles long."

Virginia thought about that. How long would it take them to walk through the forest? A human being only traveled a mile every twenty minutes or so, maybe slower if she was with her father who was dragging a solid gold dog on a cart. That meant, at best, three miles an hour. There were twenty-four hours in a day, but a person could only walk about twelve of those so, three times twelve was thirty-six. A person could reasonably do thirty-six miles a day. And thirty-six went into a thousand—

Her mind boggled. She forced herself to concentrate on the math. She knew she knew it. Math was easy for her. She tried to ignore the growing darkness. The forest was spooky enough with little rays of light coming in. Now that the light was fading, the place was becoming absolutely terrifying.

Twenty-seven-point-seven times. So thirty-six into a thousand equaled twenty-seven-point-seven, which meant that it would take a month to walk through this entire place.

Virginia shuddered. She'd only been here two days. A month seemed like forever.

"We can't walk all night," Tony said.

"Yes, we can," Wolf said.

"Shhh," Virginia said. "There are lights up ahead."

They crept to a clearing deep in the forest, where three wagons formed a small encampment. They looked like gypsy wagons from old Bela Lugosi movies. Faintly, she heard music—fiddle music. It made her want to dance.

"What do we do?" Tony asked.

"Come and join us, of course."

Virginia started. The voice had come from behind them. She turned. Two men in colorful clothing stood as close to her as a person could get. They were carrying axes and firewood. They didn't seem menacing, but she didn't trust anything she saw in this place.

Wolf, on the other hand, looked very nervous. As the men led Virginia, her father, and Wolf into camp, Wolf leaned over to her and whispered, "They are all poachers. They will kill us if they so choose. Do not refuse anything they offer, but do not consume anything you have not already seen them eat first."

"It's just like eating at your grandmother's house, Virginia," Tony said.

She glared at him. He was still dragging poor Prince Wendell. She wondered what the Gypsies would think of that.

Their camp wasn't as temporary as it had seemed from the clearing. All around there were skins and drying meat from the animals the Gypsies had killed. In one area, there were six wooden cages, filled with birds. The birds were still alive. They watched as Virginia and her band came into camp.

There were about a dozen Gypsies. One of them was throwing a large knife at a tree and didn't stop as Virginia walked past.

A shy boy of nine or ten sat near one of the wagons. He watched as Virginia passed; then he saw Wolf. The boy's eyes lit up, but he didn't move. The boy had a very intense expression on his face. Wolf didn't look that unusual. Did the boy know him?

They reached the center of the camp. It was lit by lanterns and fires. Virginia didn't realize how spooky flickering light was until she saw it against the utter darkness of the forest.

The light moved, and more than once she glanced into the shadows, thinking she saw something.

The music was even more intoxicating up close. Virginia could feel it like a live thing, encouraging her to dance. The Gypsies asked her and her friends to sit, which they did. They had interrupted the Gypsies' dinner. Without asking, a Gypsy woman dished up plates for all three of them.

Virginia took hers without looking at it. Wolf held his. Her father turned his food over with his knife. He took a bite, and Virginia looked at him warningly. Had the Gypsies eaten some of theirs? She hadn't noticed.

He chewed the way he did when he was given something he hated, and then smiled unconvincingly.

"What do you call this?" he asked. "Suckling hedgehog?"

Virginia glanced at Wolf to see if he could smooth this over, but he was looking at the dark-haired boy.

At that moment, the fiddler finished a beautiful piece of music.

"Your turn, stranger," he said to Tony.

"I don't play."

"Then sing us a song," the Gypsy said.

"I'm not really a singer."

Wolf finally turned his attention back to what was going on. "Sing anything, Anthony," Wolf said softly. "Let's not insult them."

"I can't think of anything," Tony said.

Virginia couldn't either. She glanced over her shoulder. The big Gypsy in the back was sharpening his knives. He saw her look at him.

"Is our hospitality not worth a song?" he asked.

Her father grinned his little suck-up grin and glanced at Virginia. She shrugged. Then he started, in a wavery voice, to sing the old Cher song, "Gypsies, Tramps, and Thieves." Surprisingly, he remembered the verses, and even more surprisingly, his voice got stronger and became rather nice as it went along.

She hadn't heard her father sing in a long time. Even if the song was not really what she would have chosen.

As her father sang, Virginia noted another Gypsy man studying Prince Wendell. The man ran his hands along Wendell's back. Virginia wanted to stop him, to claim that Wendell was hers, but she was afraid of insulting him.

When her father finished singing, the man said to him, "Is he real gold?"

Virginia felt her heart sink. How would they get out of this one?

"Oh, no, no," Tony said. "It's gold paint. He's one of a pair I bought for my driveway, you know, they're both going to sit on the front gates."

The Gypsy man seemed to accept the explanation. Virginia stood to stretch her legs. She wasn't sure she could sleep here. It was so strange.

She walked toward the birdcages.

"Set me free."

Virginia jumped. She looked both ways, but didn't see where the voice had come from.

"Set me free."

She peered into the cage. One of the birds had spoken to her. She wasn't as surprised by that as she would have been just a few hours ago. Maybe she was getting used to this place.

"Please set us free," another bird begged. "We're just little victims."

Wolf came up behind her. She could feel him before she heard him.

"They are magic birds," he said softly. "Very rare, very hard to catch. Only the Gypsies know how to catch them."

"Little victims," one bird said. "You understand that, girlie? Little victims."

Virginia felt Wolf's warmth against her back. "What will happen to them?"

"They will have their wings broken and then be sold to rich people."

"We won't, will we?" one bird asked. "That's awful."

"Some people eat them," Wolf said, "believing they absorb their magic."

"They don't, do they?" the bird said. "That's terrible."

"I have six little babies waiting to be fed," the other bird said. "They're starving to death without me."

"It's so cruel," Virginia said.

Suddenly the door to one of the caravans opened, and an ancient crone emerged. Virginia would never have used that word, not even mentally, but she knew of no other. The woman looked like she was six hundred years old and had been the meanest person on the planet for five hundred and ninety-nine of those years. Virginia felt her heart begin to race.

The crone fixed her glare on Wolf, then Tony, and then Virginia. Virginia had never seen eyes like that, and she knew her own fear showed in her face.

This woman, or so someone whispered, was the Gypsies' Queen. Virginia was beginning to think being a Queen in this place was not a good idea.

"Set up the table," the Gypsy Queen said.

The other Gypsies hurried to do her bidding. Quickly they set up a table with a cloth over it and a chair at one end. They placed a tarot deck in front of her, and a bowl of red liquid. She beckoned Virginia's father to sit in the chair. Virginia was relieved that the crone didn't ask her to sit.

The Gypsy Queen dealt the cards. "I see great wealth coming to you," she said to Tony.

He smiled. "I like the sound of that."

"And passing straight through," the Gypsy Queen said.

"That was just the bean I had," Tony said. "What about the future?"

"I find The Fool," the Gypsy Queen said as she turned over another card.

"What's that card?" Tony asked, pointing to the next card she turned over.

"The Fool's friend, The Oaf," the Queen said, turning over

more cards. "He is joined by The Buffoon and The Village Idiot. And behind him, The Cret—"

"Can we get back to the financial advice?" Tony asked.

"There is nothing beneath the surface," the Gypsy Queen said. "I will read the girl."

Virginia shook her head. She didn't want this woman looking into her life. "No, thanks."

The Gypsy Queen stared at Virginia. Virginia stared back. The Queen's stare grew more and more malevolent. Or perhaps Virginia only feared that was what was happening.

Finally she took a deep breath. What would it hurt? Tarot cards existed in her world. They didn't work.

Virginia sat in the chair her father had just vacated.

The Gypsy Queen dealt some cards, then stared at them for a moment before speaking. "You are full of anger. You conceal much about yourself."

The Gypsy Queen reached into her dress and removed a pair of scissors. With age-crabbed hands she reached forward and grabbed a lock of Virginia's hair. Virginia tried not to cringe as the Gypsy Queen snipped it off. She threw the lock of hair in the red liquid.

"You have a great destiny that reaches way back in time," she said.

Virginia snorted. "I'm a waitress, so no prizes so far."

The Gypsy Queen looked at her hair as the strands separated in the liquid. "You have never forgiven your mother for leaving you."

That was enough. Virginia stood. "As I said, I don't really want my fortune read."

Wolf slipped into the chair, a smile on his face. He held his hand out like a child. Virginia moved out of the way, relieved that he had taken her place.

"Love and romance, please," Wolf said as the Gypsy Queen took his hand. "Marriage, children, how long I will have to wait until the creamy girl of my dreams says yes, that sort of thing."

"I see death," the Gypsy Queen said. "A young girl dead. Torn to pieces."

Wolf's smile faded. "Oh, no. I was thinking more along the lines of two boys and three girls—you know, a family—"

"I see a fire being built," the Gypsy Queen said. "You are going to be burnt on it."

"No." Wolf tried to pull his hand away, but the Gypsy Queen kept a firm grip on it.

"You are not what you seem. You are a wolf!"

Knives came out all over camp. Virginia had never seen so many weapons in one place. They glinted in the moving light, like the eyes of the Gypsies themselves.

Wolf didn't seem alarmed by this. He had stopped struggling. He was looking at the Gypsy Queen. "I am a wolf," he said softly, "and so is your grandson."

Virginia looked at the boy in the corner. He was watching just as intently.

The Gypsy Queen gazed at Wolf for a long moment, then smiled and released his hand. "You must stay with us tonight," she said. "Friends must stay together in the dangerous forest."

The word "friend" reassured Virginia a little. She would rather be in this heavily guarded place, trying to get some sleep, than walking through the forest in the dark. She said as much to Wolf later, who gave her a measuring look, as if he wasn't sure he would rather be here.

Eventually, Virginia lay down by the fire. Her father was beside her, and Wolf was nowhere to be seen. She craned her neck and finally saw Wolf talking to the young boy. There was a tenderness and patience in Wolf's manner that Virginia had never seen before.

She smiled and watched for a time. But her eyelids got heavier and heavier, and eventually she fell asleep.

She dreamed she was in the forest. It was twilight or perhaps full daylight. She couldn't tell. But she could see Wolf about twenty feet away from her. In the strange light, he looked very predatory. She closed her eyes for an instant, and when she opened them, her heart jumped. Wolf was closer.

"You moved," she said.

"No, I didn't." Wolf was standing absolutely still, just as he had before. The darkness was becoming night. The light was fading fast, and Virginia did not want to be in the woods in the dark. She glanced over her shoulder and when she looked back, she saw Wolf.

"You moved," she said.

"I haven't moved an inch," Wolf said.

But he had. He was only ten feet away from her. And he was standing still, smiling a weird smile. She felt as if she were prey. She finally understood why people talked of deer getting trapped in the headlights. She had this funny feeling that, if she moved, he would be right beside her.

But that was silly. She tested it, and when she turned back around, he was only six feet away. She glanced at the path to see if she could escape, and now he was only three feet away.

She didn't want him to get any closer. She was afraid of what he would do.

She was afraid of what she would do.

She stared at him, and didn't move.

She didn't move at all.

Chapter Twenty-Two

A hand over her mouth awoke Virginia. She opened her eyes and was startled to see Wolf so close. For a moment, she was back in her dream. He must have seen the panic in her eyes, for he held his hand in place a moment longer than he probably should have.

Her father was gathering their things. A bit of light had seeped into the clearing. It was dawn. But the Gypsies still slept. Virginia sat up. Wolf put a finger to his lips just in case she didn't understand the importance of remaining silent. But she did. She wanted to get out of there as much as he did.

She finger-combed her hair, wished for a toothbrush, and dusted herself off. Her father already had Prince Wendell and his little cart pointed in the right direction; Virginia could only hope that the cart's squeaking wheels didn't wake up the Gypsies. Wolf and her father apparently had the same thought. They started to carry Prince Wendell out of camp.

"Set us free," one of the magic birds said. "Please set us free."

Virginia looked over her shoulder. Wolf and her father had Wendell safely out of earshot. She glanced at the birds. Their tiny bodies were pressed against the cages.

They'd have their wings broken, or worse. All because of what they were.

She couldn't stand it. She'd never be able to live with herself. Quickly she opened the cages, and the birds flew free.

"Virginia," Wolf whispered.

Virginia heard him, but she pretended she didn't. There were a lot of cages, and a lot of birds. She knew she was ruining someone's work, but she didn't care.

Lives were at stake.

She had gotten all the cages. And then she looked at the Gypsy Queen's caravan. One more cage hung over the door.

"Oh, no, please," Tony said to her. "That's enough."

He was right. But that single birdcage would bother her as much as all the others did. She bit her lower lip. Three wooden steps led to the door. She climbed the stairs carefully, trying to avoid the creaks she knew were there. When she reached the stoop, she reached up. She had to stand on tiptoe to reach the cage door. For a moment, her fingers brushed against the catch. Then they hit it, and the door opened.

The magic bird flew off, but Virginia slipped. Her foot banged down on the steps. The force of her landing sounded like a gunshot in the still air.

She turned just as the caravan door ripped open. A Gypsy she had never seen before started after her. Virginia ran as fast as she could. The Gypsy was yelling and the others were waking up. She only had a short lead.

She followed Wolf and her father's path into the forest, but she couldn't see them. She knew they had seen what she did. Were they hiding?

Behind her, the Gypsies pounded through the woods, obviously not caring about how loud they were. Virginia stopped for a brief second; she had to figure out which way Wolf and her father had gone.

Something caught her ankle. She looked down, fearing it was a trap. Then the something yanked. She fell, sliding down a bank. Wolf pulled her close as the Gypsies ran past.

She was beneath a river bank overhang. The river flowed below them. The dirt had gotten into the back of her shirt. She was breathing hard, and Wolf put a finger to his lips for silence. She was trying, she really was, but she needed air.

"They can't have got away," a Gypsy said above them. "Search around for them. They're hiding somewhere."

Virginia's throat went dry. They weren't hiding that well. She could hear the Gypsies in the underbrush, snapping twigs, calling to each other. She pressed herself deeper into the bank, and so did her father and Wolf.

Dirt drifted down on them. A Gypsy was above them. Virginia closed her eyes. Then she heard the Gypsy Queen's voice, faint and reedy. The Gypsy above them cursed. More dirt fell, and then Virginia heard the sounds of Gypsies moving away from them.

The woods got very silent. Virginia opened her eyes. Wolf was frowning. Her father was still hugging Wendell. If the prince were alive, Virginia wondered how he felt about all this dragging around.

Wolf motioned to them to be silent. Then he climbed up the bank and disappeared.

A moment later he returned. Virginia's father turned on him. "What did you do that for?"

Wolf didn't answer, at least not directly. He dusted himself off and shook his head. "I don't understand. The old woman has called off the hunt."

For some reason that news didn't make Virginia happy. She felt the way Wolf obviously did—the Gypsies wouldn't have called off the search without a reason.

Her father moved away from the bank. "Maybe we just got lucky," he said. "Let's get going. The sooner we're out of this forest, the better. Help me carry Prince until we get back on the path."

Wolf looked at Prince Wendell with an antipathy that he hadn't shown before, although Virginia knew he had felt it.

"Can't we bury him?" Wolf asked. "We can always come back some time in the future."

"I'm not leaving him," Tony said. "I got him into this mess, and I'll get him out."

Virginia smiled. Her father really was a gentle man, even though he was the world's biggest screw-up.

But Wolf wasn't thinking about Prince Wendell. Wolf was looking over his shoulder toward the Gypsy camp.

"I wish I knew why they gave up so easily," Wolf said. "That's not like Gypsies at all."

The Gypsy Queen stared at the empty birdcage above her caravan door. Seven years of work ruined. And to think she had shown the travelers kindness. They had shown their true natures this morning.

She took out the pot that contained a lock of Virginia's hair and sprinkled gray powder over it. The liquid caught fire even quicker than she expected it too.

The Gypsy Queen closed her eyes and began to recite: "Stretch it, twist it, make it grow. Like a river, make it flow. Make it pull and pinch and tweak. Make it grow 'til she grows weak. Make her moan and scream and cry. Make her wish that she would die."

Then she opened her eyes and watched the lock of hair burn. People should never take advantage of a Gypsy's kindness—no matter who they were.

Wolf felt uneasy. The hackles on his neck had risen and he wasn't sure why. It wasn't just the Gypsies. He knew they were no longer chasing the group, but he didn't know why. Perhaps that was what disturbed him so much—the not knowing why.

He led the others through the forest. The squeak-squeak-squeak of the cart wheels was really beginning to annoy him. Prince Wendell was a giant hunk of gold and an even bigger pain in the rear end. Tony wasn't capable of making this better. Knowing Tony's propensity for messing up, he would only make things worse.

Still, he wasn't responding to Wolf's not-so-subtle hints to get rid of Prince Wendell. In fact, Tony was acting just a little bit strange. He kept glancing at Virginia, a small frown on his face.

Virginia must have noticed it too, because she glared at her father. "What are you looking at me for?"

"Your hair looks different," Tony said.

"Right," Virginia said. "That's because I went to the beautician last night."

"No, it's grown," Tony said.

"Grown?"

Wolf looked at it too and jumped back in shock. "So it has," he said.

It hadn't grown a little bit. It had grown a lot. Virginia reached to her skull and touched her hair. She frowned. She didn't know what was going on, and he wasn't sure he wanted to tell her.

Wolf glanced at Tony, who raised his eyebrows for an explanation Wolf wasn't yet ready to give. Instead he led them forward.

They walked for nearly an hour when Wolf saw a small pond up ahead. Virginia saw it too, and rushed to it. She bent over and stared in it.

Her hair had grown to the middle of her back.

"Oh, no," Virginia said. "It's even longer than it was a half hour ago. It's growing all the time. What's happening to me? What am I going to do?"

"Braid it?" Tony said.

Wolf closed his eyes. He had to tell her now.

"The Gypsies," he said. "They had some of your hair. They have cursed you."

"What do you mean, cursed?" Virginia demanded. "Stop it. This is really freaking me out."

It wasn't his fault. Although he would probably be as upset as she was if his hair started growing like that.

He removed his knife from his pocket and held it out, silently asking her if he could cut her hair. She nodded, frightened, as if her hair were an alien thing that clung to her head instead of a part of her.

He hacked at the hair with the knife, but it was like trying to cut stone.

"Here, let me try," Tony said.

Wolf handed him the knife, then leaned back to watch. Virginia's hair was growing fast. It was nearly to her knees.

Tony sawed at her hair for several minutes, then shook his head. "It's no good," he said. "It won't cut. It's like steel."

"Maybe the knife is blunt," Virginia said.

"There's nothing wrong with the knife," Wolf said. "It's the curse."

"It's horrible," Virginia said. "I can feel it growing."

"Well," Tony said, "it never would have happened if you hadn't tried to play Miss Francis of Assisi."

"Shut up," Virginia said. Then she turned to Wolf. "How do we stop it? How do you uncurse me?"

"Curses are not my strong suit," Wolf said.

"Try pulling just one hair out," Tony said.

Wolf grabbed a single hair and tugged.

"Ow!" Virginia said after a moment. "Stop it."

"It won't budge," Wolf said.

"If we help gather it up," Tony said, "we could wrap it around you like a scarf."

Wolf gathered it. There was a lot of hair and it was very soft. Fragrant. Beautiful even in its length. But he knew better than to tell Virginia that. Right now, she was too upset.

He wrapped the hair around her, resisted the urge to kiss her furrowed brow, and then led them deeper into the forest.

They walked for some time, occasionally stopping to get Wendell out of a rut in the road or to wrap Virginia's hair around her neck again. She was becoming a walking dress of hair. It was somewhat erotic.

Wolf kept that thought to himself as well.

Then thunder boomed overhead. Virginia moaned. Wolf

looked up, and as he did, a sheet of rain fell from the sky as if some mighty being had poured it from a bucket.

He waved Tony forward—he wanted to keep an eye on Tony and Prince Wendell, figuring that in this mud, they'd get stuck—and he let Virginia shuffle past him.

She looked depressed, almost as if she had given up hope. Perhaps he should say something nice about the hair just so that she could yell at him.

Some of the hair was dragging behind her. He said nothing, just picked it up and carried it as though it were a train.

"You're jerking it," Virginia said without turning around.

"Sorry," Wolf said. "It's not easy. You've got a lot of split ends."

"How long is it now?" Tony asked.

"Don't ask," Wolf said.

The rain was really coming down now. Prince Wendell was spattered with mud, and Wolf couldn't remember the last time he had gotten this wet.

Virginia's hair was much heavier wet. He couldn't imagine what it felt like to her

"I can't go any farther," Virginia said. "We've got to stop somewhere."

"Where will we find shelter in the middle of the for—" Then Wolf saw it. "Cripes, look."

He pointed to a small cabin almost hidden by trees. Lightning flared and thunder boomed. The cabin looked abandoned. But it did have a good roof.

They ran to the door, Tony dragging Wendell behind him. The door was covered in white graffiti. Wolf had to kick it to get it to open. It fell back in a spray of dust and cobwebs.

"Anyone home?" Virginia asked.

They stepped inside. Everything was covered in misspelled graffiti, including several versions of the perennial favorite, *Elves Suck.* But that wasn't what caught Wolf's attention. His gaze landed on seven pewter mugs and seven tiny lamps. They were lined up as if someone still expected to use them, even though they were covered in eons of dust.

"What's that stink?" Tony asked.

"Trolls have been here," Wolf said, ducking under the low roof. "They like to mark their territory, rather like—dogs."

"Trolls?"

"It's all right." Wolf made sure the door was closed. The rain pounded on the ceiling. "No one's been here for a long time."

Tony went up a small flight of stairs, leaving Wendell behind. Wolf looked at the seven tiny spoons and the seven tiny bowls. Virginia was trying to get the moisture out of her hair.

"Hey, come look at this," Tony called from above.

Wolf and Virginia hurried up the stairs. There was a small hole in the roof and leaves had blown in. The upper level was damp.

But Wolf didn't give that more than a cursory glance. Instead he stared in gape-mouthed surprise at the seven tiny beds. They all were made of wood, and they all had little quilts and pillows. They were all perfectly straight and, even though they were covered with dust and leaves, they looked as if they were waiting for their little owners to return for a good night's rest.

"Are you thinking what I'm thinking?" Tony said.

Wolf grinned and stepped in deeper. He couldn't help himself. A curious joy filled him.

"This is Snow White's cottage. Goodness gracious me, this is the Seven Dwarves' house. It has been lost for a very long time."

His gaze met Virginia's. She smiled at him. "Look at the beds," she said. "They're so tiny."

"This is a great piece of our history," Wolf said. "What a pity the Prince is a stiff. This is his grandma's cottage. Cripes."

He was beginning to feel pity for the mutt. That was bad.

Still, he stood in this historic place for a moment longer before he saw Virginia shiver.

"We have to get settled for the night, and get you dry," he said to her.

She nodded. Tony gave one last look to the room, then led them down the stairs. Wolf stayed up there alone for a moment. Then he slapped a wooden beam and grinned. Hardly anyone had seen this. And he'd been lucky enough to come here. That made this entire forest worthwhile.

Then he went downstairs.

It took nearly half an hour for him and Tony to clean up the downstairs and to barricade some furniture against the door. Virginia was trying to dry her hair with anything she could find. Finally, she gave up and used the wood piled next to the fireplace to build a fire.

By the time Wolf figured out what she was doing, it was too late.

"We shouldn't really have a fire," he said.

"I don't care." Virginia held a thick strand of extremely long hair in front of the fire. "I'm not going to sleep with wet hair."

Wolf sat down next to her and started to help. He didn't want her to set her head on fire. Tony collapsed in a chair. He looked tired too.

"I can't believe I'm asking this," Tony said, "but what happened to Snow White after she married the Prince?"

Wolf looked up, surprised that Tony didn't know. "She became a great ruler. One of the Five Women Who Changed History."

"Five women?" Virginia asked, clearly intrigued. "Who were the others?"

"Cinderella, Queen Riding Hood, Rapunzel, and Gretel the Great. They formed the first Five Kingdoms and brought peace throughout the lands. But they are long gone. Some say Cinderella is still alive, but she hasn't been seen in public for nearly forty years. She would be nearly two hundred years old." Wolf sighed and looked at the roaring fire. "The days of Happy Ever After are long gone. These are dark times."

Virginia was beginning to think her hair would never dry. Fortunately the new parts, the parts around her skull, were coming out dry.

Her father had long ago gone to bed upstairs. He'd gotten Wolf's help to put four of the tiny beds together so that he could spread out on them. Her father had placed Prince Wendell at the foot of one of the beds as if he were on watch.

Virginia supposed she should go to bed too, but the fire still burned high, and the bulk of her hair was still wet. And she wasn't that tired.

Wolf was helping her dry the rest of her hair, holding up parts of it and studying it as if it were the most beautiful thing he'd ever seen. If the hair didn't frighten her so, she would like that.

But she wanted to think of something else. She leaned closer to the fire's warmth.

"What did you say to that boy?" she asked. "In the Gypsy camp?"

"Nothing much. Just wolf stuff."

"And what's wolf stuff?"

"I did not need to say anything to him," Wolf said. "I just was with him. He had never seen another wolf. He was scared. It is a lonely path in life to be different. As you know."

She made herself smile.

"Where's your mum?"

Virginia stiffened. What had made him ask that? "I have no idea. She walked out on us when I was seven."

Wolf didn't seem to notice the chill in her voice. He said softly, "How sad to be left when you were so little."

Virginia resisted the urge to pull her hair out of his grasp. "I very rarely think about her, to be honest. She's not really been part of my life."

"What happened?" Wolf rested his chin on his hand and

turned toward her. His eyes seemed paler and warmer in the firelight.

Virginia looked away from him. "She just left home. Wouldn't you if you were married to my dad? They were totally different people. You've met my grandmother. My mother was like that. It was a complete mismatch. They should have never got married. Anyway, it was a long time ago."

"Where is she now?" Wolf asked.

All this probing was beginning to give her a headache. "I haven't a clue and I couldn't care less."

"You don't wonder what she's like?"

She knew what her mother was like, just from her mother's actions so long ago. Her mother was a cold woman who only cared about herself. "She could have got back in touch if she'd wanted, but she hasn't and that's fine. She doesn't want me. I'm not going to waste energy thinking about her."

"Oh," Wolf said. He was apparently beginning to understand that Virginia found this to be a touchy subject.

"Oh, what?" Virginia asked.

"Just oh," Wolf said. "Oh, as in a noncommittal, encouraging noise. Try not to comment as you listen, as my very good self-help books tell me."

She sneezed. He stroked her hair. It felt good.

"You must do something magnificent with your life," he said.

"Oh, yeah?" Virginia asked. "Why?"

"Because your hurt is very great," Wolf said.

She yanked her hair out of his grasp. "They just split up, all right? Doesn't that ever happen where you come from?"

"Of course not," Wolf said. "We either live happily ever after or get killed by horrible curses."

That deflated her anger a bit. She put her hair back within his reach. He took it as if nothing had happened.

After a moment, he asked, "You don't trust anybody?"

"I don't trust you, no," Virginia said.

That didn't seem to surprise him. "Well, maybe you won't get hurt," he said. "But huff-puff, you won't get loved either."

Virginia snorted. "Love is such bullshit. Love is just what people say they feel because they're frightened of being on their own."

"I see," Wolf said.

The flatness of his voice caught her attention. She turned to him. He really was a handsome man. She had noticed that from the first. Handsome in a rakish sort of way.

"Have you got anything to say about that?" Virginia asked.

"Nope," Wolf said.

But she knew he did. And he was telling her without words.

Chapter Twenty-Three

The Dog Prince was tucked in bed, his hands curved like paws over the covers. In this light, he looked almost . . . cute. The Queen gazed fondly at him. He had really been a very good dog.

She only wished she could make him a better prince.

"You remember how I told you where I got my magic?" the Queen asked.

"From the nasty stepmother in the swamp?" the Dog Prince said.

"Well, when she was dead and I had mastered her mirrors," the Queen said, "I went to the White Castle. By this time Snow White herself was long dead, and her only son had married, and he himself had a newborn son, Prince Wendell."

"That's me," the Dog Prince said.

"Exactly. I became his nursemaid, and over three long years I slowly poisoned his mother, the Queen, and then for three more years I comforted the heartbroken King, and then married him. When I was called the Queen for the first time it made me feel, well . . . at home."

She could remember how good that felt as if it had happened just yesterday. When she became Queen, she had known almost immediately that she needed more.

"I was already slowly poisoning Wendell's father," she said, "and soon he too had died, and little Wendell, the last of the House of White, was the one remaining barrier to my absolute power."

With her right hand, she stroked the Dog Prince's face. He leaned into it the way he used to do when he was a dog.

"But my plan was discovered, and Wendell survived, and I was thrown in prison for ten thousand years. Thank goodness they abolished the death penalty, that's all I can say."

She leaned over and tenderly kissed the Dog Prince good night. Then she reached for the lamp, pausing for just a moment.

"I'll bet," she said softly, "he certainly wishes he'd killed me now."

She was warm for the first time in days, and she was sleeping on a soft bed. It felt very good. It felt . . . hairy.

Virginia's eyes fluttered. As she opened them, she stared at the ceiling trying to remember where she was. She rolled over and saw that she was on a sea of hair.

"Oh, my God," she said. "Oh, my God."

"What?" Wolf said, waking up. "What? Goodness me. Cripes."

The hair was in all the rooms, going up the stairs. She had never seen so much hair in her life.

"It's everywhere," Virginia said.

Wolf stared at it as if he'd never seen anything like it. She hadn't. She was beginning to hyperventilate. He put his hands on her shoulders.

"We'll solve this," he said. Then he shouted for her father. After a few moments, Tony came out of the upstairs room— and slipped on her hair. He slid partway down the stairs, catching himself with his arms on the banister.

For a moment, he stared at the sea of hair; then he ran back upstairs. Virginia felt abandoned, but only for a moment. He came down with a pair of garden shears.

"Let's take this outside," Wolf said. He helped her through all the hair. It took some work to remove the furniture from the door, but they managed.

The morning was as bright as mornings got in this awful forest. Wolf grabbed an axe and helped Virginia near a tree.

"Stay still," he warned.

She nodded. He brought the axe down on her hair again and again. Nothing happened.

She looked over her shoulder. Wolf was now using a handsaw. He brought it back and forth, and stopped as the teeth came off.

"Oh, no," she murmured.

"Try this," her father said, extending the shears to Wolf.

Wolf shook his head. He seemed to be looking for something else.

Her father came close to her and crouched beside her. He tried cutting her hair from the back. She could hear the shears working, but she knew he was having no luck. He was making that awful sound he made when he was trying too hard.

"It's no good," Tony said. "Nothing cuts through it."

She had known that, but she hadn't really *known* it. She brought her hands to her face. The panic she'd been feeling since the hair started growing had gotten worse.

"What if it never stops growing?" Virginia asked. "I'm going to die of long hair."

Through her fingers, she saw her father and Wolf exchange a worried glance. For all their bravado, they were as frightened as she was.

She began to shake.

"Don't despair," a voice said.

She looked up. One of the magic birds was sitting in an apple tree near them.

"Because you saved my life," the magic bird said, "I will tell you how to cut your hair."

She let out a small breath. Hope. "Please."

"Deep in the forest," the bird said, "there is a Woodsman with a magic axe that, when swung, never fails to cut whatever it hits, and it will cut your hair and cure the curse."

The bird then spread its wings and flew off before Virginia could say thank you.

"Let's get going," Wolf said. "Before Virginia's hair gets too long to move."

She gave him a frightened glance. She hadn't thought of that.

"Something about this place is making me ravenous," Tony said.

He reached up and plucked a beautiful red apple. He opened his mouth to take a bite and Wolf shouted, "Tony, no! What are you doing? Don't eat that apple."

Her father held the apple out in front of him and turned to Wolf. "Why not?"

"Think where you are," Wolf said. "Snow White's cottage."

"Yeah, so?" Tony asked.

"This apple tree has probably grown from the pips of the apple that poisoned her."

Virginia's breath caught in her throat. Her father threw the apple away, obviously disappointed.

"Boy," he said, "you can't be too careful in this place."

"Come along," Wolf said. "We have much to do if we are to keep up with the mirror."

The mirror. Virginia looked at him. With the hair crisis, she had forgotten all about it. She stood, hoping that this news about the Woodsman would turn their luck to the better.

Wolf was getting nervous. Their progress through the woods was painfully slow. Virginia's hair kept getting caught, and all three of them spent more time untangling it than they did walking. And to make matters worse, for the last hour or so, Wolf kept smelling something new in the air.

It was getting closer.

"I've got a scent," Wolf said. "I'm sure it is the Huntsman. He's near. We must move faster."

"I can't go any faster," Virginia said.

"Virginia," Wolf said, "this man is going to catch us, within the hour at most."

"What are we going to do?" Tony asked.

Virginia tried to free her hair from a bush. Wolf looked at it, and knew that running was out of the question. He paced back and forth, thinking for a moment. For the first time on this adventure, he was out of ideas.

Then, suddenly, he knew. "I will hide you and then lead him away. I can lose him."

"Wait a minute," Tony said. "How do we know you'll come back?"

"Because my life is dedicated to making love to your daughter."

Tony's eyes narrowed. "That's not what I want to hear."

Wolf ignored him. Reluctant fathers were a luxury at the moment. "The Huntsman is very good," Wolf said. "But he follows tracks. He cannot smell things like an animal. I will lead him in a big circle and come back for you tomorrow. Hurry. We will start with the Prince."

It took Wolf most of that hour to cover Prince Wendell, Tony, and Virginia with leaves and twigs. Prince Wendell proved the hardest. Every time Wolf thought he had finished, he saw another glint of gold.

"That's as good as I can do," Wolf said, finally. "Okay?"

There was a slight movement among the leaves and a hand—Virginia's, beautiful and small—rose up and gave a small wave. Then Tony's larger hand rose from ten feet away. Wolf half expected Wendell to raise a golden paw.

"Don't breathe at all until I return."

The hands disappeared and Wolf checked the area to make sure all trace of the three was gone. No footprints, no sneaky strands of hair, nothing.

He nodded once, then bounded off, intent on leaving a trail even the dumbest hunter could follow.

Virginia's eyes itched. Her nose was twitching too. The leaves had an autumnal smell and beneath it, mold. Mold had been bothering her ever since they got into this forest. She was mildly allergic to it, and the allergy seemed to be growing worse. She had sneezed a lot in Snow White's cottage, and she was breathing shallowly now to prevent another sneeze.

She wished she could talk with her father. He was only a few feet away and she couldn't even hear him. She was too keyed up to fall asleep. Besides, she was afraid she'd snore or talk or shift in her sleep.

And she was worried about her hair. She wasn't sure how she would keep it hidden. It had filled the cottage the night before. She was worried it would fill this part of the forest by the time Wolf returned.

Funny, she had no doubts about him. She knew he'd be back. He was sincere in his comment to her father. Wolf would be coming back for her.

Then she stiffened. There was a different sound in the forest. Not quite footsteps. The dry leaves, rustling in the slight breeze, were simply rustling more. She wondered if that was her imagination working overtime, or if it was something she had to worry about.

There were other creatures in the forest. But she knew that this was the Huntsman. She didn't know how she knew. Maybe being around Wolf had finely tuned her sense of smell. But something in the sound—its regular rhythm, perhaps—told her that someone was trying to be very, very quiet.

The leaves didn't exactly cover her eyes. She could see if she squinted. As she watched, a tall blond man appeared. She tried to hold her breath, but her heart was beating faster. It was hard to be quiet, suddenly, when it was really and truly important.

The itch in her eyes grew, and the desire to sneeze grew with it. She held her breath, hoping that would work.

The Huntsman—for who else could this stately man with the magnificent crossbow be?—stopped. For one frightening moment, Virginia thought perhaps he was standing on her father. Then she saw her father's eyes glinting from beneath the leaves. Virginia prayed that the Huntsman didn't see what she did.

Instead, he peered at the ground. He appeared to be following a trail of some sort. He walked slowly toward her, and she saw what he saw—a strand of hair poking out of the leaves.

Damn. She had known that was going to happen. She willed her hair to stop growing, but it didn't.

The Huntsman walked closer and closer until he came up beside her. His right boot landed near her face. He continued past her. She heard leaves rustle as he went deeper into the wood. In a moment, she would be safe.

Unfortunately, that thought made her breathe a little deeper and the sneeze she'd stifled came. She was unable to stop it. The sound exploded in the woods, and she actually heard the startled squawk of birds as they flew away.

She sat up. It was over now. "Run, Dad! Run!"

She managed to get to her feet just as her father bolted down the path. He was a tall man and he managed to get ahead of her quickly. As he did, he swore.

Virginia ran quietly, but as fast as she could. She felt as if she weighed five thousand pounds. The hair was a handicap, a serious one. It made her twice as heavy as she should be.

She didn't hear any footsteps behind her. Up ahead, she could see her father, blazing a fairly obvious trail. She ran faster and faster.

Suddenly something pulled on her head and knocked her feet out from under her. She landed on her back. The air left her body in a painful rush. It took a moment for her to realize what had happened.

Her hair had snagged on something.

She turned and saw, at least forty feet away, that her hair hadn't snagged on anything at all. The Huntsman was standing on the ends of it, holding his crossbow, and smiling.

Chapter Twenty-Four

The Huntsman was dragging Virginia by her hair. Her back hurt and she twisted around, trying to gain purchase on the ground. She couldn't. If the stories about cavemen bopping their women over the head and dragging them back to their caves by their hair was true, Virginia had no idea why those poor women didn't revolt. This had to be the most painful thing she had ever experienced.

"Stop it!" Virginia shouted. "You're hurting me."

He didn't seem to hear her. Finally he stopped, though, and pulled her to her feet.

They stood in front of a massive oak covered in ivy. He reached up and pressed the side. The ivy rose with a rustling sound, and then a door opened inward.

The scent of fresh wood mixed with old blood wafted out. Virginia's heart beat even faster.

The Huntsman pulled her inside, and then the door closed. Virginia couldn't even see the lines of where it had been.

He let go of her hair. She reached to the nape of her neck and rubbed. The area throbbed. He lit a small lantern, and she could see where she was.

It was a small room, filled with a butcher's block—bloodstained—many knives, obviously used, and a wooden floor covered with feathers and skin and dark blood. There were animal carcasses stretched out on various boards. Some hung upside down. There were bloodstains around the necks.

Virginia could hear her own shallow breathing. She was

terrified, and she couldn't help it. Somehow she knew that this man knew of her terror too, and probably enjoyed it.

"Why is your hair so long?" His voice startled her. It was soft and deep and cultured, not at all what she had expected.

"I think I upset the Gypsies," Virginia said.

He nodded, as if this were not unexpected news. "They will not trouble you again."

She did not find this reassuring. She looked at his hands. They had something dark, probably blood, crusted under the nails. Had he killed the Gypsies for trespassing in his woods? Or did he mean, by that cryptic statement, that she would die soon?

He picked up a knife. Virginia felt herself shiver. Then he grabbed one of the carcasses—it was a rather large rabbit— and sliced it from chin to tail.

"I rear animals to be killed," the Huntsman said. "I raise a thousand pheasants every year. I fatten them, I care for them in the winter when there is no food. From a thousand, perhaps two dozen will escape the hunt. That is as it should be. Everything must have a chance."

His tone was flat. Even though he spoke of chances, Virginia had a hunch he didn't believe in them. She wondered if this was what serial killers were like.

He separated the rabbit's flesh from its bones with his fingers, then sliced again with the knife.

"Please let me go," Virginia said. "What do you want from me? I'm not involved in this."

"Where is the dog?"

"I don't know what—"

"Make me ask again and I will skin you."

The rabbit skin dropped to the floor. She didn't know how he had done that so fast.

"I think he's dead," Virginia said.

The Huntsman's pale eyes met hers. "You're lying, but you're not lying. Is he hurt? You were dragging something on wheels, yet the tracks were too deep for the weight of just a dog.''

Suddenly he grabbed her and pulled her toward him until they were mere inches apart. He stank of fresh blood.

"The others," he said. "Will they leave you or come looking for you?"

"Me?" Virginia said, trying to make her lie sound convincing. "They don't give a damn about me."

"They will come for you." Apparently that didn't work. Somehow he saw through her. "Do they have weapons?"

"Yes," Virginia lied.

"They have no weapons," he said, letting her go. She staggered backwards. "Good."

He picked up another rabbit. Virginia leaned against the wooden wall, wondering how she was ever going to escape.

Tony was hiding behind a tree, peering back into the darkness. He had no idea how far he had run. All he knew was that after a time, he couldn't hear Virginia behind him. He'd stopped and called for her and she hadn't answered.

He wasn't sure if he should go back for her or try to find Wolf. If only he was still in New York. There, at least, he had half a chance of making the right decision. Here, all bets were off.

There was a noise behind him. Tony whirled but saw nothing.

"It's me," Wolf spoke in his ear.

Tony turned, hand over his mouth to stifle a scream. Wolf was standing in front of him, hair slightly mussed, looking winded.

"What happened?" he asked.

"He's got Virginia." The words came out angrier than Tony had planned. "That's what's happened."

Wolf clutched his hair, pulling at it. He suddenly looked like a panicked child. "Oh, no. We'll never find her. It's all my fault. It was my fault."

This was not what Tony needed. He needed a big strong Wolf, full of magic and ideas, to save his daughter.

"We've got to find her," Tony said.

Wolf nodded. Together they went back to the hiding place. And then they started to search. As they walked, Wolf was looking more and more upset.

"If you had been kidnapped, it would have been all right," Wolf said. "But Virginia! I have lost my one true love."

"You can stop all this one-true-love stuff," Tony snapped. "You're just some grubby ex-con, and you've brought us nothing but trouble."

"Don't you talk to me like that. I'll bite you in a minute."

"Come on." Tony was ready for a fight. It was this man's stupid idea that might have cost his daughter's life. "I'd like to see you try."

Suddenly Wolf stopped and raised a finger to his lips. "Listen."

Tony frowned. He heard the faint sound of chopping. He glanced at Wolf, who looked just as surprised as Tony did. They walked toward the sound. It took them only a moment to reach a clearing.

In the center of it, a tall, solid, redheaded man was standing near a large pile of wood. On a tree stump was a single piece. The man had an axe in his hand and was obviously using the mighty stump as his chopping block.

"Halt!" the Woodsman said. "Who approaches?"

He didn't wait for an answer. He brought his axe down on the bit of wood and cut it clean in half with a single, powerful blow. Some of the wood chips hit his cap, which was upside down by his chopping block.

"Forgive us, noble Woodsman," Wolf said, "but have you seen a gorgeous girl with very long hair?"

"I haven't seen anything," the Woodsman said. "I'm blind."

He grabbed another block of wood, set it on the stump,

raised his axe, and with a mighty thump, chopped the wood in half.

"You're a blind Woodsman?" Tony couldn't believe it.

"You ever seen a tree move?" The Woodsman's eyes were clouded over and he wasn't really looking at either Tony or Wolf.

"Look at his axe, Tony," Wolf said. "Is that axe by any remote chance the magic axe that can cut through anything?"

"Might be," the Woodsman said.

"How much do you want for it?" Tony asked.

"You may have my magic axe if you can guess my name." He split another log.

"But your friend must kneel down on this block, and if you do not guess my name by the time I have chopped all these logs into firewood, I will cut off his head."

"What is it with you people?" Tony asked. "What kind of twisted upbringing do you have? Why can't you just say it's a hundred gold coins or something? Why is it always only if you lay a magic egg or pluck the hair off a giant's ass?"

"You want the axe or not?" the Woodsman asked.

"Let's just carry on looking for Virginia," Wolf said.

"No, wait a minute." They needed the axe for when they found her. And Tony knew that he could get it in a matter of moments. "It's all right, I know this one. We accept."

"Don't accept on my behalf." Wolf sounded angry.

"I know it. I swear, I know it."

"Very well," the Woodsman said. "Put your head on the block while your friend guesses."

Wolf shot a dark look at Tony, then crouched beside the chopping block. Slowly Wolf put his head on the far end, as far from the axe as he could get.

The Woodsman flipped over another hinged block of wood attached to the chopping block and with a loud slam, trapped Wolf's head in a crude version of a stock.

Or, Tony thought, the thing that held the neck in place for the guillotine.

"Cripes," Wolf said. He looked helpless.

"Just making you secure," the Woodsman said.

Tony's heart was pounding. "Don't worry, Wolf." He didn't sound as reassuring as he had hoped to. Tony took a deep breath and said, "Okay, white stick merchant, your name is Rumpelstiltskin."

"Nope."

The Woodsman split another log. Wolf winced.

"I said Rumpelstiltskin." Tony spoke louder, just in case the guy hadn't heard.

"Guess again," the Woodsman said.

It had to be Rumpelstiltskin. "Rumpelstiltskin Junior? Rumpelstiltskin the Fourth!"

The Woodsman shattered another log. "No."

"Does it have a Rumple in it?"

"This was your big idea, was it?" Wolf said.

Tony looked at him and tried not to let his fear show. But he had the funny feeling that he had failed.

This time, the Huntsman held Virginia's arm as he dragged her up a circular staircase cut into the center of the tree. Her hair, getting heavier by the minute, dragged behind her. They climbed for what seemed like forever, and they finally emerged into a small tower room. The room had light, though, and Virginia was relieved to see a small hole cut into the wall.

A window large enough for her to escape from.

He dragged her over to it, and her momentary hope disappeared.

They were at least fifty feet above the forest floor.

"I was born in this forest," he said softly, "a hundred miles north of here."

She looked out. There were trees everywhere. She could actually see the extent of the forest. It seemed to go on forever. The view was breathtaking and depressing at the same time.

"When I saw the Queen for the first time, I was still a Forester. She came to my village. It was a cruel winter and

Virginia.

Law and order in the 9 Kingdoms.

Three trolls stage a prison break.

The Evil Queen.

The Troll King.

The Evil Queen and the Prince formerly known as Dog.

Prince Wendell, the grandson of Snow White.

Wolf arrives in the 10th Kingdom and stops for a bite.

The trolls capture Virginia.

The terrifying Huntsman, also tracking Prince Wendell.

Prince Wendell fills Tony in.

Be careful what you wish for.

Wolf losing his heart to Virginia.

An unusually calm moment.

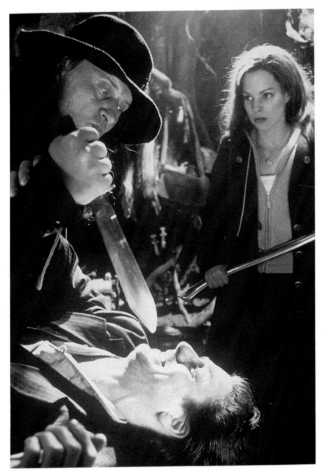
One of many dangerous encounters.

All that glitters *is* gold.

Virginia and the Beautiful Shepherdess competition.

Wanted: Wolf.

Virginia defends Wolf.

Planning and plotting

Virginia and Wolf.

Happily ever after.

everyone was starving, children grubbing in the snow for roots to eat. She stopped her hunting party to water the horses. The Queen called me forward. She saw something in me. She showed me this.''

He took out his crossbow. Virginia had seen it before, but not up close. It was made of wood and silver. In its leather harness, were many razor-sharp silver bolts. Virginia had never seen a crossbow up close before. She had no idea how terrifying they really were.

"When this crossbow is fired," he said, "the bolt will not fall until it has found the heart of a living creature. It cannot miss. In one day I could kill enough food to keep the whole village alive all winter. I said, 'What must I do to win this magic crossbow?' And she said, 'Just close your eyes and fire it wherever you wish, and it shall be yours.' ''

He plucked a bolt and placed it in position. Now the crossbow looked even more fearsome.

"I turned away from the village and all the people and fired deep into the thick of the forest. The bolt left the bow like gossamer. It sped a mile through the trees and killed a child playing in the forest.''

He stared at Virginia. It seemed as if his eyes were even more intense than they had been before.

"I remember the Queen's face as I pulled the bolt from my son's heart. She looked at me and said, 'You will be my Huntsman.' ''

Virginia held her breath in horror.

"So you understand," he said softly. "I have no interest in mercy. The hunt is the only thing that interests me. Life and death are simply matters of sport.''

Chapter Twenty-Five

The blind Woodsman had cut through more wood than Tony wanted to think about. And Wolf was beginning to look panicked.

"Dick?" Tony asked. "As in Van Dyke?"

"No," the Woodsman said and split another log.

"Bill? Ben? Jerry? Häagen-Dazs?"

"Cold," the Woodsman said, continuing to chop the wood.

"Elvis? Sammy? Frank? John? Paul? George? Ringo?"

"Ringo?" Wolf asked.

"Colder," the Woodsman said. "Way off."

"Does it begin with A?"

"I'm not playing that game."

"Tony," Wolf said, "I'm starting to lose faith in you."

"Sugar Ray? Cassius? Iron Mike?"

"Nope."

"Give me a clue," Tony said. He was beginning to hyperventilate. Everything he did in this place turned out wrong. "What fun is it for you just to kill him?"

"A lot of fun, actually," the Woodsman said. "You could almost say it was the reason for my existence."

He grinned as he brought the axe down on yet another innocent piece of wood.

"How do we know you won't lie about your name?" Wolf asked.

Tony liked that idea. Maybe they could get out of this. "Maybe I've already said it," Tony said.

"You haven't guessed my name," the Woodsman said. "You are nowhere near. My name is written in my cap."

"You sick pervert," Tony said. "You've done this before, haven't you?"

"Hundreds of times," the Woodsman said.

"And approximately what was the percentage of correct guesses?" Wolf asked.

"None have guessed," the Woodsman said.

Tony leaned over and peered at the cap. There was a white strip on it that clearly had the Woodsman's name written on it. Wolf strained to see it, but shook his head.

Tony inched closer.

"I may be blind," the Woodsman said, "but my hearing is excellent. Move any closer to it and I'll chop your friend's head off."

Virginia was very cold. The Huntsman still had his crossbow in his hands, bolt pointed out the window.

"Who is this Queen?" Virginia asked. "How can you serve somebody who made you kill your own son?"

"It was my destiny to kill my son. And hers to ask me."

He spoke so calmly. Then, slowly, he turned the crossbow toward her.

"You're crazy," Virginia said. "Everyone in this whole place is crazy."

"Everything that is meant to happen will always happen, no matter what we do," the Huntsman said. "Just as it is my destiny to kill you now."

He put a hand on her shoulder and pushed her until she bent her legs. He kept pushing until she knelt before him. He pressed the crossbow against her forehead. She could feel the coldness of the wood.

"Who are you?" the Huntsman asked.

"I am nobody," Virginia said. "I swear I'm nobody."

"Then I will kill you."

He had drawn the string back when suddenly a tiny bell went off. He brought the crossbow down.

"I have business to attend to," the Huntsman said.

He grabbed twine from a nearby table and wrapped it around her wrists, binding her to the railing in one fluid movement. He didn't make a knot.

"I will finish your interrogation later. If you attempt to break the twine, it will pull tighter and slice your wrists open and you will bleed to death."

Then he left her. Virginia stared at the twine, knowing that he had told her the truth.

She had no idea how things in this place always went from bad to worse.

There were only two pieces of wood left, and Tony was out of ideas. Wolf had his eyes closed, apparently so that he wouldn't see the final blow when it came.

"Is it the Mad Axeman?" Tony asked.

"I told you you'd never guess," the Woodsman said.

Suddenly Tony noticed one of the magic birds fly onto the chopping block and look at the Woodsman's cap. Then the bird flew off again. Was the thing just being perverse? Or was it going to help?

Tony had to stall somehow. "Is it . . . hang on a minute, a name's forming in my mind."

The Woodsman split the second log. "Running out of logs," he said. "Hurry up."

"No, wait," Tony said. "Wait just a minute. It's coming to me."

The Woodsman split the final log. "Too late," he said. "Now I will have your friend's head."

Wolf's eyes flew open and in them Tony saw a horrible look of hurt and betrayal.

The magic bird landed on Tony's shoulder and whispered in his ear. The Woodsman raised his axe over Wolf's head.

"Hold on just a minute," Tony said. "Juliet."

The Woodsman froze, and for the first time Tony felt as if the man were actually looking at him.

Wolf was looking at him as if he were crazy.

And Tony started to smile.

Very delicately, Virginia tried to wriggle the twine. If she didn't move it, maybe it wouldn't slice her skin. The movement was her only chance. Wolf and her father had no idea where she was. She had to escape on her own.

She made sure that she barely touched the twine. But it tightened anyway and a sharp pain went through her wrists. She saw a razor-thin line of blood appear on her skin.

"Damn."

Then she saw a movement at the window. The magic bird she had saved last from the Gypsies was on the sill.

"Because you helped us, we will help you again," the magic bird said. "But this really has to be the last time. You're such a lot of trouble."

"Go find my father and Wolf," Virginia said. "Tell them where I am. Tell them to come and get me."

The bird nodded once and flew off. Virginia tried very hard not to move. She only hoped that they would get there in time.

Wolf was carrying the axe over his shoulder and heading back toward the place that they had buried Prince Wendell once again. He had no idea where Virginia was, nor how to find her.

Still, he was very relieved to have his head.

"Who would have thought it?" Wolf said to Tony. "Juliet the Axeman."

"No wonder he turned into such a sick sadist," Tony said, and then he stopped. Wolf almost ran into him. Tony was looking up at a tree.

"Look," Tony said. "It's another one of those magic birds."

Actually it was the same magic bird that had told them about the Woodsman, but Wolf didn't correct him.

"I know where Virginia is," the magic bird said. "She's in a tree that is not a tree, in a place that is not a—"

"Cut the rhyming craplet," Tony said, "and just take us there, all right?"

For a moment, Wolf thought that the bird was going to fly away. Then it sighed, lifted its wings, and flew at Wolf's eye level.

Such temptation. But if he ate the magic bird, he'd never see Virginia again.

They followed the bird for some time. Then the bird stopped in front of a mighty oak.

"She's inside the tree," the magic bird said. " 'Bye."

"Wait," Tony shouted. "How can she be in a tree?"

"Virginia!" Wolf shouted at the tree. "Virginia, are you in there?"

"Wolf?" Virginia shouted back.

Her voice was very far away. It also came from above them. Wolf looked up. Virginia was looking down from a great height.

"How do we get in?" Tony shouted up at her.

"There's a door," Virginia said.

A door. Wolf went around the tree. Tony went around the tree. Neither of them saw a door.

"No, there isn't," Tony said. "There's no door, that's for definite."

"Oh, dear," Wolf said. "If he has concealed it with magic, it could take weeks to open."

"Why don't you come down and open it from the inside?" Tony asked Virginia.

"Because he's tied me up," Virginia said. "Can't you climb the tree?"

Wolf looked at the ivy. "There's no footholds."

"Well, get a ladder or something," Virginia said.

"A ladder?" Tony asked. "We're in the middle of a forest."

Wolf looked around, hoping to see something, anything that he might be able to climb.

"If this axe really cuts through anything," Tony said, "I could try chopping the tree down."

That would hurt Virginia. Besides, if the tree was magic, the pain might rebound on Tony.

"Virginia," Wolf said, "how long is your hair now?"

"It's longer than ever," Virginia said. "It's . . ."

She paused, and then Wolf knew that she understood.

"No!" she shouted.

"That's a great idea," Tony said.

"No!" Virginia said.

"I've always wanted to say this," Wolf said. "Love of my life, let down your lustrous locks."

A moment later, ten pounds of hair landed in his face. He brushed it off and held it in his hands for a moment. He'd have to use it like a rope and climb the tree as if it were a mountain.

He started at the base, and then climbed as rapidly as he could. Virginia's cries of pain were heartbreaking. Wolf was only slightly offended. He wasn't that heavy.

"Look out below," Wolf shouted down to Tony. "Close your eyes."

"What is it?" Tony asked.

"Dandruff," Wolf said.

"Ow," Virginia said. "I don't have—"

"Some people can't take a joke."

"Yeah," Tony said. "Keep your hair on."

Wolf tried to put as much weight as possible on his feet, but he knew that he was pulling awfully hard on her head. At least he knew the hair was tougher than steel, and wouldn't pull out.

Virginia was still yelling in pain.

He tried to take her mind off it. "What a moment in my life. My second opportunity to save you. My story will be immortalized in song, there is no question of that."

She didn't respond. Even her "ows" had stopped. He had to get some kind of reaction.

"Oh," Wolf said, "I've just found another gray one."

More silence. Wolf hurried the last few feet, then climbed over the windowsill and pulled himself in.

"Ta-da!" Wolf said, standing in front of her. "Your Prince has come."

He swept her off her feet. She was pale from the pain. He pulled her close and kissed her. She kissed him back for a brief second, and then she shoved him away.

"Can you untie me?" She held her bound hands up.

"Of course," Wolf said. "You get the full rescue service with me."

He grabbed her hands and bit the twine holding her wrists. The things he did for love, he thought. He shook his head, and bit even harder. The twine snapped, and Virginia was free.

Chapter Twenty-Six

The end of Virginia's hair flopped at Tony's feet as Wolf disappeared into the giant tree. Tony wasn't quite sure how they'd get out of that place. They couldn't climb back down her hair. He glanced at the axe in his hands. Maybe he should have made Wolf carry it up and then axe off her hair and tie the ends to a bedpost or something.

Tony frowned and gauged the height of the tree. He probably couldn't throw the axe that high, and Virginia wouldn't appreciate it if someone else climbed her hair. He'd wait to see if they needed his help.

Then he heard something behind him. He turned around.

A tall, pale man carrying a crossbow was walking toward the tree house. It had to be the Huntsman.

Tony cursed under his breath and hid behind the nearest tree. He held the axe in his hands. He had to do something, but he wasn't sure what. And all of his plans so far had been dismal failures.

So he bit his lower lip and waited.

"Careful you don't trip over your hair," Wolf said.

Virginia was picking her way down the stairs and Wolf was helping her. This hair thing had gotten out of control. If she had just her normal haircut, she would have been out of this tree house and far away already.

She had reached the carcasses on the first floor when the

door opened. The Huntsman came in and frowned in surprise at Wolf. Wolf jumped in front of Virginia, but over his shoulder, she could see her father running up behind the Huntsman.

Her father had an axe.

"Stay back, Virginia," Wolf shouted. Apparently Wolf had seen her father too and was trying for a diversion.

But it didn't work. The Huntsman turned as her father reached the door. He kicked the door shut, trapping her father's body half in and half out.

Tony was making horrible grunting noises and flailing with the axe, but the Huntsman managed to grab his arm. Wolf dived at both of them, knocking the Huntsman back against one of the tables. Carcasses fell everywhere. Wolf slid in the blood on the floor, but managed to retain his grip.

Knives scattered.

Virginia wasn't sure what to do. If she picked up one of the knives, she might get Wolf instead.

The Huntsman grabbed Wolf's throat with one hand and one of the knives with the other. Wolf struggled, yanking on the Huntsman's wrist.

"Virginia!" Wolf shouted. "Get the axe!"

That stopped her indecision. She ran to the door, where her father was flailing, and took the axe gently out of his hand.

"Chop his head off!" Wolf shouted. "Stick it in his back—anything."

Something banged behind her. She turned. Wolf was struggling, managing to keep the Huntsman's knife hand away, but just barely.

Virginia raised the axe and then hesitated. She'd never killed a man before. She wasn't sure she could do it.

"Do it!" Wolf shouted.

Virginia closed her eyes and brought the axe down as hard as she could. She heard a thunk and opened her eyes. She'd missed the Huntsman completely and hit the table, chopping it in half. Wolf and the Huntsman had fallen backwards onto the floor. The knife moved away from Wolf's throat, and the Huntsman started screaming.

It took a moment for Virginia to realize what was going on. The Huntsman had fallen back on one of his iron traps. It had closed on his leg. There was a lot of blood, but he was still waving the knife.

Wolf picked up a piece of wood and hit the Huntsman over the head. He fell back, unconscious.

Virginia let out a sigh of relief. Wolf wiped off his forehead. They looked at each other and she knew that if either of them had acted a moment later, one of them would be dead now.

"Open this door," Tony shouted. "I'm completely squashed."

Virginia and Wolf hurried to the door and managed to squeeze it open. Tony stumbled inside, clutching his ribs.

"What is this place?" Tony asked, looking down at the Huntsman.

"It's a bad place," Wolf said. "Let's go."

Virginia was looking at the Huntsman too. He was pale, and his leg was bleeding badly. "We can't leave him like that."

"You're right," Wolf said. "Give me the axe. I'll do it."

Wolf grabbed the axe and raised it over his head.

Virginia was appalled. "We can't kill him."

"Of course we can," Wolf said. "He'd kill us."

"That's not the point. He's helpless."

"Exactly why we should kill him." Wolf started to bring the axe down.

"Wolf," Virginia said. "No!"

"But he'll come after us."

"I don't care," Virginia said. "We're not killing him."

She couldn't stand it. The Huntsman wasn't an innocent man, but he could no longer defend himself. She knew, from all that she had been taught, all that was within her culture and her life, that killing a defenseless man was very, very wrong.

After a moment, Wolf sighed. He turned away from the

Huntsman. Then Wolf gazed at Virginia. She saw something in his face she'd never seen before. A sorrow, a worry.

"You'll regret this moment," he said.

It took Tony nearly an hour to dig out Prince Wendell. The poor dog hadn't moved an inch. Tony kept hoping that the spell would just wear off and Wendell would be talking again in his aristocratic little voice.

But Wendell was saying nothing.

Tony wiped the golden dog off, making sure he got all the dirt and twigs from Wendell's cold, smooth surface. Then he patted Prince Wendell on the head.

"Welcome back, boy," Tony murmured. "Time for walkies."

At that moment, he heard something behind him. He turned quickly, still spooked by that horrible Huntsman fellow. When he saw Wolf carrying the axe, he relaxed.

"How did the haircut go?" Tony asked.

"Well," Wolf said, "I think I might have overdone the axe trim a little."

Virginia followed. Her hair was as short—maybe shorter— than Tony's. Her hair had never been that short in her life.

Apparently she saw his horrified reaction before he could hide it. She held up a hand. "Don't say a word."

So he didn't. At least, not to her.

"What have you done to her?" Tony asked Wolf. "She spent years growing her hair."

"No, she didn't," Wolf said. "It was about a day and a half at most."

"She looks like a boy," Tony said. "You're doing too many things to my daughter. I don't like it. You stay off of her."

"Oh, don't you start," Virginia said to her father. "What do you know about anything?"

"Now, now, come on, everybody," Wolf said. "I know we've all had our differences, but from now on I want us to be friends. You know what the old biddy was saying about the three sticks? You can't break them when they stay together. It's time for us to bury the hatchet. What do you say?"

Tony stared at Wolf for a moment. The guy was too interested in Virginia. But he had helped them a lot. Except for that dung bean. Tony shuddered. "I don't know," he said. "I guess so."

"All right," Virginia said.

Wolf held out the axe. "And here's the hatchet. I mean I know it's really an axe, but it'll do."

He walked toward Tony. Tony took a small step backwards. Wolf ignored him and placed the axe in the hole where Prince Wendell had been.

"I would like to say a few words as we bury it." Wolf closed his eyes. After a moment, Virginia did too. Tony made a face and then followed suit.

"Dear animals of the forest who look after us and protect us, and appear to us in many guises," Wolf said, "Virginia, Tony, and I have decided to be the best of friends. And the gift Tony has given me, namely his gorgeous, dreamy, creamy daughter, Virginia—"

Tony's eyes flew open. Virginia's cheeks were flushed. She was enjoying this.

"There you are," Tony said. "You're getting right off the point again."

Wolf opened his eyes too. "Sorry." He didn't sound at all contrite. "You can cover it with earth now, Tone."

Tony wondered why he got all the horrible jobs, no matter what world he was in. But he didn't complain, at least not out loud. He started to cover the axe with leaves and dirt.

"Shouldn't we keep it?" Virginia asked.

"Oh, no," Wolf said. "When magic has served you, it's best to pass it on. Anyway, it's been used to kill people. It might bring us bad luck."

Tony shuddered, but Virginia didn't seem perturbed.

"Oh, yes, bad luck," she said. "We wouldn't want any of that, would we?"

Finally, a break in the trees. Wolf grinned. He could see daylight ahead. It had taken a half day longer than he had thought it would.

"It's the end of the damned forest," Tony said, amazed. "I thought you said it was a thousand miles?"

"And it is," Wolf said. "A thousand miles long. But not very wide."

Virginia looked positively stunned. She looked good stunned. Of course, she looked good all of the time. She followed Wolf out of the trees and stopped.

Ahead was a large valley and open pasture land. It was beautiful after the darkness of the forest. Wolf wanted to stretch his arms toward the sun.

Then he frowned. There was something unusual parked by the crossroads.

"I don't believe it," Tony said.

"It's Acorn's wagon," Virginia said, pointing. "There it is. That's him."

Virginia and Tony started to run, leaving Prince Wendell behind on his little cart. Wolf glanced at Wendell, tempted to leave him behind, but knowing that Virginia would never ever forgive him.

She was too tenderhearted by half.

Wolf grabbed the rope and gave Wendell a tug. The damn dog was heavy. Wolf had to struggle to catch up to Tony and Virginia.

"What if he won't give the mirror back to us?" Virginia was asking Tony.

"Then we'll club him to death," Tony said. "This is not a matter for debate. We're going home."

Wolf slowed a little. The time of reckoning was finally here. He'd have to show Tony and Virginia how to turn on the mirror, and then they'd leave him.

He wasn't sure how he'd live without Virginia. And he'd only known her a few days.

Tony and Virginia had already gotten to the wagon. It was tiny up close. The dwarf was sitting in it, rolling some shag into a pipe and brewing a cup of tea.

"Hey, Acorn,"Tony said. "Remember me?"

"Anthony!"Acorn the Dwarf was a homely fellow, with a scarred face and metal in place of his teeth. He leaned toward Tony. "You got out of prison. How unlikely."

And, apparently, he had known Tony well. Wolf caught up to them and stood beside the wagon. He stared at Virginia, trying to memorize her face.

"Where's our mirror?"Tony asked.

"Mirror?"Acorn said, clearly puzzled.

"It belongs to us,"Virginia said.

Acorn lit his pipe. The smell of shag permeated the air. Wolf resisted the urge to rub his nose.

"Is it valuable, then?"Acorn asked.

"No, it's worthless."Virginia was such a terrible liar. Wolf smiled fondly. He would even miss that about her.

"You've come an awful long way to get back a worthless mirror,"Acorn said.

Virginia frowned. Wolf recognized that look too. It was her "decision"look. He knew every detail about her. He had never known anyone else so well.

"It's a magic mirror,"Virginia said. "We traveled here through it. We've been trapped in this world ever since."

"Virginia,"Tony said.

"All we want to do is go home,"Virginia said. "We won't take it. We'll just go home and then you can do whatever you want with it."

The way she said "home"made it sound as if her heart was there. If she left, Wolf's would be too.

"I am moved by what you say,"Acorn said.

"Then please let us go home,"Virginia begged.

"But I don't have it anymore."

Wolf let out a small breath. He didn't want to look too pleased about this. But Virginia didn't even notice him. Instead, she ran around the back of the miniature wagon. She looked panicked. Tony just looked defeated.

"I'm afraid I swapped it with someone in the village down the road there, not half an hour ago."

Acorn sounded apologetic. But apparently Tony had had enough. He grabbed Acorn by the throat. Wolf raised an eyebrow. All this going-home stuff was quite important to these two.

"Swapped it?" Tony shouted into Acorn's face. "Swapped it for what?"

Acorn looked behind him. Virginia had already found the trade. A small lamb stood in the back of the wagon. It had a pink bow around its neck. It opened its mouth and bleated.

Wolf felt a shudder run through him. He clenched his fists. Sheep and lambs were the greatest temptation of all. He stepped away from the wagon to clear his head.

"Wolf, do you think you can simply ignore me?"

It was the Queen's voice. Wolf looked down at a puddle and saw her face reflected in it.

"I've changed," Wolf said. "I'm no longer under your influence. You cannot touch me now."

"Oh, really?" the Queen asked, then laughed. "It's a full moon tonight. Your blood is already hot. You are a wolf. What will you do when the wild moon calls you? What will you do then to your new friends?"

Wolf hurried past the puddle and waited for Tony and Virginia. What would he do? For the first time, he wished they had found the mirror. He didn't want to betray them. He didn't want to hurt anyone, least of all Virginia.

And he wasn't sure he could stop himself.

Chapter Twenty-Seven

Wolf felt himself walking slower and slower.

The forest had given way to gentle pasture land. A way up the hill, someone had built a log fence that rose waist-high. White cottages with thatched roofs dotted the countryside. A little white sign up ahead said, LITTLE LAMB VILLAGE 3 MILES.

"That's it," Tony said. "That's the place."

"I don't think we should go into this village," Wolf said. He didn't know how to convey his worry to them.

Virginia didn't even turn around. "But Acorn said the mirror is here."

Wolf bounced in front of her, hoping she would understand. "A wolf goes by his instincts and I don't like it."

Virginia looked over his shoulder. Wolf followed her gaze. There was a scarecrow on one of the fields, only it had a ram's skull on top, and fur carcasses below. Similar scarecrows—or scarewolves, to be more accurate—dotted the landscape.

Several farmers stopped their work, pitchforks gripped in their hands, watching as the trio and solid little Prince Wendell passed.

If Virginia didn't understand those looks, she didn't understand anything. "It's farming land," Wolf said, "and farmers don't like wolfies. Huff-puff, no siree. Let's stop for breakfast and think what to do."

"You just had breakfast." Virginia walked past him. She sounded amused.

He'd had enough. "I want another breakfast, all right? What are you, my mother? Do you tell me when I can eat or not? Why don't you draw up a list of rules of things I can and can't do."

He hadn't expected that last to come out like that. The full moon. He cursed it. He could feel the edge.

Virginia looked at her father. Tony frowned. Wolf could read their expressions as clearly as if they'd spoken: *What's gotten into Wolf?*

"We're going into the village," Virginia said. "End of discussion. You can do what you like."

Tony and Virginia continued on. Wolf glanced around him. Farmers, scarewolves, sheep. He closed his eyes and then sighed. Nowhere here would be good for him. He might as well stick with Virginia and Tony.

Wolf walked after them, feeling dejected. The sound of the wheels on Wendell's cart pulled him forward. Virginia would hate him now. She'd think him crazy. And what would she do when night fell?

Wolf shuddered. He needed her. He needed her on his side now.

He had to tell her what was going on.

He picked a small bouquet of wildflowers and hurried to catch up to her. When he reached her, he thrust them under her nose.

"Virginia, forgive me," Wolf said. "I didn't mean to be so rude. It's just my cycle coming on. Once a month I get very irrational and angry, and I want to pick a fight with anyone who comes near me."

Virginia smiled a small private smile. "Sounds familiar."

This was where he asked for her help. He sure hoped she understood. "I'll be perfectly all right as long as you keep me away from temptation."

They crested a hill. On the other side were meadows filled with flocks of sheep. Pretty, lovely, curly sheep, all with white bows.

"Ohhhhh," Wolf said, very low, like a moan.

Shepherdesses carried their crooks as they skipped after their flocks. It felt as if they were moving in slow motion. Delectable, delicious, delightful.

Oh, he wasn't going to survive this.

"Look at those sheep," he mumbled. "Trollops. It shouldn't be allowed."

Virginia was watching him quizzically.

One of the shepherdesses saw him look at them. She giggled at him. Her blouse was straining at her chest, and she had the most lovely eyes, the most beautiful skin.

She came toward him, a smile on her stunning face. "Mornin'. My name is Sally Peep. I'm a shepherdess."

"No question about it," Wolf said to himself.

The other shepherdesses apparently saw her, and followed. They climbed over a nearby gate so that they could see him. He caught a glimpse of leg, of well-turned ankles, of soft flesh. . . .

"My, what hairy, strong arms you've got," said Sally Peep. "If my door wasn't locked, I'd be scared you'd come into my house and huff and puff and blow my clothes off."

"Where do you live?" Wolf asked.

"Come on," Virginia said, pulling him away. Apparently her amusement had left her. Wolf looked at the shepherdesses behind him and longed for the missed opportunity. But part of him—the sane part—was glad that Virginia had pulled him away.

They went around a corner and found themselves inside Little Lamb Village. It was made up of white cottages and looked entirely too wholesome. The Peeps seemed to own everything. Wolf saw signs that listed a Bill Peep as a butcher, a Gordon Peep as a grocer, and a Felicity Peep as a florist before he stopped reading signs.

People were leading sheep around on leashes as if they were dogs. Wolf bit his lower lip, trying to restrain himself. Letting sheep loose in the village like that should have been a crime.

Couldn't they see the temptation it caused? It just wasn't healthy.

Virginia kept a firm grip on his arm. She was smiling at people as they passed, returning their cheery little greetings. Such friendliness wasn't healthy either. Such niceness should be outlawed.

All these sheep were obscene.

Wolf bit down on his knuckle to hold himself back. He made himself focus on a banner overhead that announced the Annual Little Lamb Village Competition.

For what? he wondered. The tastiest sheep?

Virginia managed to drag him to the center of the village. There were tables set up, but Wolf didn't know why. Instead, he focused on the small well. Someone had built a roof over it, and there was a bar for holding a rope to help lower buckets.

Beside the well was the only strange-looking person in the entire village. He was lumpish and he had a stupid expression on his face.

"Is there someone in charge around here?" Tony asked. He pulled Wendell close behind him.

"I am the village idiot, and I am in charge of the wishing well."

Tony rolled his eyes. "What, are we carrying magnets or something? How do we attract these people?"

If Wolf had been feeling better, he might actually have tried to answer that.

"Nice dog you got there," the village idiot said, petting Prince on the head. "He reminds me of someone."

At that moment, several villagers went by. They wheeled a cart with a cloak in it that had to be twenty feet long. It was made of pure lamb's wool. Wolf could smell it. He started salivating. He turned away so that no one would see.

"What's that for?" Tony asked.

"The village's gift for Prince Wendell," the village idiot said. "It be his coronation cloak, made out of finest lamb's wool."

Tony looked down at the golden dog. "Let's hope he likes it."

"Are you going to make a wish, then?" the village idiot asked. "It's very bad luck to pass without making a wish."

Virginia reached into their savings and pulled out a coin for Tony and for Wolf. Of course she would. She believed anything. Wolf believed it too, only not quite as much.

"This is money we shouldn't be wasting," Virginia said.

"You are very prim," Wolf said. "But my wish will change all that."

He grinned wolfishly. He wasn't sure if he was going to wish for that or for help getting through the full moon tonight. Virginia closed her eyes. She squinched up her face, and Wolf got the sense that her wish was very important to her. Then she tossed her coin.

Tony tossed his at the same time and he had a similar look on his face. His eyes were closed too.

Wolf closed his and wished—hard—then tossed the coin. He opened his eyes as it flew through the air. At that moment, the others landed with a dull clump. His landed a minute later, making the same tinkling sound.

"It don't work," the village idiot said. "It used to be a real magic wishing well, and folks traveled from all over the kingdoms to have things blessed in it. But it's all dried up now. It hasn't flowed in years. I have made it my life's work—"

"Thrilling though your story is," Tony said, "what we're really interested in is a mirror."

Wolf was glad Tony interrupted because Wolf was about to make the village idiot the former village idiot. On good days, Wolf didn't suffer fools gladly. This was not a good day.

"The mirror," Tony was saying, "is about so big and black. We were told someone in the village bought it off Acorn."

"I have made it my life's work to wait by this well until it fills up again. What do you think of that?" The village idiot grinned. It seemed as if he hadn't heard Tony at all.

Wolf clenched his fists as Tony turned to face him. "We

have a problem here," Tony said. "This man is a complete idiot."

"If only," the village idiot said. "My father was a complete idiot, but I am still a half-wit."

They'd searched all afternoon and found no one who'd seen the mirror. Virginia was feeling tired and discouraged. Her father was reduced to talking to the golden Wendell. And Wolf—well, Wolf was acting strange.

Virginia had taken it upon herself to find a place to sleep that night. No one seemed to have rooms. The annual competition, whatever it was, seemed to have filled the village. Finally she met Fidelity, one of the farm wives, and Fidelity claimed to have something for them.

Fidelity led them to a small barn. Wolf's eyes seemed to glow. Virginia wasn't sure she liked that. Fidelity didn't even seem to notice.

"You can stay here if you like," Fidelity said. "Might not be posh like what you're used to."

"This place smells of pigs," Tony said.

Her father was never satisfied. They'd stayed in worse places on this trip.

"It's great," Virginia said to the woman. "Thanks."

Fidelity nodded. She was amazingly cheery. She had the rosy-cheeked look Virginia had previously associated only with Mrs. Santa Claus.

She was about to leave when Virginia said, "You don't know if anyone's bought a mirror from a traveling trader recently?"

"You'll want to talk to the local judge. He bought a load of things off that dwarf for prizes for the competition. You'll find him across the road in the inn. They do lovely food there, too. Well, that's the understatement of the year." Fidelity smiled. In fact, she'd been smiling all along. She waved happily at them and closed the barn door.

"It's like the Stepford Wives," Virginia's father muttered.

Wolf moaned and clutched his stomach. He had turned frighteningly pale.

"What's wrong?" Virginia asked.

"Cramps," Wolf said. "I have to go to bed. I need to lie down immediately." He collapsed on a bed of straw, groaning. He looked awful.

Virginia crouched beside him and put her hand on his forehead. "You're running a terrible temperature."

"Stop fussing over me!" Wolf snapped. "You're not my mother. Stop mothering and smothering and cupboard loving everybody like a little dwarf housewife. Go out! Leave me alone!"

Virginia took her hand off his forehead in surprise.

"Don't you talk to my daughter like that," her father said. He looked ready for a fight. Virginia was about to calm him— she had a hunch she knew what Wolf was going through— when there was a scream outside.

"There's a wolf!" a woman yelled. "Wolf!"

Wolf buried his head in the straw. Virginia and Tony ran outside.

"Wolf! Wolf! Wolf!"

They rounded a corner and stopped in the center of town. Apparently, as part of the festivities, a game was going on. A local man wore a wolf's head and was knocking on doors. Women peered out the window and screamed. Virginia recognized some of them who had smiled so provocatively at Wolf that morning. Had they known who he was?

Other village men arrived on the other side of the street. They were carrying pitchforks, and were searching for the wolf. The wolf continued down the street and there was laughter and more shouting in the distance.

Virginia looked at her father. He shook his head. She glanced over her shoulder toward the barn. Wolf had said he wanted to be alone. She'd leave him for a while. Maybe he could sleep.

Across the street was a local pub. It was called, of all things,

The Baa-Bar, and it listed Barbara Peep as the manager. In there, perhaps, they might find word of the mirror.

Her father seemed to have the same idea. He led her across the street and into the bar. It was loud and smelled of milk and beer, and fried food. The bar had a lot of tables, but most everyone was crowded around the barstools.

Virginia had never seen so many middle-aged farmers who all had the same look. Their wives were not just pleasingly plump like some of the younger women in the village, but verging on fat. Young men with the same dull look as the farmers wore their shirts open to the navel, rather like young Jethro in *The Beverly Hillbillies*. And there were certainly enough shepherdesses and milkmaids to go about.

Virginia half expected her father to start in on some joke about the farmer's daughter, and was glad he didn't.

She turned toward him and, for the first time, realized that through all the commotion, he'd dragged Prince Wendell with him.

"Are you going everywhere with Prince?" Virginia asked.

Her father looked slightly embarrassed. "He's gold. I can't leave him around. Anyway, it's good to keep him moving, you know, like coma patients. Keep turning them over and playing their favorite records."

He stopped in front of a sign. "Look," he said, "here's tomorrow's events."

Virginia peered at the information written in chalk on a blackboard. One listing caught her eye.

11:00 A.M. BEAUTIFUL SHEEP AND SHEPHERDESS
COMPETITION.
PRIZE: FULL-LENGTH MIRROR.

She was about to say something when she realized her father had waded into the crowd and was leaning across the bar.

"Excuse me," he said. His voice carried. Virginia hurried toward him. "Is the Judge about?"

The bartender, who could only be Barbara Peep, said, "Judge will be in for his dinner, eight o'clock on the dot. Take a seat. Your food will be with you in a jiffy."

"We haven't ordered any food," Virginia said.

Her father shushed her and led her to an empty table. The commotion from the bar sounded fainter here. She could actually hear her own thoughts.

She settled back in her chair, but her father was looking at the couple beside them. They seemed fairly typical of the group inside the bar. The man had that same round face all the others had, and his wife had passed pleasing several meals ago. The man was reading a newspaper, the first Virginia had seen since she came through the mirror. It was called *The Fourth Kingdom Gazette*.

The man looked up, apparently sensing their interest. "They're saying the Trolls have claimed the whole of the southwest region."

Oh, dear, Virginia thought. She wondered how much of that was connected to them. Still, she had learned in New York that talking about politics with strangers was dangerous.

"I wouldn't know about that," Virginia said politely.

"We're not very political," her father said.

The couple didn't seem to notice the brush-off. "I heard the Queen's escaped," the farmer's wife said, "and she's behind it all, and they're talking about all-out war between the Nine Kingdoms."

"Where's Wendell, I say?" the farmer shouted. "If he's not careful, he's going to lose his kingdom."

Virginia tried not to look at the golden dog, but her father put his hand on Prince Wendell's head. Her father was hiding his face, but Virginia recognized his expression.

It was one of deep and profound guilt.

Chapter Twenty-Eight

The Judge was a somber man who liked his food. Virginia understood why. In the Baa-Bar, she'd just had the most fantastic meal of her life.

She and her father hadn't ordered, not really. They'd just been waiting for the Judge as Barbara Peep had instructed them to do. But Barbara Peep had brought them food—the most incredible food Virginia had ever eaten. And it was plain: potatoes, lamb, squash, and cider. Her father had had too much of the cider, but Virginia couldn't blame him. It had all tasted so good.

The one she could blame was Wolf. He wasn't looking well, but he had left the barn anyway and joined them. He'd eaten like an absolute pig. He'd gone through racks of lamb like a sheering machine, and he had more bones on his plate than Virginia and her father combined—and they'd been in the bar much longer than he had.

In fact, Wolf had continued eating even after the Judge had come in. Virginia and her father had gone to the Judge's side, intent on talking him out of the mirror. But the man focused on his food.

The Peeps grew the food, and they all seemed quite proud of it. Virginia finally understood why the older women were so heavy and everyone had such a healthy glow. They ate better here than most people in the fancy restaurants in Manhattan. She almost didn't believe it.

Almost.

She'd seen too many strange things already to discount any of them.

But now her attention had to be on the Judge. Virginia explained as best she could the entire story of the mirror. She had to speak loudly because people were singing and yodeling on the other side of the bar.

Through it all, the Judge kept eating.

"So you see," she finished, "in a way, that mirror really belongs to us."

"No, it doesn't," the Judge said. "I bought it fair and square. I buy a whole batch of things every year for the village prizes."

"I know how these things work, Your Honor," Tony said. "What about if we slip you a few gold coins?"

"I'm a Judge and I don't like people trying to bribe me," the Judge said. "Now not another word or I'll have you thrown out of the village."

He turned them away from his table. Virginia stood and started back for her own to see if Wolf had any ideas. But he was no longer sitting there. She cast about anxiously—he'd been so sick—and finally she saw him, watching a pair of yodeling milkmaids.

Virginia walked toward him. He still looked sick. His skin was pale and sweaty, his eyes almost beady. He was standing too close to the milkmaids, watching them, his tongue lolling out the side of his mouth.

Sally Peep, the buxom shepherdess who had approached Wolf that morning, brushed against him. Virginia clenched a fist. She didn't like how she felt when other women got too close to Wolf.

But she also didn't like this Peep girl. She was too forward, and she was too interested in Wolf.

"You're new here, aren't you?" Sally said as she touched Wolf's arm. She handed him a jar of candy. "I can't get these sherbet dips undone. Could you help me, Mr. . . . ?"

Wolf swallowed, apparently unable to answer. His gaze met

Virginia's for just a moment. She wasn't going to help him with this.

Another buxom Peep girl sidled up to him. Didn't they ever get strange men in this town? They were all acting like Wolf was fresh meat.

"What is your name?" the second girl asked.

"Uh, Wolfson is my name," Wolf said.

That was lame, Virginia thought. And possibly dangerous.

"Wolfson?" Sally asked.

"Warren Wolfson," Wolf said.

The Peep girls didn't seem to see anything wrong with the name. Virginia crossed her arms and leaned against a nearby table, watching and trying to swallow the anger that was building inside her. These girls—women, actually—were pressing every possible body part against Wolf.

"It's my eighteenth birthday today," Sally said. "Bet you don't know what's going to happen to me tonight?"

Virginia's eyes widened. If she'd talked like that at eighteen, her father would have put her in a cage.

The other girl shushed Sally, but it seemed to do no good.

"Is it the bumps?" Wolf asked.

Sally paused and ran a hand along Wolf's back. Virginia nearly went over to her and threw her aside. What was wrong with her anyway? She'd never acted like that over a man.

"What's that sticking out of the back of your trousers?" Sally asked. "It's quite a bulge."

Wolf moved out of her reach. He almost seemed embarrassed. "I must get back," he said. "I think I left a chop on my plate."

Suddenly, two of the big-chested young men grabbed Wolf by the arms and slammed him against the wall. Virginia put a hand over her mouth, but it was partly to cover a smile. He deserved a bit of shoving around.

"No outsiders mess with Peep girls, you understand?" one big guy said.

"What are you doing around here, anyway, Mr. Wolfson?" the second asked.

"Let's take him out back and ask him properly," the first said.

They were going to do some serious damage. Virginia felt the smile leave her face. The men had Wolf by the arms and were going to drag him outside. For all the flirting he'd done, he didn't deserve being beaten into a bloody pulp.

Unless it was by her.

Virginia walked behind the men and tapped one on the shoulder. "What are you doing with my husband?" she asked.

"Your husband?" The big guy sounded surprised. Wolf was grinning at her.

"Yes," Virginia said. "He's not feeling at all well. That's why we're leaving now. Good night."

She took Wolf's arm and led him to the door. Her grip was harder than she'd planned. She wanted to bruise him, she really did.

"Oh, Virginia," Wolf said, "when you said I was your husband, I went all hard and soft at the same time."

"I only said it to get you out of trouble," she snapped.

She looked for her father and finally saw him, in a corner, playing darts with the Judge and two other men. She hoped her father's ploy worked because hers certainly hadn't.

Then she shoved Wolf through the front door and followed him into the cool night.

The moon was full and beautiful, a solid oval against the darkness of the sky. It filled the streets with almost as much light as day and cast eerie silver shadows between the buildings.

Wolf shook free of Virginia's grasp, and she tried to catch him again. Whatever this sickness was, it was making him act very strange.

"I feel so alive! I can see everything for miles around." Wolf raised his arms and looked skyward. "Look at the moon. Doesn't it make you want to howl, it's so beautiful?"

"Not really," Virginia said.

Wolf grabbed a nearby fence post and leaned against it. Something about his face was different—harsher, narrower. He looked dangerous, just as he had when they first met. Virginia was intrigued and more than a little bit frightened.

"My mama was obsessed with the moon," Wolf said. "She used to drag us all out to watch it when we were cubs. The moon makes me hungry for everything."

He stared at it the way he had stared at the yodeling milkmaids.

Virginia took his arm and pried him away from the fence post. "Time for bed," she said softly, and this time she managed to get him to the barn.

Tony pulled Prince out of the bar, along with the last of the patrons. The ale had been as good as the food, maybe better, and had certainly affected his dart play. Tony wished the Judge would listen to him, but the old man was bent on not discussing work when he was out of court.

Tony gazed down the empty streets. "You want to go walkies?" Tony asked Prince Wendell.

The golden dog, of course, didn't move. His face was permanently locked in a look of determination mixed with just a hint of anger.

"Don't look at me like that," Tony said as he started down the street. "You can't blame me. This kind of stuff probably happens all the time in your world. I mean, you were a dog when I met you."

He got to the wishing well. The village idiot was peering down its sides.

"Ever hopeful?" Tony asked.

"Oh, yes," the idiot said. "Your dog really reminds me of somebody, you know."

Tony had no response to that. He shook his head and continued walking.

The full moon cast a beautiful silver light over the entire town. The place actually looked magical. Tony never saw vistas like this in New York. The cool air was clearing his head and making him relax. All those adventures had tied both his stomach and his back up in knots. He was relieved to have just a bit of time to himself before he returned to Virginia and Wolf.

Tony reached the village limits and was just about to turn back when he saw an old wooden sign.

PEEP FARM
KEEP OUT
DOGS LOOSE

He peered over the fence. Across the field was a forbidding farmhouse. It wasn't pleasant-looking at all, not like the other buildings around. Tony thought that odd in and of itself, especially considering what wonderful food the Peeps grew.

But what was odder was the procession of Peeps walking from the house to the barn, holding lanterns but keeping their light carefully shaded from the road.

"Wait here." Tony patted Prince on the head and climbed over the fence. Then he carefully crept across the field toward the barn.

It didn't take him long to get there. The barn was poorly built, and there were cracks separating the boards. Tony peered through one of them.

The barn was lit like the middle of the day. All of the adult Peeps were gathered there, and all of them were holding baskets filled with produce. Only this produce was nothing like the magnificent stuff he'd seen at the Baa-Bar. This was the kind of stuff he'd seen grown in window-box gardens in Manhattan—wretched thin carrots, spindly potatoes, dull, worm-eaten tomatoes.

Tony felt his stomach turn. He looked at the rest of the barn, and realized it was the strangest place he'd seen yet on this trip. Rubble, rocks, and dirt were piled throughout, as if some major excavation had gone on. Wooden posts and supports stopped the huge bank of dirt from collapsing—but just barely.

One of the older Peeps—Wilfred, Tony thought, trying to remember all the names of his dart-playing buddies—peered around at the assembled family. Tony leaned back slightly, unsure whether they could see him through the crack or not.

"Where's the birthday girl?" Wilfred asked.

Sally Peep came forward, holding a dirty, scrawny sheep. She seemed nervous.

"Why do you think everything the Peeps make tastes so good, Sally Shepherdess?" Wilfred asked.

"I don't right know," Sally said. "Used to be that there was a magic well in the town, but the well's dried up. Everyone knows that."

"Do they now?" Wilfred grinned. So did the other older Peeps. They seemed to be sharing a joke. "Well, since you're eighteen, I'm going to let you into the family secret."

Tony leaned forward. His heart was pounding harder than usual. He had a hunch that if they caught him, he'd be in horrible trouble, but he couldn't bear to move. This had to be important.

Wilfred Peep was nodding and several younger male Peeps swept straw from the floor. They revealed a wooden hatch at the base of the dirt pile.

"The reason there's no more magic water in the village well is 'cause me and my brother diverted the stream forty years ago," Wilfred said, his grin growing. "The Peeps have all the magic now."

He bent down and lifted the wooden cover, revealing a hole in the ground. Lights, like multicolored fireflies, flew toward the ceiling, and the entire barn grew brighter.

Tony put a hand against the cracked barn wall, intrigued.

"Now, let's have a look at your sheep," Wilfred said. "Ugly bugger, isn't he? Can't see him winning you the Lovely Shepherdess Competition."

The other Peeps laughed as Wilfred grabbed the sheep by the neck. Another familiar male Peep—Filbert? Tony wasn't sure. They all had such goofy names—grabbed a rope and lowered a bucket that was suspended on a pulley system.

The sheep was struggling. Wilfred hung on tighter. "Help me get him in that bucket."

It took three men to get that sheep into the bucket. Filbert manned the pulley system and they lowered the poor bleating sheep into the darkness of the well. Finally, Tony heard a splash.

Then an echoey voice came out of the well. "What do you wash in my magic waters?"

Wilfred leaned forward. "Fill this sheep with your goodness and life, oh magic wishing well."

The waters thrashed—sounding to Tony like waves in the middle of a serious storm—and lights flew all around the barn. Finally Wilfred Peep wound the bucket back up.

Tony gasped. Fortunately, so did everyone else. A gorgeous, golden-fleeced lamb jumped out of the bucket and into Sally Peep's arms.

She giggled in delight. "Wilf, it's amazing."

Wilfred stood over her, and Tony felt his own smile fade. Wilfred looked absolutely terrifying. Who knew that the old guy had it in him?

"Don't you ever breathe a word to anyone," Wilfred said, "or I'll cut your throat, grandchild or no grandchild."

Okay. That was enough for Tony. He backed away from the crack in the barn, then ran across the field. He couldn't believe he had left Prince Wendell alone for that long anyway. He bounded over the fence, patted Prince on the head, and then hurried toward the village.

If Wilfred Peep was willing to kill his own granddaughter to keep the secret, he certainly wouldn't have any qualms about executing Tony.

All Tony had to do was make sure he wouldn't get caught.

* * *

Virginia was ready to pull out what hair she had left. Wolf was not acting normally. He was being completely unreasonable, and she didn't know what to do with him. She could barely manage to keep him in the barn.

She stood in front of the door. He was careening around the barn like a drunken man, only she knew he hadn't had much to drink. She wondered if she was this crazy at her time of the month.

"Do you have any idea what you do to me?" Wolf asked. "You will never know love like mine. I am your mate for life."

"Wolf," Virginia said, "you don't know what you're saying. I know you're changing."

"Oh, you know, do you?" Wolf asked. "You know everything. You're little miss perfect who sticks her hand up and can answer every question but knows nothing. You're pretending to live, Virginia. You're doing everything but actually living. You're driving me crazy."

He put out a hand. She pushed it away.

"Stop bullying me," Virginia said. "I don't like it. Now go to bed."

He froze and a sly look she had never seen before crossed his face.

"Or what?" he asked. "Will you scream? That's what most people do when they see a wolf. Scream and scream and scream."

For the first time since they'd gone through the mirror, she was actually afraid of him. There were green lights in his eyes, and his hair seemed thicker than before. And there was something not-human about him.

Virginia grabbed the nearest thing she could find—a pitchfork—and held it in front of her like a weapon.

Wolf ripped it from her hands. "What are you going to do? Stick it in me? That's what people do when there's a wolf about. Stick it, stab it, smoke it out."

He pulled her forward, holding her tight. His eyes were glazed.

"They burnt my parents good," he said. Virginia was horrified. "The good people. The nice farmers. They made a great big fire and burnt them both."

He snarled, and Virginia thought he would have bitten her except that the barn door banged open and her father walked in.

"Hey," her father said, "you'll never guess what I've just seen."

Wolf froze and some life grew in his eyes. Virginia reached toward him.

"I know why the Peeps win everything," her father was saying. But Wolf thrust Virginia backwards, then pushed past her father and hurried out of the barn.

Both she and her father stared after Wolf for a moment.

"Is he feeling better, then?" her father asked.

Chapter Twenty-Nine

Wolf ran until he reached the edge of town. Then he stopped near a fence, breathing hard. He had no idea what he had been about to do to Virginia. He just knew it couldn't have been good.

He put his hands in his hair and pulled, mumbling to himself. "Fine mess fine mess fine mess now she hates you now she hates you and you deserve it you animal. Animal. You nasty animal."

It took him a moment to gather himself. He looked down. There was a horse trough near the edge of the fence, filled with water. He could see himself in it, himself and the full moon behind.

The evil moon. It made him like this. He didn't even recognize himself anymore.

Then the moon smiled. "Hello, Wolf," it said with the Queen's voice.

His mouth fell open and he gripped the wooden rail hard.

"My mirror will still not show me who you travel with," the Queen said. "Who are your companions?"

Finally he got enough control of himself to answer. "I'm not telling you."

"What is their power?" the Queen asked. "Why should they conceal themselves?"

"I'm not telling you anything about her."

"Her?" the Queen asked, smiling. "What's she like? Is she tasty?"

"You're evil," Wolf said. "Stay away from me."

"Look at the moon and then tell me what you'd really like to do to her. Let your wildness out. Serve me and let the wolf out."

Let the wolf out. He looked up. The full moon was beautiful, alluring, right. Let the wolf out.

He wanted to close his eyes, but couldn't.

Let the wolf out, she had said. So he did.

The hay scratched at her face. Virginia, wanting to sleep some more, brushed it away. She heard footsteps and an odd bleating, but she didn't want to think of that.

Then there was a musty smell and her father's voice, somewhere near her.

"Well," he said, "what do you think?"

Virginia opened her eyes. There was a sheep's face inches from hers. She screamed and pushed it away.

Her father shushed her. He had the sheep on a string leash. He pulled the sheep away from Virginia and took out a knife. "It took me about three hours to actually catch one. It shouldn't take long to get the markings off."

Virginia sat up and wiped the sleep from her eyes. "Why have you stolen a sheep?"

Her father shaved the red identifying "P" from the sheep's wool. "For the competition of course. Beautiful sheep and shepherdess. How else are we going to get the mirror?"

Virginia wished she had not woken up. "I'm not a shepherdess. I'm a waitress. I don't know anything about sheep."

"You don't have to. That's the beauty of my plan." Her father finished shaving the sheep. The smell in the barn had grown.

"This sheep stinks," Virginia said. "It's not going to win anything. It looks like it's going to die any second."

"It won't when it's been down the magic wishing well," her father said. "Now you get to making your costume while I go and get it dipped."

"My costume?"

Her father pointed to three large squares of white material hanging in the corner of the barn. "Look at that and tell me anyone could guess it was once curtains. Hurry up and get changed."

Virginia got up, brushed the remaining hay off herself, and peered at the material. It wasn't that pretty, and *she* would have been able to guess it had once been curtains.

She walked over to it and pulled it back—and leapt backwards. Wolf had been hiding behind the material. He had startled her.

"Hello," Wolf said.

"H-How are you feeling?" Virginia asked. She had been worried about him all night.

He looked at her strangely. Not quite as crazily as the night before, though. But he had cuts and scratches on his hands, and his hair was tangled.

"Not too good," Wolf said. "Things are very hazy at the moment."

He tottered toward her. He looked desperate.

"I must fight what I am. I can't remember what I've done. You'd better tie me up. That way I can't escape."

"What do you mean, tie you up?" Virginia asked.

"Tie me up!" Wolf shouted at her. "Stop me escaping. Which bit don't you understand? Tie me up now, while you can."

"All right, all right." Virginia didn't have to be told again. It sounded like the best solution for all of them. She got a rope from the floor of the barn and made Wolf lean against a thick wooden post next to a water trough. Then she tied his hands behind his back.

"Tighter," Wolf said. "If I struggle, I can get free."

Virginia pulled the ropes tighter.

"Tighter."

She pulled again.

Then Wolf smiled at her. "What's the worst thing you've ever done?"

His tone was colder than usual. Virginia made another knot in the ropes.

"Tighter or I'll eat you up," Wolf said.

He was still smiling, and the smile was not a very nice one. Virginia pulled the ropes as tight as she could. Wolf watched her every movement.

She finally backed away, and found herself praying that the ropes would hold him.

Tony had to stay to the back roads as he dragged the sheep back to the Peeps' farm. The Peeps were already at the competition—he'd seen them go by with their magically perfect vegetables and Sally Peep's unbelievably golden sheep.

But they hadn't seen him, and that was what counted.

He reached the barn in what he believed to be record time. The door was latched, but he picked up a spade and bashed the door in. The sheep was rolling its eyes and bleating in fright.

He pushed it inside, then followed. The straw was back over the hatch, but he brushed the straw aside, grasped the ring, and yanked the hatch open.

The fireflies floated out of the well. Up close, they looked like tiny stars.

"It's time for Well of Fortune," Tony said as he shoved the terrified sheep into the bucket.

Then he lowered the sheep into the dark well, and smiled as he heard the splash.

Virginia had no idea where her father was. She felt awkward in her full shepherdess gear, from her white gown with its smocked bodice to the white bonnet and shepherd's crook. There was a large crowd around the competition area, but only two other entrants: Sally Peep, who was holding a golden lamb, and Mary Ramley, who was holding an ordinary looking sheep.

The crowd was conversing, the sound carrying over the entire village. Some were admiring the miraculous Peep vegetables. Others were ogling Virginia. Her father would pay for this—if he'd only show up.

The Judge got onto the podium and banged the gavel, silencing the crowd. "Due to the appalling chicken massacre this morning, we are bringing forward the Beautiful Shepherdess competition."

Chicken massacre? Virginia tried not to look alarmed. Wolf had had scratches all over his hands. Then she glanced over the crowd again. Her father wasn't here, and the competition had been moved up. Now what was she going to do?

"We have three contestants," the Judge said. "Goodness gracious me. Well, the more the merrier, I say."

He seemed a lot cheerier than the man she had met the night before.

Then he peered at Virginia. "Where's your sheep, miss?"

"It's on the way," Virginia said.

"She hasn't got one," Sally Peep said.

"I have," Virginia said. "He's in the barn."

"Well, go fetch him, girl," the Judge said. "And smartish, or I'll have to disqualify you. This is a sheep and shepherdess competition."

Virginia silently cursed her father as she made her way off the stage. She didn't know how she was going to fix this one. As she hurried toward the barn, she heard the Judge continue.

"Now," he said, "to start the competition, I'll ask all entrants, as is the age-old custom, to sing their favorite sheep song. Young Mary Ramley, will you start off?"

A wobbly female voice started into a soft rendition of "Baa-Baa Black Sheep." Virginia winced. She hurried to the barn to discover her father had just gotten there.

He was holding a pink-rinsed lamb.

"What the hell is that?" Virginia asked.

"It's a mirror-winning sheep, that's what it is," her father said.

She hoped he was right. She snatched the lamb from him, and then realized she had a new problem. "What sheep songs are there?"

" 'Baa-Baa Black Sheep?' " her father said.

"She's already doing that."

" 'Mary Had a Little Lamb?' "

"What's the tune?" Virginia asked. "It doesn't have a tune."

"I don't know," her father said. "Make one up. Sing it to some other tune."

"Like what?"

" 'Sailing,' " her father said. "The Rod Stewart song. You can sing any lyrics in the world to that song."

Virginia closed her eyes and shook her head. "I can't go through with this. I'm not going to win."

"Virginia, look at me," her father said.

She opened her eyes. He was looking like her father of old, the man she believed, when she was just a little girl, could conquer the universe.

"If you ever want to go home again," he said, "do what it takes to win this competition."

Virginia nodded. She paused, then made some adjustments to her costume. She clutched her lamb and hurried back to the competition. She made it just as Sally Peep was finishing her song.

As Virginia climbed the stage, she watched in disbelief as Sally turned an innocent sheep song into a siren song. The shepherdess was pouting and bending and finger-wagging seductively.

When Sally finished, she waved at the crowd, then turned her back on them. Her smile faded as she saw Virginia.

"And now contestant number three," the Judge said.

As Virginia stepped onto the stage, the men started cat-calling. She had ripped out the smock bodice and pulled it down to show what cleavage she had. She'd also raised the skirt, knowing her legs were better than the other contestants'.

Only the Peeps looked upset. They all had identically angry expressions on their faces.

She took a deep breath—and forgot the tune to "Sailing." Then she saw the mirror, leaning beside the trophies, and she cleared her throat. The melody was in her head now.

She sang,

> *"Mary had a . . . little lamb and . . .*
> *"It was whi-ite, white as snow,*
> *"Everywhere-ere that,*
> *"Mary went that*
> *"Little la-amb was sure to go . . ."*

Slowly the crowd got into it. Her voice got stronger the more she sang, and she knew she had all of them. Her father had joined the edge of the crowd, and he was singing too.

Some of the farmers had lit matches and were holding them up the way people did at Billy Joel concerts. She switched poems midstream and no one, not even her father, seemed to notice.

> *"We are lambing, we are lambing,*
> *"Home again, cross the fields,*
> *"We are lambing . . . stormy pastures,*
> *"To be near you, to be free . . ."*

She ended on that last warbling note and everyone else did too. There was a moment of silence, and then the crowd exploded into applause. Virginia flushed, grabbed the edges of her very short skirt, and curtsied.

And that was when she noticed the Peep family, staring at her as if she'd just murdered a sheep.

Wolf had fallen into the straw near the post, not willing to move. He was sweating. He had to control himself. Had to.

Had to. The blackout the night before terrified him. The way he had yelled at Virginia terrified him more.

He was dying of thirst and hunger and—

There was a trough nearby. Something to drink would help. Those books he'd been reading said that water cut a man's appetite in half.

He rolled onto his knees and bent over the trough. The water shimmered, and suddenly the Queen appeared.

"Wolf," she said. "You're making me angry. Obey me."

This day couldn't get any worse. He stared at her shimmery face in horror. "No."

"Time is running out," the Queen said. "Kill the girl and get me the dog. Do it."

It took all of his effort to fall away from the trough. He lay for a moment; then he felt the change coming over him. He struggled, struggled, struggled as hard as he could, but he couldn't stop it.

His body shifted and altered, his head growing into its wolf shape. And even though his mind was against it, his teeth were already snapping his bonds.

Before he could even think about what he was doing, he was running from the barn, blessedly free. A real wolf at last.

Chapter Thirty

The Judge was kneeling and inspecting the teeth of the sheep. For the first time, Tony was glad he didn't have the Judge's job. Virginia was standing uncomfortably beside Sally Peep, who kept shooting her little hate-filled glances. Tony was less worried about Sally than he was about the rest of the Peep family. They were pointing at Virginia's lamb and muttering angrily to themselves.

Finally the Judge stood. "Three beautiful girls, and three beautiful lambs. It's the hardest competition to judge so far by a long chalk." He glanced at the contestants. "But I give Mary and her sheep eight of ten and a well-earned third place."

There was polite applause, and Mary looked like she was going to cry. Tony had to take his gaze off her, poor thing. She had no idea the entire competition was rigged.

The Judge put a hand first on Sally's gold lamb, then on Virginia's pink one. "Both of these lambs are so beautiful," he said. "How do I make a decision? I have to give Sally Peep ten out of ten."

Tony cursed. They'd have to find another way to get the mirror now. But the Peep family cheered and whooped and gave each other high-fives. The Judge waited patiently until the cheering was over, and then said, "But I have to give Virginia Lewis ten out of ten as well."

"A tie?" Wilfred said. "You can't have a tie. Someone has to win."

There was shouting and arguing in the crowd. Some people

were running, yelling the news to those who hadn't heard. Tony watched it all in wonder. Apparently no one had taken on the Peep family in years.

"I have to win," Sally Peep said. "Peeps always win."

"How about if you keep the trophy and I have the mirror?" Virginia asked.

"They're both mine!" Sally bounced up and down, literally. "It's not fair!"

The entire area erupted into verbal fighting. Tony stood back, listening to the Peeps hurl insults at the Judge and at Virginia. Virginia kept glancing at the mirror, as if she were thinking of just running off with it.

The Judge banged his gavel for silence.

Everyone stopped yelling and turned toward him.

"This is a shepherdess competition," the Judge said. "We'll set up an obstacle course, and whoever guides her sheep through the pen in the shortest time is the winner, using only sheepdogs and commands. Sound fair enough?"

"No!" Virginia said. "I haven't got a sheepdog."

" 'Spect I'll win then, won't I?" Sally said.

The Peep family laughed. A little Peep girl kicked Virginia in the shin. She grabbed her leg and looked down. The little girl snarled. Tony was appalled.

But the villagers didn't seem to notice. Apparently the Peeps' lack of sportsmanship didn't bother anyone but him and Virginia. Several of the village men were setting up an obstacle course. Someone asked Tony to help, but he ducked out of it.

He clenched a fist and started pacing. He had to do something. But what? This had seemed like such a good idea this morning.

"Damn!" he muttered. "Damn. Where in God's name can we get a sheepdog at short notice?"

"Excuse me." The village idiot had crept up beside him and tugged his sleeve.

"Not now," Tony snapped. "I've got to think quickly."

"But you've got a dog," the idiot said.

This guy was not called the village idiot for nothing. "In case you haven't noticed," Tony started, "this dog is—"

Tony stopped himself. He had a hand on Prince Wendell's golden head. In less than thirty seconds he put it all together.

He grabbed the idiot's hand and shook it. "Of course. You're a genius," Tony said to the idiot. The idiot looked dumbfounded. But Tony didn't care. He grabbed Prince Wendell's rope, and shouted to Virginia, "Stall them. I'll be back."

Then he ran down the road. Fortunately, all of the Peeps were still getting ready for the competition. Tony figured he had maybe fifteen minutes. He had no idea how long Sally Peep's shepherding would take.

It seemed to take him forever to get to the farm, and even longer to get Prince Wendell inside the barn. The wheels on the cart kept getting stuck. Finally, Tony picked Wendell up and carried him inside.

Wendell was certainly easier to get into the bucket than that blasted sheep had been, but as Tony started to winch the dog down, the weight of the gold pulled on the rope, and the lever broke. The basket spun out of control, hitting the well with a giant splash.

Tony peered over. He couldn't see anything in the darkness, not even the little fireflies of light. What would he do if the Peeps came back and nothing had happened and there was a gold dog in their well?

He didn't want to screw this one up. Not this time.

"Wishing Well," he said, trying not to sound desperate. "Oh magic wishing well, use your healing—um, whatever—water to bring back to life this poor dog trapped in a gold body."

"You've just had a wish." The wishing well's echoey voice sounded horribly disapproving.

"I know, I know," Tony said. "But this is very important."

"Oh, all right," the well said. "But you swear this is the last wish today?"

"Yes, yes, I swear."

There was a groaning and bubbling of water. Only a few stars came up, and those were dim. Tony clenched his hands together. After a few moments, the sound stopped.

Tony pulled the rope, winching it as best he could. The dog was heavy, and he wished he had some help. He tried hard not to focus on the millions of ways this could have gone wrong.

He finally winched the bucket into view, and his heart literally sank. Prince Wendell was still a gold statue.

"I don't believe it," Tony said.

Then the statue gave a little tremor and fine gold cracks appeared. Prince Wendell shook his head like a dog trying to dry itself, and gold flew through the air like droplets.

"It worked!" Tony screamed. "It worked!"

Wendell jumped out of the bucket and landed on the ground. He gave one more shake, and the last of the gold fell off him. He turned and looked groggily at Tony.

"Hey, Prince, my boy, welcome back," Tony said. "What does it feel like to be back in the real world?"

Prince Wendell lunged at Tony and bit him on the ankle so hard that Tony screamed in pain. Prince backed off, and Tony hopped on one foot, clutching his injury.

"You moron," Prince Wendell said. "Why did you turn me into gold?"

"It was a heat-of-the-moment thing," Tony said, checking the skin around his ankle. It was broken and seeping blood. "I was trying to save you from those Trolls."

"You are really the most incompetent manservant I have ever had. You are a complete imbecile."

"You have to help me, Prince."

"Help you?" Prince Wendell said. "You must be joking."

Virginia watched as they finished setting up the obstacle course and the little pen; then she watched as they set up a crude timer. It reminded her of a metronome. Then she watched as Sally Peep led her dog, with a series of whistles and commands, to guide the sheep into the pen.

The Judge had thought it splendid. Sally finished in a count of eighty-five.

Virginia wondered if they'd disqualify her because she didn't have a dog. She didn't see her father anywhere. She had no way to consult him.

The Judge was watching her. Virginia was going to ask him for a few more minutes, some kind of stall, but he wouldn't meet her gaze. The villagers had taken her lamb to the other side of the village, and she could barely see it.

"Time starts now," the Judge said.

Oh, no, Virginia thought. The lamb even had its back to her.

"Here, sheep," Virginia said. "Here, sheep."

The lamb did not move. Virginia could hear the little clicks of the clock as the time went by.

"Coming up on thirty," the Judge said.

Virginia whistled and shouted, but the lamb didn't even seem to notice. The Peeps were beginning to chuckle. A few of the villagers walked away.

"Coming up to fifty."

Then she heard barking. Virginia glanced toward the edge of town and saw Prince running at top speed toward the lamb. The lamb saw him too and scurried away from him toward the pen, running as fast as its little legs would carry it.

"Where did he come from?" Sally asked.

"Go, Prince, go," Virginia shouted.

"Count of seventy," the Judge said.

The lamb tried to escape sideways, but Prince didn't let him. Prince shoved and nipped and bit at the lamb, forcing it relentlessly toward the pen.

"Count of eighty," the Judge said.

They were close.

"Eighty-one."

Prince got the lamb inside the pen.

"Eighty-two."

"Pen's closed," Virginia said, feeling incredible relief.

"Eighty-three," the Judge said. "Virginia the Shepherdess is this year's winner."

The villagers cheered and shouted and high-fived each other. The celebration was raucous. They must have wanted the Peeps to lose for a very long time.

"No, no," Sally said, "it's not fair."

Virginia hurried to Prince Wendell. She hadn't realized how much she missed him. She hugged him tightly, and he let her. "Well done, Prince," Virginia said.

Sally Peep stormed down the stage and shouted something at one of the older Peeps. Then she huffed away. Virginia buried her face in Prince's ruff.

"Come and get your prize, lass," the Judge said.

The mirror. In the excitement of seeing Prince Wendell alive, she had almost forgotten. She and Prince went across the stage, and her father joined them.

Her father was the one who made the speech. "Thank you, thank you," Tony said. "It was a team effort. No one person could have done it. Thank you."

The Judge handed Virginia the mirror. It was heavier than she expected, and she could see herself in the glass. She looked ridiculous in her shepherdess outfit, but she didn't care.

She could finally go home.

Tony could barely contain his elation. It took all of his self-control to keep from jumping through the mirror right there in the center of the crowd. But Virginia got him out of the area and led him back to the barn. Prince Wendell followed.

Tony yanked the barn door open and stepped inside. "Wolf!" he yelled. "We got the mirror back."

There was no answer. Tony peered around the entire area. He didn't see Wolf at all.

"He's got out," Virginia said. She looked perplexed and more than a little worried.

"Never mind," Tony said. "Let's get this mirror working."

Virginia leaned the mirror against a post. It just reflected them. No magical scenes of Central Park, no nothing. Tony's hands had gone clammy.

"Why isn't it showing our world?" Tony asked.

"Because it's not turned on," Prince Wendell said. Every word he spoke since he got de-golded, except for the insults he'd yelled at that poor lamb, had dripped sarcasm. "There's probably a secret catch somewhere."

Tony started examining the frame. After a moment, Virginia did too.

"How did you get through in the first place?" Tony asked Prince.

"I fell on it," Prince said. "The switch can't be that hard to find."

Virginia pressed part of the cornicing, and suddenly there was a click. The mirror started to vibrate and fizz like an ancient black-and-white television set. Tony crouched, peering at the fuzzy image. It gradually came into focus, complete with color.

"That's Central Park," Virginia said.

"It's Wolman Rink," Tony said.

The image was becoming even clearer when suddenly Tony heard terrible screams.

Wolf! Wolf!

It sounded like a woman's voice. Tony looked at Virginia. She seemed alarmed. Prince Wendell was already running for the door. Tony and Virginia followed.

As they stepped outside, a distraught farmer was running into town. He looked wild.

"Sally Peep's been murdered!" he shouted.

A mob of angry Peeps followed him, dragging someone.

"We've got him," another farmer shouted. "We've got him."

It took Tony a moment to see what was happening. Wolf was in the center of that mob. He was being kicked and slapped and punched and dragged as they pulled him toward the center of the village. His gaze caught Tony's and he mouthed—or

maybe he shouted, it was impossible to tell over the noise—
Help! Help me!

"Caught him red-handed," the farmer shouted. "The murdering bastard."

The crowd was too thick to get through. Virginia started forward, but Tony held her back. Wolf struggled, but he couldn't get away.

"Burn him," the crowd shouted. "Burn the wolf!"

Part Three

Enter the Dragon

Chapter Thirty-One

Virginia paused just outside the cell. She had never seen Wolf look so depressed. He sat with his hands hanging between his knees, his head down. He still clasped *Feel the Fear and Do It Anyway* in his right hand, but it was clear that he couldn't keep his mind on the book.

Virginia didn't know how he could concentrate on anything, what with all the shouting and pounding outside. She would have thought the sound of the chanting villagers would have been fainter in here. Instead it seemed like a constant drip of water: *Burn the Wolf! Burn the Wolf!*

She didn't know how to tell him what was going to happen next.

The turnkey let her into the cell. Wolf looked up, and when he saw her, hope filled his eyes. He stood.

"Virginia. There's been the most terrible mistake."

"Look, Wolf," Virginia started, but he talked over her.

"How's my case progressing?"

She walked to the cell window and peered out. He came up beside her. The chanting villagers had mounted a wooden pole in the ground. Now they were dragging enough wood around it to create a bonfire.

She looked over at Wolf. "We're going home."

If she had thought he looked depressed before, she realized he looked worse now. "Huff-puff, you can't."

"We don't belong in this world," Virginia said. "This isn't

anything to do with us. Whatever mess you've got yourself into, it's . . ."

His entire body shook, and he turned away from her. She put a hand to her mouth. She hadn't wanted to hurt Wolf, but she knew there was no choice. She didn't belong here, and Wolf would have gotten into trouble like this before. In fact, he had; that was why he was in the Snow White Memorial Prison.

"Oh, don't start to cry, please," she said softly, helplessly.

He didn't respond. He kept shaking, and he refused to look at her.

There was nothing more she could do. She took a deep breath and told him the truth. "I'm sorry, but nothing you can say will change my mind."

The mirror held him. Central Park in all its glory, if you wanted to call it that. If Tony squinted, he could see a Mounds Bar wrapper crumpled up next to the path.

"Look, Prince," Tony said. "That's home."

"It's not home for me, Anthony," Prince Wendell said. "And you can't think of going home while you remain my manservant."

Tony kept his attention focused on the mirror. Next to the wrapper was a Nathan's napkin. His mouth watered for an authentic hot dog. "For the very last time," Tony said, "I am not your manservant. I don't know why I changed you back from gold. I was just getting used to a bit of peace and quiet."

"Peace and quiet?" Prince said. "It wasn't peace and quiet for me, it was like being buried alive. I couldn't speak, I couldn't move, but guess what? I could hear everything, every inane, stupid comment you made."

Tony froze. He hadn't realized that. "Everything?"

"Yes," Prince said. "And make no mistake, you really are the most boring man I have ever come across."

The barn door opened, and Virginia stepped inside. She seemed subdued. Tony didn't like that, but he knew that she had grown fond of Wolf. Saying good-bye must have been hard.

"Well, did you break the bad news to him?" Tony asked.

"Yes," she said. Then closed her eyes. "Well, sort of."

"Sort of what?"

"Sort of agreed to represent him," Virginia said.

"Virginia!" Just when he was tasting a hot dog. Just when Central Park was in his reach, his daughter decided to defend a felon.

"I don't think he killed anybody." She sounded defensive.

"That's what you want to think," Tony said. "There's a dead girl out there, and it could have been you. He's a wolf. That's what wolves do."

"That's the first intelligent thing you've said," Prince said.

"We've got the mirror," Virginia said. "We can go home any time."

"So let's go now," Tony said. He had to make this clear to her. "Now, this minute, before we're turned into giant pigs or trodden on by goblins or whatever the next thing in this madhouse is."

Virginia crossed her arms. "I'm not leaving without trying to help him."

Tony swore and shut off the mirror. Central Park vanished, along with his dreams of home. Virginia had never acted like her mother before. And, to be fair, she wasn't now. But she reminded him of her mother all the same.

At least, he was reacting the way he used to react to her. He grabbed the mirror and looked over his shoulder. They were alone in the barn. Then he lifted the mirror and put it in the back of an old wagon Prince Wendell had discovered earlier. With both hands, he began covering it with straw.

But no matter how hard he tried, he couldn't keep quiet.

"You never used to be this obstinate," Tony said. "That's something he's taught you."

"Yes." Virginia seemed almost serene. Her gaze met his. "Someone had to, didn't they?"

* * *

The courtroom doubled as the village council chamber. Virginia learned that when she learned as much as she could of what was expected of her as Wolf's legal council. She was waiting outside the closed courtroom door, holding her argument in one hand, and her wig in the other.

She adjusted her black cloak, then put the lambswool wig on her head. She had seen such wigs in British movies where the characters went to court, but she had never imagined she would be wearing one.

It took a moment for her father to notice. "What are you wearing?" Tony asked.

"I didn't have any choice," she said. "You have to." She sounded more defensive than she wanted to. This was the first time she remembered defying her father, and she was not comfortable with it.

"You don't know the first thing about the law here," Tony said. "Or anywhere, come to that. I should have represented him."

"Who got you off those parking tickets?" Virginia asked. "Who took the Polaroid showing the broken parking meter?"

"This is a murder case," Tony said.

"Justice is universal," Virginia said.

At that moment, two guards brought Wolf to her in shackles. He didn't seem as depressed as he had the day before—the fact that she had stayed to defend him had buoyed him up—but he still looked terrible. She knew he hadn't slept at all.

"It's no good, my creamy counsel," Wolf said. "We've lost already. The local jury are certain to be biased against me."

"That's what I don't want to hear. Negative thinking." Virginia waggled a finger beneath his nose. Then she pushed the door to the courtroom open. From inside she could hear the Peeps starting to chant *Burn the wolf!* "Any jury can be swayed, all you need is a b—"

She didn't finish the sentence. She was going to say, all

you needed was a bunch of sheep, but that was exactly what she faced. Twelve sheep, sitting in the jury box.

The courtroom smelled like wet wool.

Virginia led Wolf through the tiny, packed courtroom to the defense table. The place was full of Peeps, and they all looked alike. It gave Virginia the creeps. She couldn't imagine how Wolf felt.

The clerk of the court called out, ''All rise for the honorable Judge.''

Everyone stood. A Peep behind Virginia whispered loudly, ''Burn the wolf.''

The Judge entered, took stock of the crowd, and then sat down. Everyone else sat as well.

The Judge gaveled the session into order. Then he leaned forward and said, ''It gives me no great pleasure to sentence this wolf to death for the terrible crime he committed.''

Virginia was shocked. She jumped to her feet. ''Objection, Your Honor. We haven't heard any evidence yet.''

''Oh, all right then,'' the Judge said. ''But move it along, nice and brisk, please.''

That surprised her. This whole thing surprised her. She had expected this to be a bit more like Perry Mason. Only the problem here was that she was supposed to be Perry, which meant that she had to find a way to get Wolf free.

Virginia walked to the jury box and tried not to sneeze as the smell of wet wool grew stronger.

''Ladies and gentlemen of the jury, ewes and rams, before you leave this courtroom today, I will not only have proved my client's innocence beyond any reasonable doubt, but also unmasked the real killer.''

Virginia was beginning to get into this. She turned to the Judge with a flourish, and then realized he hadn't been paying any attention at all. He was talking with an usher.

''Just a pot of lemon tea,'' the Judge was saying, ''and a slice of Rosie Peep's ginger cake, thank you.''

Virginia waited until he was done before going on. ''Look

at this poor man before you. Is he a wolf? No! He's a stranger. And stranger equals wolf and wolf equals killer—is that what we're saying?''

"Very well put." The Judge smiled at her. "Now to sentencing."

"Your Honor," Virginia said. "I'm only just beginning. I'd like to call my first witness."

"Sorry," the Judge said, "I thought you were finished."

Virginia was acting out parts she'd seen on television. Tony knew this because he'd watched the same shows with her. She was currently interrogating Wilfred Peep, trying to prove that he couldn't have identified Wolf in the dark.

Only her trick wasn't working. She wanted him to read from a card to prove his eyesight was bad, and the other Peeps were mouthing the information to him.

The Judge was convinced of Wolf's guilt—and Tony wasn't so sure he was wrong—and he was commiserating with the Peeps instead of listening to the evidence. And who would trust a sheep jury when faced with a wolf?

This was rigged, and no matter how hard Virginia tried, she wasn't going to succeed. Tony saw that from the moment he and Prince Wendell had taken their seats several rows back.

Now he was feeling a little guilty that he had told Virginia to give up. She was the only one who was trying to help Wolf. If they had left Wolf here to his fate, he'd be burning by now.

Tony shuddered and turned to Wendell. "We've got to help him out," Tony whispered.

Prince Wendell shook his shaggy head. "He's a wolf. What do you expect? He's only done exactly what I said he'd do all along."

"Virginia believes in him," Tony said. "And, well, I *want* to believe in him."

Tony started to stand. Prince Wendell gave him a withering look that was somehow more effective coming from that dog face.

"Nothing you can say," Wendell said imperiously, "will make me help him."

"Then I'll do it," Tony whispered, and slid out of the row. After a moment, Prince Wendell followed him. As Tony walked up the aisle, he heard his daughter call Betty Peep to the stand.

The Judge swore in Betty Peep, and then Virginia asked, "What is your profession?"

"Shepherdess," Betty Peep said.

"Shepherdess or temptress?" Virginia asked.

"I'm a good girl!" Betty Peep was saying as Tony went out the door. "That Wolf came up to us girls, and he kept trying to touch us and show us his tail."

The door banged shut as Wolf shouted, "That's a lie! They provoked me."

"And it didn't take much, I'll wager," Prince Wendell said in the silence of the hallway.

"Shhh," Tony said. He led Wendell outside and down the street until they reached the edge of the Peep farm. He walked until he found the murder site. It wasn't as hard as he thought it would be. Sally Peep's outline had been marked in paint, complete with her crook.

They were nothing here if not thorough.

Tony stood over the spot and looked at Prince Wendell. Wendell seemed a little confused.

"What can you smell?" Tony asked Prince.

"Your body odor," Prince said.

Tony crossed his arms. He was going to help Wolf, and he was going to use Prince Wendell to do it.

"You haven't even tried," Tony said, imitating Wendell's imperious tone. "Go on, see what you can smell."

"Why don't you get down on all fours and see what you can smell?" Prince said. "It's mainly feet and excrement at ground level—had that ever occurred to you?"

Tony glared at him. Wendell sighed and then, reluctantly, bent his head down and sniffed.

"Can you pick up a scent?" Tony asked.

"There's hundreds of scents," Prince said.

He walked around the painted spot, sniffing loudly.

"Yes, but only a great hunting Prince like yourself could distinguish that special scent."

"Correct!" Prince Wendell raised his head, his tail wagging. He had smelled something. He took off as fast as his four legs could carry him.

Tony ran after him, too elated to ask Prince Wendell to slow down.

It looked so easy when Perry Mason did it. Virginia tried to run a hand through her hair, but succeeded only in knocking off her wig. She caught it with one hand and put it back on. Somehow, she had made matters worse for Wolf.

Then she had called him to the stand. He had seemed eager enough. She had a good list of questions. She just hadn't expected the Judge to ask a few of his own.

The Judge held up a book so that both Wolf and the audience could see it. "Do you know what this is?"

"I have never seen it before in my whole life," Wolf said.

"It is the infamous *Wolf Four Seasons Recipe Book,* and I draw your attention to the ingredients for Shepherd's Pie on page thirty-seven. Carrots, potatoes, pepper, coriander—and one pert shepherdess, if in season."

Peeps rose to their feet and started screaming. The handful of non-Peeps in the audience talked loudly to themselves. Wolf cringed.

"That book is inadmissible evidence, Your Honor," Virginia said.

The Judge ignored her. "How would you describe Sally Peep?"

"Objection!" Virginia said.

"Sally?" Wolf said. "Very cute, succulent. Nice girl, a very tasty little birdie and no mistake."

"Nice enough to eat?"

"Oh, yes." Wolf blinked, then looked panicked. "No, I didn't mean that."

"She was asking for it, is that what you're saying?" the Judge asked.

"No, she was begging for it. She was gagging for it. No, no I just meant they're very provocative, some of the girls. They know that a wolf—well, it's like thrusting a steak in front of a starving man."

"Is it indeed," the Judge said dryly.

Virginia hadn't expected Wolf to be such a bad witness. She had no idea how she'd get him out of this.

"No, I didn't mean that either," Wolf said. "I'm twisting everything I'm saying."

Finally she decided on an oldie but a goodie. "He's suffering from post-menstrual tension, Your Honor."

The Judge continued to ignore her. He leaned closer to Wolf. "The night before the murder there was a henhouse homicide resulting in the death of ten chickens. Anything to do with that?"

"No, sir," Wolf said.

"You didn't kill the chickens?"

"No, sir."

"You didn't go near the henhouse?"

"Absolutely not, sir," Wolf said.

"Then how do you explain this?" The Judge held up a ripped bit of blue cloth that looked like part of Wolf's shirt. Virginia closed her eyes for a brief moment, and wished herself somewhere else. Then she opened her eyes to watch more of Wolf's destruction.

"This is a piece of shirt recovered from inside the Peeps' chicken coup," the Judge said.

Wolf studied the shirt. "Oh, the chickens."

In that moment, Virginia knew that Wolf had been on the Peeps' farm. She had been wrong. He had been there all along.

Wolf said, "Let me think. Yes, yes, I might have eaten all the chickens."

He had just signed his own death warrant. Virginia was too shocked to speak.

But the Judge wasn't. "And then you killed Sally Peep."

"A couple of drumsticks doesn't make me a killer," Wolf said. "I had chicken for dinner, I admit it. But I didn't touch any girl. I swear."

"Then why did you lie?" the Judge asked.

"Because if I said yes to the chickens, you'd think I wolfed down the girl as well."

"That's exactly what we think," the Judge said.

Peeps rose to their feet shouting, "Burn the wolf! Kill the wolf!" They were shaking their fists. Spittle was coming out of their mouths. Virginia had never been in the middle of a mob scene before.

"I didn't do it," Wolf shouted back at the crowd. "I didn't do it."

That was it. She had to do something. Virginia leapt to her feet and tried to bluster her way through the crowd. She believed him. She believed he killed the chickens and didn't kill Sally Peep.

But somehow she had to prove it.

"Of course he didn't do it!" Virginia shouted. The courtroom got quiet, except for an occasional Burn-the-Wolf outburst. "But if he didn't kill Sally Peep, then who did? I hear myself asking. Because the time has come for me to point the finger at the real killer. Last night there was another man going around dressed as a wolf. Oh, yes. The man in the wolf mask, and the real killer."

The entire courtroom gasped.

Emboldened, Virginia shook her fist. "And that murdering piece of filth is the one who should be on that stand now."

"The honor of playing the Wolf in the annual fair has always gone to an unimpeachable member of our society," the Judge said.

"I don't care," Virginia said. "Bring the sleezebag in, let

me cross-examine him and I guarantee we'll have our murderer.''

"And when that honor was bestowed on me last week," the Judge continued, "I was only too pleased to accept."

The silence was so intense that Virginia could hear her own breathing. She flushed. "I'm most dreadfully sorry, Your Honor."

She sat down. She had lost the case, and she didn't know what else to do. But she squeezed Wolf's arm and leaned over to reassure him as best she could.

"It's in the bag," she whispered.

Then someone hit her on the head with a juicy tomato.

"Burn her too!" a Peep shouted.

The rest of the Peeps took up the cry. "Burn them both! Burn them both!"

"Members of the jury, you have heard the evidence, most of it quite ridiculous," the Judge said to the sheep. He was speaking loudly so that his voice carried over the shouting.

As he spoke, a bailiff unlocked the doors on either side of the jury box.

"Those who believe he is innocent, go into the right-hand pen. Those who know he is guilty, go into the left-hand pen."

Virginia leaned forward and stared at the two pens. She stood to object. "The left pen's full of food!"

But no one seemed to care, except Wolf, who put his head in his hands. All of the sheep went to the left-hand pen.

"Oh, no," Wolf said, "the Gypsy was right. A girl dead. A wolf burns."

Virginia shuddered, and then took his hand.

"By a unanimous verdict," the Judge said, "I pronounce you guilty of murder most heinous. I sentence you to be burnt at the stake. Let's do it immediately before the Marvelous Marrow contest."

"Burn the wolf!" the crowd chanted. They sounded gleeful. "Burn the wolf!"

Chapter Thirty-Two

Prince Wendell led Tony to the Peeps' barn. Tony followed, feeling nervous. He flashed on Wilfred's threat to harm his own granddaughter if she told anyone about the well. Tony was really pushing his luck coming here three separate times.

Prince Wendell had already been inside, but he couldn't be dissuaded. He wanted Tony to come in too.

"Look, I know about the well," Tony said. "So what?"

"This is where she came from," Prince Wendell said. "She was here just before she was murdered. I can smell her here."

Tony followed Wendell inside the barn. Then Tony froze in place. Everything was different. The support beams were gone from the dirt mound. The hatch door was open, and the dirt had spilled inside.

Someone had wrecked the well.

Wolf struggled as hard as he could, but two burly Peeps held him tightly. Several more surrounded him as they dragged him toward the stake in the center of town. Villagers with torches stood all around.

Virginia was following, shouting, "You can't do this. You haven't given him a fair trial." As if they were going to listen to her. No one who continually chanted *Burn the wolf! Burn the wolf!* as these idiots were doing would care about fairness.

He'd tried to explain that to her. Somehow her disillusionment mattered almost as much to him as the fact that he was going to burn to death.

Very soon.

They dragged him over a huge pile of kindling and tied him roughly to the wooden stake. A splinter dug into his hand. His feet crunched through the pile of sticks below him, and suddenly he didn't care so much about Virginia's feelings.

This mob was really going to kill him.

"No!" he shouted. "No, not me, big mistake, not me, didn't do it, no! No! No!"

"Shut up, you murdering wolf." Wilfred Peep grabbed Wolf by the throat and slammed his head against the post. Then more ropes bound him, and other farmers—not even Peeps— began tossing more kindling around him.

This wasn't just going to be a bonfire. It was going to be an inferno.

Virginia was at the edge of the crowd, begging with whoever would listen. But no one was. They were all joining the chant.

Burn the wolf! Burn the wolf!

Then the Judge walked toward the pile. He was carrying a bigger torch than anyone else, and he was smiling, the old hypocrite.

"Justice will be served," the Judge said as he handed the torch to Wilfred. "Only seems right that family should do it, Wilf."

It was really going to happen this time. No nice prison, no pact with a Queen to save himself. Not even a wonderful, passionate kiss with Virginia.

"Virginia," Wolf said, "I want you to remember me all nice please? Forever?"

Virginia's eyes were filled with tears. "No!" Virginia shouted. "No! Stop it!" That last wasn't directed at him. It was meant for Wilfred Peep, who was bending over the kindling, about to light it with the torch.

"Wait!"

Wolf looked toward the back of the crowd. Tony was running toward them, Prince Wendell at his side.

"Wait! Stop! Wait!"

Tony pushed through the villagers to the edge of the bonfire. He stepped right beside Wilfred Peep.

"Wolf didn't kill Sally Peep, and I can prove it!" Tony said.

"He'll say anything." Wilfred Peep thrust the torch into the kindling. Wolf moaned. But Tony grabbed the torch and kicked the singed kindling out of the way.

"The Peep family have been cheating all of you for years," Tony shouted. "They've had their own magic wishing well and stopped the rest of you having any water."

He was struggling with Wilfred Peep for the torch. Wolf wasn't listening so much as he was watching. Tony was clumsy, and if he dropped that thing it would be all over no matter what.

"It's a lie!" Wilfred Peep shouted. He tried to force the torch back down to light the bonfire. Tony fought to keep it away.

"When Sally Peep lost the competition, she wrecked your well," Tony shouted. "And when you saw what she'd done, you chased her into the fields and killed her—didn't you, Wilfred?"

"I don't know what you're talking about," Wilfred shouted. "We don't have no magic well."

Tony finally managed to wrest the torch out of Wilfred's hands. He held it above his head. Sparks flew off it and landed near the kindling. Wolf struggled against his bonds.

"Why do you think they win everything?" Tony shouted to the crowd. "Or their food is so wonderful?"

The crowd started muttering, looking at the Peeps. Now, if only Tony would move away from the kindling, Wolf would feel a lot better.

"I believe him," one woman shouted. "You Peeps have cheated us for too long."

"Where's the proof to any of this?" Wilfred Peep demanded. "Prove I killed Sally."

Tony whistled, and Prince Wendell came forward like the dog he was. Wolf was startled to see Wendell so docile. In Wendell's mouth was a long bit of cloth.

"Where's your coat, Wilf?" Tony asked. "The one you were wearing last night?"

Wilfred looked around nervously. Prince Wendell stopped in front of him and dropped the cloth. It was Wilfred's coat, and it was covered with blood.

The villagers gasped. Wolf checked the position of that torch again, relieved to see that Tony still had a firm grip on it.

"Poor Sally wasn't screaming 'Wolf' at all, was she, Wilfred?" Tony asked. "She was crying out your name. Wilf! Wilf!"

Wilfred backed away from the others, looking frightened. "She ruined the well, the dirty little vixen. She destroyed the magic."

The other Peeps looked at him in horror.

"You killed our Sally?" Barbara Peep asked. But she didn't wait for an answer. She lunged at Wilfred. So did the other Peeps. Tony got out of the way. Wolf held his breath. That torch looked mighty precarious.

Then Wolf felt fingers brush his. Virginia was untying him.

"Time to go," she said.

They climbed off the kindling as the battle raged on. Tony dropped the torch in a nearby horse trough, and Prince Wendell rinsed his mouth out. Then they hurried toward the barn.

"My three friends," Wolf said, "how can I ever thank you enough. You saved my bacon."

He patted Wendell. The dog looked disgusted.

"Thanks, old chap," Wolf said. "I owe you a very big bone. Oh, yes, from now on, we are friends for life. As for you, Virginia, what a courtroom drama."

She looked at him hesitantly. "Are you cured now?"

Tony pulled the barn door open. Wolf went inside first, grinning. He hadn't felt this good in years.

"Oh, completely," Wolf said. "Back to my old self. Can't remember much at all about it, to tell the truth. But I remember that you and Tony both laid down your—"

"Look!" Tony said.

The big back doors of the barn were wide open.

"What's happened?" Tony asked. "Where's it gone?"

Wolf glanced at Virginia, confused. She looked extremely upset. Then he remembered. When she had first come to him in the cell, she had said they had gotten the mirror. And now, apparently, it was missing.

Fidelity, the farmer's wife who'd let them stay in the barn, peeked in through the double doors. She smiled in her rosy-cheeked way, oblivious to the courtroom drama that had gone on before. Wolf was the only one who smiled back at her. Virginia went to her in a clear panic.

"Where's the cart gone?" Virginia asked.

"Oh, my son, John," Fidelity said, "he's just taken his pigs to market. Set off a couple of hours ago."

Virginia looked at her father, who sighed. Wolf sighed louder. If he had known what they'd done, he would have warned them against it. Magic liked to move around.

"Which way and how far?" Virginia asked.

"Well, it's not a journey you'd want to make on foot," Fidelity said.

As if they had any choice. Virginia talked to the farmer's wife and got directions. Wolf took a deep breath and got himself back together. It had been a stressful morning. Actually, it had been a stressful few days.

He was relieved he hadn't killed Sally Peep. He really didn't remember much after the chickens.

Finally Virginia got the directions and the small group headed out, making sure to avoid the other villagers. They went past the wishing well. The village idiot waved at Tony.

"Did you have a nice stay in our village?" the idiot asked.

"Not exactly," Virginia said.

"I wish I could remember who that dog reminds me of," the idiot said.

"Let me make a suggestion," Tony said. "Prince Wendell, your ruler?"

Wolf shot a surprised glance at Tony. Wendell positively glowered at him. The village idiot crouched and looked Wendell in the face. Then he giggled.

"Prince Wendell?" the idiot asked. "Don't be daft. No, it was a puppy I once knew called Mr. Fleas."

Prince Wendell made a horrible sound of disgust and started off on his own. Virginia followed him, which meant that Wolf had to follow her. Tony walked beside him.

The village idiot called after them. "Aren't you going to make a wish?"

Virginia took out a coin and flicked it over her shoulder as they kept walking. "You make it for us," she said.

Wolf turned. The village idiot tossed the coin into the well. And, surprisingly, a moment later there was a splash.

Now Virginia and Tony turned as well.

"Sounds like our well's getting some water back in it!" the idiot said. "Oh, joy! Water's back on!"

There was a sound like a rushing wall of water down below, and tiny stars started to spiral slowly out of the well. The villagers rushed out, and Wolf moved behind Virginia. He wasn't going to get near those people again.

Suddenly, a jet of water burst out of the well, destroying its little roof, and flew thirty feet into the air. The village idiot ran under it as if it were a shower.

"Finally!" the idiot said. "I am a complete idiot!"

Funny, Wolf thought, the man had seemed like a complete idiot before.

Then he turned and caught up to Virginia, Tony, and Prince Wendell, who were already making their way out of Little Lamb Village. Wolf resisted the urge to shake the dust of the village off his feet. But he knew he'd do everything he could to make sure he never came back to this place again.

The Queen stood before her mirror, watching Wendell's incompetent advisors dithering over the Troll problem. The Troll King's armies had advanced through half the Fourth Kingdom, and Wendell's royal advisors were in a tizzy.

They were waiting for Wendell to appear to save them. That much amused her. What didn't amuse her was the fact that they were bargaining with the First and Ninth Kingdoms. Fortunately their price to help was high indeed. They wanted to divide the Fourth Kingdom into quarters, to be run by the council of the Nine Kingdoms in perpetuity. Wendell's throne would be gone forever.

And if it was gone, so was her opportunity.

"No!" she shouted at the mirror. "I'm not ready. This is falling apart. Get me the Troll King. Immediately."

The mirror remained static. "He still rejects your calls. He grows stronger every day."

"Get him," the Queen said. "Get him or I will bury you all back in the darkness."

The mirror did not respond. Only blinks of light in its surface showed that it was even trying. She threaded her fingers together, feeling the beginnings of an unfamiliar panic. Nothing had gone the way she had planned it. Nothing. She had to regain control, and she had to do it soon.

Then the Troll King appeared in her mirror. He had caked blood on his nose and down his shirt. When he saw her, he raised a fist and shook it.

"You're dead!" he shouted. "The next time I see you, you're dead!"

He was holding a shard of rusty mirror in his hand. His palm was bleeding too.

"Wendell's council are calling in the other armies." The Queen had to struggle to keep her voice level. "Cease fighting immediately or you will be overrun and we will lose this kingdom forever. Do you understand, cretin?''

The Troll King raised the shard of mirror and looked at her for a moment. Then he spat on the mirror. His spittle was a disgusting green. It ran down her mirror like a live thing.

''I'm taking the kingdom,'' the Troll King said. ''Then I'm coming for you, you evil pig.''

He vanished. The Queen stepped away from the mirror, stunned and shocked. How had she lost control so very quickly? And to imbeciles. Was it all that time in prison? Had she lost her edge?

''It's gone wrong,'' the Queen said to herself. ''It's all gone wrong. My plan is in ruins.''

Her mirror remained before her, silent. But another mirror, one she had never used, started to hum. It was older than the others, and she hadn't been certain of its powers, so she hadn't touched it. Little crackles, like distant thunder, made her sit up and stare at it.

The mirror came slowly to life. It turned red, not green like the others, and the dark room filled with a blood-red glow.

The Queen went to the mirror. A horrible face appeared in the red surface of the glass.

''Come to me.''

The Queen approached the red mirror.

''Come to me and your mind will clear.''

The Queen stretched out her hand to touch the full-length mirror. The surface rippled, and then she put her hand through the mirror itself.

Then she followed her hand inside. She was stepping into a memory. An old memory. She recognized this place. It was a long time since she had seen it. A wooden shack in the middle of a swamp. In front of her was a crone so familiar that the Queen had to suppress a gasp. Snow White's evil stepmother.

''I am dead,'' the stepmother said, ''but my work is unfinished. The House of Snow White survives.''

Around her, five mirrors rose out of the swamp.

"These are my gifts. They give you my power."

She indicated one of the mirrors.

"Mirrors to travel . . ."

And another.

"Mirrors to spy . . ."

And another.

"Mirrors to remember . . ."

And another.

"Mirrors to forget . . ."

And the last.

"Mirrors to rule the world."

The Queen turned toward all of them. She remembered everything now, including what she had to do. The scene before her faded, and she stepped back to her palace.

As she got out of the mirror, she was covered in blood. It felt good. She wiped the blood off her face and smiled.

"Let the battle commence," she said.

Chapter Thirty-Three

The trip on the back of the hay wagon was a long one, but they were lucky that the farmer had picked them up. Virginia sat against one hay bale, Wolf against another, Tony against a third, and Wendell was curled up beside him. They had long since run out of things to talk about, and Wolf had shared his books.

Virginia read *What Do Women Want?* Tony was reading an affirmation from one of the other books, and Wendell was looking over his shoulder. Tony hadn't known that until Wendell yelled at him for turning a page too soon.

As they came into a town, Wolf claimed he had finished the final page of the final chapter of his final book, saying that he now completely understood women, top to bottom.

Tony didn't have the heart to tell him there was no way a man would ever, ever completely understand women. And Tony certainly didn't tell him the derogatory things that Wendell said about wolves and their relationship to their women.

Beyond the town was a high mountain range. Tony had never seen mountains so spectacular and foreboding. Then he glanced at the area the wagon was bringing them into.

It was a town, and it had a wall around it. Tony thought that miraculous at first, but not nearly as spectacular as the town itself. It was beautiful, with tall buildings and lots of shops and restaurants and fountains. There were heart balloons everywhere, and places advertising things like Kissing Lessons.

And for a town, it smelled very fresh, like roses and cinnamon and freshly baked bread.

The people were also amazing. They seemed happy and prosperous and extremely well dressed. For the first time, Tony felt uncomfortable in his jeans and flannel shirt.

The wagon stopped at an intersection, and the group climbed down. They stood on the cobblestone street, staring at all the choices before them.

"Where exactly are we?" Tony asked.

"We have entered the most romantic town in the whole of the Nine Kingdoms," Wolf said. "The Kissing Town, where everyone falls in love. Truly fate has led us here."

He looked at Virginia and sighed.

Virginia glared at him. "Dream on."

Tony grinned. That was his girl.

"You'll see," Wolf said.

A married couple dashed past, followed by another. Confetti was falling everywhere and people were laughing.

"Anthony," Prince Wendell said, "my castle is over the other side of those mountains."

Tony looked again at the mountains. They made the Alps seem small—and Tony had never really been a mountain person anyway.

"Well, we're not going there," Tony said. "We're here for the mirror."

"It's a hundred-and-fifty miles, at most," Prince said. "Look at the map."

He pointed. Tony turned. He hadn't realized that they were standing near a huge framed map of the Nine Kingdoms. It showed the green of Wendell's Fourth Kingdom and had an arrow pointing to a spot two-thirds of the way to the northern-most section of the kingdom. With traditional Fourth Kingdom helpfulness, the arrow had the words YOU ARE ROMANTICALLY HERE written in its center.

"Have we walked all that way?" Virginia asked.

"What's this kingdom underneath all the others?" Tony asked.

"Don't bother with that," Prince said. "It's the Dwarves' Ninth Kingdom. Entirely underground. Very unsavory."

A man dressed all in pink hurried past them, hawking perfume. As he walked along, he sprayed the scent of lilacs from a bottle. People turned toward it or toward each other, sighing heavily, as if their hearts were full of love.

At the intersection, three couples kissed. Full body kisses— lots of tongue and pawing. Tony glanced at the elderly couple and quickly turned away.

"Can't they do that in private?" Tony asked.

"They can't help it, Tony," Wolf said. "Love is in the air."

A chubby little girl dressed as Cupid skipped up to them. She had an arrow and homemade wings strapped to her back.

"Hello," she said, "I have been looking for you all day. I can see love and fortune coming your way."

"It's slice-the-fruitcake time again." Tony shook his head. They really did attract the crazies like bees to honey. "How much do you want?"

The girl smiled at Virginia. "Great romance and wealth before this very night is out. I can sense it in your auras."

"Yeah?" Tony asked. "Who's going to make the money?"

The girl turned to him as if she hadn't really seen him before. "Your aura is cloudy. Just give me a couple of coins."

"It's the old cloudy-aura routine," Tony said.

Virginia gave her a few coins. He'd have to pull his daughter aside at some point and talk to her about giving money to panhandlers. She seemed to have a penchant for it.

"She is such a soft touch," Tony said, putting a little sarcasm into it. But no one else seemed to notice.

"Oh, yes, a very soft touch," Wolf said. "Sensuous, creamy touch."

"Thank you very much," the girl said to Virginia. "Now,

if you look over there, you might find what you're looking for.
Good-bye.''

The girl had pointed away from the sign. Tony looked in
that direction, and his jaw dropped. ''That's the pig wagon
with the mirror in it, I'm sure.''

''But how did she know?'' Virginia asked.

They walked over to the wagon and peered into its back.
It was empty. No pigs—although the smell remained, faintly
sour—no straw, and no mirror.

The farmer who had driven the wagon here—what had his
mother said his name was? John?—came out of a butcher shop,
counting his coins. He was so obviously from Little Lamb
Village that Tony shouted at him.

''You! Where's our mirror?''

''Yours, is it?'' Farmer John had his mother's charming
smile. ''I wondered what it was doing with all my pigs.''

''Where is it?'' Tony asked.

John's smile left. He looked from Tony to Virginia to Wolf.
''I didn't know it was yours, did I?''

''Where is it?'' Tony could hear the edge in his voice. He
tried to keep control of himself.

''You wouldn't want it now, anyway.'' John was backing
toward the front of his wagon. ''It's covered in pig shit.''

''Where is it?'' Virginia yelled. Tony looked at her in
surprise. He thought *he* was overreacting.

''I don't rightly know,'' John said, staring at her. ''Fellow
gave me five coppers for it this morning.''

''What fellow?'' Tony asked.

''Dunno,'' John said. ''He was just passing with a wheelbar-
row full of bricky-brac. Probably came for the antiques
market.''

All of them looked around, as if they could conjure the
fellow up with a single glance. Instead, they saw how daunting
their task was going to be. This part of town was absolutely
full of antique shops and market stalls.

Tony couldn't believe their bad luck.

"You'll never find it now, Anthony," the Prince said. "Let's head for my castle instead."

John climbed into his wagon. Tony ignored Prince Wendell and stared at the shops. What an impossible task.

"Anthony," Wendell said.

"No," Tony snapped. He crossed the road. He would find that mirror if it meant he had to look at every trinket in every antique shop in Kissing Town.

Wendell followed him. For a while, so did Virginia and Wolf. But they soon realized it would take them forever to find the mirror if they stayed together.

So they split up. Tony would have gone with Virginia, but Wolf couldn't understand Wendell. So reluctantly, Tony stayed with the Prince while his daughter disappeared with the wolf.

He was liking this pairing less and less. And somehow, he felt he had nothing to say about it.

Wolf had flagged them down a buggy. It was lovely, and Virginia could tell it was usually used for courting couples. Wolf didn't seem to mind. In fact, that could have been part of his plan.

"Wouldn't it be quicker to walk?" Virginia asked.

Wolf didn't answer her. Instead, he looked at the town around them. "You remember the story of Snow White, when she swallowed the poisoned apple and everybody thought she was dead? The seven dwarves brought her here and put her in a glass coffin in the hope that someone might be able to bring her back to life."

"Here?" Virginia asked. "To this town?"

"To the top of this very hill," Wolf said. "Prince's grand-mother."

The horses took the buggy to the top of the hill. Wolf casually put his arm on the seat behind Virginia. She didn't mind, even though she knew what he was doing.

"Most rulers are respected," he said. "Some are feared or held in contempt. But Snow White—she was loved like no one you have ever known. She had magic that was just to do with being around her. If she went to a town or a house or just plain was with anyone for a while, then good things happened to that person. She was super-duper in every way.''

As the buggy crested the hill, Virginia realized they were in some sort of romantic tourist trap. Souvenir sellers hawked their wares all over, and dozens of couples were walking toward a spot not too far away.

''Glass coffins!'' a souvenir man was shouting. ''Get your miniature glass coffins.''

Wolf rapped on the roof of the buggy and it stopped. He got out and helped Virginia down.

A long line of couples stood in front of a stand. Virginia watched as one of the couples paid and went beyond the stand. The woman lay on a rock and closed her eyes. The young man leaned over and kissed her. There was a glass coffin and a completely cheesy theatrical background with painted birds. The couple, Virginia realized, had dressed up in costume.

While the couple posed, a sketch artist drew their faces into pre-painted scenes. It was as corny as hell, but Virginia loved it. She had never imagined a place like this.

She turned to Wolf. ''Does Happy Ever After really mean ever after?''

''No, it's just a figure of speech,'' Wolf said. ''But all the Happy Ever After people get to be at least a hundred and fifty before they pop off gently in their sleep.''

''A hundred and fifty years old?'' Virginia asked.

''Happy Ever After is like another life, given free, for being good.''

''Where's Snow White now?'' Virginia asked. ''Is she dead?''

''Nobody knows,'' Wolf said. ''On her one-hundred-and-fiftieth birthday, she left her castle in just the clothes she stood up in, and took no food, and walked through the snow. She is surely dead, but where she lies now no one knows.''

Virginia stopped and sighed. Then she looked at Wolf. He

seemed to have lost that edge she saw in Little Lamb Village. He had a handsomeness she hadn't appreciated before.

Maybe it was the sight of all those couples. Maybe watching other people who were enjoying themselves made her feel better.

"I don't know why," Virginia said, "but I just feel so good."

Wolf smiled. "Everyone does in the Kissing Town," he said.

Tony felt filthy after going through seventeen different antique stores. Why didn't those dealers clean the stuff they bought? There was enough dust in those places to build entire rooms. Prince Wendell was just as disgusted and had suggested that they try something different.

He led Tony to an auction hall. It was jammed with all sorts of things, but unlike the stuff in the antique stores, this merchandise seemed to be magic. Tony saw jars of authenticated dragon beans, golden eggs, and a gingerbread door claiming to be from the original gingerbread cottage.

But it was Lot 8 that caught Prince Wendell's attention. Tony couldn't see it clearly until he came up beside Wendell. Then Tony gasped.

The three Trolls who had been chasing Wendell were here. They were still gold, still stuck in their tableau. The only difference was that an identification tag hung from one finger. There were a lot of stamps on them and writing as well, making it seem as if they had been shipped through the mail.

"Not very attractive work, I'll grant you."

Tony jumped at the sound of the voice. He turned. The auctioneer was standing behind him, hands behind his back, contemplating the Trolls.

"But still full of vitality and life." The auctioneer smiled at Tony. "Frozen Rage would grace the gardens of any fine house. Does it tickle your fancy?"

"Far from it," Tony said. "I never want to see it again.

But have you had a mirror come in recently, about my height, black?''

The auctioneer's eyes glazed over. Apparently Tony had just shown himself to be a cretin. The auctioneer waved a hand toward the far corner. "I seem to remember a job lot of junk over there.''

Tony and Wendell walked in that direction. The auctioneer wasn't kidding. Piles of junk, most of it in boxes, were scattered all over the floor. More dust. Tony rolled up his sleeves and dug in.

He didn't know how long he searched. Wendell pushed things aside with his nose. Tony was just beginning to think of giving up when he saw:

JOB LOT 101
MIRROR. UNKNOWN ORIGIN. NEEDS RESTORATION.
ESTIMATE 10-15 GOLD COINS

"This is it,'' Tony said. "This is it.''

"Don't attract attention,'' Prince Wendell said.

"Ten to fifteen crowns,'' Tony said. "It's priced really low. No one knows what it is.''

Tony glanced around. Maybe, if no one was watching, he could just carry it out of there. Then he noticed the guards near the door. They were watching him.

He pulled the mirror out of its crate and stared at it. His own image stared back at him. He reached for the secret catch.

"Don't turn it on in here, you moron,'' Prince Wendell warned. "Everyone will see.''

Wendell was right, of course. Tony turned around to look for the auctioneer. Instead, he bumped into an elderly Elf. The Elf was well dressed. He was peering down at the mirror with a monocle. Tony found himself staring at the Elf's pointed ears.

The Elf used a silver-headed cane to tap the side of the mirror. "Mmm . . . what do you think?'' the Elf asked.

"Of what?" Tony asked. "Of this? Piece of garbage. Don't waste your time."

Tony put the mirror back.

The Elf continued to peer through his monocle. "At first, I thought it was a reproduction, Late Naked Emperor at best, but I think it's older than that. Quite a lot older. Maybe even early Cinderellan. And quite a lot more special."

He scraped away the black paint with his long fingernails. Gold writing gleamed beneath the ancient paint job.

"Dwarf runes," the Elf said. "It's almost like someone's concealed its true origins."

"I think it's definitely a reproduction," Tony said.

The Elf gave him a thin smile. "No, you don't."

Wendell tugged at Tony's leg. They had to find Virginia. She was the one carrying the coins. Tony wasn't pleased at the idea of leaving. The Elf was a little too interested in the mirror. But Tony let Wendell lead him out of the auction hall anyway.

As they walked toward the door, Tony thought he saw a familiar figure. The Huntsman? Tony shuddered. It wasn't possible. The man had been too badly injured to make it this far.

Tony nodded once, and then headed out onto the street.

It took nearly an hour to find Virginia and Wolf. They weren't looking for the mirror at all. They had paid some ungodly amount of money to dress in costume and have their portraits painted. Virginia was lying on a rock, and Wolf was too close to kissing her for Tony's comfort.

So Tony said in his loudest voice, "Hey, you two! Stop clowning around. We've found the mirror."

Virginia looked over at him, a bit bleary, then moved away from Wolf. She took off the costume—it only covered her clothes—and came toward them. Wolf looked horribly disappointed, but he followed as well.

As Tony hustled them down the hill, he told them all about finding the mirror. Wendell kept them moving quickly. They got back to the auction hall in less than twenty minutes.

Tony hurried back to the far corner. The box of bric-a-brac remained, but he couldn't find the mirror anywhere.

"It's gone!" Tony shouted.

The auctioneer came over to see what the commotion was.

"Where's the mirror?" Tony asked.

The auctioneer smiled his supercilious little smile. "Oh, the magic mirror, you mean? What a find. We're all tremendously excited about it."

He led them toward the center of the hall. There, on a pedestal, sat the mirror. Restoration experts were cleaning it, carefully scraping away the black paint and pig poop to reveal the gold leaf and delicate writing beneath. A crowd of people were watching and talking excitedly.

Tony's heart was pounding hard as he and Virginia approached the mirror. It had a new description. Tony read it silently.

LOT 7
VERY FINE MAGIC MIRROR, EARLY CINDERELLAN
DWARF WROUGHT AND RUNED
ESTIMATE 5,000 GOLD WENDELLS

"Five thousand?" Tony said.

"We'll never raise that," Virginia said.

And Tony knew that she was right.

Chapter Thirty-Four

The Queen stood before her magic mirrors. She had cleaned herself off. The vision she had been granted had given her a new determination. She was ready to take what was rightfully hers.

She waved an arm and said to the mirror, "Get me the Troll King."

"He will not speak to us," the mirror replied.

The Queen smiled a small, private smile. "Tell him his children are dead."

The mirror rippled and suddenly an image appeared. A burning field, smoke-inky and roiling, dominated the image. Toward the edge of the field, the Queen believed she saw heads on pikes. War drums beat in the distance, and Troll armies marched along the road, almost hidden in the smoke.

Suddenly Relish the Troll King leapt in front of the mirror. His face was streaked with soot and blood, his eyes narrow.

"Dead!" the Troll King shouted into the mirror. "Dead?"

The Queen suppressed her smile. "They are dead unless you agree to meet me for talks."

The Troll King head-butted his mirror, splintering it. The Queen had to take a step back from hers before she realized the splintering would not happen on her end.

"You evil pig!" he shouted.

The Queen folded her hands beneath the long sleeves of her purple gown. "Meet me at the Apple Orchard outside Little

Lamb Village at dawn tomorrow. Come alone and unarmed, or I will slit their throats.''

''If you hurt a—''

She waved a hand and cut him off. It felt good to control their conversations again. ''Well, that's that.''

She turned to the servant who cowered near the door. Someday she would get servants who didn't cower and were still efficient. ''Pack everything so no one knows we've been here.''

The servant nodded.

She allowed her smile to come back, contemplating her future. ''We'll leave,'' she said, ''when darkness falls.''

The group sat in the town square, beneath a large ancient statue of Snow White and the Seven Dwarves. The statue was gray and covered with pigeon poop. No one had cleaned the thing for fifty years. Tony worried about sitting so close to it.

Virginia and Wolf were too close together, and Prince Wendell lay at their feet, his head on his paws. They all looked dejected, but not as dejected as Tony felt.

He sat at the very edge of the bench, staring at the nearby newsstand. He knew Wendell had already seen the headlines: *Wendell's Disgrace: Coronation Cancelled.* Looking at the words just made the dog even more depressed.

''All is lost,'' Prince Wendell said for probably the fifteenth time.

''How much do we have between us?'' Tony asked.

He kept hoping that they would somehow come up with the cash they needed for the mirror. If only he had found a way to buy it before searching for Virginia. It was amazing how much difference an hour made.

Virginia counted their combined wealth. She put the coins in different stacks to show the different denominations. Tony still wasn't sure how she kept track of all this play money, but he was glad she could.

''Exactly thirty gold Wendells,'' Virginia said. ''How can we turn thirty coins into five thousand by tomorrow morning?''

Wendell sighed. Wolf frowned. Virginia stared at the money. Tony thought. How did they increase their holdings? Finding a job that paid that well would be as difficult as winning the lottery.

Then he sat up straighter. "I've got an idea," he said. "Follow me."

They went to the other side of the town square. As they walked, he told them his plan. Virginia didn't like it. Wolf shrugged. Wendell had no opinion at all, which wasn't like him. But Tony was determined.

Tony stopped them in front of the building that he had only barely noticed before. The Lucky-in-Love Casino. Outside, people were selling lucky charms—literally. A rabbit's foot for one gold Wendell. Four-leaf clovers for four gold Wendells.

Virginia shook her head and mumbled something about the only people who made money being the charm sellers.

Tony ignored that. He made sure that Wolf and Virginia got ten gold coins. He kept ten for himself.

"Okay," he said. "One of us has to make a fortune before daybreak."

"I've had an idea for Prince." Virginia knelt beside the royal dog. Tony couldn't see what she was doing, but he could tell that Prince Wendell was getting quite agitated.

"No, Tony," Prince said. "Tell her I refuse. I absolutely refuse. It's so humiliating."

"Every little bit helps." Virginia stood. Tony peered down. She had placed a sign around Wendell's neck. It read:

LUCKY GAMBLING DOG
PLEASE SPLIT WINNINGS 50/50

Prince Wendell looked completely humiliated, and somehow that added to the charm. Tony smiled. This just might work.

In the open bell tower that overlooked the square, the Huntsman leaned back and let the pain run through him. His leg was nearly ruined, and he was losing too much blood. But he had to finish this job for the Queen. Somehow he had not expected these incompetents to be as much trouble as they had been.

His crossbow was beside him. His other weapons were laid out and ready for use. He could see most of the town from up here.

He could see Virginia and Tony and their Wolf go into the casino, along with Prince Wendell.

He had time to rest before he did the work he had been hired for.

Carefully he unwrapped the bandages around his injured leg. The trap had ripped through the muscle down to the bone. It had been an efficient trap. He had just never expected to be caught in it. Fortunately, he knew how to release the lever and set himself free.

Which was more than those he chased knew. From now on, he took any advantage he could. They would die quickly and silently. He would finish this work, even if it killed him.

The torches and oil lamps made this casino darker than any other Wolf had ever been in. Perhaps it was the small space. He was used to outdoor casinos, not one like this, where the games were played in semi-darkness.

All around were people throwing dice and laughing or putting coins into machines. The chink-chink-chink of winnings was intoxicating.

Tony had just come from the window where he had converted the coins to chips. "Okay, team," he said. "Let's make money."

Virginia went in one direction, Tony in another, with Wendell at his heels. Wolf frowned, looking for something that interested him. Finally he saw his favorite, the Wheel of Fortune.

He walked over to it and asked the croupier who ran the wheel, "Miss, what is the highest return possible from one gold Wendell bet?"

"Well, sir," the croupier said, "you'd want to bet on the grand Jack Rabbit Jackpot at ten-thousand-to-one odds. But it's only ever come up once."

"That's the one for me."

Wolf put one of his coins on the jackpot square but didn't watch as the wheel turned. Instead he looked over at Virginia, who was playing racing rabbits. She was completely into it, shouting and waving her fist. She looked so relaxed.

He crossed his fingers as the wheel clicked around him. If he won, Virginia would love him even more. But if he won too much, she'd buy the mirror and go home. She would leave him. . . .

"Bad luck, sir," the croupier said.

Wolf looked at the wheel. He had lost. "Oh, thank you," he said, relieved.

"Do you wish to bet again?"

Wolf glanced at Virginia. If he lost it all, she would at least know he tried.

"Sir? Again?"

He smiled at the croupier. "Absolutely," he said.

Virginia was leaning over the Racin' Rabbits table, watching as the Rabbit Checker made certain the four bunnies who ran this course were secure in their harnesses. Virginia couldn't help wondering if this wasn't just a bit cruel, forcing rabbits to run an obstacle course as if they were horses.

But she couldn't think of the morality of this now. Not when she had to win enough money to get home.

"Racin' rabbits, racin' rabbits, pick the winner and win the pot," said the man in charge of the betting.

Virginia had studied the odds and picked her rabbit. His name was Solvig and he had done well in the past.

The rabbits were lined up, and then a little bell went off. The rabbits shuffled forward.

"Come on, Solvig!" Virginia shouted. "Come on, Solvig. Come on, Solvig."

The man in charge announced the race like Howard Cosell on speed. "Solvig leading from Tidbit as they approach the last hurdle . . ."

Virginia tuned him out. She was watching Solvig. He made it through the final hurdle and had beaten Tidbit in the stretch. And then, suddenly, out of nowhere, Rumpus pulled forward. Rumpus caught up to Solvig and—

"—it's Rumpus by a whisker."

Virginia closed her eyes and sighed. Then she ran her fingers over her chips. Only five left.

This was all beginning to seem quite hopeless.

Tony sat in the deep smoke near the back of the casino. The lamps gave everything a faintly oily smell, and Tony wasn't sure of the safety laws in here. There were too many cigar smokers for his taste.

But he couldn't concentrate on that. He was in the middle of a high-stakes game with four other players. He had a stack of eighty chips before him, and he was doing well.

Prince Wendell was watching from the floor, but hadn't yet given any advice.

"I raise you twenty," said one of the players. Like the rest, he held his cards very close to his face.

"I sneer at your twenty and raise you fifty," Tony said.

A crowd was gathering. Apparently, high-stakes games like this were rare in the Lucky-in-Love.

"I match your fifty," the man said. "Call it."

Tony gave him a malicious smile. "Have you got Mr. Bun The Baker?"

The man cursed and threw the card at Tony. Slowly, Tony laid out a complete set of Happy Families.

"Read 'em and weep," Tony said, raking in the money.

"Sorry, sir," the croupier said, "not your lucky night."

Wolf smiled at her. In fact, he beamed. "Not to worry."

"I have never seen anyone as happy to lose as you, sir."

"Ah, but have you ever been in love, miss?"

"Just the once, sir," she said. "To a knight. But he was married."

Wolf placed his last chip on the jackpot space. "You see that girl over there? She is the other half of my heart. I would do anything in the world for her."

The croupier spun the wheel. It click-click-clicked, and Wolf let the sound engulf him.

He looked at Virginia. Apparently she was losing too. She looked so very sad.

"Oh, my goodness! Sir, you've won the Jack Rabbit Jackpot."

It took a moment for the words to register. Wolf turned back to the croupier. "I have?"

He glanced at the wheel. Sure enough, the jackpot had lined up with his coin.

"Oh, yes, sir." The croupier seemed more excited than he was. "Congratulations. Ten thousand gold coins. If you'd like to go to the cash desk, you can pick up your winnings. Sir?"

Suddenly Wolf grinned. "I've won! Wait until I tell my girl. Ten thousand gold coins."

He walked across the casino, past the card players and the dart players and the lucky-charm sellers. Virginia was still at the Racin' Rabbits table.

"More than enough to buy the mirror," he said to himself. "Now she will . . ."

Wolf slowed down.

". . . leave you. Yes. That's what she's going to do. She doesn't really love you—she just wants you to help her go home. She loves you . . . not."

He was almost to the Racin' Rabbits table. Virginia was only a few feet away.

"No, no, she adores you. Your wolf instincts are never wrong. She loves you."

Wolf stopped behind her and tapped her on the shoulder as

the obnoxious guy running the race said, "Can you believe it? Rumpus romps home for the third time running."

There were no more chips in front of Virginia. She saw Wolf and sighed. "Well, that's it. I've lost it all."

He looked at her. She was so beautiful. He really didn't want her to leave.

Wolves did mate for life. What would he do without her?

"How are you doing?" she asked.

"Yes . . . yes, me too," Wolf said.

She took his arm. "I have to get some air."

He nodded, still amazed at the lie that had come out of his mouth. What had he been thinking? He let her lead him to the balcony.

It overlooked the entire town. There were people on the streets but no one else on the balcony. And Virginia had been right. The air smelled much better out here. It was cooler too.

Wolf watched her stare over the city. She was so very beautiful.

"Don't be sad," Wolf said.

She shook. "I'm never going to get home. I'm going to end up spending the rest of my life stuck with you here. I can see it all."

Then she turned to him and caught him looking at her. Her features softened and he knew, suddenly, that she understood. That staying with him was going to be all right.

She asked, "Is it just this place, or . . . ?"

He held his breath. He didn't want to lose the moment.

"I feel like something . . . momentous is happening," Virginia said. "I can't describe it. I feel like there's a huge wall of water coming toward me, but I can't see it. I feel like it's going to engulf me."

She turned away from him and faced the town again. It felt as if the connection broke.

He couldn't leave the lie between them.

"Virginia," Wolf said, "I can't conceal it from you any longer. Something has just happened to me."

"Me, too," she said. She sounded both happy and sad at the same time.

"I have just—It has?"

She turned toward him. Her eyes were very soft. "Tell me it's just this town."

In this, he told her the truth. "Well, it is a magic love town, but flowers only grow where there are seeds. Fireworks only happen where there is stuff in the rockets already."

She smiled. And he knew, for the first time, really knew, that she was falling in love with him.

"Maybe there is destiny," Virginia said.

"There most certainly is," Wolf said.

Behind him, the lamps turned pink. Tiny birds appeared out of nowhere and started to tweet. It was a sign of his affection for her that he found the sappiness inspiring and didn't think of the birds as lunch.

"Maybe I am supposed to be with you," she said.

"You most certainly are."

He leaned toward her. She closed her eyes and parted her lips slightly. He was actually going to get to kiss her. His lips were almost touching hers when her eyes flew open and she turned away.

"We'd better see how Dad's getting on."

The pink light faded. The birds vanished. And Wolf felt a deep disappointment. He didn't know how to recapture the moment—and then he had no choice. Virginia was leaving the balcony. He stood for a moment, thinking how close he'd been to heaven, and then he followed her inside.

It had taken a few moments to find her father. He was in a dark, smoky room with several difficult characters. A crowd was gathered behind him. Virginia had to push through it to get close to her father. Wolf was right behind her.

"Mrs. Bone The Butcher's Wife completes the set," Tony said, as he laid down his cards. Then he chuckled as he pulled in money. The other players threw down their cards. They left, and so did the crowd. The dealer looked at Tony expectantly.

"Dad," Virginia said, "well done."

"I think I'm up to nearly six hundred, but it's no good. I'm not going to break the bank playing Happy Families. I have to move on to the top table." He pointed at a private table in the corner. It was marked for high rollers. The area was so full of smoke that Virginia could barely see the players. And what she did see, she didn't like.

"What are they playing there?" Virginia asked.

"It doesn't matter," Tony said, "there's no card game in the world scares me. You remember our week in Las Vegas in '93?"

"When we sold the car?"

"No, no, the year before that."

She remembered. She helped him pick up his winnings and move to the new table. The players there looked forebidding. There were only three of them: a huge Troll, a mean-looking Dwarf smoking a smelly cigar, and a very rich old lady. They grinned wolfishly as Tony arrived.

Virginia was going to ask Wolf what he thought of them, but when she turned around, he had vanished.

Chapter Thirty-Five

Wolf couldn't stand being inside the casino a moment longer. He had gotten his winnings and they were hiding in his pocket. He had no idea how he was going to handle this. For the first time, he wished he had someone to talk to, like that doctor back near Virginia's home.

The only person he had to talk to now was himself.

He paced back and forth in front of the casino, weaving in and among the lucky-charm vendors. Most of them, when they saw the look in his eyes, steered him a wide berth.

"What am I going to do? What am I going to do?" he muttered.

Then he straightened. "Yes, what are you going to do?"

He bent over. This felt like a dialogue between his animal self and his good, human self. "I'll give her the money, even if it means I will lose her. It's the only honorable thing to do."

He clenched a fist and nodded. "Yes, then she can go home safely and the Queen will not get to her."

A newlywed couple walked by, giggling and nuzzling. They were so in love. He and Virginia were in love. She was his life's mate.

"Of course," he muttered, "you will have to kill yourself the moment she's gone. Your life won't be worth living."

The couple stopped and kissed. He had almost kissed Virginia. She had wanted him to before she remembered herself and turned away.

An idea struck him. He could propose marriage. What did

he have to lose? He could give her enough money to buy the mirror, but spend the rest on presents for a marriage proposal. Then he would be fair and she would have a choice.

The idea made him smile. He glanced at the casino door. Tony and Virginia were still inside. They wouldn't come out for a while. He had time to do some planning.

He hurried across the street, stopping to ask couples for their recommendations. Finally he found the restaurant everyone mentioned.

He pounded on the door, hard, harder still, until he heard footsteps. A man pulled the door open and yawned.

"Is this the best restaurant in town?" Wolf asked.

The man looked at Wolf as if he were crazy. "It's four o'clock in the morning. Go away."

"I wish to make a reservation. I need the whole restaurant. It's for a marriage proposal."

"Go away!"

He closed the door and Wolf saw him through the window, heading back to bed. Wolf reached into his pocket and put money against the glass. The man didn't turn, so Wolf pounded on the window with his fists.

The man whirled; then his mouth opened when he saw the cash.

Wolf returned to the door. The man opened it, obviously wide awake now.

"You have to start work immediately," Wolf said. "The dishes I have in mind will need obsessive attention and a great deal of marinating and preparing."

The man let him inside, then went and woke up the rest of the restaurant staff. In a few moments, Wolf was standing in the large kitchen with a lot of sleepy people who were still in their nightclothes. He handed all of them some money.

"I want romantic food, you understand. Food that will sweep her off her feet, but also glue her to her seat. I want her to feel she has had a meal that has changed her life. This must be the finest meal ever cooked."

The chef, who apparently even slept in his big white hat, glared at Wolf. "I am the greatest chef in the Nine Kingdoms. Folks travel hundreds of miles to eat my food."

"Yeah?" Wolf was unimpressed. "Well, my date's from a different dimension, so don't slip up."

Relish the Troll King inspected the apple orchard. It was a lovely orchard, with large, fruit-bearing trees. The apples were firm and red and ripe.

He hadn't been to this part of the Fourth Kingdom in a long time. This orchard, near the Merrypips Cider House, was only thirty miles or so from Little Lamb Village—a place where he had heard Trolls were completely unwelcome.

He smiled. He would show them welcome. As soon as he got rid of the Queen.

Relish turned and beckoned with his right hand. A dozen armed Trolls followed him into the orchard, walking carefully on the grass so that they wouldn't reveal their presence. He had instructed them in that, just as he had instructed them in many things.

His nearest advisor, at least on this mission, slunk up to Relish. "Why are we here so early, Your Majesty? We are not meeting the Queen for another hour."

"Shut up!" Relish narrowed his eyes. The advisor had just lost his position, but he wouldn't know it until this mission was done. "Conceal yourself and your men all around. When she arrives, she must see only me, unarmed, or she will not approach. Do you understand?"

The advisor nodded. So did the other Trolls. "Yes, Your Majesty."

They scurried among the trees, snatching apples as they went. This was a well-fed army and becoming accustomed to all the fine food in the Fourth Kingdom.

So was Relish. He picked a round apple and took a healthy bite. Juice ran down his chin. He smiled.

All of this would be his.

Soon. Very soon.

Virginia had never known that watching cards could be so tiring. Especially when the players were playing a game of War for high stakes.

Over the last few hours, her father had eliminated the Troll and then the Dwarf. Only the old lady was left, and she didn't look tired at all.

"Please stop, Dad," Virginia said. "Please. We've won over four thousand."

"Four might not be enough," her father said. "One more game."

"Dad, stop," Virginia said. "You've been playing all night. You're too tired."

"One more. For the whole pot. I can take her."

This was typical of her father. Virginia should have known this was going to happen. Both he and the old lady had a mountain of chips. They stared at each other. Virginia sighed. Her father had clearly forgotten that the point was to get the mirror back, not to be the best player in the casino.

"One more for the pot, dearie," the old woman said.

Her father shoved in his chips. So did the old woman. Virginia put her hands over her face. She couldn't watch.

The sun was rising over Kissing Town. Wolf had never seen a more beautiful dawn. He hurried back to the casino, wondering if Virginia had missed him as much as he had missed her.

As he got close, he ran through the plan in his mind.

"Everything is done, prepared and ready, and I still have tons and tons of money left. I will give the rest to Virginia and she can still buy the . . ."

He was walking past a jeweler's and he stopped, stunned at his own stupidity.

"Cripes," he muttered. "You fool. You nearly forgot the most important thing."

He went inside the jeweler's. The shop was filled with stones and necklaces and clocks of all types. The cuckoo clocks seemed to have real birds in them.

Wolf went immediately to the ring display. Inside a glass case were velvet boxes filled with all sorts of rings, from plain ones to very elaborate ones. Some were even nestled in a nest of tiny flowers. He hadn't expected this much choice.

The jeweler leaned his hands on the glass display case and smiled at Wolf. "A very good morning to you, sir. How may I serve you?"

"I want an engagement ring," Wolf said. "And not just any ordinary ring."

The jeweler put a hand on his heart, as if Wolf's words had offended him. "We don't sell ordinary rings, sir. Tell me a little about the lady. Is she a big girl?"

"No," Wolf said. "She's very slender."

"Plain or pretty?"

"She's gorgeous," Wolf said. "Are you trying to insult me?"

"Most assuredly not, sir," the jeweler said. "I am simply trying to fit the ring to the lady. Some rings might overwhelm a lady."

"No ring is more beautiful than my girl."

"Oh, sir, how romantic," the jeweler said. "She sounds like a girl in a million."

"She is."

"Then I shouldn't insult you by showing you these ordinary, everyday gold and diamond engagement rings."

He reached inside the glass display and closed the box with the plain rings.

"Or even these, handmade by Royal Dwarves."

He closed the box with the flower-encased rings.

"Feast your eyes instead on these."

The jeweler opened a satin box that had previously been

closed. Just six rings were inside it. They sparkled magically. Little stars bounced off them to add to the glitter.

The jeweler brought the box to the top of the display case, and the rings bobbed up and down as Wolf looked at them.

"Choose me," one ring said.

"No, choose me," a second ring said.

They spoke in tiny little voices. Wolf was charmed.

"Sir, I don't wish to be indelicate, but these rings are disgracefully expensive."

"Money is no object," Wolf said.

"You're my kind of gentleman, sir." The jeweler slammed the box closed, almost trapping Wolf's fingers.

"They looked pretty nice to—"

"Oh, no, no, sir," the jeweler said. "I have something quite unique in mind for you."

The jeweler turned with a flourish and pulled back some purple curtains beneath the cuckoo clocks. Behind the curtains was a nest of duck down and inside it was the biggest, most beautiful engagement ring Wolf had ever seen. It sent off a shower of sparkles that lit up the room.

"It is a singing ring, sir."

Wolf smiled. "Huff-puff. A singing ring. I have to have it."

As he leaned over the ring, it twinkled.

"How I long to linger, on your sweetheart's finger . . ." the ring sang.

The jeweler leaned beside him and said, "The lady who slips this on her finger will have no choice. She will simply say, I do."

"Will she?"

"No singing ring has ever received a rejection."

"Ever?"

"It comes with a lifetime love guarantee," the jeweler said.

"I'll take it," Wolf said.

"It's yours. For the paltry sum of seven thousand gold Wendells."

Seven thousand gold Wendells? Wolf put a hand over his heart. It was either the ring or the mirror. But if Virginia put the ring on, she would forget the mirror.

Still. Perhaps he could bargain.

"Seven thousand?"

"Is there a problem, sir? There are more modest rings for less important ladies if—"

"No," Wolf said. "No, I'll take it."

Dawn in an apple orchard. The Queen almost smiled. Across the row from her stood Relish, the Troll King. He looked less fearsome than he did through her mirror. When he saw her, he started walking toward her.

She walked toward him as well. Might as well meet him halfway. It would be the last time.

He opened his jacket to show his hips. "I am unarmed and alone."

She opened her cloak. "As am I."

They stopped ten feet from each other. She was glad. She didn't want to get too close to him.

"I have done as you asked," the Troll King said. "Now where are my children?"

The Queen smiled. "To be quite honest, I have no idea. I simply used them as an excuse to get you to meet me."

The Troll King frowned. "Then I will kill you."

"Don't you wish to know my great plan first?" she asked.

"I have known your plan all along," he said. "To put the imposter prince on the throne and rule the Fourth Kingdom yourself."

She took a step closer to him. He was as stupid as she had thought he was. Good.

"Do you think I spent seven years rotting in jail, just to rule one of the Nine Kingdoms? I'm going to have them all."

"But where do I fit in?" he asked.

"Yes, well." That was the problem, wasn't it? "I see what you mean."

"I have heard enough," he said. "Trolls, arise!"

A dozen Trolls came out of the orchard and surrounded her. They were all carrying weapons, and some of them pointed the weapons at her.

She was hopelessly trapped.

The Troll King sauntered over to her, secure in his victory. The idiot.

"You didn't expect that, did you?" he asked. "My men have been hiding here for the last hour."

"I am impressed at your foresight." She looked up at him and smiled very, very slowly. "And had you arrived *two* hours earlier, you would have met me, poisoning all the apples."

The Troll King put a hand to his throat, and looked afraid for the first time since she met him. All around him the other Trolls started to gag and fall.

"Poison is something of a science with me," she said, smiling. "And I seem to have timed it just right."

The Troll King sank to his knees. The hand at his throat had started clutching it. His men had eaten more and were dying faster. They fell forward, on their stomachs, weapons forgotten. Only the Troll King remained, eyes bugging out of his head, filled with disbelief.

"You know what they say. An army marches on its stomach." She plucked one of the apples from the tree, and stuck it in the Troll King's open mouth. Then he fell forward.

She surveyed the mess. So easy, once she remembered how to do it. Then she leaned over and picked up a sword. She cradled it against her for a moment, and then she brought it down with the full force of her unspoken anger.

A girl always needed a trophy. It made any other dissenters so much more civilized.

The game had gone on all night. Virginia had no idea what time it was, but judging by her body's clock, it had been forever. Everyone in the casino was gathered around this table. Her father still seemed alert. He would snap a card as the old lady would snap a card. Virginia felt as if she had lost the thread of the game.

Then someone brushed against her. She looked behind her. Wolf was standing there with a wide grin on his face.

"Where have you been?" she whispered.

"I just popped out for a walk," he said.

Her father laid down a card. Then the old lady did. Then her father did. And then—snap!—her father's hand slammed on top of the deck.

But when Virginia looked, she realized that the old lady's hand was beneath his.

"Sorry, dearie," the old lady said to Tony. "Better luck next time."

Her father put his head in his hands as the old lady swept up the mountain of chips. There had to be thousands upon thousands of gold Wendells in there, enough to buy the mirror twice over.

And her father had lost it all.

"Oh, no," Virginia said. She was out of money. Wolf was clearly out of money. Her father was out of money. He couldn't even play another hand.

The old lady scooped the chips toward her, then started separating them into two equal piles. "Well," she said as she worked, "you certainly have been lucky for me, so a deal's a deal. I expect you want a biscuit more than you want this money, though."

Virginia looked at her father. His eyes had widened. Together she and her father peeked beneath the table.

Sitting at the other end, beside the old lady, was—

"Prince!" Tony said.

He was still wearing his placard proclaiming him the lucky gambling dog.

" 'Bye, then," the old lady said. She left half her earnings on the table for Prince Wendell and walked away. Prince Wendell rose on his hind legs to survey the money. Wolf was staring at him as if he'd never seen a dog before.

But Virginia lunged for the chips. "What time is it?" Virginia asked. "We may be too late."

Somehow they managed to cash in the chips and get to the auction hall. The auction had already started when they entered.

And, on the block, was their mirror.

"Oh, no!" Virginia muttered.

"For the final time," the auctioneer was saying, "I am bid three thousand, eight hundred gold pieces. Any advance?"

A large antique dealer in the front row put his hands over his ample stomach. Obviously he thought the mirror was going to be his.

"Going once . . . going twice . . ."

"Five thousand gold pieces," Tony shouted from behind Virginia.

The huge hall echoed with gasps from the audience.

"Five thousand," the auctioneer said. "Will anyone increase on five thousand gold Wendells?"

The antiques dealer shook his head in disgust.

"Five thousand," the auctioneer said. "Any advance on five thousand?"

Virginia clasped her hands together. They had it. No one else was going to bid.

"Going once . . . going twice . . ."

"Ten thousand," a voice said from the other side of the room.

Virginia felt a chill run down her back. She knew that voice. She turned. The Huntsman was standing in the back, his pale eyes on her. He was holding a pipe and he didn't seem injured at all.

"It's him," she said to her father.

"Going once," the auctioneer said.

Her father looked lost. They didn't have enough to buy the mirror. But he turned anyway.

"Going twice," the auctioneer said. "Sold to the gentleman with the pipe. Your name, sir?"

"Mr. Hunter. I will pay immediately." He stood and followed the auctioneer's assistants as they carried the mirror into the back office.

"That's ours," Tony said.

"And the next item for auction," the auctioneer said, "is a remarkable Troll work in 22-carat gold, entitled Frozen Rage."

Virginia hadn't seen the Trolls before. She frowned at them, then shook her head. Wolf was staring at them openmouthed. Her father was looking at Prince Wendell.

"Come on," Virginia said. "What are we standing around for?"

They hurried to the office, but the two guards outside stopped them.

"Only purchasers allowed in here," a guard said.

Virginia felt a familiar frustration. She led them through the front door and around back. There had to be an exit back here somewhere. Finally she found it.

It too was guarded.

Her father caught up to her, panting hard. "Is there a man in there buying a mirror?" he asked the guard.

"Was," the guard said. "Just left this second."

"No," Tony said. "Which way did he go?"

The guard shrugged. Virginia looked one way down the street, her father the other.

"You go that way," Virginia said. "I'll go this way."

She hurried down the street, Wolf at her side, but they saw no one. Nothing.

The Huntsman had vanished, taking their mirror with him.

Chapter Thirty-Six

Virginia wasn't sure how Wolf managed to talk her into going out with him. She was horribly depressed. The loss of the mirror to the Huntsman meant that she would never go home again. She certainly wouldn't chase after the Huntsman to find the mirror.

She could only hope that was all he wanted.

Her father and Prince Wendell were sitting at the bar in the Ho Ho Ho Hotel, getting drunk. Apparently the bartender had told them there was no beer in the place, so when Virginia came down the stairs, she had found them drinking some frothy pink concoction, her father from a glass, Prince Wendell from a saucer. They had been talking to Wolf, who was dressed up, his hair slicked back.

He was the one who was sober, and he was the one who looked nervous.

For some reason, taking her to dinner was important to him. So she had gone.

She hadn't expected the carriage, though. It was beautiful, stuffed full of flowers and chocolates. Somewhere nearby, a string quartet was playing a melody she had never heard before.

Wolf eased her into the seat of the carriage, then clutched his pocket. His eyes were big and he seemed subdued. He held her hand tightly as the carriage started.

"To the restaurant, driver," Wolf said. "And please drive as romantically as possible."

Virginia smiled. As they pulled away from the hotel, the music stayed with them. "Where's the music coming from?"

"Do you like it?" It seemed to matter to Wolf that she did. Suddenly she realized that he had something to do with it. She looked out the carriage window. On the roof, the string quartet sat, playing as comfortably as if they always played from a carriage top.

As she eased back into the carriage, Wolf said, "It's a tune I had specially composed for you. It's called 'A Time for Commitment.' "

She gave him a funny look. He had a small, warm smile on his face. She had trouble turning away, but she did as the carriage pulled to a stop.

Wolf got out and then helped her down. The string quartet continued to play as he led her into a restaurant.

The restaurant was stunning. A thousand candles lit the interior. Live frogs leapt out of individual ponds placed on top of every table. As Virginia took it all in, waiters swooped down on them, taking their coats and then lining up to greet them as the maitre d' led them to a table.

"Are we the only people eating?" she asked.

"It certainly seems that way," Wolf said.

As Virginia sat down, more musicians showed up. They started to play the same tune. A wine steward came by and poured champagne.

The maitre d' bowed, and said to Wolf, "Would you like your food served now?"

"Do we get menus?" Virginia asked.

"I have chosen for us already, my darling," Wolf said.

She smiled at him, feeling slightly confused. He smiled back. He had never looked handsomer.

The bar in the Ho Ho Ho Hotel lived up to its name. At first, Tony had thought the place garish, but it was beginning to grow on him. The grotto theme and the brightly painted gnome-sized dwarves just added to the charm.

Or maybe it was the six empty cocktail glasses lined up on the bar. He could feel them, yes indeedy. It wasn't as nice a buzz as the one he got with good beer, but it was certainly better than thinking about the loss of the mirror.

He leaned toward Prince Wendell, who had been keeping up with him, surprisingly enough. Tony would have thought royalty too snooty to get drunk.

"I had a perfectly good business," Tony said to Prince, "but I expanded too soon, and then the recession hit me and I lost everything—my business, my self-respect, my wife." He lifted his glass. "To Tony Lewis, the biggest failure you could ever hope to meet in all Ten Kingdoms."

He drained the ugly pink drink. It tasted like rum and refined sugar. That was growing on him too.

"No, Anthony, my failure is much worse than yours," Prince Wendell said. "This has been a test of kinghood, and I have failed dismally."

"It's not your fault you're a dog. It could happen to anybody."

Prince Wendell put his head on his paws. He seemed quite forlorn. "Anthony, I'm starting to forget things. Like my parents' names, and great big chunks of my life. It's like somebody's stealing my life from me."

Tony looked at him in alarm. He hoped it was just the drink talking, and not the dog himself. Wendell was so much better than a dog.

"A message for you, sir." The bartender handed Tony a note, which he opened, thinking perhaps it was from Virginia. She shouldn't have gone out with that Wolf tonight, but Tony had been in no mood to stop her.

He read the note, then stopped and read it again. Prince Wendell sat up, trying to see it. Tony read it to him.

"Take the dog and tie him to the post in the center of the town square. If you have not done this within fifteen minutes, I will smash the mirror into a hundred thousand pieces."

Tony turned around. They were alone in the bar. How had the Huntsman known they were here?

He grabbed the bartender. "Where is he? Who gave you this?"

"It was handed to the doorman, sir," the bartender said.

Tony sank back into his chair, regretting each and every one of those frothy pink drinks. "Oh, Wendell," he said. "What do we do now?"

Virginia looked at the mashed potato castle before her. She particularly liked the sausages that studded the turrets. This food was too beautiful to eat, but she had managed so far. And it had been good.

Still, she spent more time looking at Wolf. He was handsome. The kind of man who had just a bit of danger to him. The kind that all the books said a woman should fall in love with.

And he cared about her. He had planned this. He had been there for her ever since they had come through that mirror.

"You haven't touched your third helping," Virginia said.

Wolf smiled warmly. "Haven't I?" He looked down at his untouched plate and sighed. "You are, without a doubt, the most corky girl in the whole of the Nine Kingdoms."

Now it was Virginia's turn to smile. "I bet you say that to all your girlfriends."

"You are my first girlfriend," Wolf said.

"What?" Virginia asked, stunned. "First, as in first ever?"

"Oh, yes," Wolf said. "A wolf mates for life. Am I not your first boyfriend?"

"No, I've been out with loads of guys."

"Oh." He looked absolutely crestfallen. She hadn't expected that.

"But nothing serious," Virginia said. In this she was completely truthful. "I'm not very good at trusting people. I never want to jump unless I'm sure someone's going to catch me."

"I'll catch you," Wolf said. "And if I miss for any reason, I'll sit at your bedside and nurse you back to health."

Behind them the music swelled romantically. The lights turned pink. Virginia thought this was the most wonderful night she had ever had. She leaned toward Wolf, and this time, as they were about to kiss, she didn't pull away.

When his lips met hers, she felt it all the way through her entire body. It seemed right. She had never been kissed like this before. She didn't want the kiss to end, and it didn't for the longest time.

Then, finally, they separated. Wolf's eyes opened, and he looked as stunned as she felt.

"Cripes," he said.

The town square was dark, and Tony didn't have his balance yet. He was slightly drunk and it made him uncomfortable. He wasn't the most competent guy even when he was sober.

He was only a few feet from the square. Wendell was beside him. Prince Wendell, who had just made the most ridiculous plan.

"No, I won't let you do it," Tony said to Prince. "How do we know he's not going to put a crossbow bolt through both of us? We could be walking into a trap."

"I can only be killed once," Prince Wendell said. "Sacrifice is the greatest achievement of the hero."

"You're as drunk as I am," Tony said. "You don't know what you're saying."

The square was empty. Tony stopped. "Wait a minute. The square. He's got to be able to see that I'm leaving you in the square, hasn't he?"

"So?" Prince asked.

"So he's got to have a clear view of the square. He's got to be watching from—"

"Somewhere high," Prince said.

"Exactly," Tony said.

They both looked up. There was only one tall building in the entire town.

"The tower of the auction house," Prince said.

Tony nodded. He kept walking, but every now and then he would flick his eyes toward the tower.

"Don't look up," Tony said. "That's where he'll have the mirror. Don't look up. Just pretend to struggle."

Wendell threw his entire self into his performance. He dragged his doggy feet, he pulled on the rope lead that Tony had found, and he barked, an angry growling bark that Tony would never have taken from any other dog.

When they reached the central post, Tony began to tie him. Prince Wendell still struggled, but between growls, he said, "Just do a loose knot. I'll be faster than him."

"Where will you go?" Tony asked. "What if I don't see you again?"

"You will," Prince said.

"Good luck, your highness," Tony said.

He pretended to secure the knot and walked away. Prince Wendell barked as if he had been left there against his will. Tony tried not to listen. He wasn't really sure if this would work.

Virginia smiled as she finished her dessert. The carved meringue swan filled with fruits and sorbets seemed to please her. So did the flowers that the waiters had arranged during the meal. And she had even hummed when the music kept playing. She was enjoying herself, and Wolf thought that quite an accomplishment considering the day they'd had.

"What a meal," Virginia said. "And the flowers. Everything. It was amazing."

Wolf reached out his hand. To his surprise, Virginia slipped her fingers into his. She had fallen for him. He knew it now.

"Virginia," Wolf said, "I have something very important to ask you. Really, really, really important."

At that moment, the waiters brought out the cake. It was

covered in candles and sparklers and shaped like a heart. The frosting paintings of him and Virginia weren't as realistic as he had hoped, but they would do.

He wished the interruption hadn't happened—this was hard enough as it was—but then Virginia gazed fondly at him, and even the interruption became worthwhile.

"I can't believe this evening," Virginia said. "This must have cost an absolute fortune."

"It was nothing compared to what you're worth."

"How are we going to pay for it all?" The light left her eyes. She was only partially joking. "We'll have to wash dishes for the next ten years."

He had to get her past this moment. "It's all paid, done for, don't worry your gorgeous head about it. Now, as I said—"

The ring started bouncing in his pocket, interrupting his train of thought.

"Go for it," the singing ring said. "I'm hot to trot."

"Paid for?" Virginia asked. "How?"

"I have a present for you," Wolf said, ignoring her question. "A very special present."

He took a deep breath and put the box on the table. She watched as he opened it, but she wasn't smiling. The ring pinged and released a halo of gold. Then it started to sing.

"Beauty that could break a million hearts. Beauty that could—"

Virginia slammed the box closed. "How have you paid for all of this?"

He had vowed not to lie to her anymore. Besides, he couldn't think of a lie that would work. "Uh, oh, yes, I won the Jack Rabbit Jackpot last night."

"Last night? But you said you lost all your money."

"Did I?" Oh, huff-puff. This wasn't going at all the way he wanted it to. "Well, I did win some."

"You said you'd lost everything."

"Yes, but look what I bought you."

"Let me out!" the singing ring shouted. "Let me out!"

"Outside, when you were telling me how much you loved me—you liar!"

"You messed it up, you idiot," the ring said.

"How much money did you win?"

He didn't expect her to get this angry. "I can't really remember."

"Get me out before it's too late," the singing ring said.

"How much?" Virginia asked.

"I think it was around ten thousand."

"Ten thousand!" Virginia shouted. "We could have got the mirror back and you spent it on food?"

"I didn't spend it on food," Wolf said. "I spent it on you."

"We could have gone home," Virginia said. "We could have gone home. Don't you understand? I don't belong here. I want to go home."

"No, please, we've got lots more treats. I've got a gondola out back. And fireworks and more fizzy stuff."

Virginia started to cry. Wolf had never seen Virginia cry before. He didn't know what to do.

"You don't care about me," Virginia said. "You just care about yourself."

"No, that's not true." He reached for the ring. He would prove to her how much he cared.

But Virginia stood. "I don't want to see you anymore."

"No!" Wolf stood too. But Virginia was already hurrying out of the restaurant. "Please don't go, Virginia."

She slammed the door so hard, the thousand candle flames shook.

"You loser," the ring said. "Where's my finger? Where's my finger?"

Wolf stared at the slammed door, then at Virginia's empty seat, and then at the ring.

"I hate you. I hate you," the ring said.

"Why was I ever stupid enough to think a girl like her would fall for an animal like me." He sank into his chair and started to howl. He hadn't howled like this since he was a pup and he had to leave the den. He tried to stop and he couldn't, so he snuffled, then howled, then snuffled again.

Finally a waiter approached him. "Would you—um—like to see the dessert trolley?"

"No, thank you," Wolf said. "My life is over."

He wiped his eyes, put the ring in his pocket, and walked out of the restaurant. His life really was over.

He had no idea what he would do.

Chapter Thirty-Seven

Prince Wendell waited in the town square, the rope chafing at the back of his neck. He hoped that the loose knot wouldn't be that obvious to the Huntsman.

He also hoped that he would be able to concentrate long enough to make his escape. For he had been completely honest with Anthony. Wendell was beginning to forget things, and he had horrible dog-like impulses. He could hear the Queen's voice over and over again in his mind.

Do you like dogs, Wendell? Because you're going to spend the rest of your life as one.

Until recently, he had thought he would escape, his faculties intact. Now he wasn't so sure.

Finally he heard a noise. The Huntsman walked across the square. Wendell could get a faint whiff of the man, the smell of pain and dried blood and old death. It wasn't a pleasant odor.

The Huntsman was limping. The wound the others had given him in that tree house had apparently been quite severe.

Wendell looked up. He saw Anthony on the roof of the auction house. Then Wendell looked down again. The Huntsman was very close.

Wendell waited until the Huntsman was just about to reach him, then slipped off his lead. The pretend knot slipped open, just as it was supposed to, and Wendell ran.

He glanced over his shoulder and saw the Huntsman pull out his crossbow. Then Wendell hurried around a corner. Maybe he had lied to Tony. Maybe he couldn't stay ahead of the Huntsman. He hadn't counted on the bow.

But Wendell suddenly found himself in a sea of people. They were coming out of buildings, flowing into the streets, shouting and yelling and celebrating.

Overhead, fireworks went off. He had no idea what this was for. It was not a holiday, was it? Had he forgotten that too?

Bells were ringing in the distance and people were shouting. Wendell glanced over his shoulder. The Huntsman was watching, but couldn't shoot, not with all these people around.

Then Wendell focused on what the crowd was saying.

"The Troll King is dead!" someone in the crowd yelled. "Prince Wendell has killed the Troll King and twelve of his men. He's on his way home. The crisis is over!"

"Get your souvenir copy of *The Kingdom Times*," a newspaper man shouted. "Return of the Prince. Happy Ever After."

Wendell felt his tail go between his legs.

"This can't be," Wendell said to himself. "This is a lie. I'm Prince Wendell. That's me!"

"Here he comes!" a man shouted. "Here he comes!"

Wendell turned. There was his carriage. And there was the Dog Prince, leaning out of the window, tongue lolling. He was holding something and waving.

"Born to be King!" the crowd shouted. "Born to be King!"

As the carriage passed, Wendell finally saw what it was. The head of the Troll King dangled from the Dog Prince's hand.

"Long live Prince Wendell. Long live Prince Wendell."

Wendell watched the carriage disappear around a corner, like his life.

The Huntsman was nowhere to be seen.

Wolf walked away from the restaurant alone. It was dark, and his limbs felt so heavy that he could barely move. His life was over. It truly was.

He stopped in front of the river and took the ring out of his pocket. Then he pried the ring from its box.

"What are you doing?" the ring asked. "What do you think you're doing, you loser?"

He gazed at the ring for a moment. It was right. He was a loser. He should never, ever have hoped to make Virginia his wife. She deserved so much better than him.

With a single arc, he threw the ring into the water. There was a ripple, and then a fish rose, holding the ring in its mouth. The fish flipped its tail and disappeared into the darkness forever.

Wolf stared at the ripples for a moment. Then they coalesced into a familiar face.

The Queen. She smiled at him. "Now you see what I told you all along. You are nothing without me. Come back to me. Will you turn back to me?"

"Yes," Wolf said, and wandered off, alone, into the night.

He was too drunk to be climbing on a roof. Too drunk and too old. Of course, if he hadn't been drunk, he might not have gotten to the roof in the first place. He might have remained by the locked door down below.

Tony slipped, sending an ancient tile skittering to the street below. It landed with a bang.

"Be careful," Tony said to himself.

He hoped the Huntsman hadn't heard it. Tony found the open tower and slipped inside. There were weapons here, but not the crossbow. He hoped Prince Wendell could fend for himself on that.

Tony reached the Huntsman's bag. He opened it and grinned. Inside was the mirror.

He lifted it. The damn thing was heavy. Great. Now he was too old, too drunk, and not balanced. He had to hope the luck gods were with him tonight.

He climbed back out onto the roof. He started across the tiles when he lost his balance, slipped, and fell on his back.

Tony screamed and slid down the roof for a few feet before he reached for a loose tile. He got it, and lost his hold on the mirror. It slid to the edge of the roof and stopped there, hanging off the ledge.

He stared at the mirror for a long moment. Okay. So the luck gods weren't with him. But they had to be with someone in the troop. Someone, maybe Virginia. Tony had to do this for his daughter.

He inched down the roof to get to the mirror. His fingers nearly touched the gilded edge. He slid farther forward and his fingers brushed the metal.

The mirror slipped slightly, until the bulk of its weight was over the edge. It kept tottering up and down like a demented seesaw.

Tony strained, reaching for the mirror. He finally touched it when it slid over the roof and disappeared into the darkness.

Virginia sat on a bench in the town square. She had never gone from happiness to sorrow so fast in her life. She was still crying. Wolf hadn't realized what he had done. He had ruined her faith in men and destroyed her hope for going home all in one quick stroke.

"Well, at least things can't get any worse," she said to herself.

Suddenly something fell past her in the darkness. It landed and shattered into a thousand pieces. She crouched and then realized that what had smashed before her was the magic mirror.

She looked up and saw her father, looking forlornly from the roof above.

Now she really was well and truly trapped here. Alone. Forever.

"It's entirely possible to mend anything with a bit of glue," Tony said.

He was trying to pick up the shattered pieces of the mirror. He was trying to put them into a bag he'd found. Virginia hadn't moved. In fact, she stared at him with a look he'd never seen on her face before. Anger, fury, complete and total rage. Yet she wasn't saying a word.

"Are you going to help me?" Tony asked Virginia. "Are you going to stand there all day and say nothing?"

"Don't make me say anything." Her voice was low, husky. "Where's Wolf gone?"

"He's just gone, all right? He's gone back to wherever he came from."

Tony continued to pick up the pieces. He was completely sober. More sober than he had ever been in his life. He didn't really even have a hangover. He supposed adrenaline had done that.

"You idiot," Virginia said. "That mirror was our only way home."

Well, at least she told him how she felt. But he already knew what he had done wrong. He was just trying to make it better, trying to find some kind of solution.

It was beginning to look as if there wasn't any.

Then Prince Wendell came up, tail between his legs. He looked as upset as Tony felt.

"Anthony," Prince Wendell said.

Tony couldn't deal with an aristocratic dog. "Not now."

"Anthony," Prince said, "what's being scared like? What does it feel like?"

"What do you mean, what's it like?" Tony asked. "It's like being scared."

Suddenly he realized what he was saying—and what Prince Wendell was asking. Something was happening. Tony looked at Wendell, really looked at him. He wasn't looking at a Prince. He was looking at a frightened little dog.

"Careful of your paws with all the glass," Tony said gently.

"My mind is going," Prince said. "My brain is shrinking."

Tony couldn't handle another crisis. "You're imagining it."

"My dreams are getting more and more dog-like. And when

I wake up, it takes longer and longer to remember who I am. And instead of calling you Anthony, I wanted to call you Biscuit Giver.''

That just made Tony sad. He looked at Virginia, but she— of course—hadn't heard a word that Prince Wendell had said. She was still staring at the broken pieces of glass as though she had lost everything.

Maybe she had.

Then there was a shout behind him. Tony turned. A crowd was gathering.

''Look,'' a man shouted. ''The mirror-breaker.''

''He's broken a magic mirror,'' a boy said. ''Seven years bad luck.''

''I don't believe in silly superstition,'' Tony said. Then he heard the strangest sound. It was the sound of breaking glass, only more so. It was as if there was a tinkling, shattering wave of breaking glass coming toward him. The sound shook him and enveloped him.

He looked at Virginia. She was staring dully at the crowd. She didn't seem to hear the glass sound at all.

''What you don't believe in can't hurt you,'' Tony said with more bravado than he felt.

Then something hit him hard on the head.

''Ow!''

He staggered about, clutching his forehead. It was bleeding. There was a stone at his feet.

''What?'' Virginia asked.

''It was a great big rock,'' Tony said, looking up. A bird was flying away from him, as if it had dropped the rock. ''What are the chances of that happening?''

The crowd was starting to advance on them. This crowd looked ugly. Not quite as bad as the crowd that had tried to kill Wolf, but close.

''Mirror-breaker,'' a man said. ''Get out of the town. We don't want your bad luck here.''

''Get out of town!''

Tony reached for Wendell. Virginia shook her head, and then they all started to run. The crowd chased them to the edge of the cobblestone streets, but didn't follow into the mountains beyond.

The road was windy and narrow and not nearly as pleasant as Tony could have hoped. He'd left with only the bag in his hand, the bits of the mirror that he'd been able to salvage. He hoped that Virginia had something else with her.

"It's no good just walking," Virginia said. "Where are we going?"

"I don't know," Tony said. "But we can't stay in town, can we?"

"Anthony," Prince Wendell said, "you see that stick over there? Just coming up to it now. Perfect size. Be a good man and pick it up and throw it into the grass over there."

"I'm not going to start throwing sticks for you," Tony said, "or you'll completely forget who you are."

"Oh, go on. Just throw one stick."

"No."

"Just one," Prince Wendell begged. He wagged his tail and looked quite appealing.

"All right," Tony said. "Just one."

He picked up the stick Wendell had been talking about and threw it. Wendell ran after it and brought it back, his tail wagging so hard, his entire backside moved.

"That was great!" Prince Wendell said, sounding more like a dog voice-over in a commercial than a prince. "Throw it again!"

"No."

"Go on," Prince Wendell said. "You know you want to."

The broken glass sound began again. It grew louder and louder. Tony looked around for its source, but he had a hunch he wouldn't find it.

"Oh, no," Tony said, "I can hear that sound again, that bad-luck sound."

"Well, I can't hear anything," Virginia said.

He looked all around him, stepping back to see if anyone was following them. Then he screamed in pain and fell to the ground, clutching his foot.

"What?" Virginia asked.

"My foot! My foot!" He rolled over on his back yelping in pain.

Virginia bent down to investigate. "Keep still." She caught his waving foot and examined it. "It's just a nail."

She pulled it out and Tony screamed again. He could feel the blood flowing in his shoes. They both examined the huge, rusty nail. They looked at each other, and then thunder boomed.

The heavens opened and within an instant both he and Virginia were soaking wet. Tony looked skyward. A giant cloud hung above them, but ahead and behind, the sky was blue.

"Look," Tony said, pointing upward. "This is the only place it's raining. On me. It's clear skies over there. I'm cursed. I'm doomed. Seven years' bad luck. I'm not going to last the week out."

Virginia gave him a withering look. "It is also raining on me, Dad," she said, heading off.

Virginia had found a barn just down the road. It wasn't much of a barn: the roof was nearly gone and the walls barely held together, but it did provide some shelter from the rain. She didn't tell her father about her greatest fear for him—that for the next seven years it would rain on him and anyone who was near him.

She wouldn't be able to take that.

There was a farmhouse about a quarter mile away. Maybe when the rain stopped, she would ask them for food.

Her father was crouched on the barn floor, trying to put the mirror back together. He was working it the way he worked his jigsaw puzzles at home. He'd used most of the pieces, but there were still large gaps.

"We're going to have to go back," Tony said. "There's so many pieces missing."

Virginia looked at the hundreds of pieces that they had and slumped. Even if they had all the pieces, they would never be able to reassemble the mirror. They were stuck here forever.

Her father watched her. He was as scared as she was, only in his usual way he was trying to find a solution. But he knew as well as she did that there was no solution, and there never would be.

She picked up one of the larger pieces and turned it over. "What's on the back?" she asked, not sure what compelled her to ask the question.

Still, she turned over piece after piece. All of them had black backing.

"What are you doing?" her father yelled. "It took me hours to put those in the right place. You're mixing them up."

She didn't pay any attention. She kept turning pieces over until she found one with writing on the back.

"Look," she said.

He stared at it for a moment, and then he helped her. They turned over piece after piece until they had a line of mirror pieces, backs showing. There was a small red dragon emblem followed by parts of words.

"It's some kind of cryptic clue," Tony said. "Man red by the war . . . It's probably a reference to bleeding."

"Bleeding?" Virginia asked. "It's a mirror. It's not a clue, it's a maker's seal. Man red . . . Manufactured. That's it. Manufactured by the War . . ."

"Manufactured by the War of Rag Mounties?"

"Mountain," Virginia said.

"That looks like the tip of a 'd' . . . The Warves of Drago Mountain."

"No. It's a bigger gap." She moved the pieces until she saw something she liked. "Manufactured by the Dwarves of Dragon Mountain."

Prince Wendell leaned over to look at the pieces.

"Do you know it?" Tony asked Prince. Tony paused for

a moment, and then he said to Virginia, "He thinks he knows it."

She smiled.

"Well, let's go there," Tony said. "Quick, before I have any more bad luck."

Virginia looked through the open barn doors at the farm-house beyond.

"Let's see if we can beg some eggs and cheese from that farmhouse there," Virginia said.

Her father shook his head. "It's that broken glass sound again," he said, "fading in and out like a radio signal. Let's go. Maybe it won't find us."

Virginia sighed and shook her head. Hoping for that was like hoping it would never rain again.

The farmer sat on an ancient chair, watching as the metal merchant he'd hired worked with his new statue. The room was extremely hot. The merchant had a fire going, and he used a winch to hold the statue over the flames. The gold was dripping, which the farmer took to be a bad sign.

"That's not gold," the merchant said.

"It is," the farmer said, but he didn't really have the convic-tion he'd had just a moment before. He rather liked the statue—called Frozen Rage—even though the three Trolls in it were the ugliest creatures he had ever seen.

"Nope," the merchant said. "That's fool's gold."

"I got it at a knockdown price on account of it being the ugliest thing you've ever seen."

Outside, a man's voice yelled, "Ow! Ow!" The farmer looked at the merchant. The merchant's eyes were wide.

"Where's those noises coming from?" the farmer asked.

The bubbling statue suddenly started to shake and split. The merchant swore, and the farmer watched in horror. Then the statue exploded, sending gold everywhere.

It landed on the farmer, drenching him in hot gold. When he wiped his eyes, he saw three Trolls lying on the floor, clutching their legs and arms like people whose limbs had gone to sleep.

"Suck an Elf troop!" the large male Troll shouted.

The farmer got up and kicked his chair aside. The merchant was wiping the gold from his eyes. He looked terrified.

"Rubber legs," said the female Troll. She stood up and fell over. The third Troll threw up all over his shirt. They were acting drunk and, the farmer knew, drunken Trolls were dangerous.

"We have shamed the Troll nation," said the first Troll.

"Only temporarily," said the female.

"We'll disgrace our way back to the top!" said the third as he staggered backwards.

The farmer was just thinking about escape when there was a knock at the door.

"I don't think there's anyone home," Tony said. He hadn't really escaped the broken-glass sound. It had caught him in the middle of the field and twisted his ankle. Now he was standing on a farmer's porch, begging for food. How low could he go?

"There is," Virginia said. "I can hear banging."

She knocked on the door again. Tony heard the broken glass sound coming at him like a freight train. He tried to pull Virginia back as the door opened.

The three Trolls stood inside, along with two men covered in melted gold.

"Oh, my God!" Tony shouted. "They're back!"

"Sniff a sandal," said Burly. "It's them."

"Kill them!" Blabberwort shouted.

Virginia was already off like a shot. So was Prince Wendell. Tony brought up the rear. He glanced over his shoulder. The Trolls were rolling on the ground, clutching their legs.

They hadn't gotten their land legs back. A tiny, tiny stroke of good fortune. Tony ran after Virginia. They had to get as far away as possible, because now that those Trolls were back, they were never going to give up.

Chapter Thirty-Eight

The mountains all around them were the biggest mountains Tony had ever seen. Tall and gray and forebidding. He adjusted the pack on his back, thankful that he and Virginia had been able to find camping gear, and stared at the sign ahead of them.

DRAGON MOUNTAIN
QUESTING PERMITS REQUIRED

The sign had the same little dragon symbol, but it all looked very old. Just like the tents around them, frayed and wrecked by the winds. This area had obviously once been a base camp for climbers. And just as obviously it was no longer.

"There's nothing here," Virginia said. She sounded panicked.

"Let's not make any hasty judgments," Tony said. "It's probably just up the mountain a bit."

He didn't believe that, though. There wasn't a building in sight. And the path going up the mountain was steep. He hoped they wouldn't have to do regular climbing. With all the walking they'd been doing this last week, he'd gotten into shape, but he wasn't in that good a shape.

Besides, one of them would have to carry Wendell, and that wouldn't be pretty.

They didn't talk much as they went up the path. It was hard

to climb, and narrow. The farther up they went, the thinner the air got too. Tony had read somewhere that there was some kind of illness connected to thin air. He hoped he didn't get it.

As they walked, he could think about all he'd done. The worst was breaking the mirror. Maybe. He hadn't had a productive life. The only thing he felt he'd done right was Virginia. She at least stuck by him. And she was the best thing that had ever happened to him.

Even if she was mad at him.

She wasn't talking as they made their ascent. She was focused, sure, but there was more to it than that. He knew his daughter. Her temper was boiling.

They walked for hours. The views of the mountains and the valleys beyond were gorgeous, but after a while even the view got tiresome.

The path grew narrow and Virginia, who had taken the lead, stopped. She looked up. Tony followed her gaze. The mountain was huge and daunting, and to go up a rabbit path like the one that was facing them was nearly impossible.

"If we go any farther," Virginia said, "we may not be able to get back."

"My paws are sore," Prince Wendell said.

Tony was wheezing. He hadn't realized it until they stopped. "One more hour," he said, "and then we'll give up. All right?"

No one answered. He assumed that meant they agreed. He started up the rabbit path, hoping that his luck would hold.

Wendell's castle was at least cleaner than her own. The Queen stood in Wendell's bedroom, peering down at the courtyard below. She had hidden in the carriage as it made its triumphal journey across the Fourth Kingdom. The Dog Prince had enjoyed the trip, although toward the end she had to prevent him from rolling on the Troll King's head.

When they had arrived at the castle, the Dog Prince had provided cover for her, talking—poorly—with the advisors, and leading them off so she could sneak into the castle. Now she was making certain no one saw her, hiding behind curtains and staying out of the way.

They'd find out about her presence soon enough.

"This is a lot better than the other place," the Dog Prince said from behind her. "I'll tell you that for nothing."

The Queen turned away from the window. The Dog Prince stood in the middle of Wendell's bedroom. His shirt was buttoned wrong, and his hair stuck up in a weird quaff.

"Nobody helped me," he said. "I did it myself. What do you think?"

He really was horribly dog-like. So eager to please, so upset when someone yelled at him. She was trying to choose an appropriate response when she heard tapping.

It seemed to be coming from one of her mirrors. She took the cloth off it to reveal Burly the Troll and his two siblings, covered in the remains of some gold dust, knocking on the mirror glass as if it were someone's front door.

"Hello! Hello! Anyone there?" Burly said.

Then they saw her and they grinned. What an ugly lot they were.

"We're back, Your Majesty," Burly said.

"Alive and kicking," Blabberwort said.

"And madder than ever," Bluebell said.

The Queen couldn't help herself. She started to laugh. When she got control of herself, she said, "I must say, I am most surprised to see you."

They looked at each other, obviously pleased that she was smiling. There seemed to be someone else kicking behind them. She could barely make out the shapes of two men, hanging upside down from their feet.

"Your Majesty," Bluebell said, "could we use one of your mirrors to contact our dad?"

"He'll be very worried about us," Burly said.

"Just a quickie to tell him we're okay," Bluebell said.

The Queen stopped smiling. What to tell them? They might

be somewhat useful. She would have to keep them on her side. "You haven't heard the awful news, then?"

"We haven't heard anything," Bluebell said. "We've been gold."

She sighed and made the words as gentle as possible. "Your father has been murdered."

They staggered backwards away from the mirror. They didn't say anything and then, in unison, they started to cry. It took them several moments to get control of themselves. Burly, the eldest, managed first.

"Who did it?" Burly asked.

Their reaction had given her time to concoct the right story. "That girl," the Queen said. "She poisoned him."

The Trolls stared at her, obviously unable to accept the news. She had to control them now. If she didn't, they would make a mess of everything.

"Many terrible things have happened since I last spoke to you," the Queen said. "My friends, if only for your father, swear you will track her down."

"We swear it!" they shouted.

She smiled. This was a piece of luck she hadn't anticipated at all.

It wasn't a path anymore. It was a mountainside, slanted enough so that Prince Wendell could try to scramble up it. Virginia went first, using rocks for leverage, which meant that Tony had been staring up a dog's butt for the better part of the last hour.

He put his hand on Wendell's haunches and shoved the dog over the last precipice. Wendell disappeared, but Tony heard the broken glass sound again.

Then he felt his pack shift. Both straps ripped, and before he could react, his rucksack fell off his back and tumbled down the mountain.

"No! No! *No!*"

He watched as it burst open hundreds of feet below. Food,

drinks, pans, and his sleeping roll tumbled in a thousand different directions.

Virginia was watching from above. "Anything important inside?"

Such sarcasm. You'd think his daughter would give him a little sympathy. Tony pulled himself over the last rise and lay down for just a moment. "How could both straps break at exactly the same time? The chances of that must be a billion to one."

"Or maybe you just didn't tie it properly." Virginia's tone was icy.

"Of course I did," Tony said. "It's just my bad luck."

"Yeah," Virginia said. "Well, I've got the worst luck of all, traveling with you."

"Oh, please just say it," Tony said. "Get it off your chest. Anything is better than sulking."

"I'm not sulking."

She adjusted her rucksack and made sure the straps were secure. Then she started up the narrowest of paths. Prince Wendell was ahead of them, blazing the trail. Sort of. He did seem more enthusiastic about this than he would have been a week ago.

Tony rather missed the complaining aristocrat.

"What were you doing on the roof of that building, drunk, with the mirror?" Virginia finally asked. Of course, she waited until they were alone on a mountainside. "It was our only way home."

"Oh, you still can't be mad about the mirror," Tony said. "It's done."

"I spend my whole life looking after you," Virginia said. "You're on your own for five minutes and—"

"Looking after me!" Tony shouted. "Who brought you up? Twenty years I've looked after you. And if I hadn't had to do that as well as work a full week, then maybe my business wouldn't have gone down the drain. Did you ever think of that? Or do you only think of poor little Virginia, me, me, me.''

"I really hate you sometimes," Virginia said.

"Yeah, well, I'm used to it, so hate away. You have a good long hate if it makes you feel better."

It didn't make him feel better. He needed some sympathy. Just a little. He knew it would get harder and harder as these seven years progressed. Didn't she see that? Didn't she know they needed to stick together?

The narrow path they had been following forked. Prince Wendell stood at the fork, waiting for them. Virginia stopped beside him. Tony stopped too and surveyed the area.

"The path is this way," Tony said.

"That path goes down," Virginia said. "It's sloping downwards. This is the way up."

Prince Wendell was looking anxiously from Virginia to Tony and back to Virginia again.

"That's not a path," Tony said. "That's a goat track."

"Prince, am I right?" Virginia asked.

"Anthony," Prince said, "I know this is highly irregular, but would you give me a cuddle, please?"

Tony shuddered. Wendell was no longer any help. Tony would have to take the leadership role. "This is the way. I'm right."

"You go your way, I'll go mine," Virginia said.

"I will," Tony said. "And don't blame me if the dragons get you."

Virginia walked along her path. Tony watched her go. He wasn't going to back down on this. He needed to get some self-esteem from somewhere.

"I'm serious," Tony shouted after her. "I'm not going that way, because it's wrong."

Tony started down his path. Prince Wendell still stood at the fork looking at Virginia, then at Tony.

"Oh, no—decisions," Prince said.

The poor dog didn't sound happy or princely at all. Tony whistled, feeling odd, and Prince Wendell came.

They walked together on the narrow path. Tony was grateful, at least, for Wendell's company. He was worried about Virginia, but he wasn't going to admit it.

"Now, it's on the tip of my tongue," Prince Wendell said softly, "but who am I?"

It was the fifth time he'd asked that in the last hour.

"Oh, God," Tony said, "don't start that again. You're Prince Wendell, all right? You rule all this land around us. You're the most important person in the kingdom."

"Top dog?" Prince asked.

"Yeah," Tony said, not liking this at all. It was getting worse. "That's right. Top dog."

"Dominant dog," Prince said. "I thought so."

They walked in silence for a few moments. Tony kept thinking of Virginia. He had no idea that she would defy him like that. This place was changing her and not for the better.

"Prince Wendell," Tony said, "you came with me because you knew I was going the right way, isn't that right?"

"No," Prince said.

"No?" Tony asked.

"I only came with you because she doesn't understand anything I say."

"Yeah," Tony said. "Well, she doesn't understand me either."

Then, from behind him, he heard the broken glass sound. He winced in advance. He hoped it wouldn't catch up to him, but he knew it would.

He would keep going, that's what he would do. Like the intrepid adventurer. He put his hand on a nearby rock and screamed in pain.

He pulled his hand back. It was covered with a live, active wasp nest. The pain was incredible. He shook his hand and the wasps flew off, except for the ones stuck inside the nest, who kept stinging him.

Weren't they like bees? Didn't they die after they stung someone? He hoped so.

"Since when do wasps build nests halfway up mountains? Of all the places I could put my hand. It's beyond belief."

With his other hand, he picked the wasp's nest apart, bit by bit, leaving chunks of it—and dying wasps—on the ground behind him.

He finally got the last bit of nest off his hand. It was horribly swollen. He hoped he wasn't allergic.

Prince Wendell looked up at him. "I'm losing my mind."

"You're not," Tony said. "Give it a rest."

"Can we stop for a cuddle?" Prince asked.

Tony sighed. The poor prince. The poor dog. Tony stopped and sat down against the rock face. Prince Wendell came up beside him and leaned against him. Tony put his arm around him.

"Combined cuddle and stroke, please," Prince said.

With his good hand, Tony stroked the dog. He sucked on his sore hand while he did so.

Then a shudder ran through Prince Wendell. "I'm going dog," he said. "I'm going dog, and there's no going back."

Tony didn't know what to say about that, so he just kept cuddling his dog.

"Tired now," Prince said. "Sleepies."

"I'd like to be a dog," Tony said. "I'd like to have someone who looked after me, fed me so I didn't have to worry about anything. That would be my idea of heaven."

Suddenly there was a crunching sound behind him. Tony started. Hands appeared beneath him, and then Virginia pulled herself up.

She looked dirty and windblown.

"Oh, you made it," Virginia said.

"I was going to say the same to you," Tony said. "I've been here quite a while."

"Really?" Virginia asked.

"Yes, about an hour."

"I didn't know it was a race."

Tony peered over the ledge. "I didn't know that was a path."

Blabberwort was tired, and her muscles ached. Every time she got into the same position she had been in when she had been turned to gold, her muscles screamed in agony.

She was trying to ignore it. If she thought about anything, she thought about her dad, and that was a bad thing.

She and her brothers were walking along the mountain road, following the trail left by the awful witch and her companions. Blabberwort was focused on revenge, but Burly was a wreck. He kept cutting nicks in his arm with his knife and crying at the same time.

"There's more paw prints here," Blabberwort said. "They came this way."

The other two really didn't seem to care. They were coming with her because they didn't know what else to do.

"Dad's dead," Burly said.

Blabberwort didn't know what to say to that. Neither, apparently, did Bluebell. Finally, Blabberwort decided to try. "Look on the bright side. No more beatings."

"We can fail totally without fear of punishment," Burly said.

"Good riddance to the old bastard," Bluebell said.

They smiled at each other. Then Burly's smile faded.

"Wait! Wait! What are we saying?" Burly asked. "He was our dad. He took us hunting."

"He gave us our first weapons," Blabberwort said.

"He taught us how to keep a torture victim conscious for hours," Bluebell said.

They all started to sob. Blabberwort felt the tears run down her face like molten gold.

"Wait until we get hold of that little witch," Burly said. "We'll tear her apart."

* * *

Bad weather had found them again. Or perhaps more rightly, it had found her father. Virginia stopped under a huge rock overhang and hoped that the storm clouds wouldn't try to chase Tony in here.

She sat down on a pile of rocks and didn't help her father as he climbed under the overhang to join her. Prince Wendell followed. Something about him made him seem more and more like a dog.

"Hey, you're sitting on somebody," her father said.

Virginia got up and saw that there were more piles of rocks all around. Each one had a sword or spear stuck in the middle of it, and a rotting pennant.

"Do you think these people found the dragon of the mountain?" Virginia asked. "Or it found them?"

Her father bent down and read the carved wooden inscription leaning against one of the piles. "Here lies Ivan the Optimist."

"These graves are really old," Virginia said. "I don't think there's still any dragon up there."

And then, suddenly, there was a roar high up on the mountain.

"This is insane," Virginia said. "We must have climbed a thousand feet."

"Have we?" Tony asked.

He walked to the edge of the ledge and looked down. She joined him. The bottom of the valley was very far away.

He twitched the way he sometimes did when he heard that awful sound. She hoped that wasn't what it was, but then, as if on cue, her father said, "We should think about staying here for the night."

"In a graveyard?"

"The light will be gone in an hour. I mean, it's fading now."

"You think so?" Virginia asked, looking around. "I think there's just a lot of clouds."

But she was tired. She didn't want to go any farther. They

were too high up to gather wood, and she didn't like the idea of taking the grave markers. So she huddled next to her father and Prince Wendell for warmth.

"It was a stupid idea of mine to come up here," Tony said. "I'm sorry."

A wolf howled in the distance. Virginia looked up. When she had been climbing alone, she had seen a young wolf on a distant ledge. It had made her long for Wolf. She shouldn't have driven him off like that.

"You miss that Wolf, don't you?" Tony asked.

"Yes."

She looked out into the darkness. How her life had changed in such a very short time.

"I think this is the end of the line," Tony said. "I'm not going to survive seven years of bad luck. I'm proud of you, Virginia. We wouldn't have gotten this far if it wasn't for you."

"I'm cold," she said. "Give us a hug."

He hugged her. They hadn't hugged each other in a long time. It felt good.

Then she realized that they were alone. "Where's Prince?"

"Oh, my God," Tony said.

They looked around. She couldn't see him. She shouted, "Prince! Prince!"

But there was no answer in the darkness.

Chapter Thirty-Nine

Tony couldn't remember the last time he had fallen asleep sitting up. He woke, stiff and cold, huddled against his daughter. The wind on the ledge was fierce.

Then he saw what had awakened him. Prince Wendell— more Prince the dog now than Prince Wendell—coming down the path toward them. He clutched an enormous bone in his teeth.

"Virginia, wake up. Prince is back."

Prince stopped in front of Tony and dropped the bone at his feet.

"What is it, boy?" Tony said, somehow knowing that this tone was appropriate. "What have you got?"

"Big bone big bone," Prince said.

Tony picked it up and looked at it in amazement. "It *is* a big bone. I've never seen anything like it before. Where did you get this from?"

Prince started barking furiously. Tony winced. He had been hoping for an answer in English.

Virginia stared sleepily at Prince and Tony. She was even colder than he was. He had to shake her a little to get her to follow the dog.

Prince took them on a winding path. There were rusted helmets and armor littering its sides. Then they rounded a corner and came upon it—the huge skeletal head of a dragon, thrusting out of a cave.

It was as big as a brontosaurus and probably more impressive. Tony took a step closer. The dragon had been dead a long time. Its mouth was wide open, forming an entrance into the mountain. A rusty sword was sticking through what had once been the dragon's eye.

The place was eerie, with the remains of knights and the wind blowing through it. The dragon's head itself was the creepiest part of all.

Tony followed Prince forward and Virginia followed. They picked their way along the path until they reached the dragon's mouth. It was huge. Each of the jagged teeth was nearly as big as Virginia.

Tony stepped around them and helped Virginia through. Then they made their way through the skeleton, walking down the dragon's gullet.

Other creatures had come this way. The bones were scattered. There was no smell, which made sense, Tony supposed, considering how long the dragon had been dead.

Finally they reached the tail. After they climbed down it, they were inside the cave proper. It smelled musty and was warmer than Tony had expected.

Virginia stopped beside him, and together they stared into the darkness.

"People have been in here," Virginia said. "Look, there are shovels and things."

Not to mention wooden supports farther down in the cave. Virginia dug in the pile of tools. After a moment, she pulled out something that Tony had to stare at before he figured out what it was. An old-style wooden torch with a wick made of hessian soaked in oil. The tip was encased in an iron frame. It could double as a weapon.

Virginia lit it with one of their matches. Tony had never been so glad to see light in his life.

The flame only illuminated the area they were in. Hanging from a roof beam above them was another sign with a dragon painted against a red circle. The sign was blackened and burnt as if someone had tossed a flame-thrower at it, but Tony could still make out the words:

KEEP OUT! DRAGONS!
TRESPASSERS WILL BE EATEN!

"Dragons," Tony said. "That means there is more than one dragon."

"It's a very old sign," Virginia said. "They're probably all dead now."

"Oh, what are you, the dragon expert? Dragons might live for thousands of years. With my luck, I might as well season myself now."

Virginia ignored him, which, he supposed, he deserved. She stepped into the tunnel. Tony followed, and he heard Prince's claws scrabble on the stone beside him.

The tunnel descended very deep into the mountain. Virginia looked at Tony. She was scared. He hadn't known her to get scared.

"What do you think?" she asked.

He shrugged. What choice did they have, really? He didn't want to go back down the mountain.

So Virginia led them through the tunnel. It twisted and turned, and once or twice the flame guttered. When it did, Tony got a hint of the complete darkness they would be in if the flame went out.

"I hate confined spaces," Tony said. "This tunnel is getting narrower. It can't be right. Let's go back. I'm finding it hard to breathe."

"Look," Virginia said. "It stops ahead."

They reached a hole where their tunnel joined with another, bigger tunnel. Virginia lifted the torch, and Tony stepped up beside her. They looked in both directions, but their light didn't extend far enough for them to make a good decision.

"Which way now?" Virginia asked.

He had no idea. In the distance, he could hear rumbling.

"Do you hear that?" Tony asked. "It's a dragon."

The rumbling grew louder until it became a roar. A breeze preceded it and Tony thought of nothing more than subway tunnels. He pushed Virginia against the wall as hot air hit them. Then a train went by.

It was full of Dwarves who sat astride. The train was little more than a wooden bench with wheels and an engine. The Dwarves wore miner's helmets complete with lamps. They were all singing.

Tony pushed Virginia as far back as he could. She shielded their lantern with her hand, maintaining the flame.

After the train passed, they looked at each other in amazement. They now knew which direction to go. They crossed into the new tunnel and followed the tracks.

They didn't have to walk far before they found the train. It was empty now, except for the last few Dwarves who walked under a large archway. Above the archway was a carved sign.

9TH KINGDOM ROYAL DWARF MINES
ENTRANCE SHAFT 761

"Ninth Kingdom?" Tony asked. "When did we leave the Fourth Kingdom?"

"I'm not sure we have," Virginia said. "You remember that map in the Kissing Town? The Ninth Kingdom is all underground. Maybe we can get through this mountain and out the other side."

It sounded like a good idea to Tony.

They walked up to the train. It had stopped at an underground station, marked by the dragon symbol again, this time decorated with a mining hammer and pick cut into it. The huge sign was illuminated from behind by lamps. It reminded Tony of nothing more than a spooky entrance to hell.

On the other side of the arch was a changing area. There was no sign of the Dwarves. Just a black hole disappearing down into the dirt.

"Where did they go?" Tony asked.

"They must have gone down there," Virginia said.

She pointed into the hole. Tony peered down it. There was a slide that disappeared into the darkness. It was highly polished and wooden and would have been a lot of fun when he was, oh, say, twelve.

"I am not going down there," Tony said. "You can't see the bottom. Not with my bad luck."

Prince peered over the edge too. He wagged his tail uncertainly.

"Well, there's nothing up here, is there?" Virginia asked. "It's the only way down."

The broken glass sound came toward him. "I don't think so," Tony said.

Virginia climbed on the slide. "Dad, get on behind me. If the Dwarves went down, it must be safe."

"Why does that follow? It might have a very low ceiling."

Prince looked at Tony, then padded over to the slide and sat down behind Virginia.

"Dad?"

"I could die," he said. "Let's stay up here."

She gave him that doleful look again. He didn't like it. Then she pushed off—

"Don't!" he shouted.

—and disappeared into the darkness.

Virginia hurtled down the wooden miner's slide for what seemed like forever. Prince Wendell was pressed against her back, making sounds that she took to be doggy joy. Her torch went out halfway, but long before she reached the bottom she knew where she was going was lit. She saw the lights as she approached.

The slide leveled off and slowed them down. She got off at the bottom and moved out of the way, hoping her father would be right along. He wasn't. Prince Wendell stood beside the slide too, looking up hopefully.

"Come on, Dad," she said to herself. "You can do it."

The slide ended in a large tunnel, but there were still no Dwarves. Up ahead, she heard a lot of banging and noise. They had to be there.

She took her torch to one of the lit torches. She had to stand on her toes to relight it, but it worked.

Then she heard a cry from behind her. She turned. Her father overshot the slide and rammed into a post on the end. He doubled up in agony.

"You made it then," she said.

She helped him up. They walked to the end of the tunnel and around a corner. Then Virginia stopped. Up ahead was an amazing sight.

A vast chamber, illuminated with lamps, was filled with Dwarves. There were wooden frames that enabled the Dwarves to reach the rock surface. The area had already been mined extensively with wooden ramps and balconies linking most of the chamber.

On the ground, dozens of miners were smashing up large pieces of rock. They all wore red uniforms and little black fez-type hats.

"What do you think they're mining?" her father whispered.

Virginia had no idea. Another group of Dwarves was refining the rocks, crushing them to separate the rock from a silver substance. Farther along, a group of Dwarves examined and graded the silver, removing impurities—she assumed that's what they were doing—with ladles.

In the middle of the cavern was a huge vat of bubbling silver liquid. The air smelled faintly of sulfur and of sweat.

As Virginia watched, the Dwarves lowered something into the vat. Then someone shouted an order, and three Dwarves hauled that something out with a winch.

Slowly and magically, a glistening mirror emerged from the bubbles. All of the Dwarves stopped what they were doing to watch. Virginia felt her breath catch in her throat.

The mirror hung in midair for a few moments, and then it

wobbled. Virginia took a step forward so that she could see better.

The mirror coughed, and then it started crying like a baby.

"Behold," a Dwarf said, "Prince Wendell's coronation gift."

The entire cavernful of Dwarves shouted and applauded. The noise was deafening.

"You hear that, Prince?" Virginia said over the noise. "That's for you."

Then there was a crack above her. She moved out of the way, but her father wasn't so lucky. A stalactite fell on his head.

He shouted in pain and clutched his skull.

Every single Dwarf in the chamber heard him and turned around.

Virginia moaned. Having her father around was becoming a serious liability.

Several Dwarves came toward them. Virginia didn't even try to run. She had no idea where they would go. Her father was in too much pain to notice that they were in trouble until the Dwarves were upon them.

They grabbed her, Prince Wendell, and her father and dragged them toward an office. As they went, Virginia saw the other Dwarves put the new mirror in a drying rack outside the office.

Inside, they found themselves in a small room. A Dwarf who seemed to be the leader sat behind a big desk covered in papers. Behind him was a union-style woven banner, depicting Dwarves heroically constructing mirrors in all their stages.

"You realize the penalty for entering our secret mirror mines, comrade?" the Dwarf asked.

"Is it a heavy fine?" Tony asked.

"It is death. This is our mountain."

"You can have it," Tony said. "We just want to get back to the Fourth Kingdom."

"We didn't know we were trespassing," Virginia said.

"Ignorance is no excuse," he said. "You have illegally entered the underground Ninth Kingdom, and anyone who tries to steal our secrets will die."

"We don't want your secrets," Virginia said. "We just want to ask for your help. You see, there was this magic mirror recently which had a little accident."

The Dwarves who had carried them in gasped. The Dwarf behind the desk stood up in outrage.

"You!" the Dwarf shouted. "It was you. We heard a magic mirror had got smashed. Were you responsible for this outrage?"

"No, not at all," Tony said. "It was nothing to do with us."

The other Dwarves shook their heads in horror. Virginia moved closer to her father. One wrong move, and they were both dead.

"Do you realize what you have done?" the Dwarf asked. "You have destroyed one of the great traveling mirrors. It is irreplaceable. It is part of Dwarf legend."

"I told you," Tony said, "I wasn't even there when it happened."

"Wait a minute," Virginia said. She hoped she had heard the Dwarf correctly. "Did you say *one* of the traveling mirrors?"

"One, as in there are others?" Tony asked.

Virginia couldn't repress her smile. But that offended the Dwarf leader.

"Why, are you not happy with your handiwork?" the Dwarf asked. "Do you wish to smash the other two as well?"

"Where are they?" Tony asked. "We must find them."

"You will find only death here," the Dwarf said. "Take them to the old shaft and throw them in."

"No!" Tony shouted.

The Dwarves grabbed Virginia and her father. She tried to struggle, but there were too many of them. Prince Wendell followed beside them, looking confused. Virginia didn't even know how to ask him for help—as if there was anything he could do. The Dwarves were dragging them into the cavern when one of the Dwarves yelled, "Wait! Look!"

All of the Dwarves gasped and fell to their knees. Virginia had no idea why.

"Look in the Truth mirror," the Dwarf yelled. "Look!"

Virginia looked in the same direction as the Dwarves. They were all staring at the new mirror. Prince was standing in front of it. He was reflected in the mirror, not as a dog, but as a man, a handsome blond man kneeling on all fours.

It was an exact mirror image.

She had known that the dog was Prince Wendell, and had even come to accept that he could talk. But until that moment, she had not really understood, deep down, that the dog who followed her was a true Prince.

"It is Prince Wendell," the Dwarf said. "Grandson of the greatest woman who ever lived."

"That's right," Tony said. "That's the guy. I'm his indispensable translator."

The crowd gathered around the mirror. Prince Wendell barked at his own reflection.

"What magic is this?" one of the Dwarves asked.

Virginia was still staring at his image. "You didn't tell me you looked like that."

Prince Wendell looked at himself and barked, very excited. He raised a paw and the human in the mirror raised an arm.

"Who are you, strange travelers?" the first Dwarf asked.

"We are involved in a secret mission to restore Prince Wendell to his rightful form," Virginia's father said. "I am a very important person."

"Long have the stories told of the day when the proud Prince would stand before us on four legs," said the second Dwarf.

"And this is the day," Tony said. "And we have questions that must be answered."

There was much commotion as the Dwarves realized that the

group in their midst was very important. Finally, they decided to let Virginia, Tony, and Prince Wendell get the tour, given by the Librarian. He was the best, the Dwarves decided, to answer all of their questions.

Virginia had only one. Whether or not they could find a mirror that would take them home.

The Dwarves gave Tony and Virginia torches as they started them on the tour, then introduced them to the Librarian.

The Librarian took them into an underground library filled with thousands of ledgers. It was really a hall of mirrors. Every single type of mirror Virginia had ever imagined, and some she hadn't, were here.

"Mirrors, mirrors, mirrors," the Librarian said. "Here is every kind of magic mirror you could ever want."

Virginia followed her father, watching their images change in the various mirrors. It was like a funhouse. Some of the mirrors made them fat, some thin.

The Librarian gave them the history of the mirrors. Some were Vanity mirrors to make a person more beautiful—and, Virginia noted, it worked. There were many talking mirrors and even more spying mirrors. But Virginia was fascinated by the trick mirrors, her father by the erotic mirrors, and Prince Wendell by the water mirror.

The Librarian explained how the Dwarves had mined this area for thousands of years, searching for the quicksilver, fighting off male dragons who, the Librarian said, were addicted to quicksilver.

He was holding up a vial of quicksilver, letting Virginia look at it, as he explained it. "This is extremely quicksilver," he was saying. "Ordinary quicksilver is much too slow for magic mirrors. Most attempts to make a magic mirror fail completely. But—"

"Ow!"

Virginia turned. Her father had been running his finger along the frame of a mirror and he had gotten a sliver.

"You're clumsy," the Librarian said.

"Yes, sorry about that," Tony said.

"You're not suffering from bad luck, are you?"

"We're looking for a Traveling mirror," Virginia said, as much to cover for her father as to get them out of there fast. "To match the one that was broken."

"Which was nothing to do with us," Tony added.

The Librarian studied Tony suspiciously. Then he scanned a shelf of ancient red-leather ledgers. "Traveling mirrors . . . Traveling mirrors haven't been made for hundreds of years. I doubt our records go that far back."

He opened one of the volumes, ran his finger down the entries, closed it, and shook his head.

"As I thought," the Librarian said. "There is one other slender hope. Let's see if we can raise Gustav."

Virginia looked at her father, who shrugged. Wendell wagged his tail as if he understood.

The Librarian led them across the cavern. He stopped in front of an ancient mirror. Its frame was rotting, and it smelled like decaying teeth. Most of its silver was gone. Someone had wrapped a shawl around it as if it were a very old man.

The Librarian coughed. Then he gave the frame a gentle shake. "Gustav. You have a visitor."

Slowly the mirror shimmered to life. Virginia watched in fascination.

"You have to speak up," the Librarian said to her. "He's going a bit deaf."

She nodded once and stepped before the mirror. "Great Record Keeper," Virginia said, "we need to ask you a question."

"Eh?" the mirror said.

"Question?" Tony shouted. "We need to ask you a question. About Traveling mirrors."

"An answer only will I chime, when questions put are asked in rhyme," the mirror said.

"All early mirrors talk in verse," the Dwarf said.

Virginia leaned back. She wasn't good at rhyme. But her

father shouted, "Were there any other Traveling mirrors made, that might help us on our escapade?"

"Escapade?" Virginia said to herself.

"Three fine mirrors there were made, to make them such a price was paid."

"We're on the case," Tony said. "Where were the other two?"

"Eh?" the old mirror said.

Her father looked impatient. "Our mirror's smashed. What can we do? Where the hell are the other two?"

"Mirror one is smashed forever, by an idiot dressed in leather."

Virginia looked at her father. He wouldn't meet her gaze.

"Mirror two is on a bed, with barnacles upon its head."

"A bed?" Tony asked, glancing at Virginia. "With barnacles on it?"

"The sea bed," Virginia said.

"Yes," the Librarian said. "One fell into the Great Northern Sea. I think you can safely discount that one."

"Mirror three, stolen be," the old mirror said.

"Stolen?"

"Who's stolen it?" Tony asked. He was looking nervous. Virginia felt her stomach twist. She was beginning to recognize that expression. It was the bad-luck expression.

Apparently the mirror hadn't heard him, so Tony yelled, "Could you please get off your ass, and tell us who has got the glass?"

"What you seek has not been seen, since it was stolen by the Queen."

"The Queen," Tony said. "That's all we need."

He glanced over his shoulder, as he had done all the times before. Virginia felt her palms grow clammy.

"Very helpful you have been," her father said, "but for Chrissake tell us where we'll find the Queen."

He strained for the rhyme. Virginia never thought "been"

and "Queen" matched, even though they were spelled similarly. But apparently that was good enough for the mirror.

"Near she is and not alone, in a place that's not her home, in a castle out of sight, where once the Queen was called Snow White."

"Wendell's castle," Tony said. He clapped his hands together and stepped backwards. "I knew it!"

His hand clipped a nearby mirror. Virginia reached forward to stop it, but she couldn't. The mirror toppled backwards. It was one of a long stack of magic mirrors. They tipped over like a stack of dominoes. All Virginia could do was watch.

"Oh, no!" her father said. "Oh, no. No. No."

The noise was astounding as mirror after mirror banged against another. Then they all crashed, breaking into thousands of pieces.

"Murderers!" the Librarian shouted. "You have murdered my mirrors."

"No," Tony said. "It was an accident."

"Mirror-murderers. Kill them. Kill them."

All around the mine, Dwarves looked up. Someone pulled a cord and a large horn rang, echoing through the tunnels.

"Come on," Tony said. "Let's get out of here."

Virginia pushed at Prince and they all ran, even though she had no idea where they would go.

"The next person to look up will be executed," the Queen said.

She was facing Wendell's entire staff. They shook in fear as she walked up and down the line. They had discovered her, and because of that, they now would pay—some of them with their lives.

"Messengers will be sent today to every King, Queen, Emperor, and dignitary throughout the Nine Kingdoms, inviting them to Prince Wendell's coronation ball."

The Dog Prince stood behind her. He clapped his hands in pleasure.

"That's me," he said.

"No one will leave the castle between now and then unless you are instructed to do so by me and me alone," the Queen said. "If asked, you will simply say that your master has returned and is well. If I hear one rumor, one whisper that anything is amiss, I will kill your children in front of you. Return to your duties."

The staff turned and walked away in silence. They wouldn't be much more trouble. Most of them had been around her before. They knew that she meant what she said.

She went to the desk and heated Prince Wendell's seal over a candle. In front of her were a large pile of embossed invitation cards.

"Are we going to have a party?" the Dog Prince asked. "Great. What do we do when everyone gets here?"

She slammed the sizzling seal on the first invitation before her. "Kill them all," she said.

"Look, there they are!" a Dwarf shouted behind them.

"Mirror-murderers!" another shouted.

Virginia was running as fast as she could. Her father had stopped ahead. The tunnel dead-ended. Their only chance was to go down another set of slides.

She grabbed Prince and jumped onto the slide, flattening out as she went into the darkness. Her father followed. She slowed as she reached the bottom and got off.

Her father plummeted past her and flew onto the floor.

"My wrist," Tony said. "I've broken my wrist. I can't take much more of this. I've broken my wrist."

"You've got to be more careful," Virginia said.

"It's not my fault. It's my bad luck." Then his face fell. He had had seven years of bad luck. Now he had thirty times that. "Oh, my God. What's it going to be like *noowwww?*"

As he spoke that last sentence, he disappeared down a hole. Virginia ran to its lip. "Dad? Dad?"

She peered down the hole and saw the tiny flickering light

of her father's torch at the bottom, and the shape of his motionless body thirty feet below.

He looked dead, but she couldn't tell. She looked at Prince. He was staring down as well.

Then she sighed. She grabbed Prince and slowly, carefully, climbed down the hole. She slipped and fell the last six feet, landing in a cloud of dust.

"Dad, are you all right?"

She grabbed their only torch from the ground. It had burned out. She used several matches trying to light it. When she did, she realized she had used the last match.

Then she heard a faint sound. It was her father. Tears were running down his cheeks. "I've done something awful, seriously, I'm not exaggerating, something went crack. I can't move."

"I'll help you," Virginia said. "Try and—"

"No!" He screamed in pain. "I think my back is broken."

Virginia crouched beside her father. He had a look of terror on his face. Prince was peering at him as well.

"If we can't go back up," Virginia said, "we'll just find another way out of here."

She held her torch up. It illuminated no more than twelve feet of blackness. The tunnel they were in forked almost immediately. Virginia looked down both tunnels, equally dark. She had no idea which was the best way to go.

The torch started to flicker. It was only a stump, nearly done. There wasn't more than twenty minutes left in it at the most.

"I don't want to die down here," her father said.

"We won't," Virginia said. "We'll find the way out, and if the light starts to go, we'll crawl in the darkness until we find a way out."

"I can't crawl," Tony said. "I can't move."

"Then I'll drag you."

She put her hands under his shoulders, and he screamed.

She eased him down. She didn't know what to do. He would die down here, and she didn't want to leave him alone.

But she had no other choice. She needed help. It wouldn't come from the Dwarves.

"Okay, I'm going to go on and find a way out," Virginia said. "And then I'll come straight back for you. Maybe Prince can sniff out fresh air. I'll go with him and—"

"No," Tony said, "there are hundreds of tunnels. You'll get lost."

She shook her head. "Dad, we don't have any choice."

He was shaking with fear. But she had to tell him the other thing, the one that would only make things worse.

"And," she said, "I have to take the torch."

"It's pitch black in here," Tony said. "You'll never find me again."

He grabbed her arm like a drowning man. She pulled his fingers away one by one. He gulped. He looked about seven years old.

"I will find the way out and come back for you," she said. "I promise."

She dug through her rucksack and found the last of their bread.

"I'm going to leave a trail of breadcrumbs so I can find you again."

He looked at her, and he was strangely calm. He knew— hell, she knew—that this was it. They would both probably die down here. But at least they would die trying.

"You get out, Virginia," Tony said.

She nodded, then kissed his forehead. Prince Wendell watched. Then she stood and walked off into the darkness. When she reached the fork in the path, she chose the left one without hesitation. If she second-guessed herself now, this journey would take forever.

And she didn't have forever.

Chapter Forty

Who was it that told her the Dwarf Kingdom was a horrible place? Wolf? Virginia's heart twisted. He was right in so many ways. She had walked for what seemed like miles now, marking her path with breadcrumbs, Prince padding along beside her.

Her torch was still guttering, and even when the flame burned high it didn't give much protection against the darkness. The cave tunnels were dark and cold and, for the most part, silent. She was grateful for Prince's doggy presence beside her, for his warmth and his breathing.

She had never been so frightened in her life. Her father's back was broken. They were stuck in a place that had no medical facilities to speak of, and she had no idea how to get out of these caves let alone get out of the Nine Kingdoms.

She wanted to go back to New York so badly, she could feel it. Or, at least, see a friendly face. Why had she turned Wolf away? If he were here now, she could have stayed with her father while Wolf found them a way out.

The path narrowed up ahead. As Virginia got closer, she realized that it narrowed into a space about the size of a manhole. She stopped. She was done then. There was nowhere to go except back. How could she tell her father that she failed?

Prince went through the hole. She peered after him, but didn't see him. Then she waited for him to come back.

He didn't.

She couldn't go back. If she gave up now, her father would

die. She took a deep breath and squeezed through the hole, torch first.

For a moment, she thought she would have to crawl until the tunnel ended in front of her. Then she saw an opening. She crawled toward it, feeling a chill that was so incredible, it made the air in her lungs freeze.

She stepped out of the hole into an ice cave. It was stunningly beautiful. Above her, stalactites glistened, giving off a magical light. She didn't need her torch anymore. She was glad for the light. The darkness had creeped her out more than she wanted to admit.

Prince Wendell was in the center of the cave. He barked when he saw her. She approached him, and realized he was standing near a circle about fifteen feet wide. A faint bluish light was coming from it. As she approached, she realized there was writing all around the circle.

"For seven men she gave her life," Virginia read. "For one good man she was his wife. Beneath the ice by Snow White Falls, there lies the fairest of them all."

Virginia looked into the circle. It was ice, and below the surface was an old woman with jet-black hair. She was beautiful in her long sleep, buried in the ice itself.

"Hello, Virginia."

Virginia turned. The old woman was behind her, sitting on a throne built into the rock of the cave. She was even more beautiful in life, with her tissue-paper skin, wrinkled and soft, and her stunning blue eyes.

"Who are you?" Virginia asked.

"You know me," Snow White said. "I was the old woman gathering sticks in the forest. I was the little Cupid girl in the Kissing Town. Your journey was once my journey, and I have tried to help you."

"Are you dead?"

"Well, yes, I think you'd have to say so. I am more into the fairy-godmother occasional appearance sort of thing now. But I can still influence things. And I have protected you in other ways, shielding your image from the mirrors of the Queen. But soon you will have to see and be seen."

"I don't understand," Virginia said.

The old woman opened her arms, and Prince Wendell went to her, tail wagging. She cuddled him and stroked his head. "What do you think of my grandson?"

Virginia smiled. The old woman was Snow White. One of the five great women, Wolf had said.

Snow White was waiting for Virginia's answer. "I like him."

"I think being a dog has been very good for him," Snow White said.

"But he's lost his mind," Virginia said.

"That's why you must now take charge," Snow White said. "He needs you to save his kingdom. We all do."

"Oh, no," Virginia said. "You've got the wrong person."

"My mother was a Queen," Snow White said, "and every day she sewed by a window, staring at the falling snow, longing to have a baby girl. But one day she pricked her finger with her needle, and into the snow fell three drops of blood, and she knew she would die giving birth to me."

Virginia took a step forward. Snow White's words were compelling.

"My father was sad for a very long time, but eventually he remarried because he was lonely. My new mother brought no possessions to the castle except for her magic mirrors."

Virginia frowned. Mirrors were everywhere in this place.

"And every day she locked her bedroom door and took all her clothes off and said, 'Mirror, mirror, on the wall, who is the fairest of them all?' And the mirror would gaze at her, and shudder and scan all the other mirrors in the world, and all the people looking at themselves and then answer, 'My lady is the fairest of them all.' "

The story was so familiar, and yet so intriguing to hear this way. Virginia walked to Snow White and sat down beside her.

"This satisfied her, for she knew that the mirror spoke the

truth. That is the function of mirrors, even wayward, willful mirrors, Virginia. To let you see yourself as you truly are. But you must be sure you wish to know the truth.''

Virginia wrapped her hands around her knees and listened. Snow White went through the fairy tale, changing only small parts of it, from the moment she grew up to the moment the mirror told Snow White's stepmother that Snow White was now the fairest of them all.

When Snow White mentioned how her stepmother had brought in the Huntsman to kill her, Virginia shuddered and thought of the man who had been chasing them. She recognized so much of this as both a tale and as events she was now living.

''The Huntsman said he was going to show me the wild animals,'' Snow White said, ''but the wild animals were in his eyes, and I knew as he took me deeper and deeper into the forest that he was going to kill me. Can you imagine that moment, Virginia, when you realize that you are so awful that your stepmother is going to have you murdered?''

Virginia shuddered. She could imagine it.

''As he drew his knife, I fell to my knees and I said, 'Let me live. Let me live.' And he put away his knife and on the way home he came across a young boar and killed it and cut out its lungs and liver and took them to the Queen. And that night she ate them, believing that by eating me, she would acquire my beauty.''

Snow White reached out and took Virginia's hand. Snow White's hand was warm, surprisingly, and the skin was delicate and soft. Her grip was firm, though.

''Have you ever been in the forest, all alone, in the darkest dark?'' she asked.

''Yes,'' Virginia said, thinking just how recent that had been.

''I was so terrified, I just ran in the darkness. I ran until I was exhausted, and there, in front of me, was a tiny cottage.''

''The cottage we found!'' Virginia said. She remembered how it had seemed like such a refuge.

Snow White described it that way too. Again, the tale she told merged with the fairy tale and became eerily familiar. Virginia's father used to tell her stories at bedtime, but her mother never had. This story-telling soothed something in Virginia, and made her feel loved.

Snow White told Virginia all about the Dwarves, how the Dwarves were pleased to see Snow White and how they had a soft spot for children because of their height. She made Virginia laugh by telling her how Dwarves were champion windbreakers, always wafting their sheets at night and doing the "he who smelt it dealt it" routine.

Virginia could imagine life in that little cottage with those seven men. She could also imagine how tedious it got, doing all the housework. But Snow White hadn't seemed to find it tedious.

"I thought I had found my true vocation and happiness," Snow White said. "But in a strange way, they were just like my stepmother because they didn't want me to grow up either. This is really important you understand, Virginia, because I had gone from something very bad to something very good, but it was only halfway right. They loved me, but they wanted me to stay small, like them."

Virginia nodded. Prince sighed and curled up closer to his grandmother's feet, like a child enjoying a good story.

Snow White continued, telling Virginia how she had warned the Dwarves about her stepmother, and how they became completely paranoid about her. And how their fears became her own.

"She did come for you, though," Virginia said. "You were right to be scared."

Snow White smiled faintly, sadly. "Her mirrors found me eventually. She dressed as an old peddler and walked over the seven hills to my house. Twice she came, once with a corset to crush my ribs, and then with a poisoned comb to drug me. Both times I fell for her tricks, but the Dwarves returned just in time to save my life."

Virginia had forgotten that part of the fairy tale. She leaned closer, listening.

"But the last time she came with the most beautiful apples you ever saw," Snow White said, voice trembling with the memory, "and this time she stayed to watch me die to make sure. She held me until I died in front of her, choking on a piece of apple."

Snow White paused, then sighed. Virginia squeezed her hand. Snow White squeezed back.

"I often think, why did I let her in? Didn't I know she was bad? And I did, of course I did, but I also knew that I couldn't keep that door shut all my life, just because it was dangerous, just because there was a chance of getting hurt."

She smiled at Virginia, and her eyes filled with tears. She could barely tell Virginia how the Dwarves found her and mourned for her, and Virginia had trouble listening to a tale of such grief. The Dwarves mourned for three days and three nights, crying until their eyes bled. They couldn't bear to put Snow White in the ground, so they made her a glass coffin.

"They wrote my name on it in gold letters," she said, "and that I was a Princess, which was something I had long forgotten myself. Then they put the coffin on the top of a hill at the base of this mountain."

"In the Kissing Town," Virginia said.

Snow White nodded. "One day a Prince came and fell in love with me and offered to buy the coffin."

"The Dwarves didn't sell, did they?" Virginia asked.

"Not at first," Snow White said. "They told him that he couldn't have it for all the gold in the world, but he came back day after day for a year, and in the end they saw he had fallen in love with me just as they once had. And he brought his friends to move the coffin, but they stumbled and dropped me, and the jolt moved the lump of poisoned apple that had stuck in my throat, and suddenly I opened my eyes."

Virginia found that she was holding her breath, spellbound by a story she had known all her life.

"At our wedding, the Dwarves gave me away, and I saw in their eyes that gleam of pride and hurt, and I realized I had received something very special. The love of people who do not give their love easily, or do not give it often. But I had to leave them to fulfill my destiny. There are a great many lies, but the biggest of them is the lie of obedience."

Snow White was speaking forcefully now. Virginia frowned. She knew that Snow White was making a point, but not exactly sure why she thought this point would be important to Virginia.

"Obedience is not a virtue. I wanted to please everyone but myself, and I had to lose everything to learn that lesson. For my pride I had to lie in a glass coffin for twenty years to learn my lesson. By the time I was released, I understood. My husband was a good man, but he did not rescue me. I rescued myself."

"What's all this got to do with me?" Virginia asked.

"Everything," Snow White said. "You're cold, Virginia. How have you let yourself become so cold?"

Virginia shivered. Snow White put her arms around her, and Virginia felt tears stream down her face. It was as if she had melted. The tears fell and became sobs, and Snow White held her and rocked her like a child.

"You're still lost in the forest," Snow White said. "But lonely, lost girls like us can be rescued. You are standing on the edge of greatness."

"I'm not," Virginia said, trying to stifle her tears. "I'm useless. I'm a nobody."

"You will one day be like me," Snow White said, "a great adviser to other lost girls. Now stand up."

Virginia stood up. She wiped the tears off her face with the back of her hand.

Snow White reached into her pocket and gave Virginia a beautifully carved hand mirror. "This mirror will show what you do and do not want to see."

Virginia looked at it, but turned the glass away so that she couldn't see herself.

"Poison is the way the Queen will strike," Snow White said. "And the way she must be defeated. You must find the poisoned comb my stepmother tried to kill me with."

"But what can I do on my own?"

"Do not cling to what you know," Snow White said. "I turned away from ordinary life myself. I know the price. Do not think. Become."

Virginia nodded. Then her torch flickered. How much time had she been here? She only had the one light.

"My light is going out," Virginia said. "I'm going to die down here."

"Let the light go out," Snow White said. "Embrace the darkness."

"I can't find my way out in the dark." There was only a tiny flame left. She wouldn't be able to find help now.

Snow White put a gentle hand on Virginia's arm. "Now you may ask for one wish and I will try and grant it."

Virginia looked up. Snow White had given her hope.

Snow White smiled. "But ask for the right thing."

Virginia knew what she had to ask for. "I wish Dad's bad luck was over and his back wasn't broken anymore."

"Strictly speaking, that's two wishes," Snow White said, "but it's done."

Suddenly, she turned and looked away from Virginia. Her pale skin grew even paler, as if a terrible thought had crossed her mind. "Your father is in danger. Go to him."

"I know, but—"

"Go to him. Now. Immediately," Snow White said.

And Virginia did.

Tony had never experienced pain like this before, pain so severe that it was actually a companion. He'd heard that such pain would fade because the body couldn't handle it, and it was true. If he didn't move, he didn't feel anything below the neck at all.

Sometimes that terrified him even more.

He had to find things to do in the darkness. He counted his breaths. He tried to sleep.

He had no idea how much time had gone by when he saw a faint light in the distance. His heart leapt. He had thought he was going to die here, slowly and alone.

"Virginia," Tony said. "Oh, thank God. I was going out of my mind."

His cheeks were wet. He wished he could reach to his daughter, but it would hurt too much.

"I gave up all hope," Tony said.

"That was the right thing to do." That wasn't Virginia's voice. It belonged to the Huntsman.

"Oh, my God," Tony said. He couldn't do anything. He was trapped here with this monster.

He was going to die.

"I move slowly," the Huntsman said, "but I always get what I want."

The Huntsman set down his lamp and gazed at Tony. There was no compassion in the Huntsman's pale eyes. "Where did she take the dog?"

Tony didn't answer. The only thing he had was his silence.

The Huntsman looked at the forked tunnels. "Which way did she go?"

"Go to hell," Tony said. "You might as well kill me, with my luck."

"I will not ask you again." The Huntsman grabbed Tony by the throat. The movement sent ripples of pain through Tony's back. The Huntsman put his knife to Tony's skin.

"Go on, do it," Tony said. "I don't care anymore."

"You'll tell me long before you die." He dug his knife into the skin near Tony's Adam's apple. Tony braced himself when suddenly—wham! Something hit the Huntsman over the head.

The Huntsman loosened his grip, his pale eyes moving. Then two more hits and the Huntsman went down. He lay completely still.

His torch had fallen with him. Tony peered into the flickering light to see Virginia, clutching her own torch, the iron top bent out of shape by the force of the blows. Prince Wendell barked his encouragement as Virginia looked down at the Huntsman.

"I think you've killed him," Tony said, feeling more relief than he ever had in his life.

Virginia looked different. Distracted, almost distant. She didn't seem as happy to see Tony as he was to see her.

"Get up and come with me," Virginia said.

"My back's broken," Tony said. "I told you."

"No, it's not," Virginia said.

"Yes, it—" He moved. There was no answering pain. He could lift his arm, bend his legs. He almost cried with joy. "It's better. How did you know it was better?"

He stood up and grinned, feeling a bit goofy.

"That's not possible. My back was broken."

"I've found the most wonderful thing," Virginia said. "Come with me."

"Did you find the way out?"

"Better than that." She picked up the Huntsman's torch and went down the left fork. Tony followed. His body felt stronger than it ever had. Or maybe he was just noticing it for the first time, noticing how nice it was when everything worked right.

"There's something better than a way out?" Tony asked.

She didn't answer. She led him quickly through the tunnel to a place that became a man-sized hole. She crawled through it, and Tony followed.

They ended up in a huge cavern.

"Look," Virginia said, holding up her torch.

It was a cavern. A few stalactites, some rocks. Nothing more.

"At what?" Tony asked.

Virginia whirled, clearly upset. "But it was . . ."

"I thought you'd found the way out."

"Yes." She sounded distracted again. She raised the torch to her lips and blew it out.

The darkness was complete and immense. Tony had never wanted to see darkness like that again. "What have you done? We haven't got any matches left."

"Be quiet," Virginia said. "Listen."

All Tony heard was silence. Silence and darkness. At least his back wasn't broken anymore. This was nightmare enough.

"Can you hear that?" Virginia asked.

"What?" Tony asked. "Hear what?"

Then he heard a faint sound. A rumble in the distance.

Virginia took his hand, and Prince butted his head against Tony's free palm. Together they walked toward the rumble. It grew louder and louder, like the rumble of thunder.

Eventually the darkness ceased to be so complete. Tony began to realize he could see shapes of rocks, Virginia, and Prince. The light got stronger, and as they got closer to it, Tony recognized the sound as the rush of water.

Suddenly they stepped into the daylight. It blinded them after the darkness of the cave. Tony put a hand to his eyes, then brought it down and almost fainted.

They had emerged at the top of a waterfall which cascaded hundreds of feet below. Spray hit him in the face. The wind here was bracing, and the rocks they stood on were wet.

"Don't look down," Tony said. "Stay back from the edge, Prince."

Virginia grinned. Then Tony laughed. They were alive. He hadn't thought they were going to make it, and yet they stood here, in the light, outside of the caves. Whole.

"We're back in the Fourth Kingdom," Tony said.

Virginia looked back toward the cave. That distracted expression crossed her face again. She pulled a beautiful hand mirror out of her pocket.

"Where did you get that?" Tony asked.

Virginia held the mirror to her face and smiled. "Mirror mirror, in my hand, Who's the fairest in the land?"

The mirror started to cloud. Tony leaned over and watched. Virginia's smile faded. They both watched nervously as the outline of a person formed in the glass.

Then Virginia nearly dropped the mirror in shock. Tony had to grab her wrist to hold the mirror up.

"No, no, no," Virginia said. "It can't be . . ."

Tony turned the mirror so that he could see the image. And what he saw almost stopped his heart.

"Oh, my God," Tony said. "It's your mother."

Part Four

THE PRINCE

FORMERLY KNOWN

AS DOG

Chapter Forty-One

She had been only seven when her mother left, but she would recognize that face, that form, anywhere. Her mother, wearing purple and looking a decade older, was in the Nine Kingdoms.

"No, no, no, it can't be," Virginia said.

Her mother walked toward the hand mirror. As she got closer, Virginia's father grabbed the mirror and tossed it away. It flew into the waterfall before them and vanished under a white froth.

"It was Mom!" Virginia said. "She's here. How can that be possible?"

Her father said nothing. He stared at the waterfall, shaking his head in disbelief.

For the longest time, they didn't speak. They had to concentrate on the treacherous climb down the side of the falls. It took some maneuvering to get Wendell down, but they managed.

At the bottom, they found a ravine. The falls dumped into a river that frothed and boomed around them. Virginia was damp with spray. She kept walking, but she couldn't stop thinking about her mother.

Neither, apparently, could her father. He looked sadder than she had seen him look in a long time.

"You said she was living in Miami," Virginia said.

"I had to say something," Tony said. "You kept asking me all the time."

Prince Wendell sniffed the ground, tail wagging. He was becoming more and more dog-like.

"Why did you throw the mirror away?" Virginia asked.

"If we could see her," Tony said, "then maybe she could see us, and—"

"And what?" Virginia demanded. "What do you think she's going to do?"

Her father shook his head. Wendell stopped before them and sniffed at a mound of dirt. His tail was wagging even harder. All around them the mountains rose. This was a gloomy place, even with the sun shining.

"How did she get here?" Virginia asked.

"She's got the other mirror, hasn't she?" Tony asked. "The one we're after."

Virginia had thought of that, but she hadn't wanted to acknowledge it. What it meant. All the implications.

Her father stopped and turned around. Prince Wendell was still sniffing that one spot.

"Prince," Tony called. "Here, boy."

Prince bounded toward her father, wagging his tail. Her father crouched and scratched the dog's ears.

"Are we still going the right way for your castle?"

Her father cocked his head and then looked very sad.

"No," Tony said to Prince. "No stick throwing. Big things are going on. Your stepmother is my wife—what do you make of that? The Queen, your stepmother, is—"

He stopped as if Prince Wendell had spoken again. Then Tony shook his head. "More sticks," he said to Virginia. "He's going fast."

Blabberwort held a torch and made her way through the darkness. She hated the mountain. She hated the Dwarf Kingdom. She hated the Dwarves. Pursuing the witch hadn't been fun. If the witch hadn't killed her father, Blabberwort would have stopped long ago.

Her brothers held their torches tightly. They hadn't whined in the past five minutes. It was time for them to start.

And then, as if he'd heard her thought, Burly said, "Suck an Elf. We're completely lost. We've been walking round in circles for hours."

"No," Blabberwort said. "Lookee here." She pointed to the faint form she saw ahead. The Huntsman was lying on the ground, looking dead.

"How the mighty have fallen," Bluebell said.

Blabberwort prodded his body with her foot. Her brothers did the same.

"I bagsie his boots," Burly said.

"They're mine," Blabberwort said.

"You two," Bluebell said. "Don't start a stupid fight over my new boots."

Burly shoved Blabberwort. She shoved him back. Bluebell got into the middle of it, and then they all shoved each other. Burly shoved the hardest and bent over the Huntsman. The Huntsman's hand rose and grabbed Burly on the wrist.

"I am alive," the Huntsman said.

Blabberwort leapt backwards, then bent over, staring at him. He was badly hurt and bleeding.

"Help me," he said.

"Help yourself," Burly said.

"Yeah," Blabberwort said. "Since when have you ever helped us?"

She walked off, and her brothers followed. There was a fork ahead in the tunnel.

"You will not find them," the Huntsman said.

"What's it to you?" Blabberwort asked. "You can't hunt anybody now. You're finished."

"I cannot fight," the Huntsman said, "but I can find them for you. There is a way. Get me to daylight."

She stopped. She didn't want to go through that tunnel and pick a direction. It had been getting harder and harder to track the witch in this darkness.

Her brothers turned toward the Huntsman.

"What if we do help you?" Bluebell asked. "What are you proposing?"

"A partnership," the Huntsman said.

Virginia and her father walked down a narrow path on the other side of the mountain range. Below them, the river raged. Prince Wendell walked in front of them, stopping to sniff stones, lift his leg, or bring a stick back to Tony.

Her father ignored Prince as much as he could. Tony and Virginia were talking openly for the first time in Virginia's life.

"Christine was the kind of woman who woke up beautiful," Tony said. "She never seemed to have to try. But she was so neurotic, she spent her whole life in front of a mirror. She said when you're beautiful, you never know why people like you."

Virginia had never heard this about her mother. Her father had barely spoken of her.

"It was my fault," her father said. "I rushed into marriage because I couldn't believe that this beautiful girl liked me. But she was sick, even then. She was seeing a shrink. Every day she was taking pills. I knew she slept with other guys. She wasn't even discreet about it."

Virginia closed her eyes. Her poor father. She'd had no idea.

"I was just crazy about her. But you don't want to hear that. You want to hear how nice she was, because she was your mother. The truth is, she walked out on us when she'd had enough, and I don't think she gave it a second thought."

"I don't believe that," Virginia said.

Her father looked at her sadly, and then Prince started barking. She glanced up. Ahead of them was a woods that looked slightly cultivated, like the forests of England. Prince was standing in front of a fence that stretched for miles, and a wooden sign that said,

PRINCE WENDELL'S ROYAL ESTATE
HUNTING BY PERMIT ONLY

"Hey, Prince," Tony shouted. "Recognize this? You own all this. This is your estate, your home."

Prince barked and wagged his tail.

"What's he saying?" Virginia asked.

"Sadly," Tony said, "nothing. He's just barking."

Virginia was silent for a few moments. She and her father joined Prince. He bounded up to her father's hand, and her father petted him absently, as one would do with a dog.

They walked along the path, which ran through the woods.

"I can't remember the night she left," Virginia said, wanting this conversation to continue. She felt as if she were finally beginning to understand her past. "But I remember the morning after because you were trying to make breakfast and you didn't know where anything was."

Her father nodded. "Your grandma came round to look after you because I had to go to work and she said, 'Look, she's playing with her bears. She's coping fine.' But you had three bears and you'd put one of them apart from the other two and told him he had to be all on his own."

Virginia remembered that too. The indescribable sadness she had felt that day had never really eased. Sadness and betrayal. Her mother had left—Virginia had known it, deep down, and had always known that her mother had never wanted her.

But she had always hoped her mother would want her, someday.

"I knew she'd come back because she left all her clothes," Virginia said. "She loved them more than anything, and I kept going to her room. And then, after a few months, you suddenly said we had to get rid of them. I remember folding them all neatly, and I kept thinking that a note was suddenly going to flutter out of one of them, written to me, just to me, telling me how much she loved me. And explaining the special, magical reason why she had to go. I still have this uncontrollable urge to go up to people and say, 'My mother left me when I was seven' as though that'll explain everything.''

There were tears on her face again. How come she was crying so much? Was it all the stress? She wiped at her face. She had never cried this much in her whole life.

"I miss her," Virginia said. "I hate her and I miss her. I feel like I was on a train and it crashed, and there was no one who came and rescued me.''

Her father was watching her. His expression was full of love. Maybe he'd been there for her, in his own bumbling way. At least he had tried.

She shrugged. "I always wanted my life to be like a fairy story, and now it is.''

Her father was looking uncomfortable now, as if there were more he had to say. "Even if you do meet her . . ." he started.

"She never wanted me, did she?" Virginia asked. "That's why she left.''

"It was my fault," Tony said. "Our marriage was going wrong and she got pregnant and she wanted to get rid of you, because of her career.''

Virginia looked at him sharply. She had never known this.

Her father ran a hand through his thinning hair. "But I wore her down. She didn't want to have a kid, and it was a mistake, and there you have it. That's the mess that life is, because if you hadn't been born, then I wouldn't have had you, but . . .''

"But you might still have her.''

He nodded, looking almost ashamed, then turned to her. Suddenly pink dust covered his face and he staggered backwards, coughing.

"Dad!" Virginia shouted. "No!''

Her father fell to the ground unconscious. The three Trolls emerged from the trees. They were firing packages of Troll dust. Virginia ducked as one hit the tree behind her.

She couldn't even help her father. She reached for Prince—

and a package hit him in the face, followed by another. He got a look of doggy surprise and toppled over.

"Kill our dad, would you!" the Trolls shouted at her. "Well, we're going to fix you proper now, you little witch."

She started to run, but before she got too far, a package of dust hit her as well. It smelled like bubble gum, and it made her dizzy. She had to keep moving. She staggered, and then fell.

Footsteps surrounded her, and she felt dull thuds. Someone was kicking her. She was losing consciousness, but she struggled against it.

The last thing she heard was the voice of the Huntsman. "Get off her. You'll get your chance later, after the Queen has finished."

Virginia came around as if she were waking from a deep sleep. She was so groggy that she didn't even know where she was. People were singing "Saturday Night Fever" at the top of their lungs, slightly out of tune. They were getting the words wrong. How annoying was that? Drunken people beneath her window mangling the Bee Gees. The bed beneath her bounced, and it took her a moment to realize she wasn't on a bed, she was on a wagon.

She opened her eyes slightly. She was manacled to her father. He was still out cold. The Trolls were up front, singing. They were drunk. They had Prince Wendell with them. He was chained too.

The Huntsman was beside them, trying to rest. He was in a bad way. His head was covered with dried blood, and so was his leg. She couldn't believe how hard he was to kill.

She was so groggy. She raised her head slightly, but that took too much effort. She closed her eyes, just for a moment—and dropped back into sleep.

She dreamed she was standing in the forest. It was nearly dark. She had a feeling she had had this dream before. Wolf was fifteen feet in front of her. She wanted to go to him, to touch him, but she didn't move.

In the dusky light he looked very predatory. She closed her eyes. When she opened them again, he was closer.

"You moved," Virginia said.

"No, I didn't," Wolf said.

He was standing absolutely still behind her. The dusk was becoming night. She reached for him.

"I miss you," she said. "I miss you so much."

Then she turned away from him. In her hand, she was holding the magic hand mirror. She raised it so that she could see behind her. Instead of Wolf reflected in the glass, she saw Snow White.

"Poison is the way the Queen will strike," Snow White said. "And the way she must be defeated. You will find your weapon in a grave."

Virginia looked down. In her other hand, she held a comb, silver and encrusted with jewels. It had razor-sharp teeth.

"Do not think. Become," Snow White said.

Virginia woke with a start. The horrible music had stopped. She glanced up. The Trolls had passed out, and the Huntsman was asleep. The horse was pulling the wagon without direction.

Virginia grabbed her father and shook him. "Dad!" she whispered. "Wake up."

He shook his head, then opened his eyes, and blinked at her. He seemed to take in their surroundings rather quickly.

"They're asleep," she whispered. "No one's watching us. We can escape."

"How?" Tony asked. "We're tied up."

"Jump off the back," Virginia said. "They won't see us."

"Jump," Tony said. "Our hands and feet are tied together."

He wriggled so that he could look over the edge of the wagon. They were only four feet off the ground, but the wagon was moving at a good clip. The road was made up of stones and hard dirt.

Virginia could almost read the fear in him.

"No way," Tony said. "Anyway, what about Prince?"

Virginia looked toward Prince. He was chained and tied in the front of the wagon, but he was resting between the Huntsman's legs. His chain was wrapped around the Huntsman's boots. There was no way to get him without waking the most dangerous man on the wagon.

"We can't get to him," Virginia whispered. "We have to escape."

Prince opened his eyes, and for the first time in a while, they were filled with intelligence.

"I'm not going without him," Tony said.

Prince shook his head.

"What did he say?" Virginia asked.

"He told me to go," Tony whispered. "I can't, Virginia. I can't leave him with these monsters."

"Don't think," Virginia said. "Just do it. One. Two. Three."

They rolled together over the back of the wagon and landed on the ground. Virginia winced as the air left her body. The jolt was incredible. Her father cursed softly, and they had to struggle for a moment to get themselves untangled. Then Virginia looked up.

The wagon had gone on without them.

It took a while, but Virginia managed to untie the ropes from her feet. She and her father were still bound together by iron manacles, but the chain that held them allowed some distance. They were in the woods, and it was early evening. Virginia even had a sense of where they were.

Apparently, so did her father. "What's the point of escaping if we're just going to walk straight to the castle?" he asked.

"We'll find a weapon," Virginia said. "I dreamt it."

"Oh, good," he said. "That puts my mind at rest."

It was getting dark as they approached a wooden sign with two arrows. The one that indicated the road they were walking on said, PRINCE WENDELL'S CASTLE — 39 MILES. The one that pointed into the woods said, PRINCE WENDELL'S CASTLE — 13 MILES.

"Oh, great," Virginia said. "A shortcut. We can catch up to them."

She started walking through the trees, pulling her father by their handcuffs.

"Woah, Virginia," Tony said. "Why do you think it's thirty-nine miles one way and thirteen the other?"

"Perhaps there's a scenic route," Virginia said. "How should I know?"

The ground was soft underneath.

"You don't think the other road might be going around something?" her father asked as his boot sank in the marshy soil, punching a hole through some rotting timber.

Virginia shrugged. "This route is probably not suitable for carts, that's all."

They walked for a long time. Virginia felt like these thirteen miles might be the longest of all. The marsh made walking difficult, and her father was making snide comments about shortcuts.

Finally, they reached an area bathed in green light. It was a swamp. The light revealed sunken trees and brackish water. The smell was thick and slightly rancid.

All around them were strange bird calls and weird cries. A shiver ran through Virginia when she heard some screeching. The marshy land gave way to waist-deep water, and Virginia had to lead them carefully, seeking little islands that rose like ghosts out of the swamp.

"Is that just me," her father asked, "or can I hear Pink Floyd?"

They stopped. Virginia listened. She heard more screeching, but no music.

"It's just you," Virginia said. "I can't hear anything."

She looked back and saw a pair of green eyes flick on and off in the trees. She frowned. Maybe she had imagined that. This certainly was a spooky enough place.

They kept walking.

"It's the Floyd," her father said. "It's 'Dark Side of the Moon.'"

Virginia stopped to listen again, but all she heard was the howl of a wolf. Wolf, she thought longingly. But she said as coolly as she could manage, "It's an animal howling."

"It's not," Tony said. "It's track four, side one. I love this!" He started swinging the chain between them in time with the music that only he was hearing.

Virginia knew better than to try to make him stop. Instead, she gazed ahead. There were tiny lights flitting about, almost too fast to follow.

"What are those lights?"

Her father peered toward them but didn't say anything.

Virginia had had enough. She had made a mistake coming this way, and she knew it. "Look, it's not too late to turn back."

"Oh, no," her father said. "I'm not going back until I've heard side two."

She glanced at him. He was losing it. What was causing that? Then lights appeared all around them, buzzing them and whizzing past in the darkness.

Suddenly three girls appeared. They were sitting in the trees that grew out of the swamp.

"Who are you?" Virginia asked.

"Who are you?" asked one of the girls.

They weren't human, but they had a human appearance. They reminded Virginia of adolescent girls, except for the pointy ears and perfect skin. They seemed to glow all over. Virginia had a sense she was looking at Elves.

"Everyone thinks they can handle the swamp," the first girl said, tugging on her earring. It was a little light, like the florescent rings Virginia had seen at concerts.

"But they all end up in the hands of the Swamp Witch," another said.

"The Swamp Witch?" her father asked.

Virginia looked at him. He shook his head slightly. More problems. That was all they needed.

"There are three things you mustn't do under any circumstances," said the first girl. "Don't drink the water."

"Don't eat the mushrooms," said the second.

"And whatever you do," said the third, "don't fall asleep."

"All right," Tony said. "Enough. Show us the way back and we'll take the long way."

"It's much too late now," said the second girl. "You're doomed."

"Too late," said the first. "Doomed. Doomed."

Then the girls vanished. The lights whizzed past Virginia, and suddenly she and her father were alone again.

She took his hand. The swamp seemed even scarier than before.

Chapter Forty-Two

He smelled of sulfur and rotten eggs, his feet were wet, and the chain was heavy. Tony was getting really tired, and he had the horrible feeling that they were lost forever. Virginia wasn't saying anything either, just moving forward with a determination that seemed forced.

Occasionally, she would slap at a mosquito or some other kind of bug, and that would be the only sound in the darkness.

Ahead was another little island. They half walked, half swam to it, then pulled themselves onto the mossy surface. They should have gotten up and walked, but neither of them did.

"That's it," Tony said. "We've got to stop, just for five minutes. There's dry wood. We can make a fire, and we've still got a couple of eggs left."

"We mustn't eat anything," Virginia said.

"I'm sure that doesn't include food we've brought in."

He sat up and took a small frying pan from Virginia's rucksack. Then he removed three eggs, cracked from the fall off the wagon. Virginia leaned against a tree. She seemed completely wiped out.

"You won't fall asleep, will you?" Tony asked.

"I'm starving," Virginia said. "I'm not going to fall asleep."

She closed her eyes.

"Don't eat any of the mushrooms," she said.

He looked around. He hadn't noticed the mushrooms before.

They were all over the island. He had thought they were moss when he climbed up, but the slimy feeling under his fingers had been actual fungus.

He shuddered a little, then went about gathering dried wood. It took a while to light a fire, but it felt so good that he warmed himself before starting the eggs. Virginia hadn't said anything yet, but she'd be all right once he fed her.

The warmth of the fire lulled him. He stretched out so that his pants could dry, and then he closed his eyes, just for a minute. He knew he shouldn't fall asleep, and he wouldn't. Not really. He'd just rest for a few minutes. . . .

It took him a while to make it through this insane swamp. When would Virginia learn to understand the signs in the Nine Kingdoms? Wolf shook his head fondly and hurried forward, eager to see her again.

But as he got close to the island, he saw only her feet. The rest of her body was covered in vines.

"Virginia!" Wolf shouted.

He climbed up beside her, and found that the vines were around Virginia's neck, choking the life out of her, and she wasn't even noticing. He yanked at the vines, pulled her free, and clasped her against him.

If she was in trouble, so was her father.

Wolf shook her awake. "Where's Tony?" he demanded. "Where's Tony?"

Virginia gasped for air with a horrible, desperate sound. She couldn't speak. Then Wolf saw the manacle and chain attached to her wrist. He followed it back to Tony's arm.

Tony was underwater. Bubbles were coming out of his mouth. Wolf wrenched Tony out of the swamp and pulled the vines away from his face.

Tony gagged and spat out a huge mouthful of water. "Lights!" he shouted. "Lights all gone out!"

Wolf tore the vines away from Tony's eyes so that he could see again. He dragged Tony closer to Virginia. She was shaking.

"Oh, my God," Virginia said. "Hold me, hold me."

Wolf held her close. She was shivering so hard that he was quivering too. Tony was looking wild-eyed.

"I died," Tony said. "I died back there. They turned out all the lights."

Wolf didn't say anything. He managed to get them calmed, and helped them pull off the remaining vines. The vines had little suckers attached to the ends, which left scratches on Virginia's beautiful skin.

As they calmed, they seemed to realize that he was there. Virginia finally looked him in the face.

"Wolf," Virginia said, "how did you get here?"

He smiled at her. "I have been following you for a long time."

She smiled back. She had missed him, that much was clear. He was glad he had come.

He hadn't been able to stand the time alone.

Virginia was still a little shaky from her near-death experience. She had had a weird dream through it all, something about being in the palace, married to, of all people, her father.

It took her a while to shake that off. She certainly didn't tell her father or Wolf about it.

Wolf. She was so glad he was back. She had missed him more than she could say. And he had saved her life.

He stayed at her side now as though he wasn't going to let her go. She waded through the swamp beside him, just enjoying his company.

Ahead, she saw what looked like a mirror graveyard. Ancient mirrors and shards of mirrors protruded from the swamp. It was like the Dwarves' hall of mirrors, only polluted somehow. Polluted and dead and dark.

Most of the mirrors were black and covered in slime. As the three came up to them, they heard incoherent voices emanating from the mirrors. Some of the voices were harsh and rasping, others were sly and beckoning. Only a few were soft and seductive.

"Look!" her father said, pointing past the mirrors. "That's the Swamp Witch's house."

In the middle of the mirror graveyard, on a tiny island, was a wooden shack.

"She's in there," Wolf said.

Virginia squinted. He was right. There was a single window, and the light inside illuminated a terrifying shadowy figure huddled over what looked like a bubbling cauldron.

"What do we do now?" Tony whispered.

"Avoid making any noise," Wolf said. "We'll just sneak past her."

"Stay where you are, or I'll shove you in my pot!" a voice announced.

Suddenly the door flung open, and a hideous giant figure was silhouetted against the light inside.

"Cripes," Wolf said.

Virginia put a hand on his arm. She had even missed that little phrase.

Her father continued walking forward, and after a moment, dragged her with him.

"Tony?" the figure said.

Her father laughed. As Virginia got closer, she realized that they weren't looking at a woman at all, but at a goblin who was horribly scarred.

"This is Clay Face the Goblin," Tony said. "We did some hard time in prison together."

"Hard time?" Virginia asked. "You were only in there overnight."

Clay Face came forward and stared at them. He took off a bad black wig made of string and rope. He peered at Wolf for a moment, then grinned.

"Yeah," Clay Face said. "You were the Wolf in E block who ate all the—"

"Yes," Wolf said. "Nice to meet you, but we must be on our way."

Clay Face looked at Virginia and then winked at her father. "Nice girlfriend."

"She's not my girlfriend," her father said, sounding indignant. "She's my daughter."

"Even better," Clay Face said. Virginia shuddered. Better for whom? But Clay Face was beckoning them. "Come in."

They climbed out of the swamp onto the island. Wolf glanced over his shoulder as if he had heard something. Clay Face noted the chains linking Virginia and her father.

"You weren't in chains when you escaped from prison, were you?" Clay Face asked.

"Oh, no," Tony said. "This is an entirely unrelated incident."

They entered the shack and Virginia found herself wondering if that was wise. It was tiny and the wood was rotted, but the place was full of stuff. Bottles and jars of potions. There was a noxious odor that seemed built in to the place. Black candles gave off what passed for light, dripping like huge stalagmites, staining the floor.

Tony picked up a jar with a bat in it. "We thought you were the Swamp Witch."

"She's been dead for years," Clay Face said. "This is a great place to hang out when you're on the run."

Virginia didn't think so. She wasn't sure how long she could stand to be here. Wolf eased up closely behind her, his body against hers.

Clay Face sat at the table. Food was scattered on the surface, and there was a huge cleaver off to the side.

"Put your hands on the table," he said to Virginia and her father.

They reluctantly put their manacled hands on the table. Clay Face adjusted the chain, then studied it for a moment. "Troll tatt," he said.

Suddenly he grabbed the huge cleaver. Virginia screamed

and cringed, and so did her father. Clay Face hit the chains with all his strength, and they split apart.

He grinned at Virginia. Her heart was racing. For the second time that night, she had thought she was going to die.

"So," her father said, trying to sound calmer than he was. "Who was this Swamp Witch?"

"Who was she?" Clay Face asked, clearly surprised at the question. "I thought everyone knew. You know the story of Snow White?"

Virginia smiled. "From the horse's mouth, actually."

Clay Face stared at her, and Virginia's smile vanished.

"Well," he said, "the Swamp Witch was the wicked step-mother who tried to kill her. All that 'mirror, mirror on the wall' stuff, that was her. This was where she crawled to after they made her dance in the red-hot slippers. She spent the rest of her life plotting revenge, but she was too weak to carry it out. Then she found someone to do it for her."

Virginia had a horrible feeling he was talking about her mother.

"And who was that?" Virginia asked.

Clay Face grinned and pushed a black candle across the table. "The Swamp Witch is buried in the basement. Why don't you go in and ask her?"

He nodded toward a rotting trapdoor. Wolf stood up quickly.

"Well, it's been a fascinating history lesson," Wolf said.

She knew what he was doing, but she also knew that she couldn't turn back now. She took the candle.

"Virginia," Tony said, "what do you want to look at a corpse for? I thought we were in a hurry to get to the castle."

"What I seek is down there," Virginia said.

"What I seek?" Tony said. "What are you talking like that for? You're from New York."

Virginia walked to the trapdoor and pulled it back. The odor of still water and mold and rotted flesh rose up out of the depths.

"My mother came here," Virginia said. "I know it."

No one said anything. Virginia took her candle and walked down the creaky steps into the darkness.

There were more mirrors down here, stained and rusted and cracked. They were silent, though. On the rotted wooden floorboards was a dark painted circle, and in the middle, half submerged amidst rotting vegetation, was a black coffin.

As Virginia got closer, she realized the coffin was partially buried in the earth. There were inscriptions around the circle. It was like an evil copy of Snow White's tomb in the ice.

Only here Virginia wasn't looking at a beautiful old woman. She was staring at a rotted skeleton.

"Are you lost, my child?" the Evil Stepmother asked.

As Virginia stared down, she saw an awful vision. . . .

Suddenly Virginia was in Central Park—only it was a slightly different Central Park. It took her a moment to realize it was the park of twenty years ago. Cans with ring tops had been discarded, and there was an old-fashioned skateboard with metal roller-skate wheels tossed to the side of the path.

Her mother, Christine, staggered into view. Her mother was younger too, exactly as Virginia remembered her, down to the expensive sweater and the long fingernails. Her mother was crying, sobbing so hard that she could barely get her breath. She fell against a tree and slid down, staring at her hands as if they belonged to someone else.

"Are you lost?" a voice asked. Virginia recognized the voice. It was the one that had spoken to her a moment ago. The Evil Stepmother.

Christine looked around. She was alone. But then the outline of a door appeared before her. Virginia recognized the shape. It looked like the one she and her father had gone through from the park so long ago.

A gnarled hand appeared in that dark doorway, fingers encrusted with black jewels. The hand reached out. "Let me show you the way."

Christine stared at the hand in horror and fascination.

"Come with me," the Evil Stepmother said, *"and you will forget your pain forever."*

Virginia, even though she knew this had already happened, found herself wishing her mother would leave. All she had to do was leave the park and go back to the apartment, to the family that loved her.

Christine extended her hand and grasped the gnarled hand. Virginia felt the disappointment as if it had happened just now.

The hand pulled Christine through the mirror and into the wooden shack in the middle of the swamp. An ancient woman stood before her—the Evil Stepmother in life. She smiled when she saw Christine, and at that moment, Virginia knew her mother had lost.

"I am dying, but my work is unfinished," the old woman said. *"The House of Snow White survives. You will do my work for me, and I will give you all my power."*

Virginia snapped out of the dream. She was queasy and heartsick. Now she knew what had happened to her mother. It didn't make things easier. Somehow it made them harder. Her mother had had a choice, and she had chosen to come here, to this evil place.

Virginia looked down. The skeleton's hand was curled into a fist, clearly holding something.

With shaking fingers, Virginia peeled back the crumbling bones. As the hand opened, Virginia found what she had been looking for: the jeweled silver comb from her dream. The teeth of the comb still looked deadly.

Virginia tore a strip of fabric from her own sleeve and wrapped it around her hand before she picked up the poison comb. Then she put it in her pocket.

As she went back up the stairs, she heard the dry dusty voice call after her, "You are nothing. She will crush you."

Clay Face turned out to be a pretty good host. He gave them something to eat and removed the manacles. He wanted them to stay, but Wolf was the one who said that they couldn't. Virginia didn't argue. She knew they had to find Prince Wendell before things got too bad.

So Clay Face led the three of them to the slim veranda and pointed out the landmarks. "Straight ahead three hundred yards, then take a left by the rotting entrails, you're out. Ten, fifteen minutes at most."

What a relief. There was a way out of this place. They thanked him, and took off.

The first three hundred yards were difficult, but once they hit the rotting entrails—whose stench was indescribable—the ground got harder. Wolf stayed at Virginia's side. She took his hand as they left the swamp and headed into the woodland.

She glanced over at her father. He was a few yards behind, maybe being sensitive, giving them time to talk.

Maybe not. She had told him what she had seen in the basement, and he had looked very sad.

"Where did you go after you left the Kissing Town?" Virginia asked Wolf.

"I, uh, went off for a while to think about a few things, then picked up your trail a few days ago."

"But how?" Virginia asked. "We went through the mountain."

"Virginia," Wolf said, "I could follow your scent across time itself."

It was poetry. No one had ever spoken to her like that before, and no one probably would again. She looked at him. He was so handsome, so serious. And to think she had almost thrown all of this away.

"You seem . . . different," she said.

"We are both different," Wolf said.

She had to tell him how she felt. Wasn't that what Snow White said? She had to take control of her life. "I didn't mean to chase you away. It was just that everything was too much, happening too quickly. I do like you. I really like you."

"Oh," Wolf said.

They had stopped walking.

"And I never want to hurt you," Virginia said.

She touched his face. He leaned into her hand.

"I think I love you," she said.

Chapter Forty-Three

The Trolls had finally served their purpose. They brought Wendell to her.

The Queen watched as they dragged her nemesis, so dog-like now that his eyes no longer looked human, down a corridor in his own palace. He was muzzled, but he still snarled and snapped at them.

The Huntsman stood beside her. He was better, but still not at full health. The girl had been tougher than any of them imagined.

But the Queen would not think of that. Instead, she watched the Trolls pull Wendell forward.

They had two iron chains on his collar, but he was strong and determined. He would escape if they gave him any chance at all.

She would give him no chance.

"So long have I waited for you," the Queen said to Wendell. "So many dull prison days."

The Trolls dragged him near, despite his struggles.

She stuck her hands in her sleeves, her gesture of calm. "In the summer I could see the sunlight on my cell wall. I longed for the summer to see the sun, and yet each time it came I knew I had lost another year of my life to you."

She smiled. Prince Wendell was still now, glaring at her.

"When all of this is over," she said, "I will put you in a little box until you curl up and die of despair."

He growled at her through his muzzle.

She turned to the Huntsman. "Where was he caught?"

"About fifteen miles away, Your Majesty," the Huntsman said.

"So near?" That surprised her. What had he been doing so close by? "What about the others?"

"Oh, we killed them," Bluebell said.

She slapped him. "Liar. Idiot!"

"We are extremely stupid, Your Majesty." Blabberwort bowed her head, revealing that ridiculous orange pouf. Poodles wore poufs, not Trolls.

"But we have the dog," Burly said.

"You fool," the Queen said, "the dog is not the threat to me. The girl is the threat."

She shook her head, and knew it wasn't over yet. "The girl," she repeated. The Queen wouldn't win until the girl was dead.

They had just crested a hill in the woods. Through the trees, Virginia could see Prince Wendell's castle. It looked like a fairy tale castle, which, she supposed, it was.

Wolf came up beside her. "Journey's end."

She nodded. The castle was only about five miles away. It was shrouded in early morning mist and surrounded by acres of lakes and hunting land. How beautiful.

"We were following the mirror all over the place," Tony said. "Who'd have thought we'd end up here?"

"We were always meant to come here," Virginia said.

Her father gave her a startled look, but she didn't care. She was trusting her instincts for the first time in her life.

Her father opened her rucksack and took out the kettle. He started carrying it to a nearby stream. "Let's have a cup of tea before we do the final stretch. Does one of you want to get some firewood?"

"I'll go," Wolf said.

"I'll go with you," Virginia said.

She didn't really want Wolf to leave again. She hadn't been

able to take being separated from him before, but she was still having trouble admitting that.

It was dawn, beautiful and silent. The woods were lovely, but not as great as being with Wolf. He kept looking at her, and she couldn't stop looking at him. She could feel the electricity between them.

"There is something I would really like you to do for me," Wolf said, "and I think I deserve it, given my multiple savings of your life."

She smiled. "I know what you want to do, and the answer is yes."

"Oh," Wolf said, as if he hadn't expected her to say that.

They were standing inches away from each other, in the lovely morning mist.

"Oh, cripes," Wolf said. "I want you so much."

"I know," Virginia said. "I want you too."

"All right," Wolf said, "you run off into the woods and I will cover my eyes."

"I'm sorry?" Virginia frowned. What had he just said?

"Into the trees and I will cover my eyes and count to a hundred."

"Are you serious?"

"Oh, yes." He seemed very serious. This whole thing seemed to mean a lot to him. "I won't cheat. I promise I won't cheat."

"That's not the point," Virginia said.

"All right, maybe I will count a little quicker after fifty, but I promise you'll get a proper—"

"I'm not playing hide-and-seek," Virginia said.

He covered his eyes with his hands and started to count.

"No!" Virginia said. And then she wondered why she was protesting so much. He was a wolf, and everyone did things differently here. Besides, it sounded like fun.

She ran off. Behind her, she heard him counting.

"Eight, nine, twenty-one, twothreefour five nine, thirty-one, two, three, four, forty, one, two, three—Commiinnng!"

She ran as fast as she could, crashing through brambles, into bushes, hurrying, hurrying. But she could hear him behind her. Eventually, the sound of his footsteps faded, and she stopped to catch her breath.

There was no sign of him. She couldn't hear anything but her own breathing. Her heart was thundering in her chest. This was silly and stupid and exciting all at the same time. She listened—and became sensitive to everything. The birds were louder, the breeze through the trees, even the scent of the nearby pine tree seemed more intense.

And then she heard Wolf a long distance away. She smiled and ran again.

She ran until she thought she lost him. Then she found a good hiding spot behind a bush. She caught her breath again and thought about strategy. Should she let him catch her or not?

Suddenly he leapt out of the trees and knocked her over. They rolled through the undergrowth, pushing and shoving and kicking and hitting at each other, just like cubs at play. She grabbed him and was biting his ear and then they were kissing and pulling at each other's clothes, and she laughed as the play turned into something she recognized, something she had been longing for.

"Wolf," she murmured and lost herself to the sensation of loving him.

It took Virginia and Wolf a very long time to find wood. Tony had given up on the tea nearly an hour before and had searched the rucksack for some kind of snack. He missed Prince Wendell. He hadn't realized how much he relied on that dog.

Then Virginia came out of the woods. She had leaves in her hair and grass stains on her jeans. She was smiling, but he had never seen her look so happy and distracted at the same time.

"Where's the wood?" Tony asked.

"Yes," she said.

"For the fire?"

"Couldn't find any," Virginia said as she walked right past him.

"You couldn't find any wood in a wood?"

She didn't answer him, but she didn't have to. Wolf came out of the woods, looking just as stunned as Virginia.

"Hello, Tony," Wolf said.

"You haven't got any wood either, I suppose," Tony said.

He walked past Tony toward Virginia. "Yes, thank you."

Tony watched him, feeling utterly confused. Then he gasped. Wolf's tail was sticking out of his trousers, wagging jauntily back and forth.

It took some coaxing, but Tony finally got his breakfast. It almost felt as if he were eating alone, however, since Wolf and Virginia didn't really have much to say.

All during their meal, they heard the distant rumble of carriage wheels. When they had finally finished eating, they walked to the edge of the woods.

Before them was a cobblestone road. The castle was less than a mile away. Guards patrolled the battlements.

There was more rumbling, and Wolf made them go back into the trees. A wagon passed, carrying supplies. Not a minute later, an incredibly beautiful black coach clipped by.

"They are all going to the castle for Wendell's coronation," Wolf said.

"Why don't we just walk in there?" Tony asked.

"Because if I'm right," Wolf said, "this is no longer Prince Wendell's castle. It is controlled by the Queen. And his guards may now be her eyes. We can trust no one."

"Wolf, I have to tell you something," Virginia said. "The Queen is . . ."

"Is what?" Wolf asked.

"She is my mother," Virginia said.

"I have guessed this since the first moment I smelt you."

Tony didn't need to hear that. He glared at Wolf, but Wolf didn't seem to notice. Wolf was taking off his coat.

"We will wait until it is dark before we try to enter the castle," he said.

"What are we going to do all day?" Tony asked.

Wolf bunched up his coat into a little ball and lay back on it, and closed his eyes. "Sleep. We are exhausted, are we not?"

"Definitely." Virginia lay down and put her head on Wolf's chest.

"Have I missed something here?" Tony asked.

The Queen stood in front of the window, watching the sun go down. She was trying to get a sense of the girl and her companions, but couldn't. It frustrated her.

"Shall I signal the start of the Coronation Ball?" the Huntsman asked.

"They will come amongst the others," she said, "when they think they are safe."

Fireworks illuminated the sky. The castle was ablaze with lights, making it look even more like a fairy tale. The strains of a waltz floated on the night air.

Virginia walked beside Wolf and her father. They had joined the guests who were going to the palace by foot. Everyone was well dressed but them. Their clothes were mud-stained, and for the first time, Virginia was aware of the twigs in her hair.

Behind them, Virginia heard the rumble of carriage wheels. All of the guests left the road as a golden coach went by. She caught a fleeting glimpse of the girl inside.

"A princess," someone whispered.

More coaches passed. The road was going to be impossible to walk, so they walked beside it. Virginia almost thought they could get through until she saw the guards at the edge of the drawbridge, looking at invitations before allowing people to enter.

"What do we do now?" Virginia whispered.

Two guards noticed them and their filthy clothes. One of the guards pointed and went to talk to a man who seemed to be in charge.

Wolf grabbed her arm and led her under the drawbridge. Tony followed. He nodded toward a grill at the other side, then got into the water and started swimming.

Swim the moat? Didn't Wolf know what they threw in these moats? Some castles didn't even have plumbing.

Virginia sighed. She guessed it wouldn't be any worse than some of the other things she had done on this trip.

She got into the cold water. Her father followed, cursing under his breath. Thank heavens he had taught her to swim in city pools. They used to play a game, seeing how silently they could swim across a pool. It came into play now.

Wolf reached the sheer castle wall a moment or two before they did. He gripped the grill and pulled on it. As Virginia reached him, treading water, she realized he couldn't get it open.

"I was hoping it might be loose," Wolf said.

"This isn't going to work," her father said.

"It's a portcullis," Wolf said. "Perhaps we can swim under it. It's bound to lead into the castle somewhere."

"Somewhere?" Virginia asked.

She peered through the grill. Inside was a passage, but the water level reached the ceiling. It was too dark to see where it led.

"Forget it," her father said.

Wolf ignored him. "Follow me. If I don't come back within a minute, I will either have got through or got stuck."

"No!" Virginia said.

But he didn't listen to her. He dove under the water and disappeared. He could drown in there. How could she bear it if he drowned?

She peered through the grill, but saw nothing.

"There is no way I am diving underwater in the dark," her father said, "in the hope that I might surface *somewhere*."

He wasn't coming back. She had waited long enough. "He must have found the way."

"Why do you assume that?" Tony asked. "He's probably run out of—"

But she didn't hear the rest. She took a huge breath and dove underwater, into the darkness. For a moment, she felt like she was doing the stupidest thing in her life, and then she realized she had to keep going.

She felt her way along the slime-covered stones. She had never been in water this dark. She moved forward, using her legs to propel her, searching for any kind of light.

Once she was under the grate, she went up, remembering that the passage was full to the ceiling. She could touch the ceiling stones. If she hadn't been touching them, she would have bumped her head on an overhang. This had once been a real passage.

Her breath was getting thin. Her lungs were straining, begging her to take in air. She kept moving forward, knowing that she had to, and then she popped up, like a cork, from beneath a wave.

She took the deepest breath of her life, breathing hard, glad to be alive.

Wolf had already pulled himself onto a ledge. There were torches burning all around. They were in some kind of cellar.

He grinned when he saw her.

"Nobody around," Wolf said as he helped her out of the water.

"I thought I was going to die down there," she said. "It was pitch black."

The seconds passed. She found herself staring at the inky black surface of the water.

"Where's Dad?"

She scanned the surface for him, hoping that he had come, hoping that he wasn't in trouble.

"That passage was very thin at the top," Wolf said.

She clenched her right hand. He had to come through. He had to.

Finally she stood. She was going to go in after him. She was poised for her dive when her father broke through the surface. He gasped great lungfuls of air.

"I almost drowned," he managed.

"Oh, don't exaggerate," Wolf said, as he helped Tony out of the water. Wolf patted her father on the back and he spat out even more water. Virginia grimaced. She certainly wasn't going to tell him what she knew of moats.

It took a few minutes for him to get ready to travel, but he did. They squished their way forward. As they rounded a corner, Virginia realized they were in Wendell's wine cellar.

"See if you can find some towels," Tony said.

"Towels?" Virginia said. "We need weapons."

"Shhhh," Wolf said.

They found the exit from the cellars, then crept up the stairs past the kitchen. Virginia peered inside. No one noticed them. The servants were all frantically preparing food. She could smell roast beef and duck, and those were the scents she could identify. Her stomach rumbled. Swimming always made her hungry.

They made their way to the first floor reception area. As some of the guests were led through, Virginia saw their chance. She beckoned her father and Wolf to follow. They hurried by, passing behind a row of butlers. Through the glass doors, Virginia could see the guests assembling in the grand ballroom beyond.

Wolf led them up a flight of stairs toward the upper floors. Virginia's heart was pounding. They'd been lucky so far, but she had no idea how long it would take before someone discovered them.

The stairs ended in a beautiful corridor. It was decorated better than anything Virginia had seen in Manhattan.

"These are the Royal chambers, unless I'm very much mistaken," Wolf whispered, "and the Queen will sleep as near her Dog Imposter as possible. My deduction is that she will have put our Prince in the very next room.''

Wolf opened a door and looked around. It was small and not decorated at all. ''Maybe I'm wrong,'' he said.

But Virginia had the feeling she had gotten in that cell weeks ago. She stepped inside. ''No, this is her room.''

Her father pushed Wolf inside and closed the door behind them. Virginia went to one of the large walk-in closets and opened it. Inside were five mirrors, leaning against the wall like corpses.

''Look at those,'' Tony said.

The mirrors were covered in sheets. Virginia pulled a sheet off a mirror, and so did her father and Wolf until all the mirrors were uncovered.

Her father stood in front of the last mirror. ''This is it,'' he said. ''This is the other Traveling mirror.''

It certainly looked familiar. The black frame was the same as the other; it was the same size and had the same markings. Wolf came up behind Virginia as her father pressed the catch on the side of the frame.

The mirror crackled into life, and slowly the reflection formed a picture. First the Statue of Liberty, then Manhattan, and finally it settled on Central Park.

''Look,'' Tony said. ''It's Manhattan. We can go home. We've done it.''

Virginia stared at it. Wolf was watching her intently. She could go now, she knew, but it wouldn't be right. Snow White had said that Virginia had to follow her heart, and her heart told her she wasn't ready to leave yet.

''What? What is it?'' Tony asked her. ''Come on, let's not hang out here. Let's go.''

She shook her head. ''I can't go back yet.''

''What are you, crazy?'' Tony asked. ''We've found it. Wolf, tell her, let's go. Let's go.''

Wolf didn't move. He had a small frown on his face.

''I have to see her first,'' Virginia said.

"Virginia, she is not your mother," Tony said. "Whatever she is now, it's not Christine, not the woman we knew."

"We've been led here all along," Virginia said. "Don't you see? It was never the mirror. It was just a way to bring us here, to meet her."

Her father grabbed her arm as if he were going to drag her into the mirror. "We have to get home while we still can."

"No." Virginia dug in her heels, literally. "I have to see her."

"Your last request is granted."

They all turned. The Queen stood behind them. Beside her was the Huntsman.

Virginia stared at her mother for a long time. She was shorter than Virginia remembered, and there were some extra lines on her face, but she was just as beautiful as she had always been.

Virginia was so intent on the Queen that it took a moment to register the fact that Wolf was bowing to her.

"Did I do well, Your Majesty?" Wolf asked.

Virginia felt a shiver run through her.

The Queen nodded. "Excellent."

Wolf went deeper into the room, took a piece of candy, and threw it in the air, catching it with his mouth. Then he smiled a cold smile that Virginia didn't recognize.

"I thought it would be safest to stay with them to make sure they didn't spoil your plans," Wolf said.

He was serious. That was why he had been so evasive. He had helped *her!*

"What have you done?" Virginia backed away from him. "No, no, no, not you."

She loved him. He loved her. He couldn't have betrayed her. He said that wolves mated for life and she was the one.

"It's simple, Virginia," Wolf said. "I obey the Queen."

It felt as if someone had stabbed her in the heart.

Her father stepped toward the Queen. "Christine," he said, "what are you doing here? Don't you recognize us?"

The Queen looked at them as if they were mad. "I've never seen either of you before."

"Of course you have," Virginia said. This was easier to deal with than Wolf. "I'm your daughter, Virginia."

"Christine, it's Tony. Don't look through me. It's Tony. Me." Her father took a step toward the Queen, and the Huntsman pushed him away.

The Queen's voice became murderously quiet. "I said I don't know who you are."

"Mom, we came from New York. Where you used to live."

The Queen seemed to falter. She looked at Virginia with a genuine uncertainty in her eyes. Then the moment passed.

"This is just magic to distract me," she said.

"Majesty, we must prepare for the Coronation Ball," the Huntsman said.

"There is time enough," the Queen said. "Leave me with the girl."

She looked at Tony. "Take him down to the dungeon, then bring Wendell to me. Wolf, go to the kitchen now."

Wolf bowed again, and didn't meet Virginia's gaze. He left. Her heart left with him. Snow White was right. She couldn't wait to be rescued.

She had to rescue herself.

The Huntsman dragged her father from the room.

The Queen stared at Virginia for a moment, then went to another adjoining door, which led to a changing room. She made no attempt to stop Virginia from escaping through the mirror. She didn't even shut the mirror off.

Virginia wasn't sure what she should do. Should she escape and try to come back later to rescue her father? Or should she stay and see what she could do now?

"I have sensed you for a long time, through the mirrors," the Queen said, as she changed clothes. "But your image has always been denied me. Why is that, do you think? You don't look very powerful to me. Has someone been helping you? Some little dead heroine puffing you up as an adversary?"

Virginia reached into her pocket and carefully took out the poisoned comb.

"Would you like to dance tonight?" the Queen asked. "I could find you something to wear. A pretty girl like you shouldn't sit on the sidelines all her life."

The Queen came back into her line of sight. Virginia concealed the comb behind her back, clutching it like a weapon.

The Queen was dressed in a beautiful white dress. She held it out to her sides like a girl.

"Do you like it?" the Queen asked. "You can wear too much black."

She walked into the closet and admired herself in one of the mirrors.

"I am your daughter," Virginia said.

The Queen laughed. "I don't have a daughter."

"You traveled through a mirror, like me," Virginia said.

The Queen looked at her slyly. "What do you know about Traveling mirrors?"

"I know they are a way home," Virginia said. "For you as well. You don't belong here any more than I do."

"You lie very well." The Queen smiled. "We should get together."

She walked over to the Traveling mirror and put her hand on its frame.

"If this is where you came from, then why don't you just go home? Go on, I won't stop you."

Virginia looked at the mirror, then at the Queen, remembering that one moment of uncertainty. If she could get through that, she might be able to speak to her real mother and end this.

"You look through it, don't you?" Virginia asked. "At night, you look at home and wonder what it's like."

The Queen pushed the catch on the mirror's frame and shut the mirror down. "Are you sure you won't have an apple? You've been eyeing them since you came in."

Virginia hadn't even noticed the apples until now. They sat

on a table, and they were as beautiful and red as the ones grown by the Peeps. Suddenly she remembered how hungry she was.

"Have one if you're hungry," the Queen said.

Virginia reached for an apple, and then stopped herself. It hadn't been her will to take one. It had been the Queen's.

"What?" the Queen asked. "You think I'm trying to poison you? Really. You've been reading too many stories."

The Queen took an apple and bit into it. She offered Virginia the rest. Virginia shook her head.

"What have people been telling you?" the Queen asked. "I'm no worse than anyone else here."

"Then why does everyone fear you?"

"There is only black and white in this world. Nothing in between. And we are all cast in our roles. Just as you are."

"I don't believe in destiny," Virginia said.

The Queen smiled. "It certainly believes in you."

Chapter Forty-Four

"**Y**ou're my mother," Virginia said.

The room was darker than it had been before. It felt odd in here, in this closet, with the woman who had once been someone else.

What had the Evil Stepmother said? That she had given all of her powers to the Queen? Which meant that Virginia was fighting a magical battle, without having any magic of her own.

"Or maybe I just look like your mother," the Queen said. "Have you ever thought about that? That this is some cruel magic trick on you? Because I'm not your mother. Nor would I want to be, frankly, because you are little Miss Nothing to me."

"Why did you leave me?"

The Queen left the Traveling mirror and walked over to Virginia. She stopped only inches away. They were closer than they had been in years. The Queen's eyes were cold, colder than any Virginia had ever seen.

"You were unwanted," the Queen said. "That's plain to see."

Virginia frowned.

"Haven't you always thought that secretly? Honestly?" The Queen's voice was soft, hypnotic. "Come and compare yourself to me in my mirror. Mirrors cannot lie."

She led Virginia to another of her mirrors. Virginia stared at her own reflection. She could actually see the blending of her father's features and her mother's and how they formed something uniquely her. The Queen stood beside her. There was a family resemblance—on both sides.

"Do you think you are fairer than me?" the Queen asked. "Shall we ask the mirror? Look in the mirror."

The room was getting darker. Everything seemed to have slowed down.

"Mirror, mirror, on the wall . . ."

Virginia swayed, struggling not to faint. Things were getting darker and slower, and the room started to swirl. "What are you doing to me?"

The mirror showed her standing right beside the smiling Queen, but something wasn't right.

"Who is the fairest . . ."

Virginia stared at the mirror, struggling with all her might to remain conscious. "What are you doing?"

She forced herself to look away from the mirror. As she turned her head sideways, she saw herself and the Queen reflected in another mirror.

Instead of the Queen standing passively beside her, the Queen had her hands around Virginia's neck, choking her. The moment had a horrible feeling of familiarity to it.

Virginia pulled herself away, and the Queen stepped back. She was obviously shocked that Virginia had saved herself. Virginia put a hand to her neck. Now she could feel the pain. Her lungs strained for air, more than they had from the swim.

The room had gotten lighter.

"You intrigue me," the Queen said. "No one has ever resisted me for so long. Why have you come here?"

"To find you," Virginia said. "To talk to you, to make you realize who—"

"You have come to kill me."

"No, of course not," Virginia said.

"But I'm going to kill you first. This moment, this instant." The Queen moved toward her.

Virginia held up a hand. "Stay back or—"

"Or what?"

Virginia opened her hand. The comb was gone.

"Were you looking for this?" The Queen laughed and produced the comb. It looked wicked in her hands, like a sparkling, razor-sharp set of teeth. "How long do you think you have been talking to me? Guess."

"Five minutes," Virginia said.

"Over an hour," the Queen said. "I know everything. Your pathetic plans. You think Snow White will protect you. She's dead. That's why she's sending a little girl after me with old magic."

The Queen examined the comb, careful to keep her hands away from the teeth.

"Such beautiful jewels," she said. "The most awful things often appear in beautiful form. Is it poisoned?"

"No."

The Queen took the comb and ran it through her hair. Virginia held her breath.

"You little liar," the Queen said. "If this comb were to break my skin it would kill me instantly. It's very beautiful, though."

She took her hair and twisted it up, using the comb to hold it in place. Then she examined herself in the mirror.

Virginia remembered what her father had said, about the way her mother was obsessed with her own beauty. Indeed, the Queen's examination of herself looked familiar.

"In your whole life," Virginia said, "did you ever once love me?"

The Queen looked away from the mirror. Her gaze met Virginia's and, like before, seemed to falter.

Then the door opened. The moment was broken.

"Milady," the Huntsman said as he entered, "we have a problem with the Prince."

The Queen blinked in obvious confusion, and then the mask fell over her face once again. Her expression grew hard. "Take the girl downstairs and lock her up. I will finish with her afterwards."

"After what?" Virginia asked. "What are you going to do to everybody?"

"No more than you would do to me," the Queen said.

The guests inside the ballroom reflected all of the Nine Kingdoms. Elves and Dwarves and other notables danced with each other. A man with hedgehog quills protruding from his tuxedo smiled at three identical dancing girls. In one corner, clearly drunk and obviously an embarrassment to the other guests, was the Naked Emperor's Great-Grandson. Servants run after him everywhere, covering him as best they could with giant ostrich feathers.

A table ran the length of the room, ready to seat all the guests except the royal ones, who had their own table in the front.

Glittering chandeliers cast light on all the beautifully dressed people. The music was stunning, the room even more so. All the guests seemed to be enjoying themselves, but they were also watchful for the guest of honor, Prince Wendell.

Lord Rupert, who had been in charge of the coronation, clapped his hands for attention. "Your Royal Highnesses, Lords and Ladies, ladies and gentlemen, may I present a vision of loveliness, the Dancing Queen, the Slipper Supreme, it's midnight madness, it's Queen Cinderella."

The people in the room gasped. No one had seen Cinderella in a long time.

They turned toward the entrance as two-hundred-year-old Cinderella entered the ballroom. She was still beautiful, but no longer young. Servants rushed to her side to help her down the steps, but she waved them away.

She walked forward, sashaying her hips from side to side. Some of the men gave her wolf whistles, and she smiled. Her glass slippers made small clinking sounds on the ballroom floor.

Cinderella took her place at the head of the table for royal guests. The Kings and Queens stood in respect and raised their glasses to her.

She turned and gave a beauty-queen wave to the crowd. Then, as she sat down, her exhaustion showed. She didn't get out much anymore, and this had been quite a strain.

Finally she looked up. "Where is Wendell?" she asked.

Each cell was worse than the others. Tony was beginning to hate prison. This cell was dark and dank and had no windows at all.

It also had mice.

He leaned against a wall and shook his head. He had never suspected Wolf would betray them. He had thought that Wolf loved his daughter. It was clear that Virginia loved Wolf.

And now, poor Virginia was alone with her mother. Tony had no idea how to help her.

Then he heard a clanging from the end of the hall. A moment later, the Huntsman appeared, dragging Virginia. The Huntsman unlocked the cell, and before Tony could rush him, threw Virginia inside.

Without a word, the Huntsman locked the door and went away.

Virginia sprawled on the floor beside Tony. He crouched beside her. "Are you okay?"

She shook her head. And then she started to cry. "Oh, Dad, what's happened to her?"

He put his arm around Virginia's shoulder. He didn't know how to comfort her. The truth was not good, but she had to know.

He pulled Virginia close and spoke softly. "In the months before she left, she got worse and worse. She was crazy. I never told anybody what happened the night she left. You didn't remember anything, so I never wanted to tell you."

It had been his own personal deep, dark secret, the thing he was both ashamed of and worried about. He had caused it, by forcing Christine to have children. He had almost lost everything he cared about.

"I came home that night and she was trying . . ."

He shook his head. After being repressed so long, the words wouldn't come out.

"She didn't know what she was doing," Tony said. "She was sick in the head. She was on all kinds of tranquilizers and . . ."

"What happened?" Virginia asked.

"I came home early and she was giving you a bath," Tony said. "The bathroom was full of steam. She looked distracted, distant. Her eyes had the craziest look. I didn't see you for a moment, and I came up to her to find out where you were."

He paused. His heart was pounding as if he had been running.

"Then I saw you under the water. Her hands were on your throat. She was trying to . . ."

He couldn't finish the sentence.

"What do you mean?" Virginia was shaking.

He looked at her, and he could see when the realization hit her that her mother—Christine, not the Queen—had been trying to kill her.

"I don't believe that," Virginia said. "That's not true."

"If I had come home a minute later, you would have been dead. And that—"

"No!" Virginia shouted. "That's not true!"

He finished anyway. "That was the night she left and never came back."

The Queen led the Dog Prince out of his room. At least he looked the part of the Prince. He was wearing a lovely white uniform, covered in medals. His hair was combed, and she had gotten him to stand up straight. Now if she could only get him to shut up.

"Stop muttering," the Queen said.

"I'm trying to remember my speech."

She held him tightly, trying to think how to control him. So many things could go wrong in the ballroom. She wouldn't be able to watch him all the time.

Finally, she leaned over, kissed him on the cheek, and whispered, ''Do this properly tonight and you can have any bitch in town.''

At that moment, the Huntsman rounded the corner. He was leading the real Prince Wendell by a metal chain. Wendell was muzzled. When he saw the Dog Prince, he froze.

''You!'' the Dog Prince said.

Wendell strained at his leash and tried to jump forward.

''Don't let them touch!'' the Queen ordered. ''Keep them apart!'' If they touched, it would ruin everything.

The Huntsman wrenched Wendell's chain and pulled him back.

''The people in the hall are beginning to become suspicious, milady,'' the Huntsman said.

''Let them wait. Take him to my hiding place. I will join you shortly. I have one last thing to do.''

She swept past him, careful to keep the Dog Prince and Wendell apart. Then she went down the back stairs. The Dog Prince followed closely, looking over his shoulder for Wendell.

The Huntsman had taken Wendell away.

The Queen yanked the Dog Prince after her. They hurried to the kitchen.

The kitchen was piled high with rotting plants, rancid roots, acid berries, and sulphurous powders. Every noxious item she had thought of filled the room, from classics like arsenic to rarities like a Dwarf poison.

Wolf held down a white slug while the cook sliced it. Then the cook put the pieces, still squirming, into a large, bubbling vat.

After a moment, Wolf noticed the Queen.

He smiled. ''All present and correct.''

She turned to the cook.

He bowed his head nervously. ''As you commanded, Majesty, the most powerful poison ever created.''

She walked over to the vat and sniffed it. It had a sickly sweet odor with a horribly sour afterscent.

"And it smells divine," she said. "Have you tasted it?"

The cook was shaking. "Of course not, Your Majesty."

"Then how do you know it is the most powerful poison ever made?"

The cook looked at her in terror.

"Well?" she asked.

With shaking hands, the cook took a teaspoon and dipped it in the pot. He put the tiniest portion, barely a touch, at the end of the spoon. He was trembling badly as he raised the spoon from the vat.

"Try it!" she commanded, using her magical Power voice.

He lowered his tongue to the mixture and took the smallest sip possible. Then his eyes widened. He took a step backwards and fell to the floor, choking. He twitched twice, and then was still.

The Queen smiled. Perfect. She needed a strong poison. If she had anything less, one of the imbeciles might survive.

"I think it's ready," the Queen said. "Wolf, you may do the honors."

He wheeled a silver trolley forward. The trolley had a hundred silver goblets on it.

"My wolf," the Queen said, watching. "My crafty little wolf. You had me worried for a while."

"When you freed me from prison, I agreed to serve you," he said. "A wolf keeps his bargain."

"After tonight, when I rule the Nine Kingdoms, wolves will be very important. I'll make them my secret police, and make you chief."

"Definitely." He had such an evil smile. "Huff-puff, it won't be the wolves who are run out of town this time. The farmers don't know what's going to bite them."

She grabbed the Dog Prince and left the room. She still had a hundred things to do. She led the Dog Prince to his place at the top of the stairs, reminding him to wait until the fanfare played and he was announced. She had practiced this with him a hundred times, giving him a bone after each one. She knew he would be able to do it this time.

Then she joined the real Wendell, who was bound and muzzled, behind the golden curtains at the other end of the hall. From there, she could see everything.

The guests were milling about, and the gossip had started. Worry, worry, that Wendell had not yet arrived. The Queen smiled. Oh, they wouldn't care about Wendell much longer.

Right about the time she expected, a fanfare silenced the crowd. The Lord Chancellor stepped forward.

"Pray silence for the future King of the Fourth Kingdom, Grandson of Snow White, Your Royal Highnesses, Lords and Ladies, all and sundry, I present to you the man of the hour, the hero of the day, he's Royal Personality of the Year, he's simply the best, Prince Wendell Winston Walter White!"

All eyes turned toward the entrance at the top of the stairs. No one appeared.

The Queen felt a familiar frustration. She had picked a dog because dogs were supposed to be obedient. Was she going to have to go after him?

Just as she was about to give up, she saw him at the top of the stairs. He was wearing that coat sent over from Little Lamb Village. She had opposed that. It smelled of wet wool. Apparently, he had defied her on this one little thing.

He stared down at everyone, and she worried that he had forgotten his lines. Then he grinned and leapt onto the banister. She wanted to close her eyes at this debacle, but couldn't. He slid all the way down and jumped off at the bottom.

All of the guests applauded. Cinderella stood up, a frown on her ancient face.

The Dog Prince strode across the room and bowed low, with a ridiculous flourish. "A right royal welcome to my Coronation!"

The applause continued as he sat on his throne, flanked on either side by Kings and Queens. So far so good, the Queen thought. Now he only had a little more to get through.

He waved his hand at the musicians, who started playing a waltz. The room was full of dancing couples.

Cinderella leaned toward the Dog Prince. The Queen had to strain to hear what was said.

"We are pleased to see you fit and well," Cinderella said. "There were rumors that some trouble had befallen you."

"Oh, no," the Dog Prince said. "I just went for a long walkies around my kingdom, as one does."

Cinderella's frown grew. The Dog Prince turned away from her and smiled at the young Princess beside him. She smiled back until she realized he was sniffing her.

The Queen longed to slap him on his pert little nose, but that would have to wait.

Her plan was nearly finished.

Virginia could hear the music high above them. A lovely waltz, the shuffle of feet. They were going to make the Dog Prince King tonight, which would give her mother too much power.

"There has to be a way to stop this," Virginia said. "I can't believe we've come all this way only to fail now."

"Look what I found while you were out," her father said. "It'll really blow your mind."

He pointed to the wall. Another prisoner with too much time on his hands had carved his name in stone.

WILHELM GRIMM, 1805

"Grimm," Virginia said. "Do you think that's—?"

"Of course it is," Tony said.

"What does it say underneath?" Virginia asked.

"It's written in German," Tony said. "I've no idea. *'Wenn Sie fliehen wollen, müssen Sie den Hebel drehen.'* "

"I can speak German," a little voice said from behind them.

"So can I," another voice said. "Cheese is *Käse.*"

Virginia looked down. Two mice had crawled into their cell through a small mousehole.

"Oh, great," Tony said. "German-speaking mice."

"What does this mean?" she asked, pointing at the inscription.

"If you to escape wish to, must you the lever turn," one mouse said.

They didn't speak German very well.

"Escape?" her father said.

"The lever?" Virginia asked.

She examined the cell. There were no levers. Then she saw the iron rings screwed into the walls to suspend prisoners from. Her father reached for one at the same time she saw them. He twisted it, but nothing happened.

"Try the other one," her father said.

Virginia grabbed the other iron ring and twisted it to the left. Nothing happened either.

"Turn it the other way," her father said.

As she twisted it to the right, a tiny secret door opened in the cell, no bigger than a garbage can lid. The stone bricks appeared to be on concealed hinges. They stopped finally, and dust poured out.

"You owe us a big piece of *Käse*," the mouse said.

For a few moments, Virginia stared at the hole. It led to a long passageway. Then she pushed her father forward violently.

"Hurry. Hurry," she said. "We still may have time."

They ducked into the tunnel and crawled toward freedom.

Chapter Forty-Five

How many balls had she attended? Cinderella had lost count at a hundred. Of course, she always remembered the first. It had been the best. From that point on, the rest had been predictable. Occasionally, something would liven things up, but that was rare.

She had a feeling, though, that this would be one of those rare occasions.

The music stopped and the Lord Chancellor, fatuous as Lord Chancellors always were, banged a ceremonial stave on the floor.

Cinderella suppressed a sigh. If she couldn't remember how many balls she'd been to, she certainly couldn't remember how many speeches she'd heard.

That part was probably a blessing.

"Until his twenty-first birthday," the Lord Chancellor said, "the throne has lain in trust for him. But before the Prince becomes King, he must first show us he has learnt the three values of courage, wisdom, and humility."

The Lord Chancellor looked up. Cinderella followed his gaze. For a moment she thought she saw a Huntsman, but that wasn't possible. There was no Huntsman in her story and never would be.

Still, the Lord Chancellor seemed nervous. Perhaps he thought that good Prince Wendell would fail his tests. *That* would certainly make things interesting.

Cinderella smiled slightly.

The Lord Chancellor continued. "Let the first challenger step forward."

Leaf Fall, the Elf Queen, rose and approached the Prince. Leaf Fall was a delicate Elf. Cinderella always made certain she stayed as far away from the Elves as possible, especially now that she was over two hundred. Elves always looked like adolescent girls, and they had that pearlescent skin. The comparison simply wasn't pretty.

"It is a very great responsibility that you take upon your young shoulders today," Leaf Fall said, "and I wonder if you are brave enough to join us?"

Cinderella raised a single eyebrow. Who would have expected such a question from an Elf?

The Lord Chancellor banged his stave three times. "His bravery is questioned."

The guests fell into the ritual. "Tell us the tale!" they shouted. "Once upon a time. Once upon a time."

The Prince seemed quite odd tonight. He put his face in his hands in mock embarrassment. Then he stood up. The audience oohed and aaahed. Cinderella suppressed a sigh. If she'd been to too many balls and heard too many speeches, she knew that she'd heard even more stories.

She braced herself for more.

"My tale is long and fluffy," Prince said, forgoing the traditional once-upon-a-time opening. "The Troll King threatened this fair kingdom. I challenged him to a fight, man to mutt, and he was huge and horrible. He drew his sword, and both of us fought, and he forced me back against a tree, and just as he was about to run me through, I wrapped my tail around his sword arm, and then I dropped to all fours. I was growling and snarling, and he lunged at me and then I clawed at him and sank my teeth in him and ripped his throat out."

Cinderella sat up. That was a surprise. She'd never heard a story told in that way.

The story was greeted with silence, and then someone started to applaud. Applause broke out all over the ballroom.

As everyone cheered, Leaf Fall said, "He has passed the first test. Wendell is King of Courage."

The applause grew and the crowd chanted that the Prince was Brave Wendell, Brave Wendell.

The dancing resumed and the Prince turned his attention back to that pathetically young Princess he'd been hounding.

She moved toward Cinderella, probably hoping for protection, the naïve thing. As she did, Cinderella overheard the Prince say to the girl, "Would you be awfully upset if I sniffed your bottom?"

Cinderella raised both eyebrows this time. Young people. What would they think of next?

The tunnel was impossibly narrow. Virginia's shoulders were scraping the sides. Her father was having even more trouble, but at least he was trying to be cheerful about it.

"I'm getting a lot of experience escaping from prisons," Tony said.

She did have to get him to move faster, though. "Come on," she said. "It gets wider as you go along."

"No, it doesn't," one of the talking mice said from behind them.

She shushed him. She wasn't sure how long her back would take being in this position. And she was scraping her knees.

Then her father reached the end of the tunnel. It opened into a stone passage. She stood gratefully. Her father had his hand on his back but, to her surprise, he didn't complain. Instead he went to the wooden door at the end of the tunnel and pulled it open.

She followed him through. They were in some sort of weapons store. Rusting weapons hung on the walls in front of them. Virginia surveyed them and finally chose an axe.

"Take a weapon," Virginia said to her father.

"Why?" he asked. "We don't know how to fight. Put it down."

She gave him a withering look and spoke very slowly. "Take. A. Weapon. Dad."

She had never spoken to him like that before. He picked a sword off the wall and tried to heft it.

The weight of the sword nearly pulled him over.

The Lord Chancellor's stave poundings were giving Cinderella a headache. She put a ringed hand to her forehead and pretended this whole event was already over.

"It is time for the Second Challenge," the Lord Chancellor said. "Queen Riding Hood III , ruler of the Second Kingdom."

Cinderella's eyes narrowed. Queen Riding Hood indeed. Queen Riding Hood herself had been a trial. She always thought she was so important. All she had done was save her grandmother from being eaten by a wolf. It wasn't quite the same as all the hardships Cinderella had endured.

Queen Riding Hood's granddaughter didn't even have a real name. She was a lovely young girl, but she wasn't of the same mettle as her grandmother.

Queen Riding Hood III stood near the Prince. She was wearing the traditional ridiculous red-hooded cloak. At least this one was new and lined with real fur.

"What wisdom have you learnt in your recent journey through your kingdom?" Queen Riding Hood asked.

"That's a tricky one," the Prince said. "I have walked every road, I have sniffed every hedgerow, I have roamed the land and found bones."

Bones? Interesting. Cinderella leaned back in her chair. She longed to pull off her glass slippers, but if she did that, she wouldn't be able to squeeze back into them.

"I found this huge pile of a hundred fresh, juicy bones," the Prince said, "but they were so big, I could only carry one back at a time, and I knew by the time I came back they would have been found, so I took one and I buried the other ninety-nine."

That made no sense. Cinderella watched as the sycophants

around her tried to figure out a reaction. Silence at first, and then mumblings of "brilliant," "cunning," "sound military thinking." For heaven's sake. He might have literally meant bones.

But silly little Riding Hood didn't think so. She said, "Build up our military reserves for times of war. Wise indeed."

The Lord Chancellor pounded again. "He has passed the second test."

Cinderella pressed a hand against her forehead as everyone around her started chanting, "Wise Wendell. Wise Wendell."

She did not join in the chant.

Wolf heard the page announce that it was now midnight. Time for the Cinderella waltz. He waited, as he was instructed, for the sound of ladies' shoes hitting the floor. Then he pushed his cart closer to the kitchen door and watched the young men as they gathered a single shoe and went to find its owner, who would then be their partner for the dance.

How stupid were they? If Wolf had been dancing, he would have noticed what shoes his beloved had been wearing before the ritual throwing of the single shoe. But that would take too much planning for these people.

Men knelt in front of women and tried to slip shoes on their feet. It didn't take as long as Wolf had anticipated. Within a few moments, the music had started and most people were on the floor, dancing.

He pushed the cart forward and handed goblets to the non-dancers. It would take most of the waltz for him to pass out all of the goblets, and when it was done, the dancers would take theirs.

Everyone needed a drink for the royal toast.

Tony was getting used to the sword. It was heavy, but he could handle it. Virginia had been right. He felt better with a weapon in his hands.

They had emerged from the weapons store into a thin stone

tower with a spiral staircase that seemed to go on forever. High above, he could hear a waltz. The music was much louder than before.

They had been climbing for a long time when they reached a passageway that went off in one direction, while the stairs kept going up.

"Which way?" Virginia asked.

"Here," Tony said, pointing to the passageway.

"No, we can't be high enough yet. We have to keep on climbing." She raced up the stairs.

He stood in front of the passageway. He didn't have half of her energy. "Why did you ask me in the first place if you weren't going to listen to me?"

She didn't hear him, of course. She kept going without him. He had to trudge to catch her. By the time he reached the top, he was breathing hard.

The music was very loud. He was beginning to realize that he hated waltzes.

"I counted the levels," Virginia said. "This must be the ballroom level."

Tony turned the handle gently and pushed against the door. It opened a few inches but he couldn't push any harder. The door slammed closed.

"It's not locked, but there's something heavy lying against it."

"Come on, Dad. We're running out of time. Push."

He pushed as hard as he could. Virginia added her weight to his, and together they forced the door open.

Inside were the three Trolls.

"Oh, shit!" Tony said and slammed the door shut.

"Skin them! Skin them alive!" the Trolls shouted through the door.

Tony jammed his sword through the handle and across the door frame, wedging the door so that it couldn't be opened from the inside.

The Trolls started to rattle it. "Smash it open!"

Tony grabbed Virginia and turned her around. "Back the way we came. Quick," Tony said. "Take the other route."

They raced down the stairs to the passage. Virginia disappeared into it. Tony followed. By the time he caught up to her, she was already trying another door.

"It's locked." She stood back and swung at it with her axe. Tony made sure he was out of the way.

After a moment, he realized that the door was extremely thick. "This is going to take too long," he said. "I'll go back to the stairs. It was narrow there. Only one of those Trolls can get through at a time."

"Don't, Dad," Virginia said. "You'll get killed."

He would, wouldn't he? He stared at her for a moment. Then he smiled. It was all right. This wasn't about him anymore.

"It's all right," he said. "It's your destiny."

"I'm not leaving you."

"Go," Tony said. "You have to save everybody. It doesn't matter about me."

He ran back toward the stairs, shouting, "Don't wait for me! Go ahead. I'll stay and keep them back."

As he passed through the corridor, he grabbed a new sword and shield. For the first time in his life, he wasn't afraid, even though he was going to face the Trolls alone.

He crept back up the stairs. He was halfway up when he heard the door he had jammed finally give way. The Trolls raced down the stairs toward him.

Tony gripped his sword, raised his shield, and suddenly the Trolls were upon him.

"Victory to the Troll nation," Burly shouted as he lunged at Tony with an axe.

Tony met the lunge with his sword. He fought like a madman, keeping them pinned against the narrow stairway. He had to buy Virginia some time. That was his only goal here.

The Trolls kept hacking at him. Sparks flew off their axes as the blades hit the wall. Somehow Tony found an opening and stabbed Burly.

Burly fell back, but Blabberwort took his place.

She was fresh in the fight and she moved quicker than her brother. She brought an axe down into Tony's arm.

The pain was sudden and intense. He screamed.

"We have him," Blabberwort shouted. "He's weakened."

They pressed forward, hacking at Tony's shield and forcing him back.

Virginia heard her father scream. She glanced over her shoulder and hesitated for a moment, wondering if she should go help him. Then she realized she couldn't. He was right. Everyone else was relying on her.

She brought her axe down hard one more time and created a hole in the door big enough to force her hand through. She unlocked the door from the other side, then pushed it open and ran through.

And then someone brought in the world's ugliest gold crown. They really should have retired it long ago. Cinderella watched as some page carried it toward the Prince.

She sighed. The crown was quite inappropriate—gaudy and too big—but somehow she couldn't quite imagine it on this Prince's head.

"If none question his appointment," the Lord Chancellor was saying, "then I do solemnly—"

"Wait!" Cinderella got to her feet. Oh, but those glass slippers were getting tight. "I question him."

The ballroom grew silent, and in the silence, she thought she heard the Prince bark.

Bark?

He had a hand to his mouth as if he had coughed. "Do you?" he said.

She peered at him. "Are you really who you say you are?"

He looked very nervous. "I am . . . I am . . ."

She frowned. "Are you really Prince Wendell White, grandson of Snow White and the man who would be King?"

He loosened his collar, looking lost. He glanced at the curtains and got a panicked expression on his face. Then he closed his eyes and said, "No! No, I am an imposter!"

Everyone gasped. There were cries throughout the hall. Cinderella waited. It was clear that he wasn't done.

"I am not a Prince," he said. "I am ordinary. I will never be great like Snow White. Some are born to lead, but I am a pack animal. I am not a leader, I am a retriever. I wish to tear off these royal clothes and run in the fields. I do not want the job. I will not take the job. I am not worthy."

There was absolute silence in the hall. Cinderella studied him for a long time. If only she had heard that speech from Riding Hood III or any of the other grandchildren of the great monarchs. They all thought they were their grandparents' betters, and of course they would never measure up.

She nodded slowly, still not quite sure why she had felt so unsettled. "He has passed the third test. He has shown humility."

Someone applauded, and then the ridiculous ritual continued as the guests shouted, "Such candor. Such honesty."

Of course, the Lord Chancellor picked that moment to pound his stupid stave.

"He has passed the three tests," the Chancellor said. "Now let him be crowned."

Tony was fighting a desperate rearguard action, hacking and swinging with his sword. The two remaining Trolls had forced him into the passage, but he wasn't going to let them get anywhere near Virginia.

Somehow he was managing to hold Blabberwort off with his shield and Bluebell off with his sword. His energy was flagging. But then he remembered how much Virginia was relying on him.

He used all his energy to renew the fight.

"It's time to kick Troll butt!" he shouted.

He waved his sword wildly, forcing them back. A blow

from Blabberwort sent him reeling, but he rallied and stabbed her in the arm with his sword.

Virginia had been confused by the sound. The passageway had opened *above* the ballroom, not into it. She was in a gallery about thirty feet above the floor. The glass ceiling, far above her, had made the music echo so that she had thought the ballroom was higher.

She ran toward the stairs that led down into the ballroom proper when a hand clamped around her mouth.

"You only get to watch," the Huntsman said.

He pulled her back against him. She struggled, but he held her tightly.

Down below, the crowd was cheering the Dog Prince as if he were Wendell.

One of the Lords pounded a staff against the floor. "Arise, King Wendell."

The Dog Prince was holding a goblet and grinning widely. Wolf stood before him. Virginia stopped struggling and watched as Wolf poured the last of the punch into the Dog Prince's goblet.

"Time for the toast, Your Majesty," Wolf said.

The Dog Prince looked behind him. Virginia followed the look. Gold curtains to the back of the room were parted slightly, and through them, she could see the Queen, holding the real Prince Wendell and smiling.

"Oh, yes," the Dog Prince said.

He stood up very slowly.

"The Royal Toast!" someone shouted.

The Dog Prince lifted his goblet. So did everyone in the room except Wolf, who had a horrible expression on his face.

Then Virginia knew. It was what Snow White had said. The Queen would poison them all. The Huntsman tightened his hold on Virginia's mouth as if he knew that she was going to scream a warning.

"To everlasting peace," the Dog Prince said, "and all the bones we can gnaw."

"To everlasting peace," everyone repeated, "and all the bones we can gnaw."

Virginia struggled really hard as the Dog Prince drained his goblet. She couldn't free herself. Everyone else in the room did the same, swallowing poison as if it were wine.

The Dog Prince sat down and grinned. "I did really well!"

An ancient woman wearing glass slippers fell across a table. People gasped. As the ladies in waiting rushed to help her, they collapsed as well. Then a beautifully dressed Elf fell backwards off her chair.

The Dog Prince tried to stand, but he collapsed too. Guests started screaming as more and more people slumped over their tables.

"Poison!" shouted a woman in a red hood. "We've been—"

She collapsed before she could finish. The remaining guests were panicking, running for the door, and falling. Those most hardy tried to climb over the others, but they fell too.

Wolf watched it all, his expression impassive. He had committed mass murder for the Queen, and it didn't seem to bother him.

The Huntsman held Virginia tightly, but she had lost the urge to struggle. She couldn't believe what she was seeing.

Only Wolf remained standing in the entire ballroom. Everyone else was dead.

Bluebell was the only Troll still fighting. Tony was bleeding from four different wounds, and he was older and weaker than the damn Troll. He didn't know how much he had left in him.

Axe and sword clashed violently time and time again. Finally the axe cut Tony's sword in half.

Bluebell laughed in triumph and raised his axe.

But Tony was taller than this little Troll and he still had a weapon. His shield. He brought it down hard on Bluebell's head. Bluebell toppled over backwards, completely unconscious.

Tony collapsed against the wall. He had never been so exhausted in his life. But he couldn't stop now.

"Come on, Tony," he said to himself.

He tripped, fell to the floor, and forced himself up.

The Huntsman dragged Virginia down the stairs. She was getting over her shock, and she was beginning to get angry. She had looked into the face of evil and realized that it belonged to her mother.

The Queen had stepped out from behind her curtain. She was dragging the real Wendell. Wolf still stood by his beverage cart. He was watching everything as if it weren't real to him.

The Queen saw Virginia and smiled.

"You certainly are persistent," the Queen said. She stopped less than a foot in front of Virginia.

Virginia raised her chin. The Huntsman had let go of her mouth, now that there was no one to warn. "Are you going to kill me as well?"

"I was going to let you go," the Queen said. "I don't know why."

"You know why," Virginia said.

"Go," the Queen said. "Get out while you can."

The Huntsman let her go. No one held her anymore. She could leave if she wanted to.

"No!" Virginia said.

"You were nothing but an accident. You should have been killed at birth."

Virginia slapped her across the face as hard as she could. There was twenty years of anger behind that blow. The Queen staggered backwards.

"How dare you talk to me like that," Virginia said. "How dare you."

The Queen rose slowly, hand to her mouth. She said to the Huntsman, "Kill her now. Now, or I'll do it myself."

"Yes, milady," the Huntsman said.

He raised his crossbow at Virginia. He was about to fire when Wolf tackled the Huntsman with crunching force that sent them both to the ground.

The crossbow bolt shot straight into the air and smashed through the ballroom's glass ceiling. The Huntsman wrestled the crossbow from Wolf and smashed him across the face, forcing him backwards.

Virginia screamed his name. He had saved her again.

The Huntsman pulled out his jagged knife, but there was a crunch from above. The crossbow bolt had come back down through the glass ceiling, and as Virginia watched, the bolt fell with deadly accuracy.

It punched straight into the Huntsman's heart. Wolf gasped as the Huntsman fell on him. The bolt pinned both of them to the floor.

"Cripes," Wolf said.

He struggled but couldn't seem to get free.

The Queen looked at the dead Huntsman in horror, then turned on Virginia. She sank her nails into Virginia's neck and started to choke her.

Virginia put her hands up, but couldn't pull the Queen off her. The Queen was exceptionally strong.

Virginia couldn't get her breath.

The Queen forced her fingers into Virginia's throat, and the pain was enormous.

Virginia had to fight to keep from blacking out.

Her vision was getting dark. She probably hadn't recovered from the last time.

Wolf was still pinned to the floor, unable to free himself.

She was going to have to do this herself, but she didn't know how.

She tried pushing the Queen away, tried hitting her, but nothing worked.

Then, as spots danced in front of her eyes, she saw the comb. She wrenched the comb out of the Queen's hair and, using all of her remaining strength, brought it down on the back of the Queen's neck.

The Queen let go of Virginia's throat.

Virginia gasped for breath.

The Queen pulled the comb out of her neck, spraying her white dress with blood. She stared at the comb's teeth, which were dark red.

"You have drawn blood." The Queen rubbed her hand on the back of her neck.

Virginia stepped back, horrified.

The Queen took an uncertain step forward, then fell to one knee. She looked up at Virginia, then down at the comb. Her hand slowly fell open, and the comb clattered to the ground.

"No, no, no, no," Virginia said, suddenly understanding what she had done. She hurried to her mother's side.

Her father appeared on the gallery above them. "Oh, my God," Tony shouted. "What's happened?"

And without waiting for an answer, he ran down the stairs.

Virginia pulled her mother close. "Oh, please don't die."

Now that the spell had been broken, they might have a chance.

"Please," Virginia said, "please remember who you really are."

"Why does it matter?" the Queen asked. Her voice was a throaty whisper.

Virginia's father had reached her side.

The Queen started to twist and thrash. For a moment, her face turned into that of the Evil Stepmother, vicious and bitter in defeat. Then that image went away, leaving a face Virginia barely remembered.

Her real mother, from so long ago. Her expression was soft and warm as she looked at Virginia. "Don't cry," she said. She bowed her head. Her voice was just a whisper. "I gave away my soul."

"No!" Virginia cried. "I'm not going to let you go! Not now!"

But it was too late. Her mother died in her arms.

Her father knelt beside her and gently eased her mother out of Virginia's grasp. Then he hugged Virginia close.

Wolf managed to free himself and crossed over to them. His face was battered. He stood near her for just a moment, looking helpless; then he moved out of her range of vision.

Then someone else stirred. Suddenly the Dog Prince sat up.

"I've had too much champagne," the Dog Prince said.

At the other end of the room, two twin sisters came to. "What's happened?" they asked in unison.

Suddenly there was movement everywhere. People were waking up as if they had been in a long sleep. Tony leaned back to watch.

Virginia sat up, stunned.

"Why aren't you all dead?" Tony asked.

"Troll dust," Wolf said. He was holding Prince Wendell, undoing the muzzle and chain. "I swapped the poison for a pinch of Troll dust, just to make it look convincing."

That was the best thing Virginia had heard all night.

Wolf finished undoing Wendell s chain. Then he let Wendell go. "Go for it," Wolf said.

Prince Wendell bounded across the room and leapt into the arms of the startled Dog Prince. Wendell shifted first. For a moment, it looked as if he were holding himself. Then he stood as the Dog Prince's arms turned into paws, his face changing back into that of a dog.

Within an instant, they were back in their true forms.

"That should do the trick," Wolf said, smiling.

Wendell felt his human body in obvious relief. "I'm back," he said. "I'm back. I'm back."

Meanwhile, the Dog Prince, back in his dog form, barked excitedly and wagged his tail so hard, it looked like it might come off.

"Wolf," Tony asked, "you were on our side all the time?"

Her father sounded relieved.

Virginia knew she was.

All around them people rose. The woman wearing glass slippers, who had to be Cinderella, said, "I knew it. There was something wrong. I knew it."

She was pointing at the dead Queen.

"It's her," the beautiful Elf said. "Prince Wendell has saved us from the wicked Queen."

Wendell advanced toward his stepmother and crouched. He touched her skin gently. She was really and truly dead. He raised his gaze to Virginia.

She recognized those eyes. She had seen them for over a week on a dog who had originally followed her home.

He had heard everything, seen everything, understood everything.

And he still did.

There was great sadness in his eyes—and even greater relief.

Chapter Forty-Six

Virginia stood at the tower window, looking at the vast forest below. The mountains were silver in the distance. She felt as if someone had hollowed her out. At least she wasn't tired anymore.

She was wearing the gown that Wendell's people had dressed her in. It was long and pretty, and someone had woven flowers in her hair. They wanted her below in a little while, and she wasn't sure she could do it.

There was a soft sound behind her, and she realized that Wolf was there. He came up to her shyly and handed her a bouquet of wildflowers.

They were beautiful.

"I sat outside your room waiting for you," Wolf said softly. "You have slept for almost two days."

"I didn't realize how tired I was." She sounded calm, but she wasn't. She turned away from him. Her body shuddered, and despite her efforts to stop them, tears flowed down her cheeks.

"I killed her," she said.

He put his arm around her. "It was not your fault. It was—"

"It was my destiny." She had told herself that a hundred times, but she still didn't understand it.

"You have done a great thing," Wolf said. "For her as well as everyone else. You have to forgive yourself."

"This whole journey," she said, wiping the tears off her

face, "none of it made sense, and then, when I found out the Queen was my mother, I thought I understood. I was going to be reunited with her. But this seems so cruel, so much worse than never finding her at all."

"This is not the end of the story," Wolf said. "It is just a chapter."

"That's just words," Virginia said.

He stroked her face. There was such tenderness in the gesture that Virginia felt the tears well again.

"Go and say good-bye to her," Wolf said. "Let her go."

"I can't," she said. "I can't."

She pulled away from him and walked off on her own.

Already someone had repaired the glass ceiling on the ballroom and cleaned the blood off the floor. But Virginia still looked at the place where she had last seen her mother's body. It was as if the spot were still marked.

There was a great crowd around her, and they were already celebrating. Her father stood beside her, wearing a beautiful suit, and Wolf stood beside him. Wolf looked more handsome than she had ever seen him. He gave her a tentative smile. She didn't smile back.

A trumpet fanfare sounded, and then King Wendell entered the ballroom. Everyone applauded, and in the back someone cheered. He was wearing his crown—it looked quite good on him—and he had a maturity that she hadn't noticed before.

He immediately started into the ceremony. He invited Virginia, Tony, and Wolf onto the stage. Someone brought the dog, whom Virginia still called Prince, to Tony's side.

One of the courtiers lined the four of them up: Virginia's father first, then Prince, then Wolf, and finally Virginia. She looked out at the audience. There had to be a couple of hundred people crowding the ballroom floor.

"And now," King Wendell said, "for the greatest bravery imaginable, for courage in the face of relentless and terrible danger, I award my dear friends the highest medals in my kingdom."

The court erupted into applause. Virginia made herself smile.

King Wendell stopped in front of her father. "Firstly," he said, "my temporary manservant, Anthony. My people, look upon my friend. No longer is he spineless and wallowing in self-pity."

"Thanks," Tony said.

"No longer is he an overweight, useless coward, who would rather run than fight."

"I think they get the picture," Tony said.

"No longer is he selfishly driven by envy and greed."

"Just the medal, please."

"He is heroically transformed. What braver man could exist than Anthony the Valiant!"

Her father looked taller than usual. The courtier opened a velvet-lined box filled with medals, and Wendell took one out. He pinned it to Tony's chest. Her father turned to Virginia and grinned. He looked quite proud of himself.

She was proud of him too. This adventure had been very good for him.

"For this long-suffering dog," King Wendell was saying, "I have a special collar medal. From this moment henceforth, this confused canine will live in a golden kennel next to his very own mountain of bones. He may urinate and defecate wherever he wishes, and my courtiers will follow him around cleaning up."

The courtiers in the front row winced. Virginia repressed a smile. King Wendell bent to give the dog his medal and then froze.

He said softly to the courtier who was helping him, "Perhaps it is better if I don't touch him. You never know what might happen."

The courtier fixed the medal on Prince's collar. The dog barked and wagged his tail.

King Wendell gave the dog a wide berth and went to Wolf. Wolf stood tall and proud, waiting.

"For this wolf, however," Wendell said, "I have no medal."

People gasped. Virginia felt herself grow cold. Wolf looked furious.

"Huff-puff, that's typical," he muttered.

"Instead," King Wendell said, "I have a Royal Pardon for all the wolves everywhere throughout my kingdom. From now on, wolves will be known as heroes. For it was a noble Wolf who saved the Nine Kingdoms."

Wolf beamed and waved at the crowd. "That's wolves for you," he said. "Good guys."

Finally, King Wendell turned to Virginia. His gaze softened as he looked at her.

"As for Virginia," he said, "how can I ever reward you for what you have done and what you have lost?"

He took something from his pocket. It was a dried flower.

"This flower was given to me by Snow White when I was seven years old, on the day she left our castle forever. She said that one day I would meet her again, though she would never return. I understand her words now."

Virginia took the flower and smiled. Her gaze met Wendell's, and the specialness of the moment they shared in that cave made this moment even more poignant. She couldn't think of a better reward for all those horrible days.

"A dried flower?" Tony whispered. "I thought you were definitely on for some of the Crown Jewels."

"Shhh," Virginia said to him, cradling the flower in her hand.

"Now, bring in those disgusting Trolls."

The three Trolls were brought in, manacled together by the wrists and ankles. All three looked terrible. Frightened, sad, and completely without hope.

"Oh, Your Majesty," said Bluebell, "we're extremely sorry about the mix-up."

"Mix-up?" King Wendell asked. "The penalty for trying to kill me is death."

"Is it really?" Burly said. "Suck an Elf, that's stiff."

"We claim diplomatic immunity," Blabberwort said.

"You will be beheaded," King Wendell said, disgusted. "Take them away."

They groveled and begged for mercy. Even Virginia was beginning to feel sorry for them. But, to her surprise, her father stepped forward.

"Your Majesty," Tony said, "what you see before you are three abused street kids from the wrong side of the tracks. This is a day to forgive and forget. A day for new beginnings."

King Wendell studied the Trolls as if he were looking at them from a new perspective. "I am moved by what you say," he said. "But not much. They're still Trolls."

"The Troll Kingdom has no leader," Tony said. "Send these three back to restore the monarchy. Give them another chance."

King Wendell sighed. "Very well, you are pardoned. Take them away."

The audience cheered as the Trolls were led away. Virginia couldn't tell if that was because Wendell had spared them or because they were leaving.

"I'm going to sit on the throne," Burly was saying to his siblings.

"You couldn't sit on a toilet," Blabberwort said.

"I can read without using my finger," Bluebell said.

They continued arguing as they were dragged out of the room.

King Wendell clapped his hands together. "Now I think it's time to eat."

While the others moved to the banquet hall, Virginia slipped out of the crowd. She went to the mausoleum. The room was huge and made of stone. The tombs of many people lined the walls. It was cold here and smelled faintly of dust.

In the middle of the floor was an open glass coffin. Her mother's body lay in it.

Virginia placed the dried flower that Wendell had given her in her mother's hand. Then she kissed her mother on the forehead.

As she knelt down, sunlight pierced the great room from a window high above and bathed the coffin in light.

"When I was little," Virginia said softly, "you had this fur coat, and you'd come into my room and I could smell your perfume. You would brush the fur backwards and forwards against my face and I knew you really, really loved me."

Tears ran down her face. This time she didn't try to stop them.

"I just want to be your little girl, and for you to love me."

She leaned against her mother's body and let herself cry. She cried until she had no more tears inside. Then she stood up to leave. She looked down at her mother one last time, and then she smiled.

The dried flower she had placed in her mother's hand had already started to bloom.

Virginia washed her face and combed her hair before returning to the banquet hall. She was feeling a lot better.

The meal was already under way. She wasn't really hungry, but she didn't want to be alone either.

Wolf was sitting beside her father. They both saw her, and Wolf waved his arm. "Over here, miss."

He scooted his chair sideways, forcing people along the extremely long table to make room for her. As she sat down, he said, "What would you like to eat?"

Virginia shrugged.

"Yes," her father said. "You must eat something."

They were both getting into this celebration. She supposed they all deserved it.

"Well," she said, smiling, "I'll have a bit of fish."

"Fish, fish, fish, yes," Wolf said. "Waiter, bring fresh fish immediately."

A waiter set a plate down before her. On it was a fat, well-cooked trout. She cut into it and saw both her father and Wolf watching her.

"I'm fine," she said. "Really."

She pulled a flaky bit of fish out with her fork and was about to eat when she stopped. There was something inside that fish, and it was . . . singing. She looked down. There was a ring in the fish's belly.

"Let me linger, on your finger," the ring sang.

Wolf clapped his hands together in delight. "It's my engagement ring. You made it."

"Of course I did," the ring said. "A singing ring never fails to get his girl."

"It's destiny," Wolf said. "Put it on. Put it on."

Virginia looked at it, speechless. The ring was even more beautiful than she remembered.

"It's come an awful long way," Tony said.

She took out the ring and looked at Wolf. "I'm just trying it on, okay?" she said. "I'm too young to get married, and I don't believe in marriage anyway."

"Me neither," Wolf said, laughing, "but put it on anyway."

"I'm a modern girl," Virginia said.

"And I'm a new man. Widely read and ready for action."

She slipped the ring on. It sparkled, and a shower of tiny stars exploded around her finger.

"What a creamy knuckle," the ring sang.

Her father chuckled and turned away, talking to the person next to him, recounting his heroic exploits.

Virginia looked at the sparkling ring and then back to Wolf. "It's lovely, but I'm not ready to—" She tried to take it off, but it was stuck.

"I'm on," the ring said. "I'm not coming off now. Not ever again."

"I'm not getting married," Virginia said.

" 'Course you are," Wolf said. "Our baby's got to have a father."

"I don't intend to have any children, thank you."

"It's a bit late for that," Wolf said, beaming at her.

She froze. "What do you mean?"

"You've got a little wolf cub growing inside you," Wolf said.

"Ha," Virginia said. "In your dreams."

"Just you wait and see," Wolf said. "A little furry chap, just like me, only much smaller. Believe me, I'm a wolf. I know these things."

He smiled and ran his hand gently across her belly. "I just know it will be a magic baby."

Virginia shook her head slowly. This was all too much.

"We're having a baby," the ring sang. "We're having a baby."

And slowly, Virginia smiled.

It felt odd to be in the Queen's bedroom. But the sense that Virginia had had when she first came here, that sense of evil, was gone.

She crouched in front of the Traveling mirror and hit the catch. In it, she saw King Wendell, Wolf, her father, and the dog reflected.

Virginia stood.

"You're really staying?" she asked her father.

"Why not?" Tony said. "What am I going home to do, be shouted at by Murray? Be a janitor? And don't forget, I'm still wanted for armed robbery back there."

He patted the dog. Her father had always wanted a dog, and now he had one. A very good one. The dog wagged his tail and grinned a doggy grin.

"Don't worry," her father said. "I'll just stay for a few weeks and then come back."

Virginia didn't believe him at all. "Is it to be near Mom?" she asked.

He shrugged. "I don't know."

The mirror began to clear. King Wendell peered into it as if he were astonished that his memories were real.

Virginia watched as the mirror showed first the Statue of Liberty, then the island of Manhattan, with its tall buildings.

She turned to her father. She didn't want to leave him. He was giving her a goofy, sad little grin.

"Anyway," he said, "you need to have a bit of time away from me."

She bent down and patted the dog. It was easier than looking at the warmth in her father's eyes. This would be the first time they would be apart.

She rose. "I'll see you soon," she said. "I really love you, Daddy."

His eyes filled with tears. "You haven't called me Daddy since you were a kid."

She kissed him and then hugged him.

He squeezed her so hard, she thought her ribs would crack. Then she eased out of the hug and took Wolf's hand.

"See you soon, Grandpa," Wolf said.

He walked with Virginia through the mirror.

As everything around them turned momentarily black, Virginia heard her father say, "Grandpa?" and she smiled. That would keep him worrying for a while.

An instant later, they emerged from the mirror's liquid into Central Park. It was dusk, and no one was around. The path was empty.

She slipped her hand through Wolf's arm as they sauntered out of the trees. "I was always frightened of walking through the Park at night, but not anymore," Virginia said.

She led him to a park bench. They sat down, and he put his arm around her.

The lights of Manhattan looked alien to her. They didn't flicker like the lights of the Nine Kingdoms. This world was new again. And yet, she had missed it.

Wolf smiled at her. "What are we going to do now?"

She smiled back.

"Nothing," she said. "Nothing at all."

She leaned her head against his shoulder. Happy Ever After wasn't a prediction. She had learned in her journey through the Nine Kingdoms that Happy Ever After was really about something else.

If she lived every day with all her heart, then she would be Happy Ever After. She stared at the park around her. Wolf was warm against her and so solid. Wolves mated for life. And most of the time, so did humans. She placed a hand over her belly, and her ring sang softly.

This truly was a magical place. She just hadn't realized how magical until now.

A major ten hour television event on NBC.

The 10th KINGDOM

by Kathryn Wesley

The 10th Kingdom is a contemporary drama set in a fantasy world where magic and fairy tale characters come to life. A young woman and her father are transported into a magical world, which is both frightening and funny. There they race to save the 9 Kingdoms, governed by trolls and goblins and the descendants of Snow White, Cinderella, Red Riding Hood and other members of the fairy tale nobility, from The Evil Queen.

And coming soon on video from Hallmark Home Entertainment.